The Hostage
Heart

Books by Gerald Green:

Fiction
The Hostage Heart
Tourist
Blockbuster
Faking It
To Brooklyn with Love
The Legion of Noble Christians
The Heartless Light
The Lotus Eaters
The Last Angry Man
The Sword and the Sun

Nonfiction
My Son the Jock
The Stones of Zion
The Artists of Terezin
The Portofino PTA
His Majesty O'Keefe (with Lawrence Klingman)

THE HOSTAGE HEART

a novel by

Gerald Green

𝖖𝖄𝖯
A Playboy Press Book

First edition.

PLAYBOY and Rabbit Head design are trademarks of Playboy, 919 North Michigan Avenue, Chicago, Illinois 60611 (U.S.A.), Reg. U.S. Pat. Off., marca registrada, marque déposée.

LIBRARY OF CONGRESS CATALOGING IN PUBLICATION DATA

Green, Gerald.
    The hostage heart.

    I. Title.
PZ3.G8227Ho [PS3513.R4493] 813'.5'4   74–33555
ISBN 0–87223–430–4

The Hostage
Heart

PART ONE

1

Driving the Ford into the parking field, Trask found his access blocked by a Sanitation Department truck. The garbage men were cursing, kicking at overloaded cans, heaving refuse bags.

The crew chief peered into the Ford's window and saw Trask and Rashid, both in white coats with the CGH insignia on the breast pockets. "Hold it a second, Doc," the garbage man said. "Them hospital people oughta take a course in packaging garbage. Look at all that crap. All over the sidewalk." His voice grew confidential. "It's the new *element.*" Then, cautioned by Rashid's black curling hair and mustache, he withdrew. Who could tell if the doctor wasn't a Puerto Rican himself? City General Hospital was filled with foreigners—Chinks, spics, spades.

"Hey, Angie," a collector called. "We just killed another rat. Fourth of the morning."

"See what I mean?" the crew chief said to Trask. The truck moved on. "Okay, Doc, take it in. Sorry about the delay. It's our city, so we keep it clean, right?"

Trask smiled. Rashid nodded.

Trask found a parking space at the edge of the muddy, ice-patched field. It was some distance from the hospital and was used by employees under medical rank. Rashid wondered for a moment, Would the garbage men remember the young physicians who parked a gray Ford in the lot?

"Lock?" Rashid asked Trask. They stood in the icy morning air. Each carried a heavy briefcase.

"No. We're finished with it." The car had been rented with stolen credit cards.

At seven in the morning it was still dark. On the streets adjacent to the hospital, sodium lights painted buildings an emetic yellow. A high-crime area. Inner city. But now, in the saffron glare, the air charged with a March mist, it seemed peaceful. On one side of the lot were the red brick dormitories where nurses, residents, and interns lived. Across the lot, the twin towers of City General Hospital pierced the sky. The colors of building and sky were oddly similar—a strange purplish-red—as if the old hospital towers had discharged a dye into the atmosphere.

"A bit cold," Rashid said.

"We shouldn't wear topcoats," Trask said. "The residents walk around just in white coats. *Machismo*. It's their sign of status."

"Exactly so," Rashid agreed. "Like a camouflage suit."

They passed a nurse, shivering inside a heavy coat, evidently coming off an overnight tour, hurrying to the warmth of her apartment. Rashid smiled at her. He had a dark, friendly face. White teeth gleamed under the furry black moustache. Short and barrel-chested, he walked lightly, jauntily.

"If we are stopped at the door," Trask said, "just follow me. There are fifteen ways of getting in. There are five security men, none of them armed, except for the city policeman in the emergency room. We'll try a side entrance or the basement."

Rashid wondered why Trask was bothering to repeat the information. They had memorized it in long sessions with Olmedo, who had been working at the hospital for six weeks. Was Trask struggling with a last-minute fear? Rashid doubted it. His voice was firm. He carried himself as stick straight as ever. A shade under six feet, slender, long-headed, with brush-cut wheat-colored hair and flat gray-green eyes, Trask always seemed a bit off balance. His bearing was so erect that the back of his head appeared to be an inch or two to the rear of his feet—as if pulling back from a blow.

The men walked into an inner courtyard, passing under a high walkway that connected City General's main buildings—built by the WPA, a reward from President Roosevelt to the Democratic machine—to the newer maternity and geriatric wings. The court served as a parking area for hospital staff, both medical and administrative. Beyond the parked cars was a squat building that housed the ambulance garage, the power plant and the methadone clinic.

More lights flooded the courtyard with yellow. For a moment Rashid thought of himself as an actor on an illuminated stage. He fingered the green insignia on his pocket—CGH inside a wreath—and found that he was enjoying the role.

Trask's bony face surveyed the area. "No guard," he said.

"The dog?"

Trask frowned. "You didn't pay attention. Olmedo told us he was taken off three months ago. Neighborhood groups objected."

"Ah. Of course."

"Let's go. We're on schedule."

The warmth of the hospital lobby buoyed Rashid. He did not mind cold—the mountains of Lebanon were hardly warm—but the damp of March in the northeastern United States jelled his blood.

Facing them was a fly-specked sign:

ALL HOSPITAL PERSONNEL MUST SHOW I.D. CARDS

In a cubicle the night security man studied racing entries. He did not look up when the two men carrying briefcases walked past him. He had not checked an ID card in four years. The community groups that had forced the withdrawal of the guard dog were now agitating for abolition of identification cards.

Trask and Rashid melted into the hospital scene. A technician pushing a tray of blood specimens brushed by them. Two nurses, chatting, yawning, nodded at Trask. Rashid was surprised by the ease with which they were accepted, although Olmedo had assured them. He touched the stethoscope in his coat pocket. It was like a set of worry beads, smooth amber to console one's fingers.

Trask glanced at the signs on doors: DIALYSIS. RENAL RESEARCH UNIT. NURSES' LOUNGE. At the nurses' island on the ground floor, Trask found what he was looking for—a bulletin board.

"Good morning, doctor," a stout nurse said to Trask.

"Good morning."

Rashid flashed his teeth at her.

The bulletin board featured community meetings; folk dance, ceramic, and consciousness-raising groups; notices to buy or sell cars, appliances, furniture. A yellow flyer welcomed hospital personnel to a session on Transcendental Meditation. Trask's eyes scanned the lower part of the board. Rashid watched him; Trask led, he followed.

"Good," Trask said. "No change." He pointed to a white, lined file card.

TO SELL.
HARMON-KARDON STEREO SET, USED.
GARRARD RECORD CHANGER, SPEAKERS,
GOOD CONDITION. $150.
CALL 656–7189 EVENINGS.

It was a signal from Olmedo: no hitches, no change in plans. If the operation were to be called off, he would have listed the stereo set as a Pioneer.

A gray-haired, red-faced physician bustled past them. He stopped short at the nurse's island, said something to the stout nurse, turned to look—momentarily puzzled—at Trask and Rashid.

"You fellows . . ." He was confounded by the endless parade of new faces, foreign tongues. "You fellows part of my cardiac conference this morning? We're moving it to the fifth floor."

"No, doctor," Trask said. He seemed to tilt backward another inch. His voice was soft. "We're in general surgery."

"I never know who's with me, who's not." He hurried off.

"Poor Dr. Evans," the nurse said. "So overworked he doesn't even recognize his own people. Find anything worth buying?"

Trask turned away from the bulletin board. "No. Not today." He spoke to Rashid. "Breakfast?"

"Oh, for the life of a resident," the nurse said.

The cafeteria was hot and crowded. The two men stood on line and pushed green cardboard trays. Trask was suddenly hungry—a great void in his gut demanding food. He ordered oatmeal, bacon and eggs, toast, coffee. Rashid wanted only coffee.

"You sweatin' a lot," the black woman behind the coffee urn informed him.

"Ah, the change in temperature. Cold outside. Much too hot in here." He gave the woman a dollar, waited for his change.

"All you residents alike. Too hot, too cold. Where you from?"

Rashid smiled at the informality. Olmedo had told them how City General had been under pressure from local activists. Orderlies and maintenance men sat on utilization committees and made decisions along with the surgeons.

"The Sudan," Rashid said. "Very hot place."

"That's a new one on me. Move it on, please."

Trask ate in silence, enjoying the crisp bacon, the runny yellow yolks. He did not sweat, found no need to make small talk or observe the people around him.

"An old place," Rashid said. He sipped the coffee. It was like acid. "The walls are sagging. One wonders why a man like Tench would come—"

Trask glared at him.

"Of course. I shall talk no more."

2

Dr. Eric Lake always anticipated the alarm. He had his own built-in wake-up mechanism. Precisely at five to six his eyes opened and he fumbled for the clock, turning it off so as not to disturb his wife. Martha needed more sleep than he did. Without eight hours, she tended to unravel toward the end of the day. "It's your low metabolism, Martha," Lake said. "Come on down to City General and we'll work you up, put you on little dosages of thyroid." His wife would laugh and respond with a standard family joke. "Not a chance, Eric. Anyone who walks through those grim doors ends up with open heart surgery."

"I hear you," Martha mumbled from the bed. "Use this bathroom. I'm awake."

Lake had begun to tiptoe to the children's bathroom. They slept like hibernating badgers. "It's okay," Lake whispered. "Go back to sleep." The surgeon glanced at his children. Little Eric, aged twelve, made an odd, high mound in the bed. *Fat.* The boy was getting fat. How? Dr. Lake wondered. He himself was lean, almost starved. Martha was slender and tall. Where did this chubby, somnolent boy come from? Their daughter, Sarah, two years younger, was like the parents—lean, active and energetic. Guilt cascaded from the shower head along with the hot water. Lake never spent enough time with the boy, did not encourage him in athletics. Other fathers played tennis and hockey with their sons. Out of the house at dawn, he came home exhausted. Too often he was silent, preoccupied, immersed in a professional journal. For three years he had been promising Eric and Sarah a camping trip to the Adirondacks.

In T-shirt and white shorts that drooped baggily around his undernourished buttocks, Lake returned to the bedroom. Groping for a shirt, he managed to dismantle a bureau drawer that had been coming loose for weeks. It clattered to the floor.

"He's at it again," his wife said. "World's fastest coronary surgeon, but he can't open a drawer without pulling it apart."

"Sorry. It's been coming apart for a month. We run out of Elmer's Glue-All?"

"No, the maid of all work, Martha Hunterden Lake, ran out of time."

Lake buttoned his shirt. "Honey, don't lay it on me. Not at six-thirty A.M. I told you to hire a girl."

"I don't like servants. It's like having strangers in this house. They sulk and pout and don't dust properly." Maids awakened anxieties about the slave trade and the plantation system in Martha Lake. They'd had the conversation many times before.

Lake, knotting his tie, reflected on his life with her. She was an honest, intelligent, competent woman, and he wondered if he ever could have married anyone else, loved anyone else. Martha had been a biologist, single at twenty-seven after two failed romances. A pretty, angular woman with large features, she suffered the inevitable damning compliment: she had an *interesting* face. She was more than that, though. Resilient and wise, she was an excellent companion.

"Please, Martha," Lake pleaded. "Hire a handyman to get these things done. The bathroom tiles are crumbling. The kitchen ceiling leaks." Possessed of superb hands, fantastic coordination, the surgeon had difficulty shoving liquid cement into tiles, or plastering a hole in the wall. Martha did most of the repairs. "And the loose boards in the porch, and the side light that keeps going out."

Martha burst into a wild guffaw. "Come here and hug me, Eric." Late-Depression children, they were still suffering poverty shock. They did not know what to do with all the money. Thank God for savings banks and the I.R.S., Martha felt.

Lake sat at the side of the bed. They embraced. Her body was fatless, lithe. Next year, she had advised Eric, she would go back to work. They'd sell the sixteen-room house with its canted floors and musty odors.

"Martha, repeat every morning: we're rich, we're rich, we're rich, a hundred times. Then telephone the tile man and tell him to fix the grouting in the bathroom so I can eat my Grape-Nuts without soapy water dripping into them."

"I'll call him today. That nice Mr. Battista."

"And also the carpenter and the electrician. For God's sake, we can spend our money better than the government. It's crazy," he said. "I'll never get used to it. Alan Motzkin loves his money. Evans, Fess, all of them. They know what to do with money."

"We're Puritans at heart." Eric stared intently at Martha for a moment. Then he said, "Listen, I was talking to Rockewicz."

Martha was on guard. Steve Rockewicz was the executive director of City General Hospital. She and Eric were of two minds about him. He was shrewd, energetic, and kept the hospital going. But he was devious, not someone she wholly trusted.

"About what?"

"I'm going to start returning a chunk of my earnings to the dump. They need equipment for the cardiac research unit. It's held together with Scotch tape. I talked to Steve and he's eager—"

"Naturally."

"Take it easy, Martha. I'd contribute one-tenth of everything I earn, right to the limit of allowable deductions, maybe a little more. I owe a lot to City General. Rockewicz gave me my head when the cardiac and coronary surgery units expanded. The money goes to the government anyway, so why not give it to the hospital? Those cardiac pumps should have been junked long ago."

"You're going to give them thirty thousand dollars a year?"

"More or less. Steve and I have to work it out."

"You could buy a lot of dogs for that," Martha said sourly.

Eric laughed. Years ago, when he had been an assistant in cardiology at an upstate New York hospital, he had fought a running battle with administrators, vivisectionists, city officials and rival physicians for dogs for research. Eric Lake had earned the reputation of a pound-haunting, street-prowling seeker of mongrel dogs. They had laughed at him only a short while; his research had led to important modifications in cardiac surgery.

"We have come a far piece from stealing dogs," Lake said.

"What does Alan Motzkin say?"

Dr. Motzkin was Lake's anesthesiologist. "Alan thinks I should incorporate. Form my own professional corporation. Eric Lake, M.D., P.C."

"Well?"

"I'm no corporation for God's sake. I'm a person."

He did not tell her what else Motzkin had said to him a few days ago after they had finished an exhausting aortic valve replacement: "Eric, you don't need the Mercedes and the Cadillac, I guess, not the way I do. You're Lake, one of the best, and you run

your own show. . . . Us gas-passers need the ego trips. . . ."
Martha Lake got out of bed, yawned, put on a robe. Lake was
patting his jacket pockets—wallet, handkerchief, two packs of
cigarettes, car keys.
"Do you think Rockewicz will finally put out some publicity on
you? No one knows about you."
"Walker Tench knew about me."
"Your old college chum. When will Rockewicz and the board
wake up and realize how great you are?" She knew it was Eric
himself who resisted the publicity heaped on the Texas-type surgeons.
Lake ignored the question and kissed her. "Tell young Eric
we'll go to a Knicks game before the season is over. I don't like
basketball, but I'll go. Can you get the tickets?"
"I'll try. Good luck with Walker."
"Routine. Nothing more than a simple procedure."
She tried to fall asleep again, listened to his three-year-old Dart
coughing its way out of the driveway. ("Get him out of a madhouse like City General," Jack Licata, the chief resident in coronary surgery, told her, "and he'd be on the cover of *Time* in a
week.")
Crossing the bridge that took him out of the state and toward
City General, Lake decided they needed a vacation. Alan and Bev
Motzkin were always running off to Caribbean islands. St.
Maarten. Antigua. He'd ask Alan for advice. As abruptly as he
entertained the idea, he abandoned it. He detested sitting around
pools with strangers. He had never owned a pair of swim trunks
that looked right on his starved body. Hot sun, cocoa butter
smeared on brown flesh, chlorinated green water: not his ideas of
fun.

3

"Jelly beans," Tench said.
"Beg pardon, Mr. Tench?" the night nurse asked. She was tall,
black, and slender, and wore a stiff white uniform.

"Those pills you gave me. They'll have all the effect of jelly beans. What are they, anyway?"

"I'm not supposed to tell."

"But I'm Dr. Lake's prize parcel. They redecorated the VIP suite for me."

"I know, I know." She patted the pillows, took his pulse. Her starchy white movements agitated him: lust intruding in the midst of pain, illness, possible death. A musky scent, a whiff of jungle passion.

"Diazepam, Mr. Tench. And plain Valium."

"Nothing will help, Miss Redpath. I'm six feet four inches tall, I weigh two hundred and forty-five pounds, and I've tried everything. No matter what you make me swallow, no matter what that anesthesiologist pumps into me, it won't have any effect. Painkillers, sleeping pills, relaxants. They'll be jelly beans."

With a gesture more of affection than of lechery, Tench put his huge hand on her rump.

She disengaged his hand, clapped it to the coverlet. "Now, now. That is not what we expect from Dr. Lake's friend. Besides, angina patients aren't supposed to get excited."

Mention of his ailment sobered him. Or was it the drugs, infusing his system with deadening effect? For the past five months he had been in agony. The corporation plane had carted him around ceaselessly—Palm Beach, northern Michigan, the Caribbean. The cardiologists had treated him with nitroglycerin and other drugs. They told him to lose weight, made him stop drinking and smoking.

Then everyone left him. His second wife, an erratic heiress to a fortune almost as staggering as his own, had run off to Switzerland with a Lebanese gold trader. Somewhere in New York State his daughter, the child of his first marriage, rusticated in a commune, trying to find the True Path.

So he had come to Eric Lake. And now he was frightened.

"Miss Redpath, when do they start shooting me full of anesthesia?"

"You'll never know what hit you. We're sneaky."

"Miss Redpath, I can't stand pain. I'm not a coward, but I have a low threshold for pain. I was a good infantry officer in World War Two, and I have a drawerful of medals to prove it, but I couldn't tolerate tight shoes, or itchy underwear, or a sprained ankle."

"Dr. Motzkin will pump you so full of pain-killers you'll be on cloud nine."

"I've heard about open heart cases who were paralyzed all over, couldn't move or talk, but felt everything."

"Don't believe it. If anybody can do coronary surgery properly it's Dr. Lake's team."

She turned to leave.

A knife sliced into Tench's heart. Under the womanish teats the blood-starved heart was protesting. His coronary arteries were blocked, defective. When the blood supply was diminished, the heart signaled its distress.

"Stay here. I want to talk to you."

"I'll be back."

Some chairman of the board, Tench thought. Can't even get a black nurse to stay with me five minutes. In the streets below, the Sanitation Department banged and slammed cans. He remembered a trip to Italy, a marvelous five weeks with a ravishing Venetian girl, after his first marriage fell apart. Raphael by day, the noise of the lower classes at night. Italians worked joy into the clamor of garbage cans.

Tench felt the tranquilizer forming a soothing fuzz around him. Oddly, it cleared his mind, summoned up colored pictures.

He was in the board room eight years ago, the new president taking over from his father. Crisp, quick, intelligent, a step ahead of the old farts on whom his father had relied. He'd learned it all too quickly, was too fast for them. Five years ago he began spending less time at board meetings. The corporation and its subsidiaries were self-perpetuating. Someone fixed the government; someone rigged the market; someone kept the unions happy; platoons of engineers and research men kept improving products; an army of salesmen kept them moving. Simple. He'd stepped up to chairman, appointed James J. Cardone, the boy wonder, the miracle maker, as new president.

But Walker Tench III was still looking, still opening doors, climbing mountains, descending to riverbeds, in search of something. Searching, Tench was stricken. His heart suffered, disabled him. There was no way out now, except through Eric Lake's hands—chest sliced open, heart stopped, vessels cut, rearranged, stitched. *Mortality rates are very low.*

Diazepam lulled him into semisleep, blotted out the accretions of gloom, rendered his mind full of flowery meadows, mountain streams. It would be fun, a prank, an escapade, part of his search. He'd put Miss Redpath on payroll—an expert on hospital supplies for Tench Medical. Motzkin would get a new Lincoln from him. Lake? A professorship at some Tench-endowed medical college. He dozed, smiling at the thought of the faces in the board room when the wandering chairman finally showed up—slim, energetic, free of pain.

4

Normally Dr. Lake avoided preoperative visits. He preferred to see his patients emerging from anesthesia in the recovery room, naked as herrings, full of tubes, wires, catheters, dripping urine, blood, water, silent, shaved and yellowed. "Can you hear me?" he would shout. "This is Dr. Lake. If you can hear me, wiggle your toes."

Walking down the corridor to Tench's penthouse suite, Lake nodded at nurses and reflected on his friend's flamboyant life. Power. Wealth. Wives. Mistresses. Drugs. Alcohol. Art galleries and musicals. Nothing seemed to have settled the man, brought him to earth. There was something new Tench had told him about—a foundation to work in the inner cities among minorities. The corporation's hot-shot president, James J. Cardone, was developing it. It was a source of pride to Tench, a source of distress to the older men on the board. And then coronary heart disease had struck Tench down, forcing him into a life of sloth and pain.

Outside the room, Dr. Lake stopped Miss Redpath. "How is he?"

"Fine. Shaved, prepped. He's a hard man to get to sleep."

"Mr. Tench has made a career of avoiding sleep. Especially at night or in the early morning."

"Hey, Eric," Tench called foggily. "What are you people doing to me?"

Lake walked in. He craved another cigarette, but was reluctant to smoke in a patient's room. Irritably, he snuffed a butt out in an ashtray.

"Listen, Eric," Tench said. His voice was distant. "Those people who shaved me last night. Where'd they learn that?"

"What do you mean?"

"Christ, those guys scraped me clean. In my nose, my armpits, my crotch, my asshole. Between the toes and the backs of my hands. The guy with the razor ran it over me like he was dressing a deerskin. I thought for sure the razor was going to slip and make me a soprano."

"I insist on total shaving. I've ordered patients reshaved in surgery if I don't like the way it's done."

Tench's half-shut eyes studied Lake's hungry face. Wounds of fatigue, gouges of concentration. From standing long hours at the table, squinting into people's hearts, arteries, lungs. And not a mark on me, Tench thought, my face as smooth as a Gucci valise.

"Those men who shaved you are as much a part of my team as Motzkin or Licata," the surgeon said. "They do their job, or they get out."

On oiled rollers, a stretcher was pushed into the room by two orderlies. They moved it to the side of Tench's bed.

"So soon? Golly. I was having a nice dream." Tench grasped Lake's forearm. "That two percent of patients you lose. I won't be in that select company, will I Eric?"

"Not a chance. You're young and healthy, even if you're over-weight. You'll be a new man."

"The old one could stand improvements, Eric. Not a word to those people at the corporation until I'm out of this. Understood?"

"It's taken care of."

Miss Redpath eased him toward the stretcher. Her dark flesh and exotic cologne drowned Tench in an awareness of the wonders of life. "If it wasn't for the honor of it, I'd just as soon walk."

"We'll help you. Put the sheet over him, Olmedo."

A sallow man with a drooping nose secured the sheet around Tench's elephantine form. The other orderly strapped his legs. Tench was floating, unable to speak or remember anything he had said in the last fifteen minutes.

They waited for an elevator. Lake smiled down at his patient. Walker might not hear them, but words of encouragement helped. "Jack Licata will be in charge until I get there. You've met Jack. Best chief resident anywhere."

The man whom the nurse had addressed as Olmedo maneuvered the stretcher, waited for the elevator door to open, and wheeled Tench in for the ride down to surgery on the third floor.

Lake walked in alongside his patient. He heard Tench trying to form words.

"All started with a good lay," the millionaire mumbled. Then he was asleep.

In his cramped office Lake put on a white coat, then fished a carton of filter cigarettes from his locker and placed it on his cluttered desk. Its presence alone was reassuring. So long as he could run to the soothing, destructive weed, he could keep going —all morning, all afternoon, into the night if need be. Periodically Martha tried to make him stop smoking—threats, schemes, substitutions. He would grow edgy, put on weight, lose his capacity for concentration. We all die in our own way, Lake told himself.

He opened a gray folder on his desk. It was cardiology service's "Cardiac Catheterization Report." He read the heading: PROCE-DURES: LCC/CA/CINE/SHON. "It didn't start with that good lay, Walker," the surgeon said to himself. He let the cigarette smoke flood his lungs. "But it helped."

This is a 51-year-old white male with a four month history of substernal chest pain. Pains first occurred during intercourse and lasted several hours after orgasm. Pains were associated with dia-phoresis and radiated from chest to back. For a month and a half there were intermittent recurrences of chest pain, usually lasting ten to fifteen minutes. In December there was an attack of severe precordial chest pain which got only minimum relief from Isordil. Severe shortness of breath and excessive sweating were evident. After bed rest of one week, the patient was admitted and main-tained medically on Isordil, nitroglycerin, and Inderal, with only a minor relief of symptoms. For the past month, almost totally disabled by recurring chest pain ten to fifteen times daily, with varying relationship to activity, but commonly occurring after meals.

FAMILY HISTORY: Father died of coronary artery disease, age 66. Mother died of diabetes.

SH: Gave up smoking, drugs, and alcohol three months ago. Had been heavy smoker and drinker. Overweight by forty pounds for height and age. Blood pressure, normal.

Apart from the chest pains and the blubber, Lake reflected, Tench was a healthy animal. His pulse was regular. His heart showed neither murmurs nor gallops nor arrhythmias. The EKG was normal.

In the corner of Lake's office was a viewing machine. Lake snuffed out his cigarette. He opened a round can, took out a 35mm X-ray motion picture of Tench's pained heart, and threaded it on the spools.

5

Trask and Rashid lingered over their breakfasts. The cafeteria was jammed and overheated. A broad-beamed security guard walked through the room, blinked at them from behind thick eyeglasses, and sat down several tables away with his doughnuts and coffee.

"Not a gun in the place," Trask said.

"The city policeman. In front."

"Never leaves the cubicle."

Rashid shoved his tray aside. Too easy. Too quick. When he and his comrades had shot up the Amsterdam airport they had had to worry about armed policemen.

"Coffee no good?" Trask asked Rashid.

"I prefer it dark and sweet. Thick on the tongue." Rashid smiled. He and Trask did not quite understand one another. Trask had been elected the leader. The rest were followers. But sometimes Rashid wondered. Trask was young, in his late twenties. Was he truly so intelligent? Were his plans always bound to work? They had worked twice already. The bombing of the stock exchange. The bank robbery. They had been successes. Now they were ready for bigger game, a blow that would make the world take notice. Trask had to be right. Strike in the right place and at the right time, and you can change history.

"Worried?" Trask asked the Arab. Rashid's eyes were closed. He ran his fingers over his bedouin moustache. His people were city people, not *bedu*, but Rashid cultivated a certain panache. He spoke good English and poetic Arabic.

"No, no. My bladder. You know how weak it is."

Trask's back stiffened. He laughed. "You'd better empty it. You'll be a long time in the operating room. The operation can run five hours or more."

"Then I had best go now."

"I'll call the office."

Trask jerked his head at Rashid to follow him. In the hallway outside the cafeteria, Trask went to a pay telephone, Rashid to a men's room.

Trask dialed a number in the city. It rang twice, three times.
Then he heard Bateman Hooks's thick voice.

"Acme Printing."

"Acme? Fairfax Business Forms. We got the shipment. It's all
in order."

"Okay. Any additional orders?"

"No. The same as the list we gave you last month. No
changes."

He hung up. They were on schedule, inside the hospital and
out.

6

On the spinning reels of the viewer, Tench's heart came alive.
The X-ray films showed it contracting, pumping, revealing its
defects when the pigtail catheter squirted dye into the ventricle.

"A double," Lake said. "Narrowing of the proximal area of the
left anterior descending artery, number one. Number two, the
diagonal branch. Routine."

He squinted at the film. The dye squirted again. The darkened
areas of the arteries indicated that Tench's heart was being deprived of blood, the condition they called ischemia. Lake, an
unemotional man, felt challenged. He was hardly the best-known
coronary surgeon in the country, stuck as he was in City General,
a victim of hospital politics. But Walker Tench had sought *him*.
"I don't want anyone to know," the millionaire had said. He was
doubled over, fearing another assault on his chest. "They'll ship
me to Houston or Cleveland. I want you to do it and to keep it
quiet."

"That'll be easy," Lake had said. "The PR staff here keeps me
a secret. Nobody is sure if I'm even a heart surgeon."

Watching the evidence unroll in front of him—the contracting
heart, the blockage as the dye failed to get through the stenosed
areas—Eric Lake recalled Tench. Memories thirty years old flitted through the surgeon's mind. He turned off the viewer. He had
seen enough. On the illuminated screen, he had a flashing vision

of a brawl at Princeton. Some undergraduate horseplay in their freshman year. Jocks playing softball around a beer barrel. And he, skinny, in dingy sweater, lugging books, a victim. The drunken athletes trying to tear his clothes off. And suddenly Walker Tench, enormous, powerful, exceedingly rich even by Princeton standards, loner and nonconformist, wading into everyone, cuffing halfbacks, stepping on shot-putters, digging Lake from under a mass of howling sadists. "Keep your fucking hands off him," Lake recalled Tench warning them. "You want to beat up on somebody, beat up on me." No one accepted the challenge.

Later he and Tench sat in Walker's room, sipping beer, listening to Bix Beiderbecke records, talking little, realizing that some bond had been forged that afternoon. Tench had gotten mildly drunk. "Lake," he said. "You don't owe any of the pricks around here apologies. Get a decent sweater."

"This sweater is good enough. It got me through high school."

Lake, putting the reel of film into its can, afforded himself a crooked smile. Over the years he and Tench had remained casual friends, neither really understanding the other. Lake could not digest the facts of Tench's wealth. Tench could only marvel at Lake's mastery of enormous skills, his insistence on excellence. He put the cath lab report into its folder, scrawled some instructions for his secretary, and lit a cigarette. "You'll be all right, Walker," Lake said. He remembered the millionaire's words to him when they had agreed on the operation. "Eric, I'm only fifty-one. I can't stand the pain and I don't want to die."

7

Bateman Hooks hung up the phone after the coded conversation with Trask. Lots of time. Two, two and a half hours before he was to make his move. Fiona would be leaving sooner. She had to be on the hospital grounds.

"Everything all right?" she asked.

"Yeah. Ole Trask okay," Hooks said.

"You didn't think so last night."

"Had me too much beer. Ratshit git on my back sayin' like, you know, I talk big, but ain't proved nothin' yet. Jes' 'cause Ratshit shoot up buses and airports."

"We're all in this together, Bateman. Trask is giving the drill."

"What kind of fancy talk is that? He drill sheet."

Hooks got up from the chair and looked at the arsenal spread on a GI blanket on one of the cots in the barren room. He had cleaned and oiled the guns, filled the magazines, checked the grenades. Rashid (whom he delighted in angering by calling Ratshit) knew a lot about weapons, and so did Carlos Olmedo. Trask talked a great deal, and the chick claimed she'd been trained in assault tactics in Belfast. But he, Bateman Hooks, ex-grunt, point man, slope-killer, was the weapons expert.

"Trask say no Armalite, but maybe we need one." Hooks picked up an M16 rifle from the bed. The other weapons were M2 automatic carbines and .38 police specials.

"You are not to use it," Fiona said.

Hooks's ebony face was cut in half sideways by a gleaming smile. "Use it on you, baby. Ole Trask gone. You want some?" He leveled the barrel at her.

"I am not afraid of you or fifteen like you, Hooks."

"I know. You shoot the balls off Limey-ass soljers, right?"

"And off you if I have to."

Hooks giggled. Fiona Regan was slight, pale white, brown-haired. Trask, he suspected, had slept with her. But Trask didn't seem to need it. Hooks wondered: Just the two of us left, and then we go out, maybe to make it big, maybe to die. He picked up the rifle and walked to the window that faced on the street. He ran the shade up. He sighted his Armalite into the street below.

"Get away from there," Fiona said.

Hooks ignored her. Below, a lavender Cadillac pulled up in front of a tenement. Hooks had seen it before. A pimp-mobile, property of a big dude in platform heels and a gold coat. *Hi, brother.* The pimp stayed inside, but two of his stable got out.

They looked beat after a hard night's work. One was a sister in a yellow wig, white leather coat, white boots. The other was a pale honky in a green cape.

"Got you in the sights, cunt." Hooks laughed. He saw the white girl's face in the cross hairs. She would look a lot different if he fired the Armalite. Like the people in 'Nam, the ones he had wasted in the village. Surprise, indignation, appeal—before realizing the mess was over.

"Get away from the window," Fiona said.

"I ain't takin' orders from you."

"Sometimes I wonder why Trask let you join us."

" 'Cause I weapons man, baby. And a Red Ball Express driver. Hooks shoot, drive, ball anything. How you in bed?"

"I have no interest in you."

"You be interested some day." He chuckled. "I better than Trask. You know what they say about spade studs."

Fiona ignored him. She turned her back, and with a felt pen, wrote on the wall: THE NEW DAY WHICH IS ALREADY AT HAND MUST FIND US FIRM, PRUDENT, AND AB-SOLUTE.

"Fuck is that?" Hooks asked.

"It's by one of your heroes, Frantz Fanon."

"He ain't shit to me, baby. I ain't no reader."

"It wouldn't hurt you to read. You could serve the revolution better."

Hooks tossed the Armalite on the bed. He felt loose, ready. "What good it do you?" he asked. "I hear what you tellin' Trask and Ratshit and Carlos other night. Your kinfolk in Ireland, they just like black people. Them Catholics like you, they eat shit in Belfast. You and all them Catholic cats, you the niggers of Ireland."

"In a sense." Hooks confounded her. She had expected a certain nobility. A primitive man, but a decent one. But there were secrets in him. Things that had happened in Vietnam, which he hinted at, that Trask knew about.

"All them books you read, all them schools you go to, papers you write. You still niggers to them Protestant mothers, right?"

"Yes, yes. Will you be still?"

"Ain't nobody badmouths black asses more than Irish cops, but they got relatives is the niggers of Ireland."

She began to write FRANTZ FANON under the quote. Trask had ordered them not to leave any trace in the apartment. Everything was to be burned, discarded, moved. But Fiona had a sense of history. Someday the miserable cold-water rooms where they had lived for six weeks would be a shrine. Like the workers' apartments in Moscow where the revolution was planned.

Hooks watched her behind jiggle as she reached high on the wall to scrawl the name of the hero of revolution. Desire provoked him. The memory of the whores in the street. Jealousy of Trask for having had her. The closeness of her contemptuous white face. From the rear she looked good—long brown hair, narrow waist in a black sweater, the tight ass bouncing as she wrote. As she stretched he could see her slim ankles, the pink soles of her feet rising from brown loafers.

With the stealth of an old jungle hand, Hooks tiptoed in back of her. Before she could turn he had one arm around her breasts and arms. With the other he began to yank down her slacks and underpants in an irresistible motion. The sight of her perfect white buttocks filled him less with ardor than wonder.

"Stop that, Hooks," she said coldly. "Let go of me."

"You and me goin' to ball."

"Stop that. The Committee agreed."

"Committee, sheeet. You ball Trask, you ball me."

"I'll scream."

"An' blow the job? Bring the pigs in so's they can see them pieces on the bed? C'mon baby."

She shut her eyes, clenched her teeth. It was pointless to fight him. He was forcing her, knees and elbows down, to the nearest cot. She would not resist. But she would not participate.

"You ast for it, you git it."

"I asked for nothing."

She felt the hard column, winced, forced herself not to react, not to panic, to remain inert, indifferent, cold.

8

Dr. Alan Motzkin loved his work and was proud of his eminence as one of the top anesthesiologists in the city. He always looked forward to a day's work with Eric Lake. And on days that began with a quarrel with his wife, Beverly, the towers of City General seemed to him more than ever beacons of sanity.

It had gotten worse now that the children were ready for college. Over the coffee, Bev had begun on Clarice again, their seventeen-year-old. Mrs. Motzkin shook her black curls and grimaced at the orange juice. "You could have been firmer, Alan," she said. "Last night, listening to her with her latest bulletin. No college. That's it, no college. A girl with seven-hundred boards. National Merit Scholar. Editor of the yearbook. And she informs us college is a drag, who needs it, and we can tear up the applications to Bryn Mawr and Mount Holyoke and Yale."

"Bev, darling, she'll change her mind. It's a stage."

"Stage, stage, that's all I hear. Clarice can do no wrong. Alan, you filled their heads with Thoreau and bird watching and the evils of the system, and *look.*"

Motzkin patted his lips and got up. He was a stout, sweaty man with apologetic brown eyes, and he was meticulously neat. He put the lid back on the sugar jar, returned the milk carton to the refrigerator, discarded the top of the juice can that clung to the electric opener. "Bev, Clarice will find her way. I suggest you do not antagonize her further or her attitudes will harden."

There was no appeasing Beverly. "Alan, you and I worked. Our parents in Brownsville sacrificed. We lived for the day when we'd have a house like this, and kids who didn't have to struggle, and this girl is throwing it in our face! Mark my words, Peter will do the same! Who did we do it for, if not them?"

"Ourselves, perhaps." He kissed her on the forehead. "Things work out, Bev. As Eric would say, it's all procedure."

"Ask Eric for a procedure that will send our daughter to college, instead of running off to a commune, or living in a tent in the woods."

"Promise her a Volkswagen," he laughed.

"You did already, Alan. I said no. She'd run away in it. Alan, sweetheart, she's past being bribed."

Motzkin put on his tan cashmere coat, his green Tyrolean hat with the "bart" in the band, and hugged Beverly. "Darling, we are suffering the pangs of prosperity. We came out of walkups in Brooklyn, and who ever thought we'd have this much? If the kids want to live a simpler life, not struggle the way we did—let them." It was an unconvincing speech, but it would have to suffice for an exit.

Cushioned in the air-conditioned silence of his El Dorado (he had bought it at a rock-bottom price in the teeth of the gas shortage), Motzkin tooled along, reveling in his suburban community: Tudor homes, pollarded trees, paddle-tennis courts, pedigreed retrievers. Why not be proud of it? He was more tolerant than his wife. If his kids dropped out, that was their business. Meanwhile, he would enjoy his work, his affluence, his status. Not bad, not bad at all, for a boy whose father had run a dry-cleaning store on Saratoga Avenue.

An hour later, in immaculate surgical greens, Motzkin entered operating room three. He made a mental note to call his broker later. There was a new issue, something called Total Energy, being offered. The word was that it could save them all: a conglomerate of new sources of energy, bound to soar.

He exchanged greetings with Dr. Jack Licata, the chief resident, and Dr. Gamel Mihrab, the senior resident. This early they were yawning, preoccupied, speaking softly to Flor Aquino, the circulating nurse, and Sally Moorhead, the scrub nurse. Both women were arranging instruments, bandages, sponges, surgical sutures, and the other implements of surgery at the low and high tables.

Motzkin glanced at the anesthesia cart: oxygen, nitrous oxide, lactated ringers, dextrose in saline, whole blood, Isuprel. Everything ready for the IVs. He looked around for his assistant. Flor Aquino skittered by with a green bundle of instruments. She was a beautiful Filipino girl. Only her slanted smoky eyes were visible above the yellow mask.

"Hey, Flor," Dr. Motzkin said. "You see an assistant around?"

"He was here a minute ago, doctor." She whispered to him. "You know anesthesiology. The community's department."

Dr. Licata caught the conversation. "Yep. Run like an independent outfit, hey Alan? One of these days Rockewicz'll land on them. Maybe ask you to take over."

"Not a chance."

A small Oriental man scurried in, dragging an oscilloscope, which he plugged into a wall outlet. Motzkin, unfailingly polite, thought him to be a friend of his most recent aide, Yoshiro. "Ah, *Ohayo,*" he said.

"What?"

"*Ohayo.* That's Japanese for good morning. Maybe you and Yoshiro. . . ."

"I'm Korean, Dr. Motzkin. I'm Cho. Cho Park." He extended a hand, tripped on a cable, landed in Motzkin's arms. "Sorry. New shoes."

"Cho, you can start the IVs as soon as the patient's brought in." Motzkin's eyes were tolerant over the mask.

Licata and Mihrab held their scrubbed arms and hands high. Flor Aquino draped the green gowns over them. She helped them put on the latex gloves. Licata winked at Mihrab. "Ready for Big Casino, Gamel? This is Eric's buddy. Probably the richest coronary bypass customer in the world."

"With you and Eric, why shouldn't I be ready?" Mihrab asked.

Licata was an Italian-American from the Bronx, a former football player (a 180-pound guard) under the legendary Lou Little. He had gone to Columbia's College of Physicians and Surgeons, and was now nearing the end of the interminable apprenticeship required of cardiothoracic surgeons. He was broad-shouldered, round-headed and thickly muscled.

Gamel Mihrab, the senior resident, was a native of Alexandria, Egypt. He was taller than Licata, but did not convey the same impression of strength.

Carlos Olmedo and another orderly wheeled Walker Tench III into the operating room. It was 7:15.

Motzkin and Cho stepped aside, almost in deference to the enormous sheeted figure. Tench shrunk the walls of the green room. He was larger than life, a challenge.

The orderlies pushed Tench's body onto the operating table. Flor Aquino took off the sheets. Hairless, smooth as a side of beef, Tench's chest and abdomen rose and fell in slow rhythms.

"Good Lord," Sally Moorhead said. "It's his feet. They're practically on my Mayo table. Flor, we'll need that metal extension from the autoclave room."

Jack Licata, in charge of the team until Lake's arrival, surveyed Tench's naked body. "Man, that's a big *bacala*. Extension, hell. We should have done this in the amphitheatre. How about it, Alan? A demonstration for fourth-year medical students?"

"Oh, not on someone as important as Mr. Tench."

"Yeah, guess you're right. We don't get this class around here too often. Mostly our relatives, huh Alan?"

Motzkin smiled. He and Licata understood one another. One had come up the hard way from Brooklyn, the other from the Bronx.

Flor returned with the metal platform for Tench's feet. The swiveling of her hips was always one of the pleasures of working on the Lake team, Motzkin thought. Lately, the anesthesiologist noticed, there had been less than the normal quota of flirting. Licata's pale gray eyes followed her, but he said nothing. Something going on there, Motzkin knew, some funny business involving Licata, Flor, and Mihrab.

"As Fats Waller once said, 'I hates you 'cause your feets too big.' You know that song, Gam?" Licata asked.

"Oh, yes. We sang it at the university. In Arabic, too. His feet are enormous."

"He's hung pretty good, also," the chief resident said.

Dr. Mihrab broke open two sealed packets of sponges impregnated with yellow antiseptic soap. He swabbed Tench's hairless body.

Flor sprayed Tench's body with an aerated adhesive. Then she and Mihrab floated a transparent plastic sheet over it. Sally Moorhead strapped the patient's feet to the extension.

Motzkin was putting bits and pieces together. Licata was a notorious swordsman. Despite a marriage to the stunning Mary Ann McGivern (Sacred Heart, Manhattanville, Hampton Bays), he had bedded down with almost all of the nurses in City General, a few women interns and residents, and at least two volunteer ladies. *Flor.* That was it. And it was no secret that Dr. Mihrab, self-effacing Gamel, was in love with the Filipino girl.

"Wake up, Alan," Licata said. "We're off and running."

The chief resident dug his scalpel into Walker Tench's left groin. Blood oozed freely. Sally Moorhead gave Mihrab a sponge to stop the flow.

"He is very fat," Gamel Mihrab said.

"Yep." Licata moved the scalpel downward, through skin, fat, and fascia, in search of the femoral artery. "But it's got to be down there somewhere."

In a few minutes Licata would uncover Tench's femoral artery. It would be cut, clamped, and a cannula inserted into the opening. From the cannula, a plastic tube would descend to the heart-lung machine. This would be the channel for returning oxygenated blood to Tench's body during the operation.

For about two hours, the ungainly metal contraption on the floor, full of dials, rotary pumps, levers, and coiled tubing, would serve as Tench's heart.

9

Trask and Rashid, carrying their briefcases, paused outside of a double door labeled CONFERENCE ROOM. Trask stopped a nurse wheeling a skeletal woman.

"Will this be in use?"

"Only at lunchtime," she said. "The medical residents usually eat in there."

"Thank you." He walked in. Rashid followed. They sat at a long table littered with old coffee containers, overflowing ashtrays.

"You all right?" Trask asked.

"Why should I not be?"

"It's so easy. As easy as I said it would be."

"Quite. I accepted your leadership and I see that you deserve to lead."

"But you doubted it at first." Trask's carved face managed a smile. Even seated, he seemed to tilt back, his narrow head to the rear of his spine.

"Yes. But your record has been a good one, John."

Trask spread a yellow paper in front of them. "A last look at the floor plan?"

"I have committed it to memory. Besides, Carlos will be there."

Trask frowned. "You mention Carlos all the time. Are you still unsure about me? You wanted Carlos to be in charge, didn't you? You and Fiona?"

"I did. But after . . ."

Rashid stopped. No need to review the recent past. Trask had been proven correct. All doubts had to be set aside. Trask had found his way to their headquarters in Berlin eight months ago. He had been in hiding. He smiled as he referred to himself as an "UFTAP" in the FBI files. Unlawful Flight to Avoid Prosecution. Student activist, revolutionary, visionary, the young man who five years ago had brought New York University to its knees. His picture in the papers, on television. Baiting professors, abusing the police, cursing administrators. But never beaten or jailed. He had disappeared before the heads were cracked.

The Berlin group was dubious about him. Trask had never killed, thrown a bomb, set a stick of dynamite. The others had credentials. Fiona Regan had spoken about the "beauty of terror." She could recite the occasions, the names of victims—British soldiers, even their wives and children, B-specials, a Protestant enemy in Parliament. Rashid had his own bona fides. A smoldering school bus outside of Kfar Blum, a dozen dead children. After that the airport in Amsterdam, firing into tourists at the El Al counter. Arrested by Dutch police, he had been freed when his brothers hijacked a KLM plane and threatened to execute passengers.

Carlos Olmedo had fought even more bravely. But he had been caught. Electrodes embracing his penis and his testicles. An electrical prod shoved up his anus. But he had not talked. In Argentina, he was on police lists under his real name, Vasquez. Olmedo was truly a martyr, the essence of revolution.

Hooks had not yet joined them. He would be enlisted in the cause later, sent to them by a dissident black group calling itself the Ashanti League. A specialist in weaponry and vehicles, fearless, uneducated, he was in a special category. Perhaps disposable later on.

"Yes, you had a modest record," Rashid said. "It is a tribute to your mind that we are here today."

A white-haired man in a hospital coat stuck his head through the doors and spoke to Trask. "You fellows seen Dr. Evans?"

"Which one?" Trask asked.

"Are there two? Burt Evans, cardiology."

"No. We're new. From Guadalajara."

"Hmm. Well, good luck." He vanished.

"Guadalajara?" Rashid asked. Trask, stiff, secretive, continued to amaze him. "What did that mean?"

"Where American students go. The ones who can't get into medical schools here. The hospital is full of them. Nobody remembers who they are. Just say you're from Guadalajara."

"Very good. Very good, John."

Rashid had to give him his marks. He had come to them with no record of killing, but he could offer something none of them had evolved: a revolutionary concept, a worldwide plan for revolution. Trask had created a catchment basin into which all streams of revolutionary action could flow, then rush out to nourish the desert. Like the ancient catchment systems of the Nabateans, stone cisterns and channels that he had seen in the Negev as a boy, before the invaders drove his people away. The conventional pattern of revolution was doomed to failure, Trask said. After his success at NYU and other campuses, he had watched in dismay when hard-hats, the union members, *the workingmen of America,* had beaten up the radicals in New York City. In France and Germany, the unions detested young Maoists and Trotskyites, spurned their call for revolt. Welders, machinists, mechanics, the men who should have been the heart and muscle of the revolution, were emerging as the very enemies of change.

How to regroup? How to bring down the system? Trask had evolved a thesis beautiful in its simplicity. It envisioned a bypassing of the Marxist vanguard of revolution, the industrial workers. They had been co-opted. They were part of establishment fascism.

Hence, the thrust of the world revolution had to be by way of the underdeveloped countries, the third world. They controlled much of the raw materials that capitalism needed: oil, metals, lumber. The supply would be turned off. Activists would force the governments to refuse to trade with the United States, Japan, even the traitorous communist bloc.

Simultaneously, as if unleashing a pincer movement, the masters of capitalism would be subjected to a reign of terror such as they had never seen before. Kidnappings, bombings, sabotage, robberies. Terrorized at the top, cut off from raw materials, the collapse would come sooner than anticipated. Trask spoke convincingly. Resource shortages were already putting a strain on so-called western civilization. Under double pressure, the old order would crumble.

The organization—in an amorphous state before Trask arrived in West Berlin—had suspected him at first. Was he a CIA plant?

They tested him, queried him, checked his past. He seemed a dedicated revolutionary. He appeared cool and rational, and, above all, he was the author of The Plan.

Terrorists from India, the Japanese Red Army, Tupamaros, Montoneros, fedayeen from the Middle East, Maoists, anarchists, Frelimos, black extremists from America listened as Trask expatiated. He was learned, knowledgeable, familiar with historical movements, the behavior of masses, the corrupt nature of the old order. It was Trask who gave them their name: the Wretched of the Earth, or WOTE. By Marx out of Frantz Fanon. "We will overwhelm the old order with sheer weight of numbers, starving them for oil, for tungsten and copper, terrorizing them at the top. No executive, no owner, no member of the propertied elite can ever feel safe. In time, they must succumb."

But where to start? Trask insisted they begin modestly. But they would let the world know that it was the Wretched of the Earth striking at them. The first assault, less than five months ago, had been the bombing of the Bourse, the Paris Stock Exchange. Trask and a party that included Fiona, Olmedo, and Rashid worked with a French student group. They had infiltrated a man into the night security squad. A simple pipe bomb, detonated by a windup clock, had set off the charge at three in the morning. No one was killed or injured. But thousands of documents had been destroyed, burned to cinders, files wrecked, switchboards and communications systems immobilized. Calls were made to the newspapers from isolated phone booths. "We are the Wretched of the Earth," Trask's people said. "And this is the beginning."

The cadre disbanded, met again in London: Trask, Rashid, Olmedo, Fiona. There, the second assault was planned. They would escalate into armed robbery. This time Trask's planning was more ingenious. In broad daylight, armed with M2 carbines stolen from a NATO depot in Brussels, they had walked into the United Merchants Bank of the Midlands in Manchester and had made off with $100,000 in English currency.

Fiona, posing as an Irish immigrant factory hand, was crucial to the operation. Her accent was impeccable, her appearance innocent. She had held the automatic weapon under the nose of an astonished teller, this white-skinned Irish girl, then fired a burst into the ceiling before scooping thousands of pound notes into a duffle bag. Rashid and Olmedo guarded the doors. Trask sat outside at the wheel of a stolen Rover.

They escaped by different routes to Belfast, hid in the house of one of Fiona's confederates, and planned the next move. There were uneasy moments. Fiona's friends were wary of committing her to an international movement. Again, Trask won them over. He knew more than they did. He understood the forces at work beneath the surface. The Provos were glad to see them leave for America.

"One bombing and one bank robbery," Trask told them when they reassembled in New York, "did not make a revolution." They were ready for an operation that would make the world take notice. Journalists and police officials who had written off the Wretched of the Earth as a crackpot splinter group would change their minds. They would strike to terrorize every heart in every board room.

And so, Rashid reflected, they were now in this busy hospital, two fraudulent physicians sitting in a conference room. In a few minutes the plan would be under way. Rashid, nurturing memories of the school bus and the airport, felt a calming wave wash over him, almost as if he were deep in *kif.* He studied Trask's narrow face. The eyes were emotionless. An odd sheen on the taut flesh. A strange bird, John Trask. Yet he knew something.

"You have been right, John. It was wrong to doubt you."

Trask nodded slightly.

In the corridor, nurses, doctors, and patients walked by the glass doors. There would be no innocent bystanders, Trask argued. All were guilty. All were forced to stand judgment. He had decided that six years ago when the helmeted workers had beaten up the students. No innocents. Those who would not listen to the voice of salvation would have to be eliminated.

10

Dr. Motzkin forced an endotracheal tube into Walker Tench's throat. Cho Park, his assistant, taped Tench's right hand to the edge of the table. The back of the hand was a mass of tapes and tubings—the intravenous leads. Motzkin made an incision in an artery in the patient's left arm. Into this he inserted a tube for the monitoring of Tench's arterial pressure.

At the other end of the table, a clamp opened. A stream of blood spurted from Tench's femoral artery. "Lousy hemostat," Dr. Licata said. "Give me one that works." He gave the clamp to Sally Moorhead. "Sally, send this one to general surgery. They can use it on gall bladders." Licata reclamped the artery and inserted the cannula into the opening.

"He is a huge man," Gamel Mihrab said.

"Fat, skinny, big, small," Licata said. "Allee samee Dr. Lakee."

Motzkin, who worried about foreigners' sensitivities, glanced at Cho. The Korean was adjusting the ventilator, making sure that Tench's lungs got enough oxygen. The assistant was slow, but he seemed to know his way around.

"Cho, are the rectal and esophageal thermometers in place?" the anesthesiologist asked.

"Ah. . . . Oh. Yes, doctor."

"Don't mix 'em up," Licata said gruffly. He cut deeper into Tench's thigh. "The poor guy will try to swallow through his anus."

"And is he catheterized?" Motzkin asked his assistant. "Dr. Lake insists on monitoring of urinary output."

"Soon as I get his legs up," Cho said. He tripped on the electrical saw as he crossed the room and fell against Gamel Mihrab, who frowned and helped the Korean up. "Please be careful," Dr. Mihrab said.

"Sorry, sorry."

Cho fumbled a moment with Tench's flaccid penis, then located the catheter, which fed urine into a plastic bag. "It's in, doctor," he said.

"This guy has layers of fat on top of his fat," Licata said. "It may be a long morning."

"Watch it, Jack," Motzkin laughed. "Maybe our VIP isn't unconscious. He may hear you."

"Then hit him with some more morphine, Alan."

"I was kidding. He's out."

"He better be, considering what we're doing to him," Licata sighed. "A good thing God didn't give us three assholes. We'd be shoving everything including stereo cables into them. Right speaker, left speaker."

"Tench is so rich," Motzkin said, "he may have three. He's got more of everything than anyone."

Licata glanced at the anesthesiologist. "When he comes out of the fog, maybe you could get us some stock market tips, hey Alan? Tench Consolidated? Tench Electronics?"

Motzkin did not take offense. Licata and he played the game at every operation, at least until Lake arrived.

The cannula in Tench's femoral artery began to bleed through. Licata scowled. "Secure that, will you Flor?" he asked. "This isn't my morning."

Blood had stained Licata's gown. He was a meticulous man and it annoyed him. He called to Flor for a new gown and gloves. The Filipino girl held up a gown for Licata. Facing her, he winked at the slanted eyes. She did not react. Mihrab noticed the interplay and looked away. Why had Licata talked about his conquest? At times the loneliness, the isolation, the sense of loss—of family, of homeland—drowned Dr. Mihrab in melancholy.

"Back to the drawing board," Licata said.

A stocky black man walked into the operating room. Tufts of gray hair peeked from under the green cap. He had calm brown eyes, skin the color of coffee ice cream.

"Where you been, James William?" Licata asked.

"Short a man. You know how it is. Holiday Monday. Everyone takes a three-day weekend."

"Hi, Jimmy," Dr. Motzkin said. Mihrab smiled at the new arrival.

"Good morning, Dr. Motzkin, Dr. Mihrab. Sorry I'm late. But Musgrave is hung up in the cath lab. I'll run the pump myself."

Motzkin watched him walk to the squat machine that would act as Walker Tench's heart. It was odd how Jimmy Baggs gave the team that indefinable *extra*—confidence, strength, expertise. Baggs was not a physician. His title was Chief Perfusion Technician, which meant that he and the men under him, all of whom he had trained, were in charge of the heart-lung machine and other mechanical equipment in the OR.

Watching Baggs sit on the bench and face the controls, Motzkin felt the sense of rightness and purpose that the black man brought. "Next to Eric," he had confided to Beverly, "Jimmy Baggs is the most important person in the room."

"Next to Eric and you," she corrected him.

"No, Bev, *next to Eric*. Jimmy Baggs could damn near operate if they'd let him."

Baggs was in his early forties, strong and quick, a former warrant officer in the Army medical corps. He had been a career man, resigned in a dispute with a hospital administrator, attended a junior college in California, and had found his way to Eric Lake three years ago. Lake knew talent when he saw it. Baggs was a mechanical wizard, a man with an understanding of machines, a born leader. He had put together a team of skilled technicians, men with no more than high school educations. They swore by Baggs, obeyed him, imitated his cool manner in the OR.

"He's a big one," Baggs said softly.

"But soft," Licata said. "Hemostat, Sally. Like this tackle from Cornell I played against once. Huge guy. Two-forty. I knocked him down every time we tangled. That was the old Jack Licata, one of—"

Motzkin chuckled. "We know. One of Columbia's hundred-and-eighty-pound watch-charm guards."

"That's what Dan Daniel called me. Right in the sports section of the *World-Telegram.*"

"Dr. Licata," Baggs said quietly, "Dr. Lake may be delayed. I saw him going into Mr. Rockewicz's office."

Licata groaned. "Late and in a lousy mood."

The Lake team knew about the tension between Stephen Rockewicz, the executive director, and the surgeon.

"Yeah, Steve is after the Lake empire again," Licata muttered. "Won't quit till Eric follows the rules."

Sally Moorhead nodded. "He'll wait a long time."

"This Mr. Tench," Licata said, "ought to have a saphenous vein the size of a python. We shall now find it and relieve him of a section." He took a scalpel and cut into Tench's left thigh. "Another dull tool." He gave it to Sally. "This one can go to obstetrics."

After viewing the angiograms of Walker Tench's heart, Dr. Lake went to the office of the chief attending in radiology, Dr. Fred Braff. Braff was a young man with long chestnut hair. He wore Indian tunics and sandals. He was one of Lake's favorite people at City General.

The two men looked at the X-rays of Tench's heart. "The diagonal branch," Braff said, "isn't clearly defined."

"Maybe it winds around to the rear."

"Or it might be deep."

"I hope not. I hope it isn't stenosed down the line. He's going to need all the blood I can give him."

"Shouldn't faze you, Eric. Want to see the new pictures of the Ramazotti girl?" Lake nodded. He stared at the X-ray of Tench's heart, looking for a clue to the diagonal branch of the artery. An X-ray of Angela Ramazotti's heart replaced Tench's. She was twelve, a sickly girl with an ASD, an atrial septal defect. She was scheduled for surgery that afternoon.

"This looks routine," Lake said.

Braff nodded. The surgeon read X-rays better than a lot of radiologists. Their concentration was interrupted by Steve Rockewicz's brash voice. The executive director of the hospital had thrust his shaved blond head and chunky pink face into the cubicle. He grinned and his eyes vanished. The Polack W. C. Fields, Jack Licata called him.

"Good morning, Eric. And to you too, Fred. Ah, the chief attending in radiology is wearing new sandals. But still no socks. Don't you get chilly ankles, Fred?"

Braff smiled. Rockewicz loved playing hard-hat.

"Hi, Steve," Lake said. He did not take his eyes from the X-ray of Angela Ramazotti's heart.

"Got a minute for me, Eric?"

"I'm due in surgery."

"I checked. They're not ready yet. Be my guest, huh?"

11

"We are on schedule?" Rashid asked.

"Yes," Trask said. "We are always on schedule. I told you it's a matter of planning."

"You have contacted Carlos?"

"He's expecting us. Remember, I don't want you in the room until thirty seconds after you see me enter with Lake. Understood?"

"I understand. I have done more dangerous things."

Trask's back edged away. Thus far Rashid had been cooperative, capable. But he wondered about him. This was not a matter of aimlessly spraying bullets at people. Their job required precision, discipline. Yet Rashid had been good at the bank in Manchester. Trask had lectured him before the holdup. Forget all the romantic nonsense your father taught you. This is cold, professional work. You need not prove anything about your manhood or your contempt for life. We do this so others can live decently. We make of terror the perfect weapon for good, for humanity's survival, for the end of oppression and exploitation.

"Remember the big pane of glass?" Trask said.

"Yes. I smash it inward. I will need the open space to cover the room."

12

"Eric, the board's on my tail again," Rockewicz said.

"Why?"

They were seated in the executive director's office. In contrast to the shabbiness of most of City General, this room had leather chairs, carpeting, drapes.

"Eric, don't get sore. I'm getting flak. The Lake empire. Failing to file reports. Ignoring the surgical-medical conferences. Some of the chiefs of services have been squealing."

"Evans. Can I help it if the general surgeons don't like me?" He lit a cigarette.

"Ah, the smoking lamp is lit." Rockewicz called to his secretary, Mrs. LeBlanc. "Estelle, an ashtray for Dr. Lake." He stared at the ceiling. "Eric, come on. I've told those people a hundred times our coronary and cardiac surgery department was nothing before you came. So what if you're in the big money? Like earning more than all the other chiefs combined. I don't care."

"Neither do I."

"It's hard to explain," Rockewicz said. He thanked Estelle for the ashtray and ogled her trim figure. She was reputed to be a former mistress of Steve's. Attractive, her gray hair bouffant and perfumed, she guarded his castle and did not trust Eric Lake or the loyalties he engendered.

"Frankly, Eric," Rockewicz said, "they're pissed off at the way you handled Walker Tench the Third."

The surgeon watched him run a meaty hand over his golden fuzz. Lake was not a man to underrate the executive director. Rockewicz posed as an anti-intellectual. It kept physicians, staff, nurses, the board of managers, at a distance.

"What did I do wrong?" Lake asked.

"You hid him."

"Tench wanted it that way."

"We could have gotten some mileage out of it. How about a story after the operation?"

"Only when Tench wants it."

"You could encourage him. He's your old buddy from Princeton. Why not let us tell the newspapers, oh, about four hours from now, when you've bypassed his arteries?"

"No."

Rockewicz grinned. The eyes disappeared. "Eric, you're like the late Charles Lindbergh. You don't know if you want the public eye or not. But if not for yourself, for the good of the hospital. The board wants you to hold a press conference after you revascularize Mr. Tench's arteries."

"Absolutely not."

"If Mr. Tench approves it?"

"He'll be in no condition to make decisions for a few days."

Rockewicz got up and walked around the office. He hugged his chest, paused beneath a marble frieze of Sir William Harvey. Federal programs were generous in 1936. Marble pilasters testified to the power of the New Deal. "You make it tough for a humble Polack like Big Steve."

"I won't do anything that smacks of public relations," Lake said. "This is a routine double bypass on a fifty-one-year-old man suffering from angina and coronary insufficiency. It isn't news. When I perfected the technique for aortic valve prosthesis, *that* was news, and your PR people were asleep. I know why. The medical hotshots got to them. Those cardiologists and internists who don't care for the way I cure people."

"A favor for Steve."

"I'll think about it. I've got surgery on my mind right now, not the selling of this hospital."

He got up. Rockewicz escorted him to the door, clamped an iron arm around Lake's shoulders. "One more thing, Eric. The board wants to know how come we keep getting so many foreigners in your department."

"We can't attract qualified Americans to this dump. Sorry, Steve, it's true. Besides, I like foreigners. They learn faster."

"All them little brown and yellow people with their shoes curling up in front."

"They know their jobs."

"What do I tell the board? They keep hollering for more Americans."

"Tell them Americans want to run off and become millionaires before they're properly trained."

Rockewicz opened the door. "If you weren't so good, I'd get sore. The comptroller is drawing up a schedule for you on that donation deal. Might as well get the biggest tax break possible. Besides, we need the money. Don't think I'm not grateful."

Lake frowned. "Anything else?"

"Yeah. Marvin Schlosser's Bar Mitzvah tomorrow. We're invited. I think we should put in an appearance at Temple Sinai. Just for the reading of the Torah. The Chinese food we can skip."

"Marvin's thirteen already?" Lake smiled. "He was the first patient I ever tried the aortic prosthesis on."

Walking to the elevator, Lake marveled at Steve Rockewicz's cunning talent for manipulating people. *Do this for me, I'll do that for you.* There was no denying it: He was the force holding the decrepit hospital together. A few weeks ago pharmacy had run out of Lasix, a much-prescribed diuretic. Rockewicz had borrowed a helmet from a construction worker and a motorcycle from a patient at the methadone clinic. Then he had blasted across town and wheedled a case of Lasix from the Veteran's Hospital. Such a man was worthy of respect.

13

By 7:15 A.M., James J. Cardone, president and chief operating officer of Tench Industries, Inc., was at his desk in the Tench Tower Building. He was dictating a book called *The Corporate Response*, a defense of free enterprise, bigness, conglomerates.

Cardone was a careful user of time. He spent one hour dictating notes for his book. At 7:45 he reviewed corporate reports and statements, then glanced through the *Wall Street Journal.* By 8:00 he was ready for his high command—group vice-presidents, key managers. Only thirty-eight years old, he was dismayingly

vigorous to the older board members. They considered him too
flashy in manner and dress (he favored flared suits, crocodile
loafers, flamboyant ties) and a bit dangerous in his thinking.
Against the board's wishes, but with Walker Tench's approval, he
had begun experimenting with something called the Tench Foundation for Inner Cities.

Tench had brought Cardone into the corporation. He'd looked
for a new president from outside the Tench empire and had found
Cardone running a prosperous ethical drug company in New
Jersey. Cardone had attracted attention by creating one of the
first programs for training minorities. He had made executives
spend a week in the plant, and insisted they get involved in their
local communities.

"I sneaked Jim Cardone into Tench Industries," the chairman
told a reporter from *Business Week*, "and I've never regretted it.
Look at our earnings last year."

With Cardone running the enterprise, Walker Tench III decided he would travel more, learn something about the world, get
involved with the foundation. He had been searching for a new
role for himself when coronary artery disease disabled him.

When the Tench corporate leaders assembled in Cardone's
office at 8:06, one of their number, the vice-president for public
relations, a former reporter named Randolph Hutchins, had
learned that Tench was in City General Hospital. An aunt of
Hutchins who worked in the admissions office had seen a memo-
randum on Tench. She had phoned her nephew. Hutchins informed Cardone, who at once summoned his people.

"You're certain it's Walker?" James J. Cardone asked.

"No question, Jim."

"Hmmm. I imagine he didn't want to upset us. Or affect the
new stock issue."

No one spoke. Cardone was the youngest man in the room. He
was tall and angular, with lushly waved black-gray hair. Beak-
nosed, wide-mouthed, his hollow cheeks were splotched maroon
and purple, the stigmata of hypertension. In lesser men, the

oversized features might have been deemed ugly. In Cardone they produced an aura of command. He was a genius of sorts, the old hands conceded, the man who had signed multimillion-dollar contracts with the Soviet Union, East Germany, Red China, for the marketing of Tench cosmetics and Tench appliances. *How simple it had been!* Soon Cardone was collecting modern art, lunching with cabinet officers. Little was known about him. It was rumored he was the son of a Brooklyn barber and had gone to night school.

"Randolph, have you spoken to the hospital?" Cardone asked.

"No sir."

"Do so at once. One of us should be there. How about Mrs. Tench?"

There was a laugh from somewhere in the room.

"Which one, Jim?" Hutchins asked.

Cardone smiled. "The last one, I imagine."

"She's in Davos. Or Klosters."

Cardone tapped his lips. "Daughter? That twenty-year-old girl?"

Hutchins shook his head. "Mr. Tench wasn't in touch with any of his family for some time. I'd heard the girl was living in a commune in upstate New York."

"We should try to find her. And notify the most recent Mrs. Tench."

The president walked to a mahogany lectern where he did most of his work. There was no desk in his office, just the lectern and two coffee tables hewn from ancient oaks. "What's wrong with Walker?"

"The operation is called a double bypass of the coronary arteries," Hutchins said. "They revascularize the arteries of the heart that have grown narrow and that are cutting off the blood supply."

Gallatin, a white-haired man of clerical mien, the company treasurer, cleared his throat. "Jim, it's a routine operation. My cousin had it. They do thirty thousand a year now."

"I see," Cardone said. He did not look at Gallatin. He knew his enemies. Hutchins was young, his kind of man.

"I pulled some articles out of *Time* and *Newsweek* from our library," Hutchins said. "Want me to paraphrase them?"

Cardone nodded. Fast thinking, fast moves, were in order. If Tench died, Cardone would be in peril. Gallatin, Auslander, all the older men, would be gunning for him. And what about Mrs. Tench, off in Switzerland with a Greek? Or the daughter, so long out of touch with Walker? How did they figure in the apportionment of Tench stock?

"The coronary arteries, which supply blood to the heart, suffer closure or narrowing," the public relations man said. "Less blood flows into the heart and the result is angina, pain caused by vessel spasm due to metabolic deficit. I recall Mr. Tench popping pills before he took off on this last vacation."

"Vacation, indeed," Gallatin said. "He was off to the doctors."

"If these lesions in the arteries aren't relieved," Hutchins went on, "they can become closed altogether by a clot or a spasm. That results in heart attack, destruction of part of the heart muscle. And possibly death."

"And the bypass?" Cardone asked. "That delivers more blood to the ventricle?"

"Yes, Jim," Hutchins said. He held up a diagrammatic drawing from *Time*. "It's just what the name implies. They cut sections out of a vein in the patient's leg and graft them to a point *below* the diseased artery, on to a healthy chunk. Then they connect the other end of the vein to the aorta. So the artery gets more blood from the aorta by way of the vein graft."

Gallatin cleared his throat. "May I ask who the surgeon is?"

"Man named Lake," Hutchins said. "Dr. Eric Lake."

"I've never heard of him," Gallatin said. "Jim, this is too bad. We could have gotten Mr. Tench into Houston with DeBakey or Cooley. And there are Robinson and Spencer in New York."

Another board member spoke up. "City General? That's one of those old places. It's full of junkies and unwed mothers."

Cardone looked out of his high window: dirt, haze, smoke, an iron-gray sky over New York. Why had Tench run off to City General, out of the state and into the hands of an obscure surgeon?

"Dr. Lake is an old friend," Hutchins explained. "He went to college with Mr. Tench. The way I've put it together, he got sicker and sicker, then decided he didn't want anyone to know. So he went to an unlikely place like City General and to a doctor who'd keep the story quiet."

"I wish he'd let us handle it," Cardone said.

"Lake is an able man," Hutchins said. "I checked around."

Cardone was still at the window. "Someone should be there . . . it's wrong. No family, no friends . . ."

"I'll go," Hutchins said.

Cardone's rocketing career was in jeopardy. If Tench died, or came out of surgery a wheelchair case, Cardone would be *in precarium*. Tench had appreciated him from the start. What few of the men in his office understood was how simple it was to succeed. Most among their number would have guessed that the marketing of lipstick in Leningrad—when they tried it a few years back—would have sent American patriots into the streets demanding the blood of traitors. Cardone knew otherwise. Tench had been impressed by Cardone's daring. But with Tench gone or disabled, where would Cardone be?

"I'll go to the hospital," the president said. "Order my car."

"If you want me, Jim," Hutchins said. "A press release later . . ."

"I'll send for you if you're needed."

Riding across the city in his silent chauffeured limousine, Cardone was already organizing a defense in depth if that two to three percent mortality rate claimed Walker Tench. The moisture of fear formed on his upper lip, his palms. He had come up from industrial backwaters, sooty streets like the ones he now rode through. He could fall as fast. And the market for boy wonders these days wasn't bullish.

14

Hooks released Fiona. Her silent acquiescence infuriated him. He had been unable to come. "Fuckin' bitch," Hooks muttered. "You people niggers in Belfast, but you just a dead-ass honky. No wonder ole Trask stop sleepin' with you."

She looked ludicrous, helpless, lying in front of him, bare-assed, her black slacks down to her ankles. Hooks stood up. His chest heaved. He was sweating prodigiously.

The girl turned around, pulled up her underpants and trousers, and got up from the cot. Hooks studied her bleached face. A little makeup would help. Not enough blood, not enough red meat. He was troubled by her flat blue eyes. She was not afraid.

"You a crazy chick," Hooks said. He said it almost in tribute. "You not afraid of me."

"Hooks, you are a vile and stupid man, and if it were not so late, I would demand of Trask that we get rid of you. You are unreliable. You are full of your own selfish needs. We should shoot you for what you just did."

"Cool it, baby."

Hooks sat down. He spread his long legs, clad in khaki trousers, GI boots. He wore a faded OD shirt. On his shaved ebony pate was a Navy watch cap.

"I'll tell Trask about this when we're finished," she said. "You are filth, trash."

"The brothers gonna look after me. I just on loan. They lend me to Trask 'cause ain't no one can handle weapons like Hooks."

"Anyone can shoot guns," Fiona said.

She picked up a brown duffel bag. It did not appear heavy. Alongside it was a large oblong package wrapped in brown paper. She took that, too. She set them by the door, buttoned her tan sheepskin jacket around her throat. "I'm going," she said. "If you do your job, I'll forget about what happened."

"You forget sheeet."

"Good Christ! And you represent the people we're supposed to save."

"I don' need no savin'. Not by you."

"Follow orders, Hooks."

He laughed, sprang from the seat, and grabbed her again. She was boneless in his huge hands. "I tear you to bits, baby. Send you back to Ireland in a tomato can."

Her tiny hands flew to his face. The nails dug into his dark cheeks. She spit into his astonished eyes. The black pupils seemed to melt into the whites. Twin paths of red welts bloomed on Hooks's face. He released her.

"You'll be called to account for this," she said. "We're not quits yet."

He had an urge to bash her with a gun barrel. Leave her in a lump on the floor, tell Trask and his crazies to do the thing themselves. But he hesitated. The Ashanti chief had given him the word: "You go along, Bateman. You be our Main Man. We help them to a point, then we teach them a lesson. It all end up with us."

Fiona shivered. She drew the sheepskin around her neck and trudged down the sloping stairs, inhaling the aroma of cat urine. All the same, in Belfast or here: the halls stink of pee. A moment's panic over Hooks made her shudder. He was foul-tempered, erratic. Trask was supposed to have screened everyone. He had insisted on a black on the team. The trouble with so many of the movements, Trask explained, was that they had lost contact with the blacks. He recalled his days as a student activist, the march down Wall Street. Not a black face in their ranks. They would be won back by the Wretched of the Earth.

A freezing rain had begun to fall. A line from James Joyce flitted through her mind. *Snow was general all over Ireland.* Books, teachers, classrooms. How long ago! Now she was committed. She had joined the ranks of those who were capable of "more than innocence." Shelley? Sod the poets. They confused the issue.

Wet snow oozed into her loafers. A hardy breed, inured to the vilest weather on earth. Cold feet and wet ankles could not detain her. In the street, walking toward a bus stop, she worried about

Hooks. If he deserted them, she would drive, shoot, kill. She had sent British Army trucks up in orange bursts, heard the soldiers scream, stared later at photographs of the scorched bodies. "I feel nothing for them," she told an American newsman.

She paused at an intersection. Across the street was the bus stop. First one bus, then another, then a walk to the hospital. In front of her, as she crossed, men in mustard-colored hats and damp blue overalls were excavating. Some were sipping coffee around a fire in a steel drum.

"Carry ya luggage, lady?" one hooted.

"You put out, sweetie?"

"Where's your old man? If he's on day shift, I'm available."

The workmen guffawed, whistled. Does it ever end? Fiona asked herself, this preoccupation with their bloody fat pricks? Sod them all. What would Trask say? If they were bent on changing the world, uprooting the old order and elevating the victims of oppression, what could be done with these horny laborers? Had Marx and Che and Mao missed a few subtleties?

"Eat at the Y, baby?"

15

Draped in green, all that was visible of Tench's body was a foot-square area of his flabby chest and his left leg. His head was hidden under a green cloth canopy. The rubber tubing that entered the canopy rose and fell as the machine ventilated him. His flesh was waxy smooth.

At 8:22 A.M., Dr. Licata made a vertical incision into the chest. Blood oozed discreetly. The cut widened, reddened. Suction tubes were thrust into the slit. Sponges dabbed at the scarlet rills. With no wasted motion, Licata and Mihrab snipped vessels and sizzled the bleeding ends with electrocautery.

"He is very large," Mihrab said. "I hope the standard retractor is big enough." His hands moved expertly, separating layers of fat.

"Yeah, this is what the good life does for a man," Licata said.

"Sally, you see what untold wealth, coupla wives, lots of mistresses, and all the booze you can buy results in?"

Miss Moorhead smiled. She was a Maine native, well-mannered, a maiden lady, but tolerant of Licata's crudities.

"Flor, something's wrong with suction."

Miss Aquino glided past the surgeons and past the heart-lung machine. Jimmy Baggs got up from his bench. They got to the suction tank at the same time. Baggs knew when things went wrong. He had a second sense. He and Flor adjusted the faucets on the tanks.

"Thing should be junked," Baggs said. "I told Dr. Lake again, it's in the way. It should be on trolley tracks overhead."

"And what did he say, Jimmy?" Licata asked.

"He said, 'Find me the money, James.' That's what he always says."

Baggs went back to his seat at the heart-lung machine and began to fill in forms. Normally an assistant did the paper work.

Gamel Mihrab, snipping, sponging, looked at Baggs. A remarkable man, the Egyptian thought. Intelligent, creative. Black, but never subservient or clownish. Mihrab decided that dignity and competence had been bred into Baggs. He could not help being what he was—the best perfusion man in the world.

"And the membrane oxygenator, Jimmy?" Mihrab asked. "Did you bring that up?"

"Dr. Mihrab, you needling me? We will be using these old bubble oxygenators until the end of time. Dr. Lake wants the new ones, but he's got to fight the administration for one thing at a time."

The air was laced with the odor of scorched flesh. "Smell that barbecue," Licata said. "Flor, check the suction again. It comes and goes. I don't like all this blood. Gamel, could you stick a few more hemostats on the edge of the incision? This guy has more layers than a blue whale."

Licata watched Flor dart by him again. Ah, what a rat he had been. Enticing her into an empty room, tossing her onto a mattress, peeling the white pantihose from her trembling legs. "Doctor, I am just a little girl from the provinces. I was raised in a convent." She had resisted, but only up to a point. Like skinning a rabbit. The yellow-brown skin, the slanted eyes, had driven him up a wall. He had been heavy-handed, cruel. And then he had talked about it to some residents over a beer. Gamel knew. Yet they faced each other over Tench's slit chest, cooperative, supportive—even friendly.

"We're going to buy Flor roller skates for her birthday," Licata said.

"Flor is quite fast enough," Mihrab said.

The chief resident didn't answer. Then he nodded in satisfaction. "Ah, the sternum. Had to be there somewhere. Jimmy, I'll take the saw."

Baggs left the heart-lung machine and wheeled the Stryker saw into position. The surgeon grabbed it as if he were about to cut firewood. "Stand back, folks," he said. "Jack the Ripper cuts again." Mihrab pulled the flaps of tissue apart. The saw hummed.

"Bookshelves? Anyone need a cabinet? You'd never guess I flunked woodworking in DeWitt Clinton High School." Screaming, the saw ripped into Tench's breastbone and split it vertically. It took seconds.

Mihrab took a metal retractor from Sally Moorhead.

"He's fine so far," Alan Motzkin said, squinting at the monitor. "Blood pressure is one-twenty over ninety."

"Body temp?" Licata asked.

"Normal."

"The way Dr. Lake likes his subjects," the chief resident said. "We could cool beer in the cavity."

"Jack, you are in a good mood today," Mihrab said.

"I'm a little manic. It isn't every day we do open heart on a conglomerate."

Motzkin cleared his throat. He was waiting for Jack to tease him again, but Licata and Mihrab were busy setting the metal retractor over the cavity.

"I read an interesting article on hypothermia in the *Journal of Anesthesiology*," Motzkin said. He was resting on a stool. A bit overweight, his feet tended to bother him. He wore jogging sneakers under the green paper slippers.

"Do they recommend the J. Baggs method?" Licata asked. "Cooling the patient with ice cubes?"

Baggs smiled as he checked the isolation transformer.

"That's the funny thing," Motzkin said. "It's as efficient as a heat exchanger."

Mihrab set the teeth of the spreader inside the breastbone. Winding the screw, he pulled the sternum apart. There was silence for a moment. They all stared at the bloody cavity for the first look at Tench's heart. It beat potently under the pericardium, as if straining to tear itself loose. Above it looped the hoselike aorta, pink, thick, full of power.

"Looks okay?" Licata asked Mihrab.

"Yes, Jack, fine."

"We're on schedule." He moved down the table and took a self-retaining retractor from Sally Moorhead, then anchored it to the upper end of the incision in Tench's leg.

Jimmy Baggs was taping the CV monitor to a pole. He seemed to be everywhere, reading gauges, helping the nurses, filling out forms. Lake contended that Baggs's mere presence forced others to work better. Some months ago, a *Times* reporter, observing Lake perform a resection of a ventricular aneurysm, found himself running blood gas samples to the laboratory. He was assumed by Baggs to be part of the team, and Baggs had put him to work.

Deep in Tench's chest, Mihrab found the thymus gland, a round red bulb, and tied it off. Once, early in his residency, he had failed to "exclude" the gland from the surgical field. Lake had bawled him out pitilessly, with a quiet fury that the Egyptian never forgot.

Licata probed deeper into Tench's leg for the saphenous vein. Mihrab worked on the right atrium and the vena cava. From them, catheters would lead to the heart-lung machine. Blood would flow into the tubes through simple gravitational force. Flowing downward, the dark venous blood would enter the machine where it would be cleansed and oxygenated. An electrical pump would force the blood into another tube, this one connected to the femoral artery in Tench's leg. The cycle would be complete. Tench's heart would be inert, anoxic. The metal machine with its coils and tubes and canisters would serve as his heart.

Motzkin reached beneath the canopy and adjusted the black rubber nosepiece of the ventilating hose. Tench was breathing easily. His heart rose and fell with surprising vigor. He had seen it often in people disabled by angina—a heart that acted normally, beat strongly.

Mihrab began to trim the pericardium, the covering around the heart.

"You cut nice," Licata joked. "You do that the way my mother cuts a *calamar'*." He glanced at Flor. "Flor, you know what a *calamar'* is?"

She laughed. "No. And if it's dirty I don't want to hear."

"Not dirty at all," Licata said. "It's squid. You eat squid in the Philippines?"

"We use it for bait. Or throw it away."

16

Hooks debated paying a visit to the tarts across the street. He was enraged at the Irish chick for the way she lay there, unreacting, wilting his manhood. But whores were not for him. He did not have the bread. Besides, he was proud. Black dudes, he told himself, were above that. They ran stables, collected fees, bribed the pigs. College professors were writing books about them.

"Next thing you know," he had said to Carlos Olmedo, "they be writin' about black assholes." In the bathroom, Hooks inspected the red scratches Fiona had imprinted on his face. He felt no pain, washed the traces of blood away, dabbed at the cheeks with iodine.

"Don't show on ole Hooks's black face," he laughed. "Got me natural iodine in the skin."

The last of the group to leave the tenement, Hooks locked the door. He threw the key into a drain. Apart from Fiona's scrawling on the wall—*Fanon, sheeet,* Hooks thought—there were no signs that the place had been inhabited. Neighborhood merchants barely knew them. A group of students from the community college.

Hooks found the Buick a block away, parked next to a lumberyard where mongrel dogs snarled at him. It was not a rental car. It had been bought a month ago, used but in excellent condition, with a big 350 engine. Hooks had worked on it in an alley near the tenement. It ran like a dream, never stalled, accelerated like a shot. He had bought it for cash, with money furnished by Trask. Trask and Rashid always had money available.

"Ole Ratshit, he gettin' it from them oil Ay-rabs," Hooks taunted. There was a bank somewhere in New York where Rashid drew funds. "Ratshit, I follow you to your bank someday and take it all," Hooks taunted. Rashid never responded; he did not understand the black man.

Hooks gunned the engine. Wet and cold, it roared at him. It was full of life. Like the weapons he'd used in 'Nam to shoot slopes. Armalites, M2s, Daisy Cutters, grenades, bazookas. He had enjoyed it for a long time. Sergeant Bateman Hooks, squad leader.

Then something went bad. After they killed the people in the village. He stood shoulder to shoulder with crackers, guineas, Polacks, and joined them blowing up slants. No faces. A mash of red after the M16s cut them up. Legs like sticks. And one of the white sergeants taking him aside: "Not a fuckin' word about this to anyone, Hooks, you hear? You was in it just like us, pullin' that trigger like it was your big black cock."

It had gotten muddled in Hooks's mind. Who was supposed to shoot who? A black noncom, Wallingford, got hold of him one night in a bottle club in Danang. Gave him leaflets to read. Any

VC ever call you nigger, Hooks? What you doin' shootin' them folks for?

Back in the States, he'd wandered around. An open admissions college. A playground job. Then into the Ashanti League, an organization of black veterans. The *indaba* (council) of the league picked him to join Trask's group. "A test case," the boss Ashanti called it. He carried a fly whisk and wore a lion's teeth necklace. "We usually go it alone. But maybe this Trask have something. He win two big ones already. You be his Main Man."

Hooks drove slowly through the city. He had been born in the hospital they were going to take that morning. In a charity ward. Someone had explained to him there were no more wards. The state, the government, paid for everyone. Ain't done no good, Hooks thought. We still come out angry.

They had fragged a lieutenant in Vietnam. He and a brother had tossed a grenade into the tent. Not enough left of the officer to fill a musette bag. "You kill him," Sergeant Wallingford said one night. "Yeah. I take care of him." Wallingford clucked. "Maybe you enjoy it too much, like the time you waste them slants in the village. Someday you meet a man likes to kill better than you, Hooks."

Rain spattered in chunks on his windshield. It could not make up its mind whether it was rain or snow. Driving fast would be rough, but he would do the job, especially with Carlos at his side calling the shots. Show them all who had the guts. He was sick of their bragging about the bomb they'd set off in Paris, the bank they'd robbed in England. This was his turf. They were all amateurs. Except maybe Carlos Olmedo. He'd had his balls burned by the cops in Argentina. Yanked at his tongue, shoved shit up his nose. And he never talked. Hooks wondered why Olmedo hadn't been picked to lead them. But there was some crap about Trask coming up with big ideas, selling it to revolutionary dudes in Berlin. Trask was supposed to know everything.

Hooks swung the Buick into Weaver Park. He had played

baseball there as a kid. They played in ragged sneakers, shirtless, wild and free. Once they had stolen a softball from a bunch of scared Jew-boys. How those little Goldbergs howled!

The park was empty. Trees and lawns were drenched with the snowy rain. He and Trask had scouted the location a week ago. It was under a heavy cover of trees and could not be seen from above. Off a maintenance road, so that the normal run of traffic could not see the Buick. Hooks drove the car into a muddy space between two rows of hedges. To his left the maintenance road snaked through the edge of the park and led to an exit on the opposite side of the city.

Hooks locked the car. He opened the trunk and removed a small OD duffel bag, slinging it over his shoulder. The carbines and grenades clanked against his broad back. Mud and slush oozed around his combat boots. He took a shortcut through the park and came out on a street of two-story houses. Working people. Polacks. Eye-talians. The kids he had fought when he was young.

A police car rolled by. Two white faces looked him over. Nothing suspicious—a spade in GI clothing carrying a sack. Hooks enjoyed staring down pigs. But this morning he managed an Uncle Tom smile and shifted the load to his other arm.

An urge to screw them all tickled him. Run off. Take a bus somewhere. Sell the pieces. He knew a cat who would give him a hundred dollars for the guns. Let those fuckers see how good they would do without Bateman. Trask, with his stiff back and his crazy eyes, the chick, Ratshit, Olmedo. Then he thought of the yellow people he had blasted in 'Nam. People who never did him any hurt. Standing with Zabowski and McClung and watching the bodies jerk in the ditch. The Ashantis had assured him this was one way to pay the debt.

"Git on a train or a bus, Hooks," he said to himself. "And haul ass."

17

As soon as Dr. Lake left Rockewicz's office, the director's secretary, Mrs. LeBlanc, walked in. "Well?" she asked. "Did the Great God Lake unbend?"

"Not much. No press conference. Maybe he'll go to the Bar Mitzvah. You know how he is, Estelle."

Mrs. LeBlanc and others—notably cardiologists—resented Eric Lake and his close-knit team. They did things behind her boss's back. She had it on good authority that Jimmy Baggs had been conferring with a salesman from GE about membrane oxygenators.

Rockewicz's phone rang. Estelle answered it. She covered the mouthpiece. "Mr. Cardone. President of Tench Industries. He sounds angry."

The executive director took the phone. "Mr. Cardone? Stephen Rockewicz. You want to come over? No, I don't think the hospital was under any obligation to inform you. On the contrary, Mr. Tench gave strict orders. But you're more than welcome to stand by. Come right to my office. The operation's under way. There isn't a better heart surgeon in the country than Dr. Eric Lake. . . ."

He winked at Estelle, kept talking, rubbing a hand over his golden fuzz, his voice full of confidence. Steve envisioned not only an imminent visit from James J. Cardone, but a new lab, a new ICU unit. Hell, a new building.

18

Trask led Rashid from the conference room down a flight of stairs. Two small black boys, shrieking obscenities, raced into a hallway. A door slammed.

"They have no security," Rashid said. "We come and go."

An opened door led them into a murky locker room.

Carlos Olmedo was seated on a bench, smoking. "John. Rashid. You are on time."

"Shall we undress?" Trask asked.

"Yes. This is the old locker room. It is used occasionally. People from the PM lab change here."

Olmedo was slender and stooped. He had sallow skin, damp long black hair. His eyes drooped, forever in mourning. His nose seemed to hang to his lower lip.

Trask and Rashid took off their white coats, shirts, ties, and trousers. From the briefcase they extracted two .38 police specials with two-inch barrels and inserted the weapons in leather belts around their midriffs. Olmedo gave each man a bundle of green clothing, short-sleeved tunics, loose trousers, and a green disposable cap.

"Hold the caps," Olmedo said, "until you go into surgery. It is against hospital rules to wear greens outside surgery."

Trask's back went rigid. "Why are we changing now?"

"You would be in trouble anywhere else. The dressing rooms are crowded. You would be too visible."

"What if we are stopped?"

There was noise at the entrance to the locker room. A dustpan was being banged. "Who in heah? Who usin' this room so early?" A fat black man loomed in the doorway. He seemed to enjoy clanking the dustpan against metal lockers, trash cans. The noise reverberated.

"That's all right," Olmedo said. "Visiting students, Albert. I am with them."

"Who that? Oh, Carlos."

Rashid backed away, resting his hand on the .38 under the tunic.

"You will not need it," Olmedo said. "I know the workers. They will listen to me."

From his briefcase Rashid took out an M2 carbine. It was in sections—a barrel and chamber, a folding wire stock. Olmedo gave him a green sheet and he wrapped it around the weapon. "I will show you where you get the slippers and the face masks. Put your white coats on." He looked at Rashid. "You tested the carbine?"

"Two days ago. I would have preferred a Kalashnikov. They are better."

"Are we in accord?" Trask asked. "Two on the inside, one outside?" He was annoyed with Rashid. There was no fear in Rashid, but he displayed an erratic querulousness. The reference to the Kalashnikov, the weapon favored by the *fedayeen*, was irrelevant chauvinism.

"I will go inside if you wish, John," Olmedo said.

"No. You're needed outside of the room. You know the hospital. You're one of them."

Olmedo nodded. "Rashid will come to the supply room with me until you're ready. Remember, if anyone questions you about wearing greens, just apologize."

Trask's head jerked. His spine tilted backward. "The same operating room? The one with only one entrance?"

"Yes. There is no other way of getting in or out."

"No bricked-up doors or windows?"

Olmedo shook his head. "None. I checked it carefully. There is an old air vent, but it is sealed and very narrow."

Trask took a transistor radio from his briefcase and put it in the breast pocket of the green tunic. "To monitor the newscasts," he said.

Olmedo led them into the corridor. The cleaning man was banging his dustpan against the bins outside the postmortem lab. "You are noisy today," Olmedo said.

"It don't bother the stiffs none. Have a good day, doctors."

PART TWO

1

Dr. Licata worked over Tench's thighs. Across the table, Dr. Mihrab stitched the slit pericardium to the wall of Tench's chest. The exposed heart seemed to be beating faster. The orange-red layer of fat pulsated vigorously.

Licata said, "Get a load of that epicardial fat. It's the color of a tangerine."

Mihrab removed a sponge from beneath the heart and gave it to Flor. She gave him a fresh sponge, which he placed beneath the heart. Flor moved the suction tube.

"Here's the old vein," Licata said. "It's the size of a fire hose. Gamel, how do you like it?"

"Beautiful, Jack."

The nurses looked at Tench's saphenous vein. Baggs rose from his seat at the pump. Licata, with a forceps in each hand, lifted the vein from the bed of tissue in Tench's leg. "Spare parts department," Licata said. "We aim to please. Hemostat."

Sally gave him a clamp, which he affixed to the proximal end of the vein. Then he snipped it with a scissors. He fastened a second clamp to the distal end of the vein and cut again. He held up the prize like a proud fisherman—fourteen inches of pink-white vein.

Flor Aquino offered Licata a kidney-shaped basin filled with Normosol solution. Licata dropped the vein into it. "As they say in the recipes," the chief resident said, *"reserve."*

Licata sighed and looked at the wall clock. It was 9:08. They were a little behind schedule. Tench was thick. It took time to cut into him. He took the cauterizing iron and burned the ends of the vein. The patient would not miss it. Other vessels would assume its functions.

"Ducking out for a minute," Motzkin whispered to Cho. "Keep an eye on everything."

Cho nodded sleepily. He was slumped on the stool next to the cart.

Licata leaned across Tench's body and whispered to Mihrab, "Gam, you know where Alan went? He went to call his broker. I can set my watch by it. Soon as the broker gets to the office, Alan pops out."

"Does Eric know?"

"No. And if he did, he'd ream Alan's ass. Me, I'm only a chief resident, so I don't care. If Alan gets his jollies talking about options, who am I to object?"

2

Dark and compact, Rashid blended into the halls of surgery. He walked alongside Carlos Olmedo. They could have been two Puerto Ricans. In green suits and caps, they walked through a door labeled DEPT. OF SURGERY. NO VISITORS. AUTHORIZED PERSONNEL ONLY.

"They do interesting work here," Olmedo said to the Arab. "I must close my mind to it."

Rashid smiled. "I have no such difficulty."

"One side, *amigos.*" A black orderly was pushing a stretcher past them. On it, a golden-haired girl of twelve slept, deep in anesthesia.

They paused at a drinking fountain. Rashid bent his lips to it.

"Excellent water," Olmedo said. "We have our own supply."

"I suffer dryness. Weak kidneys and so forth."

"A pity. We have one of the best urology departments in the country." Olmedo smiled. "When this is over, perhaps one of our urologists can examine you. You could use a different name."

"Perhaps." It annoyed Rashid that Olmedo identified himself with the hospital.

An elderly nurse greeted Olmedo, looked at Rashid as if she should know him, waddled by. At the entrance to surgery, the nurse stopped to chat with chief nurse McCarran. Rashid, glancing back as he followed Olmedo, thought he saw them looking at him. He tucked the wrapped carbine closer against his hip.

3

Motzkin, returning from his call to his broker, took a large syringe from Cho. "Heparin, doctor," the assistant said.

Motzkin plunged the needle into Tench's right atrium. The anticoagulant drug diffused through Tench's body. "Wow, this guy took a hundred and sixty milligrams," Motzkin said. "That would stop a whale from clotting."

Licata called for the vein. He stretched it on the green drapes above the chest cavity and studied it a moment.

Dr. Mihrab was staring at Tench's throbbing heart. "Jack, look at this," he said.

Both surgeons studied the apex of the heart. To one side there was a grayish-brown patch.

"I'll be damned," Licata said. "An old infarct. Never showed up on the cath lab tests or in the EKGs. Wait'll Eric sees this."

Licata held the proximal end of the vein with a forceps. Mihrab held the narrower end with another forceps. They worked swiftly, snipping and peeling tissue from the wormlike vessel, sealing holes with tiny sutures. Licata called for a syringe from Sally. He squeezed water into one end of the vein. It engorged but did not leak. It was ready to be grafted to Tench's heart.

"Wipe our foreheads, huh, Flor?" Licata asked.

She ran for a sterile towel, dabbed at Licata's forehead, touched Mihrab's. Mihrab tried to stop the shaking in his knees. Her eyes were looking at his. Smiling? And he had never touched her. Mossad, an Iranian resident in gynecology, had taken her out one night and reported that she had been a tiger—resistant, strong. "She has a grudge against Moslems," Mossad told Mihrab.

"Where in hell is Eric?" Licata asked.

His friend's assertive voice roused him. Mihrab did not look up. "It's all right, Jack," Mihrab said. "I need a few minutes to put the pacemaker in."

Jimmy Baggs turned in his seat and tugged at the heavy cable connecting the heart-lung machine to the wall outlet. It was secure. He turned the plug left to unlock it, took it out, and inspected the three prongs. Then he replaced it and locked it with a half turn right.

Licata watched Mihrab stitch the pacemaker into place. A good man, Gamel. Good hands, good mind. He wondered about the senior resident. Back to Egypt? What would a good heart surgeon do in Cairo, without any of the new equipment?

"You asked Flor out lately?" Licata said over Tench's thumping heart. The nurse had gone out for coffee.

"Not for some time."

"You should. None but the brave deserve the fair."

"We are ready for pacing if needed, Jack."

Not much yardage there, Licata thought, but I tried.

4

Rashid was astonished by Olmedo's medical knowledge, his grasp of the hospital. The Argentinian acted more like an eager physician than a man about to be part of a conspiracy. He spoke softly, pointing out a room where a craniotomy was in progress. "Dr. Fess is operating in there. A great neurosurgeon. But a bit tense. The doors are always closed. Dr. Lake, on the other hand, enjoys visitors."

"He will have some."

Olmedo led Rashid into the supply room. Huge multitiered carts occupied most of the space. There were two closets at the rear of the room.

"You can start stacking uniforms and sheets," Olmedo said. "Uniforms on one cart, sheets on the other. From the closets. Take your time. When you are finished I will get a mop for you."

Rashid went to work. He had known little about Olmedo. Now, he felt, he knew enough. The man was intelligent and courageous. Olmedo had blended into the hospital skillfully. Could he, Rashid, have done as well? Or was hatred so imprinted in him that he could only act violently?

"Will Dr. Lake please come to the catheterization lab? We have an emergency case, forty-year-old male with a pulmonary embolism. . . ."

The scratchy sound of the loudspeaker drifted into the supply room. Rashid turned from the cart. His eyes appealed to Olmedo, who seemed to know everything about the hospital. "This . . . ? A delay?"

"Perhaps."

"But . . . John. . . ."

"John will hear it also."

The black woman from the autoclave room poked her head in. "Carlos, we short on sheets again. It ain't like you."

"Oh, we have got sheets to spare, Mrs. Fountain." He spoke to Rashid. "*Amigo*, give Mrs. Fountain what she wishes."

5

Leaving Rockewicz's office, Eric Lake heard himself paged. He frowned. Typical of City General. They suffered from chronic misinformation. Someone should have known he was due in surgery. Some other cardiac surgeon could have been called to the cath lab.

In his office, Lake dialed the lab and explained that he could not see the emergency case. One of the senior residents should be available. He lit another cigarette. He was mocked for his orderliness, his love of procedure, but how else did one get complicated jobs done? In upstate New York, his ambitious mother, an impoverished farm manager, had bred it into him. A place for everything and everything in its place. Rockewicz had never learned this. He was an improviser, a man operating on cunning, feints, false trails. He hated to put things in writing. He reveled in keeping lines of communication muddled. Lake made a note: "Better procedure for emergency cardiac cases."

A slender young man wearing a white CGH coat was standing in the doorway. He was wearing greens under the coat. There was a stethoscope in his pocket.

"Dr. Lake?" he asked.

"Yes."

"May I see you a moment?"

"Only a moment. I'm about to go down to surgery. Sit down while I take a few more drags."

The surgeon guessed that the visitor was one of their "fourth-track" men from Guadalajara or Bologna—Americans who did their medical studies abroad. Rockewicz had worked out an intricate scheme for qualifying them for practice in the United States. They came to City General in platoons, unsure of themselves, apologetic, but ultimately useful.

But there was nothing unsure about the man sitting opposite him now. He sat bolt upright in the chair. His knees were pressed together and his slender hands were clasped in his lap.

"My name is John Trask."

"Intern?"

"No. Dr. Lake, do you mind if I close the door? What I have to discuss is of a confidential nature."

"Go ahead. But make it fast."

The door shut, Trask sat down again.

From under the green tunic he took out the .38. He leveled it at the surgeon's head. "Don't move. Don't call anyone. Don't get excited. You're not in danger if you do precisely as I order you to do."

"I believe you."

"You had better. If you don't, I'll kill you."

Lake said nothing. A risk run by all hospitals. Open, vulnerable places, drawing disturbed people the way rotting fruit draws bees. For the time being he would sit and listen and obey. Dr. Fess had experienced a similar situation some months ago. Some relative of a man who died under brain surgery. Waving a gun at him.

"Tell me what you want," Lake said.

"I'm about to." Trask stiffened in the chair. There was a hardness in his eyes. His speech was that of an educated man. The lines in the long face were sharp, there was a tautness around the mouth. Lake crushed his cigarette. The muzzle of the gun made a blue-black "O," on a line with his forehead.

6

James J. Cardone, never a man to waste hours, dictated letters during the ride from New York. He sent the driver back to the office to have them expedited, then ordered him to return to City General.

His walk through the hospital corridors dismayed him. It seemed a bedlam of hurrying nurses, foreign interns, black and Hispanic patients. He found Rockewicz's office and was greeted by Estelle LeBlanc. "Please have a seat, Mr. Cardone. Mr. Rockewicz has someone in with him."

"What about Mr. Tench? May I see him?"

"The operation is under way. He's fine."

Cardone sat down. He was not accustomed to waiting for people. People waited for him. Moreover, the door to the executive director's office was open and an argument was going on. Cardone crossed his legs. Mrs. LeBlanc admired his crocodile shoes.

"Steve, I have a right to see the cardiac catheterization report," a man was saying. "Lake kept it from me."

"An oversight, Burt. You know how Eric is with special cases."

"The Lake empire. Old Procedure. So he's a genius. But it doesn't mean he can close the medical people out. I'm no second-year med student. I'm chief attending in cardiology."

The speaker of these outraged words stood in the open doorway. Cardone saw a scarlet-faced man with a crown of steely gray hair. He was fingering a pair of calipers.

"That's Dr. Evans." Estelle smiled at Cardone. "He's a brilliant heart man."

"And an angry one." Cardone ran a tight ship. He began to fret. What kind of a hospital director left doors open so that noisy arguments could be heard?

"You'll get the cath lab data," Rockewicz was saying. "Estelle! As soon as Mr. Tench is out of surgery, will you ask Dr. Lake for the cath report for Dr. Evans?"

"Yeah," Dr. Evans growled. "After the fact."

Cardone was on his feet. "They are arguing about Mr. Tench?"

Estelle shook her bouffant hair. "It happens all the time, Mr. Cardone. Heart surgeons versus cardiologists."

Cardone was aghast. He took a step toward the door.

"It doesn't matter if the patient is a millionaire pal of Lake's or a broom pusher, Steve. Patients must go through a surgical-medical conference—"

"Rank has its privileges. Tench wanted privacy. He was Eric's friend. Anyway, it's a routine bypass."

"Yeah, routine," Cardone heard Dr. Evans say. "Just what I'm getting at. The surgeons ram these people through like they were appendectomies. We lose more of them than Lake will admit."

Rockewicz's voice was soothing. "Come on, Burt. It depends on whose statistics you use. Besides, what do you want people with heart disease to do? Suffer? They come out free of pain, able to work."

"For how long? I could have done a better job on Tench with propranolol and nitrates. Diet. Rest. Why not?"

"Come off it, Burt. Tench has been on everything—"

Dr. Evans was determined to finish his tirade. "These surgeons won't quit until every adult male is run through the bypass mill. Guy has shortness of breath, they cut. I haven't seen the data on Tench, thanks to Old Procedure, but let me tell you this, Steve, you better have a good story if his heart stops."

"Cut it out, Burt."

Cardone, full of fears, tugged at his fifty-dollar tie, tugged again at the vents in his jacket, and walked into the office.

"Mr. Rockewicz, I am James J. Cardone. I am distressed at what I have just overheard."

Rockewicz extended a hand. He introduced Dr. Evans, who looked flustered and excused himself.

"Sit down and relax, Mr. Cardone," Rockewicz said. "Don't get upset. Some cardiologists have this thing about bypass operations."

"I wish I had been contacted earlier."

Steve rolled his eyes. "Mr. Cardone, rich people have a way of enforcing their will. Mr. Tench said no. You're not next of kin. Not even his daughter knows."

"I'm disturbed by this man—Evans—by what he had to say about the operation."

The executive director shrugged. "Mr. Tench is doing fine. Dr. Lake should be in the OR any minute. The patient is prepped, open, ready to go on the heart-lung machine."

Cardone tapped his knee. He was a man who wanted assurances, the bottom line. He did not like open-ended situations. "I wish I hadn't heard what I just did. I'm concerned."

"I won't try to con you," Steve said. "There's a risk. But it's minimal. Mortality rate? Maybe two, three percent. They can come out of heart surgery with kidney malfunction, brain damage. But we try to forestall that. All the odds favor a successful bypass. Mr. Tench will be back in your board room in a month. Thinner, healthier, no pain."

"But no guarantees?"

"I don't give guarantees for a hernia."

"And the long-range prognosis?"

Rockewicz stretched his arms over his head. His chest appeared ready to pop the buttons on his shirt. "If they get through the first thirty days, they're okay for six months. If they get through six months, they're alive and healthy for five years or more."

"When will I see Mr. Tench?"

"I'll have to ask Dr. Lake."

"You'll *ask* him?"

"That's right, Mr. Cardone. This madhouse isn't like your corporation where everyone jumps when you press a buzzer. I've got floor nurses who give me lip. These people are overworked, dedicated, intelligent, most of them underpaid. I handle them politely because they're the best there are, better than that fancy crowd at Protestant Memorial. We practice a lot of medicine here and I make sure to *ask* people before ordering them."

"You've made your point."

"Good. Like to see the new wing?"

"Perhaps I should wait. . . ."

"Mr. Tench won't be out for four hours."

As Cardone preceded him out of the office, Rockewicz, pausing at Estelle's desk, scrawled on her note pad: "Eight to five I hit this guy for a new wing."

7

Fear took a few minutes to assert itself in Lake's orderly mind. But it was a controllable fear, a fear he could manage. Hospitals were fair game; psychos were drawn to it. (McFeeley, the eccentric who prowled the lobby, was Lake's own creature, a beneficiary of open heart surgery.) What disturbed the surgeon was that the man with the gun seemed intelligent and well spoken.

"You really don't want to kill me, do you?"

"No. But if you resist I will."

"I'm due in surgery."

"I'm going with you."

Eric Lake shook his head. "The gun is against hospital rules. If you put it away, maybe I can arrange for you to observe." He reached for the phone. "I'll tell the OR I'm on my way down."

Trask smashed the revolver against Lake's left forearm. The pain seared, spread upward. The surgeon dropped the telephone. An impulse to kill the intruder germinated in him: do away with him cleanly, without trace. Like excluding a diseased or dead piece of tissue. Neat stitches over the incision.

"Don't attempt to call anyone. Next time I'll shoot."

"If you tell me what you're after, none of this will be necessary." Lake rubbed his arm. It seemed all right. Bruised and red, but no injuries. To himself he promised, There will be an accounting, you lunatic. "What do you want? To watch an operation? Steal something? Drugs? If you let me go, I'll let you go. Not a word to anyone, I promise."

The phone screamed. Trask started. Lake saw the burning in his eyes. They widened, fought for a second with fear, then veiled with determination.

"Can I answer it?" the surgeon asked.

"Yes. But don't try anything. No hints. No codes. I'll kill you."

"Dr. Lake speaking. The man with the pulmonary embolism? Died in the cath lab? Sorry. Request a postmortem from the family. Get one of the residents who speaks Spanish to talk to them."

Trask was smiling. "The great Eric Lake. The great benefactor of sick people."

"What are you talking about?"

"No time for some Puerto Rican dying in your lab. But in a hurry to operate on Walker Tench, one of the richest parasites in the country. What I expected."

"Ah," Lake said. "So that's it. You're some kind of political fellow. . . ."

"Be quiet."

"Listen. You want something for your cause, whatever it is? My wallet? Credit cards?"

"I said shut up. Do you want to get hit again?"

"No. I like to be in good shape when I operate." Lake hated pain. He believed in dousing his patients with Demerol, morphine. "May I light a cigarette?"

"Go ahead."

Dragging, exhaling, Lake let the comforting smoke form a nimbus around him. "Look. There's a man down in the OR who needs my help. Whether he's rich or not is immaterial to me. I operate on anyone who needs it." He massaged his left arm. "Damnit, you hurt me. If this affects my work, you'll regret it."

"You're in no position to threaten me. You're incidental. Nothing will happen to you or your people if you obey orders."

Lake tried to place the voice: Midwest? Eastern college?

"You want to steal something? Something valuable? I don't give a damn. The hospital insures all their equipment. Just let me get to my patient. I'll explain to my people in the OR."

"I'll do the explaining. This is a political matter."

"Political?"

"An act of war."

"War? Who in hell is at war around here?"

"I have an army all over the hospital. There are ten armed men at key points. We've been infiltrating you for weeks." Trask's face reddened. The glint in his eyes brightened. "You are classified as an enemy. If you cooperate, you'll survive. The revolutionary army is giving the orders."

Lake's cigarette dropped to the desk. He let it smolder a moment. "Tench. You're after Walker."

8

They waited. Dr. Lake was due. Licata lifted Tench's pounding heart, frowned at the fat, set it down again.

"You are looking for the arteries, Jack?" Dr. Mihrab asked him. "They're deep."

"What temperature Dr. Lake wants before he cuts the heart?" Cho asked.

"It varies," Jimmy Baggs answered. "About thirty degrees centigrade." One of Baggs's perfusion workers was pushing a bin loaded with ice cubes into the room. "Give him a hand," Baggs ordered Cho.

"Ah, just in time," Licata laughed. "Mr. Baggs's portable bar. A light Scotch on the rocks, James."

Cho, pushing the bin, looked at Baggs. "Ice cubes . . . ?"

"For the pump. That's how we cool the blood fast."

"How do you know when he's cool enough?"

"We read the gauge."

Motzkin and Licata watched the two men. Baggs had little patience with fumblers. The assistant was a loser—poorly trained, inept. Baggs would work on him.

"This is an old hospital," Jimmy said. He shoveled cubes into the heart-lung machine. "No money for heat-exchangers, right Dr. Licata?"

"No money for anything, Jim."

"How do you heat the patient's blood?" the Korean asked.

"Hot water," Baggs said. "Plain old city water." He tapped his knuckles against a pipe.

The loudspeaker blared. "Dr. Evans has asked for an arteriography for five this afternoon. Will all personnel make a note of it and be at the catheterization lab?"

Baggs moaned. Another fifteen-hour day. It was only a little after ten in the morning and already he was tired. Later the fatigue would become almost pleasurable, sensual. At night, in his garden apartment, he would sleep soundly.

"You might say City General has arrived," Steve Rockewicz boasted to Cardone. They were touring the new wing.

"How so?"

"You see all this refurbishing? New wall colors, flooring, drapes? Had to get a dainty decorator to do it. In the old days, one of my wife's relatives came in with the paint buckets and drop cloths and started smearing."

Cardone did not react. He kept asking Rockewicz about bypass operations, about Tench's condition before surgery was decided upon.

"He was a definite surgical case," Steve said. "Dr. Lake worked him up thoroughly."

"But keeping it secret?"

"When men suffer heart disease, they get scared. Sometimes they're even ashamed of themselves. I can't explain it. It's as if they've failed a test. Like having done something dishonorable. So they try to hide it."

A pole-thin black man in a faded bathrobe shuffled toward them in paper scuffs. He walked as if favoring an incision. When he saw Rockewicz, he made a V sign with two fingers.

"How are you today, Mr. Montaigne?" the executive director asked.

"Hittin' on sixteen cylinders, like old Lucky Millinder."

"Good. Say hello to Mr. Cardone."

"Hi, Doc."

"Mr. Montaigne works in our maintenance department. Tell Mr. Cardone what Dr. Lake did for you last week."

"He give me a new heart is all." He placed his face an inch from Cardone's.

"Transplant?"

"No, not a transplant. Dr. Lake don't mess with them. They a hype for the newspapers. He give me a mechanical aortic valve. Right here." He touched his sternum. Under the pajamas Cardone saw a thick swath of tape. "The old valve turned to calcium. Dr. Lake dug it out and give me a new one with a plastic ball. Doc Lake is better at valve jobs than Great Bear."

"You look fine," Cardone said.

"Hang in there, Mr. Montaigne," Rockewicz said. "Dr. Lake says he's going to write you up."

"Indeed he is. In the *Journal of Thoracic and Cardiovascular Surgery*. You know when he did my valve he kept the heart full of blood? That is a surgeon for you, and I been around hospitals all my life."

When Mr. Montaigne left, Cardone smiled at Steve. "Your man doesn't keep secrets from his patients."

"He's a great surgeon, Mr. Cardone. Difficult, but great."

"I'm feeling better about things. You know, Mr. Tench could easily have gone to DeBakey or Cooley." He paused. "I know them personally."

"Eric's in their league."

"I apologize for some of the things I said, Mr. Rockewicz. And the way I barged in on your discussion with the cardiologist."

"No sweat. The staff figures they have constitutional rights to beat up on the director. I'm fair game. It doesn't do any harm being an old Marine officer."

Cardone digested the information. His own military service had been obscure: a clerk at an ordnance depot, rejected from Officers' Candidate School because of a deviated septum.

"I catch it all," Steve said, leading Cardone toward a TV lounge. "Had me a beaut yesterday, surgeons and internists raising hell with each other over an old lady with a subphrenic abcess. She was out of her head, anoxic, hypotensive. The surgeons wanted to stick drains in her. The medical men wanted her maintained on drugs."

"Who won?"

"Neither. She died." Rockewicz rubbed his head. "You get used to it. I think you do, anyway."

9

Weighted down with the two bulky packages—the sack and the flat box—Fiona Regan took two buses, then walked the wet streets of the city toward City General Hospital. In the damp air, she felt more sure of her mission. Hooks might be a problem, but there were alternatives if he failed them or became violent. Thus far John Trask had not made an error of judgment.

She looked frail in her sheepskin, black slacks, worn loafers. But her face was almost beautiful. Pale, near-transparent skin, lustrous brown hair. The beauty of deprivation, an old boyfriend in Belfast had told her. She had scant interest in her appearance. Surfaces were irrelevant; only inner substance counted. She had taught herself not to look at the debris of bombed cars and buildings, the blood and brains. They were unimportant. Do not connect, she lectured new members. Do not connect with the dead, the maimed, the blinded.

When Hooks had boasted of blowing up an officer in Vietnam, trying to outdo Rashid, she had stopped the black man in the middle of a description of the lieutenant's bloody feet coming to rest in a latrine. "Was it productive?" she asked. "Or was it counterproductive?" He had cursed and turned away.

Violence was justifiable if it produced results. Otherwise it was a negative factor. Trask understood this. He understood terror and escalation, how to choose targets. If they succeeded today, a hundred groups like theirs would be ready to strike fear into the secret masters.

Short of breath, trembling, she entered the courtyard of the hospital. Once before she had walked through it with Trask. She looked at the parked cars. Cadillacs, Lincolns, imported cars. No innocents here.

An ambulance, shiny orange and white with flashers on the roof, stood at the front of the open garage. A dispatcher lolled against the wall, talking to a driver.

She walked past them. It seemed colder and grayer in the courtyard. The hesitant rain was now a wet snow. She had been raised in cold gray weather. Dietary deficiencies, frustration, anger simmered inside the stained row houses. Maybe it would end in her lifetime. Massive changes triggered by Trask's formula.

She walked to the metal steps leading to the methadone clinic. A young man in a black slouch hat, fringed jacket and lavender bell-bottoms, lounged at the top step. He was pale tan and goateed. Gold rings dangled from his ears.

"Hey, baby," he said. He had a Spanish accent.

"Good morning."

He made no effort to help her with the packages. "You new, baby, you better look out for that methadone."

"Let me pass."

He did not move. "They hook you on that methadone, it worse than heroin. You know more junkies die off methadone than from good shit?"

Fiona wondered, Was he a cop? Did they know about her? Were Trask and Rashid under arrest? "Move. I want to go in."

"Clinic don't open till ten."

"It's after ten."

"You make a mistake, baby. I make you a better offer than Fat inside. You come work for Rico, you get all you need for your habit."

A stout man in a sweatshirt appeared behind the glass door. He opened it. "Rico, beat it," he said. "Come on in, sister." The dude grinned at Fiona. "You be part of the stable, baby. I make you happy. Fat lookin' for business. He hooks kids like you, he gets more money from the city."

The stout man came out. He brushed back lank brown hair. "Rico, how many times I told you not to use my clinic as a recruiting office? I'll call the cops."

"You shit, too, Fat." The pimp grabbed Fiona's arm, pulled her face close to his. A gold tooth winked at her. The man running the clinic made no move to come to aid her. "Let go of me," she said. He twisted her arm. The duffel bag fell.

"For Chrissake, Rico, get your hookers somewhere else."

The pimp's breath was rank with drugs. "You try what he give you, baby, then come meet me 'round the block. I give you a high. We go into business."

Fiona dropped the box. It gave her a bit more leverage. Swiftly, she brought a knee up into Rico's groin.

"Mother-fucker," he grunted.

Fat laughed. "Atta girl."

"Tough bitch," the dude said. "I get you later." He retreated to the railing, a hand on his insulted crotch.

"Come on in, sister," Fat said.

"Why don't you chase him?" Fiona asked. "He has no right to harass people."

"Rico don't mean no harm."

Fat ushered her to a table to fill in registration forms. Was there a possibility she was being observed? It was Trask's idea to use the clinic as her cover, and she wondered now if it was a safe haven.

10

"Keep walking," Trask commanded Lake. "Say hello to people, but don't stop to talk."

They had gotten off the elevator at the third floor. Trask walked a step behind and slightly to the right of the surgeon. He kept his right hand inside the white coat.

Lake's reputation for tidy thinking and cool planning was deserved. The man with the gun was either crazy or a political activist or both. How dangerous? Would he kill? The surgeon examined possibilities: jump him, scream, bolt. None appealed to him. He was Eric Lake. He did not wrestle with psychopaths or run through corridors shrieking. Sooner or later there would be an opportunity. His mind turned to Jimmy Baggs. Baggs would know how to handle it. He would get a signal to Jimmy. It would be over in seconds.

"There's time to change your mind," Lake said. "This won't work."

"I said don't talk."

"You said you have people all over the place. I don't see anyone."

"You shouldn't. They're part of the picture."

At the double door leading to surgery, Lake tried once more. "Last chance," he said. Trask's incensed eyes, the ramrod posture, the long intelligent head, the precision of his speech: this was no weakling. A nut perhaps, but a dangerous one.

"Go in," Trask said. "Don't betray me or you're dead. Don't try anything or we'll kill everyone in the operating room including Tench."

Lake pushed the doors open. He led Trask to the dressing room. Dr. Harvey Fess plodded toward them. "Hi, Eric," he said.

"Bad one, Harvey?"

"Yeah. Patient came out okay, but I'm not happy with the post-op picture."

"Sorry."

Dr. Fess made a lateral gesture of dismissal with his right hand. He seemed more an elderly garment worker than an eminent neurosurgeon. Fess squinted at Trask. "What are you doing in greens? I saw you come in the door wearing greens."

Trask's face whitened. He looked at Lake for an explanation.

"My fault, Harvey," Lake said. "Dr. West from Mass General. He was here earlier and came out to see me."

"Mass General, huh?" He eyed Trask as if he were a chiropractor or a faith healer. "Fancy place like that, they don't enforce the rule on greens?" He was having fun. "Or maybe Dr. West figures in a dump like City General it doesn't matter?"

"Not at all," Trask said. "My error."

Fess dismissed them with his hand. "Forget it. Anyway, you'll watch the best in coronary surgery when you watch Dr. Lake operate. Go back to Mass General, young man, and tell them what you saw. Maybe the heart-lung machines are old, and the CCU needs work, but this man is the *best.*"

"Some buildup," Lake said. He pushed open the door to the dressing room. Trask followed him. Two residents were slumped in ancient lounge chairs, sipping coffee. Lake did not greet them. He walked to his locker and put his white coat on a hanger.

Trask took off his own coat and put it over Lake's. The gun bulged slightly under his green blouse.

Lake was silent. He undressed. Over his underwear he put on a tunic and loose trousers. He changed from his street shoes to a pair of tennis sneakers. Trask watched but made no effort to hurry him. The surgeon slipped green paper slippers over his shoes and gave a pair to Trask. Then he lit a cigarette as Trask leaned against a radiator. Lake could see what the man was up to: He did not want to lose access to his gun for a second. He used one hand to pull the slippers on.

One of the residents was looking at Trask. "Who's that guy?" he whispered to the other.

"Beats me. Lake often has visitors."

Lake took a green cap from a shelf. They started toward the

door. Trask's hand was still over the midsection of his tunic. One of the young doctors noticed. "You got a bad stomach?" he asked.

"A little indigestion."

"Open heart surgery'll take care of that." Both residents laughed.

In the corridor Jimmy Baggs walked toward them. He looked solid, dependable. Lake was confident the crisis would soon be over. "Mr. Tench is ready, doctor. We were wondering what delayed you."

"Mr. Rockewicz delayed me."

"I bet." Baggs looked at Trask.

"This is Dr. West," Lake said. "From Massachusetts General Hospital. He's observing. This is Mr. Baggs, the chief of our perfusion team."

Trask nodded.

"Welcome, doctor. Got everything you need?" He reached into a bin on the green tile wall and took out two yellow surgical masks. He gave one to Lake and one to the visitor. Both men tied them around their noses. Trask's hands were occupied. Lake mulled the possibility of leaping at him now. Jimmy was there. Jimmy could break Trask in half. But Trask had backed away. He would be able to draw the .38.

"We're short a man today," Baggs said. "Holiday Monday."

Lake scowled. "We should go on a four-day week."

"I'll work the pump and be at the table also."

Trask was looking at Baggs. Olmedo had told him about the black man who worked for Lake. "Be very careful with him. He is extremely strong and quick, and he fears nothing."

"Also got us another one of anesthesiology's prizes," Baggs said softly. "Dr. Motzkin's got his hands full. Fellow is willing, but he's slow."

"Sounds like a great morning," Lake said. He greeted Miss McCarran, the chief nurse, but did not introduce Trask.

"I'll go ahead," Baggs said. He hustled past them, a bowlegged, impatient man. "I'll tell 'em you're here and get everything set while you scrub."

In the operating room, Baggs announced that Dr. Lake was on his way.

"About time," Licata said. "Alan, is he cool?"

"Who?" Motzkin joked. "Dr. Lake or Mr. Tench?"

"Wise guy. How'd you like to change places with me? I'll make the jokes, and you can assist Eric."

"I'd love it. But it's too late in life for me. I'm just an aging gas-passer."

Motzkin watched Cho adjust the central venous monitor, then move the defibrillator. Not a bad sort, the Korean, or whatever he was. "Cho, the ventilator," Motzkin said. "Back a little so I can get through." The assistant obliged.

There were times when Alan Motzkin found himself bored with the routine. He knew his job better than most. He was accustomed to being mocked as the "gas-passer," and all the other jokes about anesthesiologists—all the money they earned for doing so little. It wasn't true. They had to possess enormous knowledge to maintain the patient. And why should he not be well paid? He'd worked for it, out of the sad streets of Brownsville, through college and med school. Who was to say he did not have the right to his El Dorado and vacations in Antigua? These were his rewards for keeping the patient free of pain, relaxed, full of life-sustaining infusions, anticoagulants. He monitored the man's breathing, temperature, urinary output, metabolism, brain waves. Everything but his religious preferences, Licata said.

Motzkin got up and stretched. He would work with Eric that afternoon also. The Ramazotti girl with the ASD. Doubts vanished when you worked with Eric Lake. He gave the OR a certain magic. If a nurse or a physician or a technician grew irritable or indifferent, Lake's very presence changed the atmosphere. No dramatics, no piped-in rock music, no ego trips. Just superb surgery.

11

Motzkin saw the surgeon enter the scrub room and begin to wash. A tall young man was with him. He had heard nothing of a visitor. Usually Jimmy knew about departures from routine beforehand and informed the others.

"Is all of this necessary?" Trask asked Lake.

"Don't you go to movies? Don't you remember how they scrub up?"

"Hurry it along."

"No. I'll follow correct procedures. I'm a fast scrubber. Some surgeons spend fifteen minutes here. I can be sterile in three. You've got to let me make some of the ground rules." Lake looked around cautiously. "If Tench dies, you're in trouble, right? He has to live for you to get whatever it is you want."

"That's part of the plan."

"You called it a war. Even wars have rules."

"Be quiet."

Jack Licata walked toward the scrub room. He ignored Trask. "He's in good shape, Eric. But I think maybe your friend Tench should have his jaws wired after this. He could shed a fast fifty pounds."

"Walker's big," Lake said. The yellow soap foamed on the surgeon's hands, arms, elbows. Licata, without a glance at Trask, walked back to the table.

The surgeon wiped his hands. He spoke to Trask. "This is no place to start a revolution. I don't know anything about politics, but I know this is crazy. Nobody'll be on your side."

"That doesn't concern me."

"All right. If I can't discourage you, don't interfere with my operation. Don't hurt Tench or any of my people. I'll try to help you get what you want."

"That's what I had in mind." Trask stepped back. Above the mask his eyes missed nothing. Flor Aquino came toward Lake, who was holding his hands high for the opened gown.

"Thanks, Flor."

Trask half-turned. He saw Rashid's black eyes at the window of the double door. Trask nodded at him. Rashid pushed the doors open and walked in. He carried the green bundle.

Lake, arms high as Flor tied the knot behind him, understood at once. There were others. Trask had not lied.

"I told you," Trask said. He nodded at the new arrival. "Say hello to Dr. Lake."

Rashid smiled. He began to unwrap the carbine.

"What in hell is going on there?" Licata asked. "Eric, you holding some kind of press conference?"

"Go ahead," Trask ordered Rashid. He took the revolver from under his tunic and jammed it into the surgeon's waist. "Go in. Warn them not to make any move."

Rashid threw the green cloth aside. He placed the wire stock of the carbine in his side and pointed the barrel at the people in the operating room.

"Move," Trask commanded Lake. The three men walked toward the table.

"What is this?" Licata asked. "These guys have guns on Eric. Somebody talk."

"Don't panic," Lake said. "Everyone stay where you are."

Baggs, seated at the heart-lung machine, got up. "Hey, hey? Who are you guys?"

"Easy, Jimmy," Lake said. "It's all right."

Rashid walked past Baggs, past Motzkin and Cho, past Licata and Mihrab, past the nurses. Trask shoved Lake toward the table. Then he seized a tall stool and sat down at the threshold separating the scrub room from the operating room proper. He kept the pistol trained on Lake. "Anyone moves, or screams, or tries anything, I'll kill Dr. Lake." He waved it at Jimmy Baggs. "You. Sit down."

Rashid picked up a heavy stool at the other end of the room. The distant wall was of glass, fronting a gallery, once used by medical students. Inside were four rows of wooden seats and desks. With the carbine slung around his shoulder, Rashid smashed the stool into the glass twice. An enormous jagged-edged gouge grew in the echo of the falling shards.

Sally Moorhead, nearest the glass, crouched and hugged Flor. The Filipino girl was screaming, silently under the crash of glass, then in a piercing wail.

"Eric . . ." Licata was moving toward the surgeon.

"Stay where you are, Jack."

Rashid walked to the door at the side of the gallery. He opened it and entered.

"Everyone freeze," Trask said. "Anyone who moves gets shot."

Rashid walked to the top row of the gallery. He picked his way carefully amid the chunks of glass. From inside his tunic he took out two grenades and placed them on a seat. Then he leveled the muzzle of the carbine at the people in the room. Once, twice, he moved the weapon in a wide arc. Trask was right again. The area could be covered from the top row. The twenty rounds in the magazine could easily destroy everyone within range.

"Eric, who are these maniacs?" Licata shouted.

Flor's shrieking subsided. She was whimpering, backing toward the wall. "Do not move," Rashid cried.

Motzkin was shivering. He edged closer to Cho. The Korean's eyes were blank. All Motzkin could think was, Poor, dumb bastard, first day on the job, and look. . . .

"Please," Motzkin pleaded. He was nearest Trask. "This is lunacy. Who are you people? A man's life is at stake. Can't we be reasonable?"

Trask took two steps toward Motzkin and jammed the .38 into the anesthesiologist's side. "Walk to the door, but don't try to run or signal anyone. Tell the people outside to barricade the door from the outside. Tables, stretchers, cabinets. *Move.*"

Motzkin tried to walk, felt his feet turn liquid, then fought for self-control. "Sure, sure." He called into the corridor. "Barricade the door, quick. I can't explain."

Carlos Olmedo was waiting outside the operating room. He needed no urging to start moving cabinets, tables, a stretcher, to the door. He grabbed at Aaron Musgrave, one of Jimmy Baggs's perfusion team, and hurried him. "Some trouble in there. I saw a gun. A psycho is loose. Do what Dr. Motzkin says."

Musgrave wrestled a file cabinet to the door. Others helped. Olmedo moved swiftly. He warned chief nurse McCarran, who had come trotting down the corridor. "There is some kind of crazy man in there," Olmedo said. "I saw the gun. He is threatening Dr. Lake."

Miss McCarran ran to her office and dialed Rockewicz.

Trask ordered Motzkin back to the anesthesia cart. He stood at the threshold. From the corner of his eye, he could see Olmedo organizing the barricade.

"Get on with the operation," Trask said. He looked at Lake. "Tell them."

"We have to do what he wants," Lake said. "These men are part of some kind of political action. It involves Mr. Tench. We're incidental. This man says we'll be safe so long as we go ahead with the operation and try not to stop him."

"We are holding Walker Tench for ransom," Trask said. "This is an act of war, by the Wretched of the Earth. You're all irrelevant. Our only concern is Tench. We will ask ten million dollars for him. If we are denied, we'll kill him here."

"Fucking maniacs," Licata whispered.

"I don't think so, Jack," Mihrab said. He glanced at the dark man in the gallery. The eyes, the skin. *A brother.*

"All right, let's get on with it," Lake said.

"There are armed people all over this hospital," Trask said. "A dozen of us. None of you is capable of stopping us."

Dr. Licata set down his scalpel. His eyes darted from the man in the gallery, cradling the automatic weapon, to the thin man seated on the stool. The latter kept a watchful eye on the door, turning every now and then to make certain it was secure. I could take him, Licata thought. But there was no way to get to the thug in the top row of the theater. They were defenseless, as vulnerable as Tench's exposed heart.

"Eric, how did this happen?" Licata asked. "Can't we make a deal with these people?"

"Get back to the table," Trask ordered.

"You creeps are dead," Licata taunted. "You won't get out of here alive."

"Go on with the operation," Trask said. "Rashid, keep them in range."

Rashid nodded. Dr. Mihrab looked at him, trying to catch his eye. Probably a Palestinian—gentle, intelligent people, most of them.

"You're all helpless," Trask said. "This room is a dead end. There's only one door and it's barricaded. There are no other ways to get in here, no windows, nothing. Everyone stays where they are, finishes the work, until we're ready to leave."

"Jack," Lake said. "Let's go."

Motzkin held his hands out. "Look, whoever you are," he said to Trask, "surely we can talk this over like civilized men. Whoever you represent . . ."

"Alan, forget it," Lake said. "I tried."

Trask positioned himself, moving the stool to within arm's reach of the wall telephone. He could see the double door—where alarmed faces appeared, only to dart away—and could point his .38 at the operating area.

Trask took the phone off the hook. He was about to dial, when Lake spoke to him. "I understand about not coming and going. But we have to move around in here, especially the nurses and the assistants. I assume that's all right."

"Yes. But keep it to a minimum. And no one leaves."

"This is the shits, Eric," Licata said. "These guys, who are they?"

"Hold it down, Jack." The surgeon was studying the X-rays Jimmy Baggs had mounted on the side wall. He tried not to look at the armed men. A pinging in his gut bothered him. It was mandatory that he concentrate on his work, on *procedures*, that he enforce his will on the team. Saving Tench's diseased heart was paramount. Everything else was peripheral. The possibilities of death, maiming, and violence all had to be put aside. So he studied the shadows on the illuminated box, the narrowing of the left coronary artery, the peculiar way the diagonal vanished.

"What's his mean pressure?" Lake asked.

Motzkin was staring at Trask, who had started to dial, then hung up. Cho, rigid with terror, was at his side.

"I asked for his mean pressure," the surgeon snapped. "Alan! We have work to do."

"I'm sorry, Eric. It's eighty."

Sally Moorhead squirted saline solution into the incision in the femoral artery. She swabbed it, adjusted the suction tube. Lake smiled at her: an old pro, no visible panic.

"Hey, you," Jimmy Baggs was saying. He had gotten to his feet, moved a step from his seat at the controls of the heart-lung machine. "Hey you, man. Wanna rap a minute with you."

Trask had forgotten the extension he wanted to dial. He was talking to the operator. "I want Mr. Rockewicz's office," he was saying. Baggs moved closer.

"Listen, man," Jimmy said. "Hold it a second. I got a problem. I got to run these blood gas samples in and out. You dig? The lab is down the hall. I got to keep fresh ice comin' to cool the patient. If somethin' goes out on the pump, I may need help. You can't keep us locked in like this. I'm a man short as it is."

"Jimmy . . ." Lake was worried. Twice Baggs had disarmed violent junkies in City General's hallways. Moreover, he was acting, trying to lull the man at the phone. He did not normally use expressions like "you dig" or "rap."

"Sit down," Trask said. "Don't come any closer." Again he returned the phone to the hook.

"Jus' wanna rap, man."

"Get back. Stop where you are." Trask pointed the gun at Baggs's head.

"Do as he says, Jimmy," Lake said. He studied Tench's heart. "Jack, did you and Gamel notice that infarct scar? Now there's a surprise." Lake's gloved hand lifted the heart. It seemed to respond with outrage, beating faster, protesting Lake's intrusion.

"Like fishing a trout out of a pail," Lake said. "He doesn't like it when I raise the apex."

"Okay, man," Baggs said. The black eyes crinkled at the corner.

"He makes a lousy Uncle Tom," Licata muttered. In his mind, Licata envisioned himself and Baggs, communicating, working out a strategy. One of them going for the thin creep with the educated voice and the crazy eyes, the other taking on the bum in the cheap seats. But he would have to get to Jimmy. How?

"Make me a deal, man," Baggs was saying. "Gimme preferential treatment. I'm with you, baby. Right on, and all that. I come and go, but just for medical business. We all in the same bag. You want to do a number, I'll do it with you."

Dr. Mihrab was outraged. He respected Baggs the way he respected very few men. To see him playing this part mortified him.

"I'll shoot you in the head if you come any closer," Trask said.

Flor wept loudly. Her yellow mask was soaked. Sally grabbed her arm. "Be still, Flor."

"You mean nothing to me," Trask said to Baggs. "If I have to kill one of you to prove my point, I'll do it."

"Hunh," Baggs muttered. "Won't even let me carry a few test tubes out?"

"No. You'll do everything here."

Baggs retreated. He made some entries on his clipboard. No blood gas tests. A patient could survive without their knowing his pH or his pCO_2. His appeal to Trask was exactly what Trask saw it to be: a ruse. Baggs studied the room, the table, the gallery. Twice he tried to catch Dr. Licata's eye. That was the man he could work with to finish off these animals. They had invaded *his* operating room—*Dr. Eric Lake's room.* They would pay.

Trask had gotten through to Rockewicz. He turned away, covering the mouthpiece.

"Jimmy, how's the pump?" Lake asked.

"Ready, doctor."

"Is he cold enough?"

"Cold enough."

"All right. We're putting him on bypass."

"Jimmy? You with me?"

"Like always, doctor."

"Ready."

"Ready," Baggs replied.

Trask had turned his head, intent on his conversation with Rockewicz. Baggs studied him. Jump him now? Shout to everyone to hit the floor and get out of range of the carbine? Gamble that the cops were already outside with an arsenal? But Tench would be dead. They could move and hide. But not the fat man on the table.

"On," Lake said.

"On."

Baggs threw the switch marked ARTERIAL PRESSURE. The machine gave off a faint hum.

"Looks good so far," Lake said.

The heart-lung machine was an old apparatus, but a reliable one. Baggs kept it beautifully maintained. The transparent tubing carrying Tench's blood back to his body via the artery in his left leg jumped, grew fat, began to pulsate. Dark blood drained from the vena cava into the reservoir, through the oxygenator, then was pumped back into Tench. The cycle was complete. The procedure was simple. In a few minutes the heart would be an inert muscle, ready for Lake's scalpel.

12

As soon as the barricade had gone up outside the operating room, chief nurse McCarran called Rockewicz's office. There were armed men in Dr. Lake's OR. They were heard threatening to kill Mr. Tench.

A lone security guard, aged sixty-two, had come to surgery, paused at Miss McCarran's desk, and decided that he had no chance. Carlos Olmedo informed the guard he had seen the guns and heard the threats.

When the phone rang again in Rockewicz's office, he was trying to get through to the local police. On another line, he had put in a call to the special agent in charge of the local office of the Federal Bureau of Investigation, Arnold Stade.

James J. Cardone, hearing the wild reports, the anxious voices, tried to intervene. He demanded a phone. He would call Washington. He knew the Attorney General.

"John? John who?" Rockewicz was asking. He covered the mouthpiece and shouted at Estelle LeBlanc. "Tell Chief Reinhold and Mr. Stade to get over here at once. We don't know what this is, but we want them here."

"My name is John," the voice said. "I am armed. I have an armed colleague with me. We have a dozen men at key places in your hospital. All are armed and in hospital uniform. You must do as I say."

"Go ahead. I'm listening."

"We have occupied Dr. Lake's operating room. Walker Tench is our hostage. We are holding him for ransom."

"Slow down, fellah," Rockewicz said. His mind sprinted ahead. Tench had to be saved, the medical people removed from harm. Which first? No question. Eric, and Jack and Gamel, the nurses.

"Listen to me, Rockewicz." Trask's voice came over the phone with authority. "I represent the Wretched of the Earth. Tench is an oppressor. We have him at our mercy. He represents all that is corrupt in the old order. Your responsibility as chief officer of this hospital is to make certain that no attempt is made to stop us. By police, FBI, anyone. It's crowded in here. We can do away with everyone in seconds. That includes Dr. Lake. But if you cooperate and help us get what we want from Tench's corporation, everyone will survive. Clear?"

"Yeah. Sure. Anyone hurt?"

"No. So long as my orders are obeyed, no one will be hurt."

Cardone stepped in front of Rockewicz's desk. "Mr. Rockewicz, I'll take that call. I'll deal with them."

Steve held his hand up. "I understand you, John. Now *listen.* I play ball with you, you play ball with me. Can I talk to Dr. Lake?"

There was a pause. Cardone was purple. He extended his hand again. Steve shook his head and held the phone away.

"All right," Trask said. "But no signals, no codes. I'm sure the FBI will be glad to fill you in on us. We blew up the stock exchange in Paris. We are responsible for successful bank robberies. We move fast and we have support. So you and Lake must do as you're told." He hesitated again. "Dr. Lake understands."

"He could be a little colder," Lake said. He explored Tench's heart. The surface was lumpy with epicardial fat. Visitors to surgery were often puzzled. They expected a bright-red, perfectly formed organ, like the one on a Valentine card. They were dismayed by the orange-yellow lump.

"He's at thirty-one point five, doctor," Baggs said. He squinted at the gauge.

"We'll cut at thirty-one. Moist sponge, please. Are we ventilating him?"

Motzkin nudged Cho. The Korean had fallen into a walking stupor. "Are we?" he asked.

"Sure, sure," the assistant said. "Haven't stopped."

Trask spoke to Lake. "Rockewicz wants to talk to you. No one else is to move."

Lake, hungering for a cigarette, left the table. He would be unsterile once he took the phone, would need fresh gloves. In the corridor outside he could hear shouts. Once he thought he heard

Harvey Fess's voice. A face appeared at the window, vanished. Trask noticed it. He gave the phone to Lake. Then he picked up a bandage carton, ripped off two panels, and stuck them over the glass with adhesive tape. No one could look in.

"Steve?" Lake said. "No one's hurt. Yes, they're armed. For God's sake, keep the police away. We're sitting ducks. What? Two men. One's in—"

Trask ripped the phone from his hand. "That's enough. Go back to the patient."

Lake tried to find some clue in Trask's feverish eyes. He looked for a channel of communication, decided it was useless. The stiff back, the head held away. Something awry, something scrambled in the man.

Trask was talking to Rockewicz again, muffling his voice, looking across the brightly lit room to nod at Rashid occasionally.

Lake, examining Tench's heart, was glad that Rockewicz was in charge. A tough man, a resourceful man. They would come out all right. The surgeon had witnessed a great deal of pain and suffering and death. Life was always *in precarium.* The balance was infinitely more delicate than most people knew. Cardiac arrest, heart block, hemorrhage. There were all sorts of defects in the frail machine. And the crisis now? Another defect. He would have to follow the advice a professor had given him many years ago: Know your problem, isolate it, act on it.

"Cut out that sniffling," Lake said to Flor.

"I'm sorry, doctor."

"Flor, there's a job to do here. Ignore these men. They have nothing to do with us."

Baggs stared at Trask's back. Steve must be giving him an earful —cajoling, bargaining. Baggs thought, One fast move and I've got him. . . . But the other guy's got us from above. He raged inwardly at his impotence.

"Temperature?" Lake asked.

Baggs felt his palms grow moist, his biceps twitch.

"Jimmy," Lake said. "I asked you something."

"Excuse me, doctor?"

"How cool is he?"

"Right at thirty-one."

"Good. Everyone on their toes. We're cutting."

PART
THREE

1

Under the green canopy, Walker Tench III moved in a sea of warm sensations. Was it dreaming? Hallucination? The colors were too bright. The outlines were like cartoon figures, except they were wavy, irregular, assuming undersea configurations. Once he heard a crash. Loud. Resounding. The interminable tinkling of bits of glass. A chandelier? In the rich man's mind was an image of himself in a blue sailor suit. Five years old. Newport? Palm Beach? His cousin Sandy had dared him to swing from the chandelier. They had shoved a ladder under the crystal antique. Walker climbed the steps, clutched at the bangles, and had fallen. Crashing glass drowned his ears as he fell shrieking to the carpet. Bloody mouth. Bloody nose. And now again. Glass smashing, shouts . . .

The visions were excessively vivid. Tench, under heavy anesthesia, felt mystified by his rainbow imagination. He would not remember the images when he awakened. He sensed loss, a loss of youth, of daring, of the ability to see beyond what his eyes could show him. A nursery school? Somewhere in Arizona? Scottsdale? A ranch? A nursery school full of children. He was bringing his daughter for the day. But it was all wrong. The children were tots —four and five years old. And Dee-Dee was ten. Who's stupid idea had it been? Dee-Dee sniffled. Daddy, I don't want to stay with babies. He apologized, tried to make it sound attractive. A pool. A playground. Games. But she was ten years old. His wife said, Get rid of her, I don't care how or where. . . .

2

Rockewicz held the phone away from Cardone for another moment. The executive's manicured hand, the flash of gold cuff link, remained suspended over the director's desk. "Stay calm," Steve said. "They're some kind of revolutionary crowd. They're armed. They're in the operating room. You're going to be hit for a ransom is my guess."

Cardone's hand withdrew. He needed a moment to think, formulate. Cardone was a careful man, but he could also be a gambler. What now? A bluff? Play along? The older executives at Tench, the solid citizens, would blame him. He had been close to Walker. He had his ear. He should have kept him out of this dreadful place.

"This is James J. Cardone," he said. "I'm with Mr. Rockewicz."

Trask, standing between the scrub room and the operating room, paused. Why was Cardone in the hospital? Then he remembered. Tench wasn't a family man. A daughter somewhere. No parents; wives dispersed.

"You're the president?"

"That's right. Who am I talking to?"

Trask was wary. Olmedo's information was that Tench had been sneaked into the hospital. No one was supposed to know. He had imagined dealing with Cardone at the New York headquarters, not finding the man a few floors below him.

Rockewicz picked up an extension. He could see George Reinhold, the young chief of police, a broad-shouldered blond man, looming in the doorway. Behind Reinhold were two cops. They were helmeted and wore bulletproof apronlike affairs. They were carrying shotguns.

"Estelle," Rockewicz called. "Tell Reinhold to lay off. I don't want guns in sight. George, for Chrissake!"

Chief Reinhold, scowling, moved into Mrs. LeBlanc's outer room. He had a foxlike face and a reputation for being street-smart and fearless. Rockewicz called to her again. "Start taking shorthand notes. Get on your phone. Call Stade's office again."

"I'm ready to negotiate," Cardone said, "if you'll explain who you are and what it is you want."

"We are holding Tench for ransom."

"I understand."

"We want ten million dollars for his life."

"I see. And you are. . . ."

"We're prepared to take his life if the money isn't delivered in two hours."

"But—but—who are you? Why are you doing this?"

Rockewicz rolled his eyes upward, as if marveling at Cardone's insistence on credentials.

"We are the Wretched of the Earth. We represent the oppressed, hungry, downtrodden victims of the system—the dying system men like you and Tench run."

Cardone's mind hummed with notions. The innocence of these madmen! To think that he ran anything! Or to imagine they could sway masses, win workingmen, even the blacks with these acts of terror! How little they understood! Anger boiled inside him. He knew about slums, bad diets, joblessness, illiteracy, more than they did.

"Young man, can't we discuss this face to face?" he asked, trying to stifle the fury. "You sound as if you're educated. Let's talk. We can find some common ground."

"No. You understand only violence. Tench gave arms to the fascists in Vietnam, to the Zionists, to the murderers of Allende and Che."

What in God's name was he talking about? Cardone wondered. "You're mistaken," he said. "We don't manufacture arms. Maybe you're talking about our electronics division. It's possible we sold communications material to foreign governments. But you can't murder an innocent man on that basis."

"There are no innocents."

Educated. And a certain brittleness. The intelligence straining to hide—what? Fear? "If I can meet with you personally?" Cardone prided himself on his powers of persuasion.

"I won't be co-opted, Cardone. You are to give us ten million dollars in exchange for Tench's life."

"But it isn't—raising such sums—"

A medium-sized man in a suit neither blue nor gray entered the room. He had pale skin and indifferent eyes. Arnold Stade was not a man anyone would remember in a crowd. He was the special agent in charge of the local FBI office. Rockewicz motioned to him and gave him the extension.

"Ten million?" Cardone was saying. "How? Where?"

"You'll get further instructions."

"Tell me when you want it, John."

There was a pause. Was he consulting someone? "In exactly two hours. By twelve minutes past noon."

Rockewicz, who had moved into Estelle's anteroom to listen, broke in. "John? Rockewicz here. What about Dr. Lake and Dr. Motzkin and the others? They didn't sell telephones to the Israelis or the South Vietnamese."

"They are hostages."

"What?"

"If any attempt is made to trick us or attack us or intervene or impede our withdrawal, then we will execute them one at a time."

"That's murder. Those are some of the best doctors in the world in there."

Cardone interrupted. "I have an alternate proposal—"

"I'm not interested."

"You'd better be. You aren't out of here yet. I'll guarantee your departure from the hospital immediately, with no pursuit, no police interference, if you'll agree. The Tench Foundation will assign ten million dollars to feed the poor—"

Trask cut him off. "No. Not acceptable."

"Think carefully. I'm guaranteeing you your lives."

"We want the money."

"And you assure me Mr. Tench will be unharmed if I comply?"

"You have no choice but to take my word."

Rockewicz asked, "And the others?"

"They'll be safe if we aren't attacked," Trask said.

"Your demand is met," Cardone said. "You will get your ten million dollars."

"I'll call back in five minutes with additional orders. The deadline is twelve minutes past noon."

"That may be impossible to meet," Cardone said. "Be reasonable. I've agreed to everything."

"Don't you understand?" There was brittle strength in the man's voice. Cardone shivered. "You have no options. We aren't afraid to die."

"An additional hour?"

"No. When I call back, I want an assurance that the money is being raised. I'll give you *ten* minutes until I call again. That's a concession I don't have to make. Rockewicz?"

"Yes?"

"Don't try anything with the pigs. We have armed men everywhere." The phone went dead.

Stade listened a moment, put the phone down. Two more men in gray suits entered. One, an agent named Harris, began connecting a tape recorder to a telephone.

Chief Reinhold walked into the office. The policemen in quilted vests followed him, carrying their shotguns.

"Mr. Rockewicz," Reinhold said, "I think we got a matter of jurisdiction." He pointed to Stade and his aides. "The bureau's got no business here."

A third policeman, also in the padded garment, entered. He was carrying an automatic weapon with an enormous magazine. Rockewicz's face reddened. "Reinhold," he said. "I don't want those guns used."

"They may have to be."

"Not in my hospital."

Reinhold shook his head. "I heard this gentleman on the phone." He jerked a thumb at Cardone. "There's no bargaining with those germs. They understand one thing. I can get there with three or four men and shoot their heads off before they get anybody."

"No," Rockewicz said. "That's an order, chief."

Reinhold brushed back his lank blond hair. He was not yet forty. Twice he had disarmed murderous thugs single-handed, twice waded into shoot-outs between rival gangs, and come out unscathed.

"It's your hospital, Mr. Rockewicz," Reinhold said. "But I'm the chief of police, and lives are being threatened. If I can talk to a person who knows the layout of that room, I can get in. I can cut those animals down before they pull a trigger."

Stade was watching calmly, saying nothing.

"This hospital is an autonomous corporation," Rockewicz said. He was improvising. "We don't have to be bound by your orders."

"You do if there's a crime being committed," Reinhold persisted. "There are murderers in there, and the only way to get them out is to shoot them out." He pointed to his armed men. "Pinowski and Olenik with the shotguns, me with a sidearm. One man with the automatic. We holler to your people to drop, hit the floor. No one gets hurt." The foxy face seemed to relish the adventure: a lot of chickens in the coop.

Cardone came across the room fast. "Except Mr. Tench, under anesthesia while bullets fly around the room." He spun toward Stade. "Mr. Stade, you represent the FBI. I demand that you take over."

"George," Rockewicz said, "take your people outside and stay out of sight, huh? This is an FBI thing. I said no shoot-outs and I mean it. You try to assault that room and I'll burn you. I mean it, George."

Reinhold paused. Rockewicz had clout. He knew the political structure of the community. But the chief was not ready to back down. "I'm not so sure," he said.

"What? That I can burn you if you pull anything?" Rockewicz was losing patience.

"No. That the FBI's got jurisdiction. They aren't in charge until a federal law has been broken."

Cardone and Rockewicz looked at Stade. If this was true, why had the FBI agents come so quickly?

"Technically, the chief is right," Stade said laconically.

"But in fact?" asked Rockewicz.

"In fact, we make it a practice to stand by and observe. As soon as a federal law is violated, we take over. You'd be surprised how many federal laws there are that can be broken."

"Jesus," Steve said. "I mean. . . ." He stood glaring at Reinhold, as puzzled as he was furious. Then he muttered, "No offense, chief."

Stade was making notes on a pad. "Do you have a building plan and a floor plan?"

Rockewicz nibbled on a knuckle. "Mr. Stade, you with me? No shoot-out? No storming that room?"

"For the time being." He walked to his aide. "Harris, keep a line open to Washington."

"It's our case," Reinhold protested. "They got no right here."

Stade smiled. "We can handle it together, chief."

Cardone walked over to Arnold Stade and gave him his card. "It is of grave importance to me that you take over, Mr. Stade. At once."

The FBI agent looked at him blandly. Then he nodded.

"How many men can you bring in?" Cardone persisted. "I'm a friend of the Attorney General. I'm sure he will be interested in Mr. Tench's safety."

"Fifty agents in the area already. I can bring in several hundred. But we don't need the Attorney General yet."

Reinhold frowned and led his men out of the room.

"No funny business, chief," Rockewicz called after him. He shouted to Estelle, "Floor plans, Estelle. Dave Buttram has a cabinet full of them."

3

For the invaders, the assignment of operating room number three to the Tench case was an extraordinary piece of luck. The room was isolated, except for the double door leading to the main corridor of surgery. With the windows in the door covered with cardboard, no one could look in to ascertain the positioning of the gunmen. The gallery was another lucky stroke. Rashid could sit there, high above the table, and cover the area with his carbine. The rear of the room was a dead end and windowless. Nor were there windows or doors in the two auxiliary rooms—the scrub room and the supply room to the right of the operating area.

Consulting his watch, waiting for his next call to Cardone, Trask realized how fortunate they had been. He had heard about FBI snipers capable of picking off a man from a distance. But in this enclosed space, there was no way of getting a line of sight on anyone. They were encapsulated.

"Him and his oppressed people," Licata said. "What a line of crap."

"Forget him," Lake said. "We'll be out of here in a few hours."

Trask was back on the stool, within reach of the phone. He kept an eye on the doors.

"He's a goddamn nut." Licata glanced at Trask. Trask was pointing the revolver at the table. "You ever get any psychiatric help, John? You could visit the clinic on the fifth floor."

"Jack, cut it out." Lake was worried. He had seen Licata's temper rage out of control.

"I can't stand a line of crap," Licata said. "Especially when I'm working."

"Dr. Lake is right," Trask said. "Do your work. Let's not interfere with each other."

Licata shook his head. He looked across Tench's emptying heart—still beating despite the absence of blood—at Jimmy Baggs. Was Baggs trying to catch his eye? Now he noticed a faint movement of Jimmy's head. The powerful neck, the round green cap, appeared to be making short moves toward the gallery.

Licata, ligating vessels, glanced at the smashed glass. Behind it, Rashid had sat down. He moved the carbine slightly, keeping the wire stock in the crook of his arm.

"Ready to vent him," Lake said. He raised the tip of the heart. It beat feebly.

"Give me his mean pressure, Alan," Lake said.

"Exactly eighty," Motzkin responded.

Licata caught another move of Baggs's head. He had nodded at Trask and then touched his tunic. He caught Licata's eyes again. The chief resident tried to guess what Baggs was trying to say: I'll go for that one.

"Jack, Gamel," Lake said. "I'm going to vent the infarct scar." He fingered the dead tissue. "Walker had a heart attack some time ago and didn't know it. Never showed on the EKG. Scalpel."

The sharp instrument cut into the gray patch. Miss Moorhead put a suction tube into the incision. Some residual blood hissed in the cannula. The heart, losing fluid and air, began to flatten, at last surrendering.

"Sutures," Lake said.

Baggs was at the table now, straightening out the plastic tubing of the pump. Baggs did not talk. But his eyes darted from Licata to Rashid. He wants me to go for him, Jack thought. Two musclemen. Two street fighters. Licata tried to signal negatively. He shook his head.

"No," Licata said loudly.

"What are you trying to do?" Trask asked. He had been following the surgical procedure.

"Sally," Licata said. He looked at Baggs. "Not so deep with the cannula."

"It looks all right to me," Lake said. "Are we getting suction? One of those tubes isn't draining properly. Take a look at the tank."

"I'll go," Baggs said. "Flor, stay where you are."

The suction tank was to the rear of the anesthesia area. Licata

watched Baggs move between the table and the pump, past Motzkin and Cho. I tried to warn him, Licata thought. He did not dare
interrupt Eric. Don't do it, Jimmy, it's impossible. I can't get at
that guy in the gallery.

"I'll take a look at the vein," said Lake.

"The right-hand spigot," Licata called to Baggs. "It's loose.
That stuff should be overhauled."

"I worked on it last week. This equipment is fit for a museum."
Baggs knelt on one knee and tightened the valve. He got off the
knee, squatted on his muscular legs.

"Need you here, Jimmy," Licata said. "Eric . . ." He wanted
to signal to Lake. He had seen the fury generating in Jimmy.

"Lay the vein on the drape," Lake said.

Sally held the basin in front of Dr. Mihrab. Tench's saphenous
vein had turned pink-gray in the solution.

Baggs half-turned. He was trying to adjust the controls on the
suction tank. The fluids hissed as he moved the valve.

Trask came off the stool. He was watching Lake stretch the
vein on the drape above the cavity in Tench's chest.

"Hit the floor!" Baggs shouted.

Christ, he's doing it. Licata looked for something to throw at
Rashid—a stool, a basin. But it was too late.

Baggs had hurled himself at Trask, grappling for the gun.

"Rashid!" Trask screamed.

Baggs bent Trask backward, forcing him against the wall of the
operating room. Trask was surprisingly strong, stronger than
Baggs had imagined. *"Rashid!"* he shouted again.

Licata saw the Arab get up, point the carbine at the two men.
Now? Leap into the gallery over the jagged glass? Motzkin and
Cho had fallen to the floor. Mihrab grabbed at Flor and pulled
her down. Sally lowered her head.

The shots were resonant, sharp, not as loud as Licata had
expected.

"Jesus, he hit him," Licata said. "Eric, call Jimmy off."

Baggs was resting against Trask. His arms embraced the slender man. His face was an inch from Trask's yellow mask. But his body had gone soft and was sliding. He seemed to Licata like a member of a marathon dance team, slumping to the floor, gliding into unconsciousness. Two red stains bloomed on Baggs's back.

"Stand still," Rashid shouted. "No one move. I will shoot anyone else." He aimed the carbine at Baggs.

Lake shouted, "For God's sake, don't shoot again. He's helpless."

"Do not move," Rashid said.

"He's hurt," Lake said. "You want to shoot me, go ahead."

The air was charged with blue-gray smoke. The odor lingered, intensified. Motzkin, on the floor next to the anesthesia wagon, rolled aside as Lake walked past him. "Eric, plead with them, beg them," he sobbed.

Baggs's body slipped to the floor. He was lying face up. His eyes were open. Trask jerked away, leveling the gun at Lake.

"Get him out of the way," Trask said. "He wouldn't believe us. Now you see we mean what we say. Drag him away."

Licata walked to Baggs's body. In the cramped space between the wall and the suction tanks, they had difficulty moving Baggs's body. "In the supply room," Lake said.

Motzkin was on his feet. "You cowards. You shot him in the back." Alan wanted to shake a fist at Trask, threaten Rashid. But he was soft and overweight. He had none of Jimmy Baggs's courage.

Lake and Licata placed Baggs on a rubber sheet in the supply room. Licata listened to Baggs's heart. He heard nothing. Lake felt for a pulse. Nothing.

"He's dead, Jack."

"He was trying to signal to me," Licata said. "I wanted to stop him. . . . I didn't know what to say."

Trask was standing several feet from the alcove. He pointed the gun at Lake. "If he's dead, he's dead. Get back to the operating table. You were warned."

"You murdering, cowardly bastards," Lake said, hardly raising his voice. "You kill the innocent in the name of the wretched. Do you realize what Baggs meant to us? No, you'd never understand."

Licata had his lips pressed to Baggs's mouth. He tried breathing life into the black man. But already he saw the stigmata of death in Jimmy's glazed eyes. The bullets must have struck his heart, possibly the aorta. The blood was forming a puddle on the rubber sheet. Two sticky red trails led into the alcove.

Lake got up. "Listen," he said to Trask. "Get on the phone and make your deal. I want you out of here as fast as possible. Ten million, twenty. I'll talk to them if you want."

"I'll make my own schedule." Trask's voice was pitched higher. He was leaning backward as if favoring a wound, uncertain whether to argue with Lake. Suddenly he kicked Jack Licata in the side. "You, get back to the table. You knew what this man was going to do. The two of you were hatching something."

Licata refused to get up. "Go fuck yourself," he said. "Baggs should have strangled you." He looked up at the gallery. "You, too, you Arab prick. You're brave as hell shooting school kids. You'll get yours before the day is over." He bent over Baggs and kissed him. "Jimmy."

"Let's go," Lake said. "Jack, cover him. Whoever isn't sterile anymore, put on fresh gloves and gowns. Flor!"

Flor had collapsed. She lay against the leg of the table, whimpering.

"Flor, please, there is nothing we can do," Mihrab was pleading. "Jimmy is beyond our help, Flor."

Lake looked at her angrily. "On your feet. Gowns and gloves! Gamel is right. There's no helping Jimmy."

Mihrab lifted the Filipino girl. Sally Moorhead came down from her high stool and put her arms around her.

Trask said, "Get on with it."

Motzkin turned to the man. "Have you any idea what you've done? The man you just killed? He was the finest human being. . . ." He turned back to the table. His shouting would not bring Jimmy back.

Trask adjusted the face mask. He was breathing heavily. Motzkin thought, He never fired his gun. He let the Arab do the killing.

"He was a plant," Trask said suddenly. "A CIA agent."

"You're crazy," Motzkin said. "You're really crazy."

"Stop crying," Lake said to Flor. "Sally, wipe up that blood. Damn it, this operation will proceed. They won't do anything else. They want their money and they want to get out. We are going to cooperate. You hear me, Trask?"

"Yes."

Lake battled to focus his mind. His wife, Martha, an English major before she opted for biology, used to quote Dr. Johnson: "Depend upon it, sir, when a man is to be hanged in a fortnight it concentrates his mind wonderfully." Jimmy Baggs's death must not stop them.

"The pump," Motzkin said.

"Your assistant can run it," Lake said.

Motzkin looked at Cho. The Korean was resting against the wall. His arms were crossed on his chest. "Cho? Will you please handle the heart-lung machine?"

"I don't know. Not too well."

"You're elected, Alan," Lake said

"Sure, sure. I don't mind." The anesthesiologist moved across the room and settled into the seat. It was built for Baggs, low and hard. Motzkin's spreading hips were not comfortable in it. He glanced at Baggs's covered corpse. Jimmy: an old-fashioned man. He believed in work, honor, loyalty. Not just a way to make money and advance himself, but a way of life. Baggs was a reminder of human possibilities, debts paid, dialogues opened. No one ever thought of him as black or deprived.

"Clean the floor," Lake ordered Flor. "Stop crying. Jack? Gamel? Are you people awake?"

The assistant surgeons nodded.

"I'll get that son of a bitch," Licata whispered.

"Hold the vein with the forceps, Jack," Lake said. "We'll cut the pieces off for the grafts. Ready?"

4

The shots resounded in the corridor outside surgery. Dr. Fess, with Olmedo's help, cleared the area. "Everybody stay in their rooms," the neurosurgeon shouted. "No traffic except what's needed in the ORs." Chief nurse McCarran got on the phone to inform Rockewicz. There had been shouts, cries, at least two shots fired. But they could see nothing.

"Christ," Rockewicz said. "It always gets worse before it gets better." He looked at Stade. Cardone was frozen in the middle of the room. He was kneading his knuckles. His sharp face was patched with scarlet.

Reinhold walked in. "You see? You see what happens when you wait? When you give in to these people?"

"Hold it down, chief." Rockewicz wondered if Reinhold had been right all along. They were moving in the dark, blinded, at the mercy of irrational men.

Reinhold said, "My men are in helmets and armored aprons. I go in first. We take the germs in seconds. We go in shooting, no warning, no bargains."

"No, goddamn it!" Rockewicz shouted.

Reinhold's jaw tightened. "I heard you were an old Marine officer, a hard guy. You better start acting it. Those people got to be killed. We collared those bastards in the department store last month, didn't we? You read the newspapers?"

"And you killed a bystander."

"Close down the hospital," Reinhold said. "Make it secure. Get everyone out."

"No. I've got to keep it running. We'll close surgery except for cases in progress. We can't stop the hospital from functioning."

"I'm sick of hearing about this hospital running," Cardone exploded. "What about Mr. Tench? He's the only one being threatened. Can't we find out what happened down there? Call them?"

Rockewicz looked to Stade for help. The FBI agent was at the window. A half dozen blue-and-white police cars were parked below. Wooden barricades were going up. "Arnold, what do we do?" Steve asked.

"We don't go in shooting. As of now we don't even know what happened. They may have just fired warning shots. When those Japanese took hostages in The Hague, they fired thirty times and didn't hit anyone."

"Right." Rockewicz picked up the phone. "Chief, this is final. If you bust in there with your guns, I'll have your ass. Take my word, I can do it!"

Reinhold walked out. He was seething. No mercy. No bargains. And who the hell was Tench anyway that they had to worry about him? One man. Who ever worried about one cop?

Trask picked up the phone in the operating room.

"This is Rockewicz, John. There were shots down there. What happened?"

There was hesitation, then coughing, as if the young man were unable to summon up his voice. When he spoke, he sounded wary. "One of the people in here was a CIA agent. He was planted to stop us. He tried to attack us and we were forced to liquidate him."

"Who?"

"Baggs."

"Jimmy? Jimmy's dead?"

"He tried to interfere. He tried to kill me. He was an agent of the CIA."

"You're insane. Listen to me, no one's trying to stop you. Mr. Cardone agreed to get the money. We agreed to let you out." Rockewicz struggled to control himself. He wanted, more than anything in the world, to get his hands around the gunman's throat. Strangle him slowly, watch the eyes bug, the flesh turn blue.

"We can't trust any of you." Trask's voice came through stronger.

"You know what this means? You killed a man."

"We were prepared to do it. You people forced us. It should prove we mean what we say. There are to be no more delays, tricks, attacks. Or others here will go the way Baggs did."

"Listen. We're in the middle of this. I mean, my people, this hospital. I give you my word you're getting what you want. I'll come down myself and you can hold me."

"Stay where you are."

"You said you had instructions for Cardone. How about it? Right now? He's here. Let's wind it up."

"When I'm ready." He hung up.

5

Lake watched Tench's heart flatten into a shapeless orange mass. Jimmy's death was more than he could comprehend. In his orderly, compartmented mind, he tried to blot out the memories—the earnest brown face, the skillful hands, the good nature, the capacity to inspire others. Gone. No sense to it.

The man named Rashid, who had fired the shots, did not seem affected. He sat in the upper row, cross-legged, silent, his sweat staining the green cloth. An Arab, Mihrab had guessed. He would try to talk to him. But how to find common ground with Baggs's killer?

"The medical conference restudied one of our cases last week," Lake said. He had to get their minds off Baggs. "Someone left clamps on the aorta. It was embarrassing for me. Who did it?"

"It was me, Eric," Mihrab said. "I am sorry."

"Me, Eric," Licata said. "I had a bad morning."

"Well, whoever," Lake grumbled. "It was botch work. I expect better."

Mihrab knew he had been guilty of the oversight. He wondered why Licata had taken the blame. Because he thought Mihrab was less strong, less able to withstand the ordeal?

Motzkin, closest to the phone, made an entry in Jimmy's log and tried to catch Trask's eye.

"Young man," the anesthesiologist said, "may I say a few words to you?"

"No. Stay at your job."

"That's the point. To do my job I have to get tests on the patient's blood gases. We take the samples to the lab. It's down the hall. Could I be allowed to do that? You could go with me."

"I've said no already."

"Reconsider. Look, I'm a liberal. I give to the NAACP. I know about poverty and hungry people. But, my God, do you think this kind of brutality will win you friends? Shooting a person like Baggs?"

Trask grimaced. The cozy advances of liberals sickened him. They would never understand.

"Be quiet."

"I won't. And you won't kill me just for talking." Motzkin's feet were like ice. He wondered where the words were coming from. As a boy he had been fat and slow, a miserable fighter. He had been drubbed by packs of hoodlums, had his bus money stolen by blacks, his pants pulled down by Italians. "Look, we test his blood eight times. We can cut it to four. If we don't, he may become acidotic. It's a serious matter."

"I said no."

Motzkin sighed and studied the tubes of the heart-lung machine. Tench was on full bypass. All of his blood was in the apparatus, being cleansed, oxygenated, returning by way of the femoral artery. The machine hummed, working beautifully. Jimmy kept it in perfect condition. He had to. Motzkin had heard horror stories about other hospitals. At one, a badly mounted screw came loose, fell into the motor, stopped the pump. It was impossible to rig a new one in time. They had tried to run it manually but it was too late.

"Fibrillate him," Lake ordered.

Cho flicked the switch for the fibrillator. The heart quivered.

"Ready for my glasses," Lake said.

No one moved. It had always been Baggs's job to put the

magnifying glasses on the surgeon. Jimmy kept them in a leather case in the breast pocket of his tunic. It was something of an OR ritual. Jimmy would approach Lake, extend his arms, set the glasses on the surgeon's nose, fix the temple pieces.

"Ah, in Jimmy's gown." Motzkin swallowed. "I'm nearest." The anesthesiologist got up.

"Where are you going?" Trask asked.

"Just to Jimmy. Dr. Lake needs his glasses."

"Go ahead."

With an effort, Motzkin walked the few steps into the alcove. A wild hope inspired him. He would find Baggs miraculously breathing under the drape. They would work on him, restore him. What better place than Eric Lake's OR? Chest wounds. Heart trauma. Penetrating lesions. Lake would make him whole again.

But the body was already getting cold, the limbs turning rigid. Nothing seemed to give him hope. Nothing justified what was happening. He pulled back the cloth, fearful of Jimmy's open, accusing eyes. *Did we do this to him? All of us?* Impossible. Motzkin would not accept the blame. He took the leather case from Baggs's pocket and covered him again.

"Flor, I'm not so sure I'm sterile any more." The anesthesiologist held the glasses out to the circulating nurse. "Could you please put these on Dr. Lake?"

The spectacles were set in heavy metal frames. In the center of each glass was an inset, a high-powered lens. Flor held them out and hooked them over Lake's ears.

Rashid was watching from the gallery. He seemed to Mihrab to be following the surgery. He had just murdered a man, shot him in the back. Dr. Mihrab had read about them: laughing at the death of children, celebrating the murder of farmers, bragging about bombs set aboard airliners.

"*Salaam aleikim,*" Mihrab said. What was to be lost?

Rashid's eyes were like polished obsidian. "*Aleikim salaam.*"

"*Rafik, rafik,*" Mihrab said. "Why not end this?"

Rashid shook his head. "It must be done," he said. He put a

finger to his lips. "Our manhood demands it."

Lake took the first section of vein. He was ready to mend Tench's heart.

"Soul brother?" Licata asked Mihrab. "Maybe the son of a bitch will be nice if you explain to him about Jimmy. Fat fucking chance."

6

Trask called at 10:19. This time he asked for Cardone.

"This is John. I have instructions for the packaging and delivery of the reparations."

"I'm ready."

"We demand ten million dollars in unmarked bills. They are to be in standard bank packets, in denominations of one hundred. That is a thousand packages. And they are to be packed in four valises. These are to be green plaid zipper valises. They will be big enough to take the amount of money, if packaged as we demand. Are you getting this?"

"Yes. I've already alerted our treasurer." Cardone paused. "May I make a suggestion?"

"Don't try to divert me."

"I won't. I've agreed to everything. I've cautioned the police. You won't be interfered with. What I would like to suggest is that we make this a conference call with my treasurer in New York City."

"Why?"

"For your own good. He has to raise the money at the Federal Reserve Bank. He's going to oversee the operation. Why not give him direct orders? I'll listen in and I'll approve it."

Trask waited a moment. Scheme? Trap? It sounded reasonable. Trask was certain they were taping everything he said. Indeed, he wanted his voice broadcast, made known to the world. The Wretched of the Earth had power. They could bring mighty corporations, police forces, governments, the lords of the earth, to their knees.

"That sounds all right."

"Good. We'll get Mr. Gallatin, our treasurer. I've briefed him."

Arnold Stade, the FBI man, was whispering to his aide, Harris. Reinhold, lingering in the doorway, wondered what the hell they were planning. The city was his to protect. He should have been allowed to storm the operating room. So somebody might die. But what was important was that the scum in there, the germs, the hoodlums with their weapons, would also die. Rid the earth of them. He had taken off his jacket and was wearing a sidearm, a Colt .357 Magnum with a six-inch barrel.

"It's running," Reinhold heard Harris say. He was indicating the tape recorder.

"Mr. Gallatin is on," Cardone said to Trask. "You can go ahead."

"The deadline is twelve minutes past noon," Trask said. His voice rose, full of command. "Ten million dollars in unmarked hundreds, in bank packets. Packed in four twenty-nine-inch green plaid zipper valises. These four valises are to be placed on the loading platform of the main building. The unused loading area nearest Kennedy Boulevard. The people who bring the bags out are to leave at once. They are to be on the platform, I repeat, at twelve-twelve P.M."

"Young man . . ." Gallatin cleared his throat. "Jim, may I?"

"Yes, you're handling this end of it," Cardone said.

"There may be a problem at the Federal Reserve. They have that amount in cash I'm sure, but it is possible that not all of it will be available in hundreds. They may have to furnish the balance in smaller denominations."

"Unacceptable. Our terms must be met."

The line went dead.

"Jim?" Gallatin asked. "Are you on? What am I to do?"

"Do as he says. The full amount in hundreds."

"It maybe impossible with the deadline. The bank says perhaps seven million, maybe a bit more should be on hand."

"Do everything you can." Cardone spoke harshly. "I'll call the Secretary of the Treasury." He hung up.

"The case is ours," Stade said to Cardone.

"What?" Cardone looked confused.

"The phone call to New York. John gave us the opening we needed—the use of interstate facilities for extortion. It's a violation of a federal statute. He's ours now."

Chief Reinhold started to protest but was cautioned by a gesture from Rockewicz. The chief hitched his belt cowboy-style and walked out of the office. He was furious. In the hallway, he walked to his armed men.

"Do we go, chief?" one asked.

"No. Not yet. The goddamn Bureau thinks it's closing us out." He seemed to recall some connection. "Olenik, isn't your brother-in-law on the maintenance staff here, super or something, a janitor?"

"Frankie Parolo. The wife's older brother. He bowled with us last year, remember?"

"What's his job?"

"Maintenance, I think. Buildings and grounds."

"Get him." Reinhold looked around, touching the Magnum on his hip. "Meet me in the cafeteria. Just you and me and him."

7

"Somebody move the lights," Lake said. "I'm getting too many shadows." Flor slipped around the table and adjusted the overhead lamps.

"Scalpel," the surgeon said.

It was 10:26. Lake had begun to probe for the left anterior descending branch of the left coronary artery. He cut swiftly through layers of fat into Tench's fibrillating heart. With a forceps Mihrab held the tissues apart. The artery emerged. Lake lifted it from the wall of the heart. "No place to hide," Lake said. "The X-rays did not lie."

Trask, after his conversation with Cardone and the treasurer, seemed to relax. The rigidity of his head was less manifest, it seemed to Dr. Motzkin. He appeared confident, even smug, now. Everything would go his way. To Motzkin's astonishment, the man was watching the operation with apparent interest.

"Adjust the mirror," Lake said sardonically. "So our guest can see better."

Flor turned the overhead mirror again.

"I wouldn't give him the time of day," Licata growled.

We're dealing with a disturbed personality, Jack, Lake wanted to say. This is known as humoring the subject.

In the mirror, the bright bloody square was revealed—the metal frame, the shivering orange heart, the silvery instruments lifting the artery.

Trask got off his stool and peered upward at the mirror.

"John," Rashid said quietly, "be careful."

"I know what I'm doing."

Rashid coughed, changed the position of his legs. He had killed, but he did not appear disturbed. He had killed defenseless men before. By the end of the day the world would know the power of the Wretched of the Earth. They would prevail. Or would it end in a fiery blaze in the green tile room below him, a mighty sheet of flame devouring all: the rich man with the exposed heart, the doctors, nurses, all of them?

8

From Miss McCarran's office, Dr. Harvey Fess reported to Rockewicz on the phone. "I'm winding up a craniotomy. Harper's got a few minutes to go on a hysterectomy. There's an orthopedic job, a long one. That's it."

"Okay, Harvey. Close everything else. Chase everyone out. Tell those who have to finish up not to panic. I'd like you to hang around to make sure everyone goes."

"Steve, is it true? Is Baggs dead?"

"Yeah."

"Eric? The others?"

"They're all right. We're working something out."

The neurosurgeon put the phone down. He spoke to the chief nurse. "Miss McCarran, you'd better go. Rockewicz wants everyone out."

"I'm staying."

He knew it would be useless to contest her. She lived in surgery. It was everything to her. No one could remember when Miss McCarran had not been there. Tough, efficient, she was not liked, but she was admired.

Fess walked back to his craniotomy. An invasive glioblastoma. They had gotten it out, but a good part of the brain had come with it. A patient with not much to look forward to—bedridden, a vegetable.

Depressed, he approached his operating room. They did what they could. Often it wasn't enough. He saw Carlos Olmedo carrying a tray past the room where the orthopedic surgeon was working.

"Hey, you. Olmedo."

"Yes, doctor?"

"Out. The area has to be cleared. If you aren't needed, get out, *toot sweet.*"

"As soon as I bring these to room five, doctor."

"I said out. You understand English, don't you?"

Fess was sorry as soon as he said it. The place was full of foreigners. Besides, he liked Olmedo. "All right. Take that stuff in and beat it."

Olmedo delivered the tray to the operating room. He needed a moment. Outside he could hear Fess chivying nurses and technicians, ordering them out. A nurse was weeping. One of the women from the autoclave room was hysterical. She had learned about the shooting. Olmedo began emptying trash into a plastic bag. The surgical team at the table paid no attention to him.

Laden with the plastic bag, Olmedo looked up and down the

corridor, saw no one, and walked to the incinerator chute. He threw the trash away and headed for the supply closet. The carbine was there. It was hidden, but he could take no chances. More important, he had to hide from Fess, then be ready when Trask and the others left.

No one was in the supply room. Olmedo went to the closet, walked inside, closed the door. He was able to recline, with his knees drawn up, on one of the shelves. In a fetal position, he rested with the bundled carbine in the hollow formed by his torso. As if I am hatching an egg, Olmedo thought.

"Hey! Anyone in there?"

It was Dr. Fess's authoritative voice. He was in the supply room. "Anyone around? Carlos? Aaron? Any of you people?"

Olmedo held his breath. One made these decisions as the situation developed. For the moment he could only pray that the surgeon would not open the closet.

He was still debating strategy with himself when Fess yanked open the closet door.

"What the hell is this?" the surgeon shouted. "Some kind of game? Hide and go seek?"

"Dr. Fess, I—"

Fess grabbed at Olmedo's shoulders and yanked him from the shelf, as if taking down a can of vegetables. "Get out, wise guy," Fess said. "No free show today. Hanging around for some excitement, huh?"

Olmedo, wiry, powerful, fought back. He disengaged Fess's arms with explosive blows, spun the older man around, tried to slam the closet door shut. Their legs kicked at the shelves. The carbine fell to the floor. Fess saw the blue-black weapon. "So that's it," he gasped. He was exhausted from the long day at the operating table, eaten with fatigue. "So you're with them, those bastards in there . . . you little rat. . . ."

Olmedo clamped a hand over the surgeon's mouth. Fess sank his teeth into the palm of Olmedo's hand, bit deep, but could not scream as Olmedo tightened his grip. The terrorist drove his knee into the surgeon's groin. And still Fess would not stop struggling. He grabbed at the younger man's arms. Olmedo smashed his head against the tile wall. But he was still conscious. "You bastard," Fess groaned. "I'm not finished. I'll get you. Help! Someone outside. . . ."

Will he never stop resisting? Why does this old man fight so hard? Olmedo wondered. Stumbling, croaking, Fess was trying to flail his way past Olmedo to the corridor. His arms flapped. It could end for all of them now, Olmedo realized, if the surgeon escaped.

He dragged Fess into the closet. Hoarsely, Fess kept calling for help. Olmedo had no choice. He ignored Fess's hands ripping at his green tunic, trying to drag him down. Olmedo locked his fingers around the surgeon's throat. He had done this once before, killed a police spy this way, a man sent to murder him.

Fess was neither a police agent nor a spy nor a murderer. But this was no time for distinctions. Trask had to be right—there were no innocents. He locked his hands around Dr. Fess's neck, watched the eyes bulge, the lips malform in wordless appeal. Then the body went limp, the clawing hands released his blouse. Olmedo closed the closet door shut and let the remains of Dr. Harvey Fess crumple to the floor.

9

Stade had brought over a hundred men into the hospital area. Some were changing to white coats, orderlies' uniforms, maintenance men's coveralls. In front of him was a floor plan of surgery and an architect's diagram of the hospital.

"No way in or out," Rockewicz said. "They've got to leave the way they went in."

The agent was thinking ahead. Snipers might be effective later, in the open. It had worked before. There were evidently only two armed men in the room. Even if they took hostages, accurate fire might bring them down.

Rockewicz scowled at the drawings. "Christ, these are awful. Estelle, get someone from maintenance to explain them." He turned to Stade. "Are you thinking what I am? That they have to take hostages with them when they go?"

Stade nodded. "I don't see any other way."

"Eric. Motzkin. Those nurses. What do we do?"

"There's nothing we can do at the moment. We can keep talking to John. Sometimes they'll make a deal."

Cardone walked toward them. "What about Mr. Tench?"

"What about him?" Rockewicz asked.

"You said hostages. Is it conceivable . . . possible . . . they'd try to take him?"

Rockewicz frowned at him. "You mean right after surgery?"

"Yes."

"Well, it could be done." He rubbed a hand across his face. "Sure. Into an ambulance. He could be maintained. Oxygen, blood, defibrillator, pacemaker. But the odds against his making it on a bouncy ride would be a hell of a lot less than in the recovery room."

Frank Parolo, the chief of maintenance, entered the cafeteria. Chief Reinhold and Patrolman Olenik were waiting for him.

"Frank," Olenik said, "you know the chief."

They shook hands. They understood one another. They had one solution to the outrage in surgery: *kill the bastards.* Parolo was gray and furrowed, a wizard with stuffed pipes, short-circuited wires.

"Listen," Reinhold said. "We need help."

They were heading for a table when Parolo was summoned on the PA. Rockewicz wanted him. He excused himself.

"Shit," Reinhold said. "Meet us back here when you're through, okay?"

Parolo nodded. He hurried to Rockewicz's office. Estelle ushered him in. Cardone, Stade, and Rockewicz were discussing the positioning of agents. A hard-eyed FBI man named Lief was in charge of the armed squads. He was wearing a white hospital coat.

Arnold Stade studied the floor plans. The old place was a sieve —exits, entrances, stairways, ramps. "Lock the side doors," he said to Rockewicz. "Close down everything except front and rear. Start eliminating nonessential functions. Shut down the mail room, cafeteria, admitting. All patients to stay in their rooms, all nurses at the islands. Just emergency services."

"What about the garage?" Rockewicz asked. "And the methadone clinic?"

"They can stay open. The clinic might be a good place to plant a man. If they leave by way of the courtyard, it's got a good line of sight."

"*What?*" Cardone cried. "I keep hearing line of sight. I will not tolerate any shooting if Mr. Tench is being wheeled out of here on a stretcher."

"No one will be unnecessarily endangered," Stade said.

"I'm afraid I don't believe you. There have been too many of these damned shoot-outs recently."

"You have to take my word."

"Not good enough, Stade. I'm a friend of the Secretary of the Treasury. He and I—"

Cardone reached for a phone. Gently but firmly, Stade's hand closed on Cardone's. "Mr. Cardone, this is our case. I've been patient with you, but I don't have to be. You're an observer here. We have to make quick decisions and we have to make them with a minimum of interference or hysteria."

"*Hysteria?*" The president of Tench Industries reacted as if ice water had been thrown in his face.

"Maybe a strong word, but I must insist that you not raise objections to the way the Bureau handles this. We understand your concern for Mr. Tench. You will have to understand our interest in saving everyone."

Cardone spun on a raised heel and left. The crocodile leather flashed. Rockewicz winked at Stade. Then he called Parolo over to the desk to review the diagrams.

"There is absolutely no access to that room except through the main hall?" Stade asked.

"That's right," the maintenance man said. "Well, except the old vents, but it ain't really an access."

"Vents?" the FBI chief asked.

"From the old ventilating blowers before the air conditioning. It's like a space in the wall, way up, but it's covered. I don't see how anyone could get in. It's real narrow anyway."

They went back to the plans. Parolo was dismissed.

Immediately he headed back to the cafeteria where Reinhold was awaiting him. The maintenance man tried to recall how the passageways to the vents were sealed, how one got to them. It didn't matter. Anyone trying to crawl through would have to be nuts. He'd strangle in rat turds.

Cardone had sent Gallatin to the Federal Reserve Bank branch in New York. The counting of the money was proceeding. The executive took heart from the speed with which his corporation and the government responded to Tench's crisis. A bookkeeping operation. They would be given the ten million. Their account would be charged. Simple.

The executive looked up from the phone. "Mr. Rockewicz, can a helicopter land on the roof of the hospital?"

"We've done it once before."

He relayed the information to Gallatin. Things were moving quickly.

Stade listened with one ear to Cardone's conversation. Something nagged at him. He knew about hostage cases. It helped to delay, to talk, to negotiate. Criminals, political or otherwise, who took hostages were almost always psychotic. They wanted attention. They wanted recognition. The man calling himself John might want exposure, publicity, dissemination of his ideas. With Cardone rushing headlong to meet the 12:12 deadline, they might be losing an opportunity to trap the gunmen or even to negotiate their surrender.

"When you talk to him again," Stade said to Cardone, "make something of that possible delay."

"Why should I?"

"It may help."

"I'm not so sure. I want Mr. Tench out of there as soon as the operation is finished. They've killed a man already."

"I don't think they wanted to," Stade said. "If we can keep talking, we'll have a better chance of taking them."

Rockewicz watched them fence with one another. He was an interested party, too. It was his man, Baggs, who was dead, his surgeons who might be walked out of the hospital under guns. And wasn't that Cardone a piece of work! Get me the Attorney General. Get me the Secretary of the Treasury. Oh, he went first class. Vaguely Steve recalled that Tench's old man had been on trial once for price-fixing. Acquitted, of course. They ran it all, and it was necessary sometimes to take them on. But the crazies in surgery had it all wrong. You didn't do it with guns. You did it with cunning and flattery and false moves.

"More headaches," Steve said. He was looking out his window. Amid the massed police cars, a Ford station wagon had stopped. Men were unloading film and sound gear. A TV reporter was talking to a city policeman, making notes.

"Someone was tipped," Rockewicz said. "I guess you can't sit on a story like this."

Harris, Stade's assistant, joined him. "You have a PR man to talk to them?"

"The job's open. No budget. My assistant Buttram handles it."

"Better get him."

A second car pulled up. Men began to assemble cameras.

"This is going to be rough," Rockewicz said.

"We'll tell them as little as possible," Stade said. "Instruct your man to keep them in one place, a sort of press room. Not the lobby. Some isolated place. They may be a help."

"How?"

"Those radicals in your operating room have a message. We

can offer them the press. Let them get their story across. It might keep them talking. If they get itchy about delays, or foul-ups, there's always a TV show they can get on." He turned to Cardone. "See if you can raise John. Tell him the money is being counted and packaged, but that there might be a time snag."

Estelle walked in. "Mrs. Lake is on the phone, Mr. Rockewicz. Will you talk to her?"

10

Dr. Lake put his scalpel at a point on Tench's aorta about one inch above the heart. "Right here for the graft to the LAD," he said. He moved the scalpel up an inch. "And here for the graft to the diagonal. How does that look, Jack?"

"Looks fine, Eric."

Mihrab nodded. Lake would put the grafts where he wanted. But he always included the junior surgeons in his decisions.

"There's an artery that's really shot," Lake said. He touched the wider end with his gloved fingers. "Beading. A good part of the way down. Just a matter of time before it closed off. Feel it, Jack." *Beading* described the bits of hardness in a vessel grown narrow, obstructing the flow of blood.

"A little below that it's healthy," Lake observed. "There's a decent stretch here. Scissors."

The surgeon raised the artery and cut into it. Licata thrust a suction tube into the incision. The blood hissed. With a forceps Lake grasped the healthy section of the artery.

"You've worked it out?" Motzkin asked Trask. "You're getting what you want?"

"So far."

"Then—then—we'll all be free to go. I mean, when the operation is finished."

"Maybe."

"Alan," Lake said coldly. "Stick to the pump."

"He can talk to me if he wants," Trask said. "We aren't

monsters. We're more human than any of you. You save a life here and there. Rashid and I and the others will save humanity. If your man Baggs understood that he'd be alive. He'd be on our side."

"Crazier than I thought," Licata whispered. "Eric—"

"Probe," Lake said. "One-and-a-half-millimeter."

Sally gave him a curling wire probe. He inserted it into the opening he had cut into the artery and worked it downward. He guided the metal rod with his left hand. "It's open. A good lumen. Right to the end."

Licata and Mihrab were holding hemostat clamps. They were ready for the crucial step—sewing a part of Tench's saphenous vein, taken from his leg, into the artery. It was 10:42 A.M.

Licata held the incision open. Lake stitched expertly, pushing the steel-tipped sutures into the living artery and the vein. Working quickly, his hands moving deftly over the heart, he spoke to Trask. "John."

"Yes?"

"I'd like a timetable from you. They've agreed to pay you. I'll be finished by about eleven-thirty or eleven-forty-five. My assistants will need ninety minutes to two hours to finish before Mr. Tench can be moved into the recovery room. Can you give me an idea when we can start leaving?"

"It's up to them."

"Them?"

Licata shook his head. "He's nuts. Them. Us. War. The enemy. Reparations. What's the point of talking to him?"

"It's the corporation's decision. And the police's. And Rockewicz. They're the power structure. They've run your lives so far, and they still run them. Baggs was their hired stooge."

"You shut up about Jimmy," Motzkin said.

Lake continued stitching the vein to the artery, closing the incision. "I heard you say they'd agreed to pay up," he said casually.

Motzkin squinted at his monitors. The arterial pressure was

constant. He knew how quickly Lake worked. The patient could be off bypass, the coronary surgery completed in a half hour.

"You'll get your money," Motzkin said. "And we can go home, right?"

"Unless they trick us," Trask said. He seemed brittle. His movements were jerky and he swiveled on the stool. "Then you're all in trouble. You must understand that."

11

Gallatin called with distressing news: it was fairly certain that ten million dollars in hundreds, packaged in bank rolls of a hundred each, could not be assembled in time to make the deadline. What with counting, packing, loading on the helicopter, the short flight to the hospital and unloading, they could not be on time. To wait for all of the money in hundreds might mean as much as an hour's delay.

"You must talk to them," Gallatin persisted. He was old and stubborn, a contemporary of Tench's father. Cardone had wanted to early-retire him. "Many of us feel it will hurt the corporate image. The way we gave in so quickly, obeyed their demands. Some of us feel we should seek an arrangement with them or enforce our will on them."

Cardone was furious. "Gallatin, an oil company paid fourteen million dollars in Argentina for a minor executive. Mr. Tench is surely worth ten million." He paused, and then came down hard on every word. "You will follow my orders and raise the money and keep me advised, or you will be retired tomorrow. And so will any other executive who disobeys me."

Rockewicz winked at Stade. "Man knows how to eat ass. And that wasn't just a mail room clerk he was reaming out."

Trask was on the phone again. "Cardone, I want a progress report."

"The money is being counted and packaged."

"Will it be here at twelve-twelve?"

"We're doing everything possible."

"You're trying to trick us. To keep us around until Tench is out of surgery. We won't let him out of our gunsights until the money is here."

"I have to appeal to you. There may not be enough money exactly as you specified. Suppose some is in smaller denominations? Or suppose on such short notice we can't even get ten million? I guarantee you'll get the rest. This will be a personal agreement between us, John."

"You will deliver the money as ordered."

Trask's chest inflated. He stood almost at attention. This was it: bending them, making them submit and obey. Like the university president who'd put his arm around his shoulder and asked that their photograph be taken after a truce in the dormitories. (And Trask had ordered the building burned an hour later.)

"Rockewicz here," Steve said. He had picked up an extension. "May I talk to Dr. Lake?"

Trask agreed. He held the phone toward the surgeon.

"Not now," Lake said. "Tell him the first graft is just about complete."

Licata picked a blood-soaked sponge from the cavity below the heart and dropped it into a basin. The sponges were arrayed on a plastic sheet. Later Flor would weigh them to establish the patient's loss of blood.

"Look at the way these sutures curl," Lake said disgustedly. He normally was not so voluble while working. But he felt the need for small talk, anything to create a semblance of normality.

"You'd think they could invent a better suture," Licata said. "Maybe I will someday and retire on the royalties."

"While you're at it, change the color. They make them green and you can't see them on green drapes. Bright yellow would be better."

Mihrab nodded. Eric Lake's usual banter. But this time it did not seem to relieve the tension. He saw Rashid's black eyes on him. But Dr. Mihrab did not speak to him. On what basis? The man cradling the weapon had killed Baggs. He would kill them all if he had to.

Lake and his team were finishing sewing the vein into the aorta. One bypass would soon be finished.

Motzkin got up. His bones ached. Too much rich food, not enough exercise. "Can I turn the pump off for a second?" he asked Lake. "I want to make sure there's no air in the lines."

"Go ahead," Lake said.

The anesthesiologist studied the tubing leading to the artery. It was clear. "Looks okay. I'll put him back on."

Trask was off the stool. He spoke to Motzkin. "You."

"What do you want?"

"How long can a man be off the pump and live?"

"Screw him, Alan," Licata said. "He doesn't deserve answers."

"I don't know what you mean," Motzkin said.

Lake's weary eyes peered at Trask. "Wasn't it part of our agreement that you were to leave us alone? If you stop bothering us, this will go faster."

Trask walked toward the heart-lung machine. He stepped on the thick black cable that led to the outlet. "If I cut this, you'd tell me. How long?"

Motzkin drew his breath in. Trask was standing a yard away. Now? If I were stronger, braver, a hothead like Jimmy? It was useless. The Arab in the gallery . . .

"I asked a question. If the pump goes off, how long can he stay alive?"

12

Harris, Stade's assistant, was scribbling on a yellow pad. The computerized files in the Washington headquarters of the bureau had come through with a print-out on John. He read part of it to the men in Rockewicz's office.

"John is John Trask," he said. "Age twenty-nine. UFTAP— Unlawful Flight to Avoid Prosecution. From Aurora, Illinois, son of the director of a community center. Several colleges, turned up in New York, 1968, during the campus riots. Never enrolled at any school but was active in the riots at Columbia, NYU, and City College. Warrant for his arrest in Michigan after bombing of an electronics laboratory that left an instructor blinded. Vanished, believed to be in hiding in Europe and North Africa for several years."

"A middle-class boy from the middle west," Rockewicz said.

"And apparently disowned by most of the other radical outfits," Stade said. "These people are crackpots. They don't have any real support, not even on their side of the political fence."

"That doesn't make it easier for the people under the gun," Steve said. That computer in Washington, with all its stored trivia, wasn't going to bring Jimmy Baggs back to life.

13

"I'd say about four minutes," Motzkin said.

"Four minutes?" Trask nudged him with the gun. "You are saying if that machine goes dead Tench will live four minutes?"

Motzkin wiped his forehead. Sweat gathered under the gown. "I guess it varies. Other physiological conditions—"

"Alan!" Lake said. "No surgical conference." He lifted the sewn vein with a forceps. It rose in a gentle curve, paler and thicker than the artery, a healthy new conduit for blood.

"I can't help it, Eric," Motzkin said. "The gun's on me, not on you."

"Go on," Trask said. "What were you saying?"

"There are physiological variables. He might live longer, but his brain could be affected."

"Get your foot off that cable," Lake said. "You want Tench to live, don't you? You want to prove that you run a businesslike operation, don't you? Those people in Argentina returned their victims. The same in Mexico."

"Not always," Trask said. "I understand revolutionary tactics better than you do, Dr. Lake." He turned to Motzkin. "The machine is fragile? Can it be repaired if it goes out?"

"I'm not an expert. Baggs, the fellow you shot, he knew all about it."

"You do, too, doctor."

"You can plug it back in seconds. Or just turn off the arterial pressure switch and it stops."

"Is this true, Dr. Lake?" Trask asked. "After four minutes, the patient will die?"

"Generally."

"With some variations," Motzkin blurted out. "Conditions—"

Lake turned from the table. "I want you to stop bothering my anesthesiologist. Get back to the stool. Worry about your ransom money. I don't permit this in my OR."

Trask's back stiffened. Otherwise he did not react to Lake's reprimand.

Motzkin made an entry on the chart. Ah, shrewd Eric. He had cut the conversation short. Alan knew why. Yes, four minutes. But that was at normal body temperature. At lower temperatures a patient might live for eight or nine minutes without blood. He could remember Jimmy once shoveling ice cubes into the pump to lower blood temperature and keep a woman alive when the pump failed. Musgrave, one of Jimmy's assistants, had run the pump by hand.

It was a job for a very strong man. Not for him. Not Alan Motzkin.

14

On the PA system, Rockewicz ordered everything but emergency services halted. Classes were canceled. Clinics were shut down. The medical conferences were postponed. Dave Buttram, the assistant director, raced up and down stairs, trying to enforce the order. It was difficult. Some nurses refused to leave their stations. Ambulatory patients, roused from boredom by the possibility of violence, wandered into lounges, turned on radios and TV sets.

"Why they closin' us down?" Mr. Montaigne asked.

"Some bad business on the third floor," a double amputee in a wheelchair said. "Heard it's in surgery."

Teams of FBI agents began to interrogate witnesses. They spoke to the women in autoclave, the security guards, the residents in the doctors' dressing room. Descriptions emerged: a tall slender man, fair, light-eyed, and a short man, very dark, black hair. Few had heard them speak. The women from autoclave assumed the dark man was a Puerto Rican. They thought they had seen him with Carlos Olmedo.

Someone recalled hearing Dr. Lake call the thin man "Dr. West from Massachusetts General." An agent phoned Boston. There was no such physician listed. No one had planned a visit to watch Eric Lake operate.

Buttram returned to Rockewicz's office. His boss was grimacing as he listened to Cardone talk on the phone to another executive. Buttram knew what Steve was thinking: paper-pushers, corporate dummies. Except for a few terrors at the top, like Cardone, they drew huge salaries for going to meetings and playing golf.

"Absolutely not," Cardone was saying. "I don't give a damn what the stockholders think. There will be no delay. No offers to do this through the foundation or to feed children. We will deliver what they want and you will see to it that it is delivered on time. Listen to me, Gallatin. These people don't want justice. They want revenge. They want to humiliate us. I'm ready to be humiliated if it will save Walker's life."

Buttram caught Rockewicz's attention. There were a dozen reporters and TV technicians in the lobby. Someone would have to talk to them.

"You're elected," Steve said. "Move them out of the lobby. Keep 'em in the auditorium. Phones, coffee, whatever. Be nice but keep them out of the way."

"Find his daughter," Cardone was saying. "The wives should

be notified. Didn't you say the girl was in a commune? Get someone after her. . . . I know he hasn't seen her in years." He slammed the phone down.

Steve watched him narrowly. Cardone. An ethnic who came up fast. Smart, maybe too smart. Full of ideas. Someday the old bastards would hang him, send him out to be a foundation president. But before they did, long before, Old Steve was going to get something out of him, something big, for his hospital.

15

Buttram had little difficulty persuading the reporters, photographers, and technicians to set up a press room in the hospital auditorium. He gave them a one-line release written by Rockewicz: "Armed men have invaded an operating room and are holding hostages; negotiations are underway." More information would follow. They were not satisfied.

"This is for the birds, Buttram," a man from UPI said. "Who else can we talk to?"

"Suppose we look around?" a girl asked.

"No. I'm sorry."

"Negotiations?" a man asked. "Who with? Who's the hostage? What do these people want?"

Buttram apologized. "I can't say anything else."

A photographer moved to the door. Another followed.

"Hey, you fellows," Buttram said. "You agreed. No wandering around. I'll tell you something you shouldn't know. There are armed people all over the place. In hospital clothing. There may be . . . trouble."

The girl reporter squinted at him. "Sounds like the FBI. Are they in on it? Is it a kidnapping or something like that?"

"I can't tell you."

The photographers stopped. "Fellows, listen," Buttram was pleading. "There have been cases where you've meant no harm, but you got in the way of the police. Stay in this room until I have some information. I'll be back in ten minutes, I promise. Here's an extension where you can reach me."

Buttram left. As he did, a thin man with an iron-gray crew cut stuck his head into the auditorium. "Hey, reporters? Name's McFeeley. Edward J. McFeeley."

"So?" the UPI man asked.

"Know this jernt like the backa my hand. Doc Lake gimme anortic valve last year. There ain't nothin' I don't know about this place."

A man from the local paper muttered to the girl reporter, "Local nut. Hanger-on. Every hospital has one."

"They shootin' hell out of surgery," McFeeley said. "Some coon got it. I know everything. Five years inna SeaBees. I been around. Stay away from the halls, they're fulla feds. Shoot you soon's look at you."

The UPI man approached him. "Ed, is it? Ed McFeeley?"

"One of Doc Lake's best cases. Never miss a heart clinic. Buncha gunners in surgery. Gonna turn this place into a shootin' gallery before they're through."

The UPI man made a circular motion next to his head: *Nuts.*

In the lobby Buttram was distressed by the sight of Brian O'Boyle. O'Boyle was the star of a New York TV news show—brash, young, aggressive. He affected shoulder-length blond hair and an Indian headband and had won prizes for investigatory journalism. He was admired by hard-hats as well as radical students: a sort of aggregate New Yorker. A cameraman and a sound man, laden with equipment, followed O'Boyle. Buttram introduced himself and led him to the auditorium.

"Oh no," O'Boyle said. "I want to go to surgery. I want to talk to the hostages."

"Impossible, Mr. O'Boyle. It's under police security."

"Goddamn it, I don't work that way. You ought to know that!" He spoke very quickly, as if impatient with the world.

"I'm sorry. Police orders. You'll have to wait in here." Buttram opened the door to the murky auditorium. O'Boyle peered in, saw a group of his competitors, and shook his head. "I want to see the hospital director. I want to see the FBI boss. Whoever's holed up, I can get them to surrender. I've done it before."

How old was he? Buttram wondered. Thirty? "Not a chance, Mr. O'Boyle. Please wait inside."

Buttram left. O'Boyle lit a cigarette and threw the match on the floor. His cameraman and sound man began to compute their overtime. McFeeley, rejected by the reporters, came out. He fixed a red eye on O'Boyle. "Hey you, pretty boy with the hair. I seen you on the TV with the junkies. Name's McFeeley, Eighty-second Airborne. There's a coon dead in surgery. Guys with automatic weapons. They got Doc Lake."

"Yeah?" O'Boyle studied the hospital buff. "Can you take me there?"

"Jernt is fulla feds. Put me on the television? An interview?"

"You find me where they're at, you get a whole show."

The cross-hatched face lit up. "I got connections. I know this dump like the backa my hand. Had eight combat jumps." He grabbed O'Boyle's arm as he saw Chief Reinhold and Parolo walking toward them. "Stick with me, O'Boyle. I see some personal friends." His breath parted the newsman's hair.

"Who's the guy in uniform?"

"Police chief. I'll innerduce you."

16

Fiona lingered inside the methadone clinic. On the loudspeaker she had heard the orders to stop services, to clear the third floor, for patients and hospital personnel to stay out of the corridors. Now, on the clinic director's radio, she heard the single brief news bulletin. "At least two armed men have taken over an operating room at City General Hospital. . . . There has been shooting in the room, but it is uncertain whether anyone has been injured. Contact is being made by hospital director Stephen Rockewicz and. . . ."

The director of the clinic, the man the pimp had called Fat, whistled. "They never shoulda took the dogs off."

"Dogs?" Fiona asked. She huddled on a bench near the door. She could look into the courtyard.

"Yeah. We had Dobermans on patrol. Then the community groups said it was racist, so we took 'em off. Didn't have a mugging for two years while the dogs were around."

She nodded. Dogs would not have kept Trask and Rashid from Walker Tench.

"I gotta process your papers," Fat said. "Wanna come back tomorrow? It don't look so safe around here. A little girl like you, all alone."

"I'll wait if it's all right."

"Sure."

Outside the door, the pimp winked at her and made an obscene gesture. Through the door she heard him inviting her again. "You be in the stable, baby. But you kick me in the nuts again, I burn your ass."

Could he be a plant? Could someone have talked, and was this creature a cop assigned to keep her in place?

Fat had the radio pressed to his ear. "Christ, it says now there's a guy dead in surgery. They killed a guy. Or else one of them got it." He shook his head. "They never shoulda taken the dogs off."

17

Buttram returned to the auditorium with a coffee urn for the reporters. He arranged for them to use phones in unoccupied rooms nearby. Then he gave them some information. Yes, there had been shooting in the operating room. He gave them Lake's name, Tench's name, and said that a hospital employee was dead. After hesitating, he gave them Baggs's name. He had no idea of the circumstances under which he was killed.

The reporters charged out of the room to the telephones. One TV crew asked Buttram to repeat what he had just said on camera.

The young official obliged them. So far they were behaving well. One of the older reporters, the AP man, complimented him. "You got to level with these people," he said. "I covered the Weinberger case on Long Island. Kidnapping. Before your time. Nobody leveled with us. Story leaked, the kid died. You get any information, and if it won't screw up the cops or harm anyone, give it out fast."

Buttram thanked him. He was trained in administration, not journalism. But they seemed a reliable bunch. As he left, he was troubled by something. Brian O'Boyle, the long-haired kid in the suede jacket and blue jeans, had not been in the auditorium.

18

"Are you on schedule?" Trask asked Lake. He had begun to glance at the doors. It was silent in the corridor. No more footsteps and voices.

"We won't be if you keep interrupting. Gamel, take that clip off the arterial wall. It's in my way."

"I'd love to stick him," Licata said across the table.

Lake ignored the remark. "Lift the aorta, Jack. I think the graft to the diagonal should be a little higher. Vacuum pump."

Above them, Rashid shifted his legs, stood, tugged at his crotch. He'd known he would have problems with his kidneys. He needed relief. When he had fired the carbine at the black grappling with Trask, there had been a few quick spurts. It was a disgrace. He hoped no one would notice the stain on the light trousers.

"Hold the apex up, Jack," Lake said. He sounded shaky. Licata thought, not at all like Eric. Who could blame him? "We're going after the diagonal branch."

Licata lifted the shapeless heart. It quivered, barely acknowledging that it still lived. Lake squinted at the left side. "It's hidden. It's what I was afraid of when I ran the angiogram this morning."

"Isn't that the termination?" Mihrab asked.

"What there is of it." Lake shook his head. All his concentration was focused on the orange heart. A problem. A challenge.

Trask was off the stool. He took a step toward them. Cho flattened against the wall. "What's going on? Are you trying some stunt?"

Lake did not look at Trask. "Get back where you belong. You said you wanted the operation finished. Stay out of my way."

Trask did not move. "You're stalling."

"What the hell do you care?" Licata shouted. "You'd as soon kill Tench. For Chrissake, we're trying to save him."

"I want our money. I want it on schedule. That's *all* I want."

Lake did not respond. He touched the heart with his scalpel. "Gentlemen, we have here what the professors call an intramural artery. The diagonal branch of the left coronary artery is buried in the heart. All we can see is the proximal end, but the part we need, where we can make the graft, is in the heart muscle."

"You ever seen one so deep?" Licata asked.

"Not many. We have a little digging to do."

Trask waved the .38 at Lake. "What does that mean?"

"It may take a little longer," Lake said.

"Then you'd better settle for half an operation. Sew him up."

Lake stared at him. His eyes looked muddled behind the magnifying glasses. "I'll finish my work. Is that clear? You do what you want. I will finish this operation."

Trask retreated. "All right." He managed a warped smile. "There's something to be said for that kind of dedication."

Lake said, "It's inside the fat and the muscle."

"Look at the bottom," Licata said. "Less than a millimeter. Not much to work with."

Mihrab clucked his dismay. Most coronary surgeons felt that when the artery was less than a millimeter in diameter it was dangerous to cut into it because of the possibility of thrombosis. But Lake was no ordinary surgeon. He took chances. He knew more. He had been a researcher, a student of physics, body fluids, hematology, pathology. He was no mere snipper and stitcher.

Lake studied the heart. "Jack, run your finger along where you think the diagonal might go. See if you find any beading. Unlikely, but give it a whirl."

Licata did so. "Zilch, Eric. Maybe the guy doesn't have a diagonal."

"It's got a beginning and an end," Lake said. "So it's got to have a middle."

Motzkin straightened the arterial tube. "Like Aristotle's theory of drama," the anesthesiologist said. No one heard him. A try, an effort to loosen things up. Every now and then Motzkin looked at Baggs's shrouded figure. He understood now what people felt on a crashing plane, dying of hemorrhage, drowning. Why me? Why him?

"I don't like what's going on," Trask said. He sounded shrill. "You people are concocting some kind of delay."

Lake turned from the table. He pointed the scalpel at Trask. "Keep your mouth shut. And tell your friend in the grandstand to stop shifting around so much. He distracts me with that gun."

"Yeah," Licata said. "Why don't you get on the phone and see if the money's coming?"

Lake lifted the heart again. "We'll go in the back door."

He made a minute incision in the visible lower end of the artery, cutting into the tip with his scalpel.

"In medical schools all over the world," Lake said, "the experts will warn you not to cut into such a small coronary artery. But this is how reputations are made. Right, Jack?"

"I guess so. I just wonder if Jarring Jack Licata will have the guts to try it when he's on his own."

"If you don't, you'll never make the cover of *Time*. Stand by."

19

Ed McFeeley, who knew the hospital only as a hanger-on could, led Reinhold, Parolo and O'Boyle into a small conference room.

"Chief Reinhold, this here is Mr. O'Boyle. You seen him on

the TV. The guy who exposed the garbage collection rackets in Joisey."

Reinhold's foxy face was suspicious. O'Boyle was not his dish of tea. He squinted at the long yellow hair, the Indian band, the suede jacket. Normally he would have been delighted to break a nightstick over such a head.

"So?" Reinhold asked.

"He needs a story," McFeeley said. He talked out of the side of his mouth. "He'll put yez on the TV." His head swiveled toward O'Boyle. "I know the angles. Worked as a police reporter on the *Fairbanks News*. After I run champeen dog sleds."

Reinhold opened the door. "McFeeley, beat it. Keep your trap shut."

"But I made the innerductions. I set this up."

"Get out or I'll bust you."

O'Boyle watched them with contemptuous eyes. A tough city cop. A hospital buff. A stupid maintenance man. But he knew how stories were dug out. You had to look under rocks.

McFeeley left. Reinhold stared at O'Boyle. "Whaddya want?"

"What's going on?"

The chief told him. The FBI had taken over. He was being closed out. The operating room was sealed. There was to be no attempt to take it. He was bitter.

"What's Parolo got to do with it?" O'Boyle asked. He had wondered from the start. Why the maintenance man, with his metal hoop of keys?

"He was giving me a layout of the building," Reinhold said.

"Really? Can I ask why?"

The chief scowled at O'Boyle and said nothing.

"See if I can guess. You're looking for some way to bust in. Blow their heads off before they can move. Really stick it to the FBI. Make those guys in gray suits look like jerks. Do I have the picture?"

"Not bad, O'Boyle." The chief was smiling. He liked the way O'Boyle talked. The long hair, the hippie outfit, were a disguise, the way Reinhold's undercover men sometimes dressed as fags or junkies to make a collar.

"How about it, Parolo?" O'Boyle asked. "I keep hearing that that room is closed off. Is it really? Is the door the only way in?"

"Yeah."

"So we're dead. Nobody is going to charge in and get shot up, or have those doctors and nurses killed while the chief knocks off some nut with a gun."

"I'll take my chances," Reinhold said. "But not the front way."

Parolo cringed. He had no right to be with them, plotting, giving out information. Rockewicz would fire him, ruin him, if he found out. He cursed his brother-in-law, Patrolman Olenik, for getting him to talk.

"Gonna break through a wall, chief?"

"Maybe. Maybe not," Reinhold said. "Why should I tell you?"

O'Boyle adjusted his headband. "I can help."

"How?"

"A lot of ways. You want to show those FBI pricks a thing or two. It was your case. They stole it. I can see to it the media gets the story right."

"You're really beautiful," Reinhold said sarcastically.

"Level with me. You going in the front door? I've been in ORs. They're traps. Lots of people crowded around the table. Couple of shots, they're all dead. Explode the oxygen cylinders. Those lunatics in there probably have grenades, automatic weapons. You aren't going in shooting."

Reinhold looked at Parolo, then at the TV reporter. "I wouldn't tell you if I were."

"Maybe you better. Maybe I'll run right up to the FBI and to the director's office and warn them."

"You'll shit, too. You'd love to have me go in. Like at Attica. Shoot the balls off everyone. Then you'd have a story. Make the cops the heavies. What do you care if they're all dead? I care, see? I want to kill a couple of germs in there. This is my city, O'Boyle. Those fuckers understand only one thing."

"Then why is the FBI laying off? Why is everyone agreeing to pay up?"

Reinhold shrugged. "That corporation guy, Tench. He's precious to them."

"But he doesn't mean that much to Chief George Reinhold, is that it?" the reporter mocked.

Reinhold was not accustomed to such straight tough talk. Still, he appreciated the gutter courage in O'Boyle. The guy had more to him than the fag threads. And he was a hot personality. He could make Reinhold on the tube. The chief nodded at Parolo. "Tell him."

Parolo leaned forward. He had a husky voice, as if hit too often in the throat as a young man. "There's this air tunnel, see?"

O'Boyle's eyes widened. He shoved some yellow notepaper in front of the maintenance man. "Diagram it. Show me the table, the door, everything in that room."

Parolo sketched quickly. "The opening from the air shaft is about here. It was a duct for the ventilating system."

"In the ceiling?"

"No. At the top of the wall. Maybe a foot under the ceiling. It's about two feet by two."

O'Boyle asked, "Covered?"

"There's a heavy grille over it. The holes are pretty big. It ain't a screen or like that."

"Could someone shove it out?" Reinhold asked.

"Yeah, I guess so. Bang it out, maybe."

The reporter smirked. "They'd blow your head off the minute they heard it."

"Not if I move fast," the chief said. "They wouldn't know what hit them."

"How you going to separate the good guys from the bad guys?" O'Boyle asked. "There's no white hats and black hats in there. They're all in green. That's how they sneaked in. Surgical gowns and masks."

"Anyone with a gun gets shot. I won the Eastern States Fast-

Fire Competition last year. Those fuckers would be dead before they turned around."

O'Boyle rubbed his lips. He was smelling out something bigger than anything Reinhold could imagine. Something that would make two reputations.

"How wide is that duct?" the reporter asked.

"Oh, inside, maybe two anna half feet." Parolo held his hands apart. "Like so. One small guy could crawl through. I used to send Andy Fusco in to clean out the dust and crap. He useta be a jockey."

O'Boyle smiled at Reinhold. "You'll never get through, Reinhold. You'll get wedged in."

"I been in tighter places. O'Boyle, you can wait outside and I'll give you the story when I come out. You can be the first into surgery to take movies of the corpses."

"I got a better idea."

"Yeah?"

"I'm skinnier than you. Let me go in."

"You? You aren't allowed to carry a weapon."

"I won't." O'Boyle tapped the Sony recorder. "Just this and a light camera. I'll go in and bargain with them. These guys all love publicity. I'll get them to surrender."

Reinhold smiled at the newsman's innocent stupidity. "Well, you got balls, O'Boyle, but not much brains."

"I've gotten hoods to surrender. And on TV. They know who I am. These people sound like radical weirdos. I can talk to them. I'll promise them a deal with the feds if they come out. If they don't, they're dead. If they come out, they got a chance. They'll believe me before they believe a cop."

He was going too quickly for Reinhold. "You think they'll fall for that?" the chief asked.

"We won't know till we try. Look, if we can bring these lunatics in alive, we're heroes. Crack the whole gang, contacts, underground hideouts."

"Where am I all this time?" the chief asked. "While you're in there sweet-talking them, what do I do? Parolo says only one of us can get in that duct."

"You're in front of the OR with your guys. Screw the FBI. They can't keep you out of surgery. I bargain with them, make the deal, and they walk out. You put the cuffs on 'em. And no shooting."

Reinhold was hesitant. This freak with his girl's hair and sandals? Maybe you needed a freak to talk to freaks. "Suppose they try something? Suppose they come out shooting?"

"Those people watch television. They know me. They won't shoot. Reinhold, you'll never get an offer like this again. If they come out, you're a hero. If they don't, I'm the fuck-up. I'll get all the blame anyway, but what do I care? You're clean. You didn't disobey the Bureau. You saw these pricks walking out and you made the collar."

"Or waste them if they resist."

"Right. You did what any intelligent cop would do." O'Boyle leaned forward. His face was scarred and hard-boned, not a fairy's face at all. "But I'm the heavy if it gets screwed up, see? I get you off the hook."

"Gimme a minute to cover all the possibilities."

Parolo lowered his furrowed head. "What about me? I'm in the middle. Rockewicz'll find out I tipped you guys off."

O'Boyle patted his arm. "We'll cover for you, Parolo. You mentioned something about an old air duct and I went looking for it. You never heard this conversation, right, chief?"

Reinhold winked at him. A couple of the boys. O'Boyle knew the types. His father was a district leader in Queens. He squeezed Parolo's arm. "No sweat, Parolo. Like I explained to the chief, I'm the heavy. Anything gets screwed up, both you guys blame it all on me. I got big shoulders."

"And balls," Reinhold said.

PART FOUR

1

Shortly before 11:00 A.M., Martha Lake called.

On her way to a meeting of the Council on Continuing Education, she had heard the bulletin on her car radio. Eric's name had not been mentioned in the first brief accounts, nor had Tench's.

"It's bad news, Martha," Rockewicz said. "They're holding Walker Tench for ransom. Eric's okay, and so are his people. They aren't after them; they want Tench's money. The operation's on schedule, and the FBI is standing by. Martha—it'll work out."

"Has anyone been . . . hurt?"

Steve held his breath. She had to be told. The information had not yet been released. "Martha, Jimmy Baggs is dead. There was some shooting in the OR. We don't know what happened."

It is amazing, Rockewicz thought. The self-control of these WASP women. He had admired Lake's wife for a long time. Brainy, good-looking, Eric's protector and guide. But she was under pressure all the time, worried about her husband. The last time the director had talked to her at length, at a dinner at Burt Evans's, she had unburdened herself to Steve. He was one of the world's best listeners.

Eric was exhausted when he came home, falling asleep watching the 10 o'clock news, never reading a book other than a medical text, numbingly absorbed in his work, rarely spending time with the children. The huge income was fine, she told Rockewicz, the fame might follow, but what was it all for? She was determined to resume her own career as soon as the children were a year or two older. She would teach again. They would level out their lives. That's what she had said.

"Jimmy . . ." she was saying. "But what in God's name did Jimmy ever do to these people? Or Eric or Alan? What can they want from them?"

"They're after Tench, Martha. They want a ten-million-dollar ransom. Eric just . . . he just happened to be there."

"Why did the hospital let them in?" she asked. "Steve, there must be something you could have done to stop it."

"Martha, you know how this place works. It works on trust or not at all. The whole world comes and goes. These people came in like doctors."

"I want Eric out of there. I don't give a damn how much money they get from Walker Tench and his corporation. I want Eric out of there as soon as the operation is over."

"We're working on it, Martha."

"I'm coming out."

"Should I send a car?"

"I'll drive."

You bet you will, Steve thought. You will drive. You won't cry, or get hysterical, or scream. And you'll make your points when you get here.

"I'm sorry as hell, Martha," Rockewicz said. "Security stinks around here. Maybe it's my fault."

"Eric always complained about the loonies and drifters wandering around." Her voice was stern and unshaking. "Tell the FBI that I want to talk to those men in the operating room. My husband is in there. I won't permit anything to happen to him, Steve."

"Sure, Martha."

For the first time he discerned a break in her voice. "Eric is too damned good, too valuable to be threatened this way. Mr. Tench and his people can come up with twenty million, thirty, forty! And the FBI can let those maniacs get off scot free for all I care."

Rockewicz spoke gently. "Martha, I'm on your side. Come on down and give me some support."

She hung up.

Harris, Stade's assistant, came in with a sheet of yellow tele-printer copy. "More on Trask and his group."

"Let's have it," Stade said. "Maybe it'll give us some ideas."

2

"They blown up surgery," a black woman shouted. "They kilt six people."

Bateman Hooks, seated at a luncheonette counter across the street from City General, listened as he watched the crowds gathering behind the police barricades.

"What it say on the radio?" Hooks asked the counterman.

"One guy dead. They're holding hostages in surgery. Nothing about six, seven, dead. These people got an imagination."

Hooks nursed a second cup of coffee. The word was spreading. People were two and three deep behind the barricades. But the main entrance of the hospital was open. There were more fuzz on the steps, but doctors and nurses were being allowed in and out. The driveway to the courtyard had not been entirely closed. A hospital security guard—one of the old men—checked trucks and cars as they arrived. Most of them were turned away. A few got through.

Who they foolin'? Hooks thought. The FBI pigs probably had a big plan. Keep traffic going, make it look like everything was fine. And plant guns all over the place, ready to blow Bateman Hooks and Trask and Rashid to little pieces when they made their run.

Man, that hospital a big mother. The twin towers rising around the marble and glass facade seemed to Hooks like two big titties. Big mother. He was born there, screaming, wet, unwanted. Not much of a life until he went GI. He had liked the Army. He had enjoyed 'Nam. The point man, squad leader, qualified with every weapon. Until they wasted the slopes, him standing with the red-necks, pumping lead into twisting bodies. The onliest people got less than me. The onliest people Mr. Charlie hate more than he hate me. He had heard a cracker from Alabama admiring the way Hooks had joined in. "That nigger shoots okay. Got plenny guts, too. Some niggers are okay, but they ain't a gook you can trust."

Ah, they would pay for the way they'd made him one of them. In an hour or so, the world would get a good look at Bateman Hooks. Part of what he owed the yellow people. Send them a telegram. VILLAGE OF DUK LI, VIETNAM. I MAKIN' IT UP. HOOKS.

"It's only one dead," a black nurse said. She came into the luncheonette, bought cigarettes, lit one. "Jimmy Baggs, the heart-lung man. They killed him. Oh, it's so awful."

"Brother?" Hooks asked.

"Yes. And such a good man. Two children."

Hooks sipped his cold coffee. Who? Rashid probably. Rashid enjoyed killing. His eyes had lit up when he bragged about the school bus. Trask? Trask was a heavy brain, a planner. He was full of ideas, big ideas for world revolution. But Trask could have done it. Sometimes he got that hot look in his eyes, his back stiff, his head moving crazy. Like a spring winding up.

"Yeah," Hooks said. "You figure when white folks start shootin' one another, some brother get it first." He looked at the duffel bag at his feet. More good news in there: carbine, grenades, magazines. He wondered, If I walk out now, where does it leave them? Nowhere. Trask could talk and plan. He had bombed some place in Paris and hit a bank in England and was after the big haul now to finance his revolution. But suppose Hooks decided he wanted to split?

"They clearin' people away," the nurse said. "Guess I got to move."

Hooks did not leave the counter. A young cop stuck his head in the door. He looked balefully at the huge black man in Army surplus clothing. He studied Hooks's faded combat jacket, the OD trousers, the boots, the sack on the floor.

"You work around here?" he asked.

"Nope. I on welfare." He grinned. The arrogance was not lost on the cop, nor the hint of recklessness. Hooks's ebony face showed no fear.

"You got to beat it," the policeman said. He was pale. Hooks knew he could break his arm. "Orders. Clearing the street in front."

"Ain't in no street. I in here."

"You'll go if I tell you to go."

Hooks stood up. He looked overpowering. "Lemme finish my coffee, man. I paid for coffee."

The cop moved forward. "I said get outa here. Nobody stays on Kennedy Boulevard."

"Sure, man. Soon as I finish my coffee."

The counterman appealed to the cop. "I'll see he goes, Ed. Lemme handle it."

The officer retreated, glad to be relieved of the responsibility. "I'm checking back here," he said. "You be the hell out."

Hooks turned his head. "Shit-ass pig." He sat down. "After I has my coffee," he said to the counterman, "I got to use your toilet. Then I got to make a phone call. Maybe I got a whole lot to do."

"You heard what the officer said."

Hooks looked at his watch. It was 11:10. On the sidewalk, he could see the cop conferring with a sergeant. They were pointing at him.

"Got me a bad case of the GI shits," Hooks said. He walked to the men's room at the rear of the greasy spoon. The pigs were looking at him.

3

"John Trask," Stade read. "Warrant out for his arrest. SDNY 3/11/70. Southern District of New York. Did a disappearing act, and look where he surfaces."

Cardone was listening with one ear. He was shouting on the phone, accusing Gallatin of dragging his feet. "Do you know what you're doing up there?" the executive yelled. "You goddamn well better."

Rockewicz spoke softly to Stade. "Like to work for that fellah?"

Stade turned to two of his men. They wore white hospital coats. Each carried a sniper's rifle. Buttram had taken them on a tour of the areas around surgery.

"If I hear the word *delay* once more," Cardone thundered, "I'll have you fired. Who is dragging his feet? Who is holding this up? Gallatin, it is eleven-sixteen, and we have less than an hour for that money to get here. Do you understand that Mr. Tench's life is at stake? His heart is exposed and there are madmen with guns standing around him?" He slammed the phone down.

The FBI agent kept reading the print-out. Trask: an average midwestern boy. From car washes and paper routes to terror and revolution in twenty years.

Cardone walked to Rockewicz's desk. "They're having trouble counting. They can't possibly get it in hundreds, the way that maniac wants it."

Stade was diagraming his stakeouts. Men in corridors, exits, side streets. Men in cars, on foot. He had called in over two hundred agents. The director had been on the phone from D.C. Mr. Tench was no ordinary hostage.

"What about the delay?" Rockewicz asked. "Is it a problem?"

Stade looked at the ceiling. "They usually hang on. Once you agree to their demands, they're ready to wait it out. Those Japanese in The Hague hung on for days. Even in Israel, Arab terrorists usually wait for the offers."

"You mean we shouldn't be too concerned if we can't get the money here by noon?" Cardone asked.

"I don't know. I'm only going by what's happened in the past. These people are often on ego trips. They want to talk, control the situation, give orders to the police. They enjoy it."

Rockewicz thought of Lake, Licata, Motzkin, Mihrab, the nurses—defenseless, unarmed. Whatever happened, they were in the middle. When guns went off, when grenades were thrown, innocents were the ones who died. He had to regain some of the initiative. Martha Lake's accusation gnawed at him.

"Arnold," he said to the FBI man, "I've been looking at this print-out on Trask. I'm not too sure he's the same as those Japs or Arabs."

"Why do you say that?" Cardone asked sharply.

"Maybe he's nuts, but he's got a talent for getting his way, forcing his will on people." Rockewicz read from the yellow paper. "Threatened to burn NYU to the ground if demands were not met for radicalizing the faculty. When the administration met with Trask—I like that—he gave them a deadline for compliance, and after it had expired, bombs exploded in two buildings." Rockewicz looked up. "And he pulled the same stunt at City College a week later. Gave them a couple of hours to meet his nonnegotiable demands, and when they asked for an extension, he turned his troops loose with torches. Who are we to say he won't start shooting if we're late?"

"We can't say," Cardone exploded. "That's why I am going to make certain the money gets here." The president had a knack for bending people, influencing events. Now, two armed psychopaths were calling the tune. And he was dancing.

"Trask can't be that stupid," Stade said. "He was dealing with university people then. They were frightened and they were reluctant to call the police. He knows this place is full of agents. If he wants the money badly and wants to make his voice heard, he'll wait."

"But you're in no position to guarantee anything," Cardone shouted. "Mr. Tench can be killed any second—and you can't do a thing about it!" He spun around to Rockewicz. "It's your fault. I heard you on the phone with the surgeon's wife. No guards. No security." He shook a finger at Steve. "If Mr. Tench fails to survive this. . . ."

"What?" Rockewicz asked. "You'll sue? Why don't we just cool it? Maybe Mr. Stade is right and the odds are in favor of them negotiating."

But Rockewicz was not sure any more. He leafed through the teleprinter copy. There was more on Trask: "Given to impetuous acts, sudden changes of strategy." At NYU, when his movement appeared on the verge of collapse, he had rallied his followers with a march on a local police station, crystallized student opinion by getting himself arrested. Steve wondered, Would he now escalate, seek martyrdom for his cause, and, in finding it, take Eric Lake and the others with him?

4

"They had this ventilating system for surgery," Parolo said. "Before the air conditioning." He felt that by sticking to technical details he might stifle his guilt. But the chief was in on it, wasn't he? Chief Reinhold knew what he was doing.

O'Boyle, Reinhold, and Parolo were standing in a dark storage room outside of surgery. Unused beds and stretchers were stacked against the walls. It was a windowless, dusty place. No one had seen them enter. The corridors of the hospital were deserted. Patients were restricted to rooms. Doctors and nurses went out only for emergency duties.

Parolo played his flashlight against the ceiling. The circle of yellow light found a plate about a yard square outlined with a metal frame. There were screws holding it in place.

"That's how you get in," Parolo said. "I once sent a guy in to clean out a rat's nest. He almost choked to death on crap." He looked at O'Boyle. "You still wanna go?"

"Damn right."

A nervy freak, Reinhold thought.

Parolo wrestled a table from one end of the room and placed it underneath the frame in the ceiling. Reinhold helped the maintenance man up. Parolo took a screwdriver from his pocket and went to work. After a few minutes of chipping away at paint and plaster, he had pried the metal cover loose. A dark square hole loomed above them.

"How do I know when I'm there?" O'Boyle asked.

"Lemme see," Parolo said. He began to count on his fingers. "There's an outlet in the chief nurse's place, another in the doctors' dressing room, another in the nurses' dressing room. One more in the corridor, then OR one and OR two. The next is OR three. You count past six of them grilles. The seventh should be where Dr. Lake is."

"*Should* be?" Reinhold asked. "What if he misses one? Or goes too far? He ends up knocking out the screen in some empty room and everybody in the hospital hears him."

"I'm pretty sure," Parolo said. "Seventh one in. They ain't been used from before World War Two."

"Okay, we're in business," O'Boyle said. He had to play it cocky, confident. That was how he'd made his reputation: walk in, show them a microphone. Unfortunately, he could not lug the heavy sound camera with him. But he had the small recorder, and his camermen had given him a silent Filmo. He strapped the Filmo to his back and jammed the recorder into a side pocket of his suede jacket.

"You ready, George?" he asked Reinhold. "You know your number?"

"You're fuckin' right. I just wait in the hall and you talk them right out into my arms. You say you talk their language? You better talk it clear."

O'Boyle started to the table, then stopped. His mind was humming; something else had occurred to him. Early in his career the young reporter had learned a basic of his trade: When in doubt, do the obvious. The telephone, for example, was the most potent of all tools available to the journalist. And how often the old hands ignored it!

"They got a phone in there?" he asked Parolo.

"Where?"

"In surgery. Right in the OR where Dr. Lake is."

"Sure. There's a phone in every operating room."

O'Boyle grinned. "I'll call them first. Let him know I'm on my way."

Reinhold's diamond-shaped face was wary. Was this queer

going to con him at the last moment? "What the hell for? So he can be ready for you?"

"My competition might wake up. One of those idiots from the newspapers might get the same idea and beat me to it." But Reinhold had it right, too. A lunatic surprised was the most dangerous of all. "What's the extension?"

Reinhold had made a note in his memo book. "It's three-nine-four-nine. The guy's name is John. I heard the FBI call him that."

There was a phone in the supply room. O'Boyle dialed. Trask picked it up. "John?" O'Boyle asked.

"Who is this? Cardone? Police?"

"No, no, John. This is Brian O'Boyle, channel six. TV reporter. You know me, John. Didn't we meet a few years ago? Demonstration at the White House?"

"Go to hell. I'm not ready for the press. I'll call a press conference when I'm ready."

"How many of you are in there? Two? Three? How did that guy get killed?"

"Go to hell. I'll use you when I'm ready. How do I know you're not a pig?"

"No pig, baby. This is Brian O'Boyle. I have contacts with every cat in the counterculture. You don't remember when I interviewed you?" O'Boyle was faking; it often worked.

"No. I won't talk to you."

"Ah, because you want to make sure it's me. John, don't be surprised if I pay you a visit. Listen, I'm unarmed. I want your story, dig? Long blond hair and an Indian band: my trademarks. If I come around, don't blow my head off. I can save you if you let me. The world wants to know what you're after, John."

"You come around and I'll kill you. When I want you I'll let you know."

"John, I—"

Trask had hung up.

"Was that smart?" Reinhold asked

"Sure. I planted the idea in him. He'll want the world to hear his side of it. Help me into the hole."

Trask's rebuff did not deter O'Boyle. Confronted with a camera, a chance to spout his rhetoric to the world, the man would behave differently. The reporter arranged priorities in his brain: news film of the scene, then an interview, then an appeal to Trask to surrender. Reinhold was at the bottom of the list. The story would come first, then the public service.

"What if the FBI just monitored you?" Reinhold asked warily.

"So? How can they stop me now? They don't know where we are."

"Listen," Parolo begged. "Anything goes wrong, leave my name out of it, huh? Like you found this by yourself."

"Calm down. In ten minutes we'll all be heroes." O'Boyle took off his shoes and climbed on the table. Lean, wiry, he chinned his way into the entrance to the duct. Puffs of dust kicked up as he stretched out in the gloom. He took a pencil light from his pocket and turned it on. His cameramen had told him to shoot wide open. It was high-speed film and the lab could push it. With luck they'd get the picture story of the year. The tape recorder was no problem. He could let it run itself. It had a multidirectional transistor microphone.

"Move out, George," he said. "O'Boyle's on his way."

Reinhold hitched his belt and checked his Magnum. He prided himself on his marksmanship. He had the medals to prove it. He would let the kid do the crawling.

5

Trask had taken the radio out of his pocket and was listening to the news bulletins. "We're famous, Rashid," he called across the room. "They've got my name but not yours." He smiled. "We're described as a fringe revolutionary group. They'll learn."

He turned up the volume. "The Wretched of the Earth, believed to number no more than two dozen members and formed of dissident revolutionary activists who met in Europe a half year ago . . . claim credit for the bombing of the Paris stock exchange and. . . ."

"His credits," Licata said. "Christ, look at him. He's enjoying hearing about himself."

"I need the one-millimeter probe," Lake said.

"John," Rashid called. "What do they say? Is everything on schedule?"

"Cardone is saying all our demands will be met," Trask said. "We knew that already." He addressed Lake. "You see, doctor, it's working out. If the CIA hadn't sent Baggs in, no one would have gotten hurt. You can move your operation along."

Licata breathed deeply. He elevated Tench's heart. "The crazy bastards are dead and they don't know it."

"What did you say?" Trask asked. He seemed more sure of himself since hearing the radio report. He had lectured his people a great deal on the use of the media, on ways of turning the power structure against itself.

"Knock it off, Jack," Lake ordered the chief resident.

Motzkin looked at the gauges: everything was normal. "Ten million dollars, my God. What are you going to do with it?"

"Fight our war. Liberate the wretched."

"But it ends up with more killing," Motzkin said. "I was radical when I was a kid. Studied all about Lenin and Trotsky. Maybe they meant well, but what happened? Prisons, killings, torture. And then Stalin, the worst."

"So you became an anesthesiologist," Trask mocked. "And made a six-figure salary? What do they call you behind your back? The gas-passer?"

"They call me that to my face. And I don't take umbrage."

"Will everyone hold down the conversation?" Lake said angrily. "Our priority here is surgery." He turned to Trask. "Turn the radio down. I don't want to hear it."

"You should be interested," Trask laughed briefly. "It will give you some notion of how important we are. We're not run-of-the-mill radicals. We have a program." He held the radio to his ear. "They've dug up some data . . . the bombings at NYU."

"And anything about me?" Rashid asked.

"Sorry, Rashid. They don't know who you are."

"They will."

Licata could hardly believe the schoolboy bragging. Incredible. He watched Lake insert the probe in the lower end of the artery and move it upward into the heart. All the moves, Licata thought, the touch, the coordination, the uncanny knowledge of what to do, what to anticipate—like a great backcourt man, a Frazier, or a West.

"Jack is thinking what I am thinking," Mihrab said.

"And what is that?" Lake asked. "Gently, gently."

"About what other surgeons say."

Lake shrugged. "Danger of thrombosis. It's never happened to me yet."

They stared at Tench's heart. Lake's hands touched the surface above the hidden artery into which he had maneuvered the metal rod. "I think I've found an opening. Jack, feel that. You, too, Gamel."

Licata ran his fingers over the heart. "I feel the probe, Eric."

"So do I," Mihrab said. "There's an opening."

"Damn right," Lake said. "I can wiggle the wire around. He's got three millimeters there, big enough for the second graft. Not as high as I like it, but it'll do."

"Does this mean you'll finish on time?" Trask asked.

"I will if you stop bothering me."

Motzkin was worrying about something new. He had heard a note of paranoid gratification in Trask. It began when the first radio bulletin was heard. Then had come the phone call from a reporter. Trask seemed to be feeding on it, reinforcing his view of himself, moving further and further from reality.

"Beading here," Lake said. He ran his finger along the heart. "And then it stops. So there's healthy artery from here down."

Distantly, as if in an adjoining room or a room above, there was a thudding noise. Trask jumped from the stool. His hand went for the gun. He looked at the supply room, spun around to face the doors. Olmedo was supposed to keep it secure outside.

Fifty feet away, Brian O'Boyle, crawling through the vent, had dropped the tape recorder.

Rashid was standing. His black eyes were fire bright. He cocked his round head, listening. In the Galilee he could tell when Israeli patrols were coming by listening to the earth.

Trask walked to the doors, listened, heard nothing in the corridor. Reassured, he returned through the scrub room to the operating area and resumed his post near the telephone.

"Jumpy," Licata said.

"Rats," Cho announced. He smiled feebly at Trask. "Yes, rats. I saw big ones. In rooms they don't use."

Lake held the heart firmly and pointed to the spot where he had felt an opening in the embedded artery. "Right there, Jack. Keep it open for me. I'll cut in."

Trask watched them through the overhead mirror. "You people hold a man's heart in your hands. You're like us. Power of life and death, ultimate decisions. And what do you use it for? To save the life of a parasite like Tench, a man who's gotten rich on slave labor, furnishing guns to colonialists. What a waste."

"Jesus, his philosophy makes me want to puke," Licata said.

"Tench wouldn't know what you're talking about," Lake said. "Just be still, so we can all go home." The scalpel bit into the orange fat. With any luck he would get to the artery on the first try, make an incision, graft the vein.

Mihrab had worked with many heart surgeons. Most of them would have abandoned the search for the "intramural" artery. More cautious than Lake, they would conclude that the handling and cutting of the heart muscle was not worth the locating of the branch. The arguments were part of coronary surgery writ: the abused tip of such an artery could close, the heart wall could be damaged. But Lake did not hesitate and he rarely made a wrong move.

Again, a *clunk* sounded nearby. Rashid looked behind him at the green tile wall, cupped a hand to his ear. He called to Trask for guidance. "John, what do you think?"

"Our Korean friend says it's rats," Trask said. "Be alert, Rashid."

6

By the time Martha Lake reached Rockewicz's office, she was furious. A disciplined woman, she would not permit fear to dilute her anger. Steve Rockewicz introduced her to Cardone and Stade. It seemed to make her angrier.

"I want Eric released," she said.

"It isn't that easy, Martha," Rockewicz said. "He's got to finish the operation. Once Tench is out of danger and the money delivered, we're confident Eric will be okay."

"But you have no assurance?"

Stade got up from behind the desk. "Mrs. Lake, we've got to work from a distance at the moment. We can't crowd them. I can tell you that as far as the Bureau is concerned, nobody's life will be endangered. We're meeting all their demands."

Cardone approached her. "That's true, Mrs. Lake. I am insisting that there be no attacks, tricks, or delays. I'm expediting the ransom personally. Mr. Tench's safety . . . you as an old friend . . ."

They studied each other for a moment. Cardone had a lavish, high-fashion look about him—the flared jacket, crocodile shoes, the artfully shaped gray-black hair. To Martha Lake, in her tan sweater and tweed skirt, he appeared a bit exotic, a trifle . . . what? Ripe? Cardone, whose nose was sensitive to outward signs of quality, felt a vague uneasiness with her. The woman's short, unlacquered hair, the sharply defined face, the unwavering slate-blue eyes, told him that she had class, if not in terms of wealth or breeding then surely in terms of character.

"I must be frank," Martha Lake said. "I have met Mr. Tench a few times. I'm hardly a close friend. He knew my husband in college. I'm sorry he's been victimized, but my only concern is my husband. I want him out of that room."

"We're all in the same boat, Martha," Steve said.

"I don't think so," she said. "Have those men told you how they plan to get out?"

Stade sat on the edge of the desk. He looked solemn. "No. But I'd imagine they'll take hostages."

"I would imagine so, too." She remained calm. But her voice was edged. "Hostages who can walk, whom they can use to protect themselves." She turned to Cardone. "Not Mr. Tench, coming out of surgery."

"You're right to be outraged," Cardone said. "But Mr. Tench didn't will this awful thing. I didn't. He was a target. Your husband and his team were incidental. I've talked to that man Trask down there and I know how he thinks. He doesn't regard anyone as an innocent."

"It doesn't make it easier for you, Martha," Steve said. "But it's the truth. We'll do all we can to shake Eric loose. I promise you."

"Steve, let me talk to him."

"To Eric? He's on the second graft about now. Maybe later."

"No. To Trask."

The hospital director looked at Stade. The FBI man nodded his accord. It might be helpful. Trask seemed to enjoy his performances, his mastery of audiences and interrogators.

In the passageway, halfway between the first and second operating rooms, O'Boyle became wedged in the narrow crawl space. Dust clogged his nose. Accumulations of rat droppings, dead mice, pulverized insects, coated his T-shirt and jeans. At each grilled aperture—set in a dropped area, a boxlike compartment off the main passageway of the duct—he had paused to gulp fresh air. Now, with his camera caught on a warped metal rod, he struggled to free himself, raising more dust, stifling a sneeze. He could hear voices. He was getting there.

Trask picked up the phone when Martha Lake called.

"Mr. Trask. This is Dr. Lake's wife. I'm in Mr. Rockewicz's

office. May I speak to my husband? Is he all right?"

"They're all being well treated. You can tell Cardone and the others that we keep our word. I know this hospital is full of police and FBI men. I know what they're up to. If you want to see your husband alive again, you'd better help us. Will you tell that to them?"

Trask was standing almost at attention. He seemed to be in the middle of some lunatic military exercise.

"I'll help you in any way I can. I want my husband released unhurt."

"I have only limited control over that."

"But you're pointing a gun at him. You killed a man already."

"We were interfered with." The voice grew more taut. "If we are permitted to leave unhindered, if our orders are followed . . . there will be no more shooting. Do you understand, Mrs. Lake?"

"Perfectly. May I speak to Dr. Lake?"

Trask held the phone toward Lake. "Your wife."

The surgeon did not look up. "I'm busy. Tell her I'm fine. We're all okay. Tell her I'd like her to get in touch with Mrs. Baggs. If she's not at the hospital, arrange for her to be driven here. I want her to stay with Mrs. Baggs."

Trask repeated the message.

"You see?" she said. Her voice trembled for the first time. "You killed a good man. Whatever it is that drives you, you end up doing terrible things to innocent people."

"Innocent men like your husband, Mrs. Lake, who earns three hundred and fifty thousand dollars a year. Is he a millionaire yet, Mrs. Lake? Do you have your tax shelters, your corporation? You're part of the system, as corrupt as Walker Tench."

"You don't know what you're saying."

"I do. But we have nothing to tell each other. A little after noon we'll be leaving here. You can help by telling the pigs not to get too close. I'll have your husband in the cross hairs for a long time."

He hung up.

Lake looked up from the table. "You really are a merciless son of a bitch."

"No. Just political."

The surgeon squinted again at the heart. He dug the scalpel deep into the heart wall. Mihrab could see that he was operating on instinct, almost *smelling* his way toward the artery, working with some hidden radar.

7

Reinhold walked into surgery. Chief Nurse McCarran had refused to leave. She was typing, having dismissed her secretary. A man in a white coat was sitting to one side. The police chief glanced at him: one of Stade's watchdogs.

"Chief?" the man asked. "No one's allowed in. Orders."

"Who from?"

"The Bureau. I'm Agent Lief."

"I'll just take a little stroll. You guys may need me later. I want to check the layout."

Lief shrugged—what the hell. This was Reinhold's city. Leave the guy his pride.

Reinhold walked slowly, counting doors. Two weary residents walked past him. They were Dr. Harvey Fess's assistants. The craniotomy had been concluded.

"What happened to the boss?" one asked.

"I don't know. He said he was beat. This lousy job, and then the awful business in Lake's surgery." He glanced apprehensively at the barricaded doors. "They're still there. I'm getting out. Harvey probably did the same."

A hundred feet down the corridor, around a corner, Olmedo listened to footsteps. Then all was silent. Only the orthopedic case and Tench's operation were in progress. He turned off the single bulb. Light filtered through a crack under the door. He waited, cradling the carbine. In the corner of the room, under a pile of soiled green clothing, he had hidden Fess's body.

Flor Aquino saw the arterial line wobble erractically. She moved quickly from her place next to Sally and began to knead the tubing.

"Darn, I should have seen that," Motzkin said. He got up. "Let me, Flor."

Flor's hands worked faster than Motzkin's. The arterial line had been blocked. It was not harmful, Lake knew. He paid no attention to the nurse and the anesthesiologist.

"Alan," Licata said, "throw the switch a second. We can keep him off until you straighten out the line."

"Right, right," Motzkin said. "Sorry." He wanted to add, You know this isn't my regular job, but something stopped him.

Trask leveled the gun at Motzkin. "What is this? Another trick?"

"No, not at all," Motzkin said. He was surprised at the firmness of his voice. "We have to unsnarl the line, that's all."

Flor's hands fluttered on the tubing like brown birds. She worried the plastic until it snapped back into a single smooth line. Motzkin hit the arterial pressure switch. The tubing throbbed again in steady rhythms.

"Was he hurt?" Trask asked.

"No," Motzkin said. "He was just off a few seconds. No harm done. For God's sake, point that gun somewhere else!"

"Gamel, put a suture in the bottom of the diagonal," Lake said. He had ignored the trouble over the heart-lung machine. "I've found a good spot. I'll take the rest of the vein."

Inching his way forward, O'Boyle was forced to keep a handkerchief pressed around his nose and mouth. Determined not to sneeze, he did not sneeze. He had discovered in his passage that the metal grilles over the ventilating system's openings were not as heavily obscured as Parolo had led him to believe. With luck, he might even be able to film through the apertures. Perhaps he would not have to knock anything in, make any excessive noise and run the risk of drawing fire.

"John," Rashid called from the gallery. "Did you hear something again? Like last time?"

Trask listened intently. There was a recurrent hissing sound from the suction tubes, the click and snap of the metal instruments, the sighing of the ventilator. Around Tench's body, the surgeons and nurses chatted in low voices. Dr. Lake appeared to have things under control. Another twenty minutes or so and the major part of the operation would be finished. That's what they'd promised him.

"Up there?" Rashid asked. He was craning his neck toward the green ceiling, cupping his ears again. "Someone is moving furniture above us?"

Fear hazed Trask's eyes for a second. The room was enclosed. Would they dare to try to drill through, work some clumsy diversionary trick, then charge through the doors shooting? Not likely. When people like Tench were involved—or Lake for that matter —lives were protected. It was only in the Atticas of the world that the oppressors went in killing everyone in sight, prisoners, hostages, bystanders.

"I guess not," Rashid said.

"You must be calm, *rafik,*" Mihrab said. "We are almost finishing. As Allah wills it, we will survive." He said a few words in Arabic.

Licata arched his brows. "Buddies," he muttered.

"Put another suture in," Lake said.

In the passageway O'Boyle maneuvered the Filmo from his hip to his hands. He inched the tape recorder forward so that it was under his neck, with the microphone facing the room. He pushed the record button. Voices rose, now clear, now fuzzy, from the operating room. He would have the story of the year: exclusive, his alone, gotten on nerve, guts. The tape recording would not be synchronous with the film, but it wouldn't matter a damn, not on a story this dramatic.

O'Boyle inched closer, pushing the recorder. It spun silently— a high-powered model developed by technicians at the network.

He'd used it before, hiding it in a coat pocket, a briefcase.

But the film would be a problem. The correspondent squinted through the grille in the OR wall. The interstices were large. O'Boyle twisted his body and pushed the Filmo forward so that the lens was flush with the inside of the grille. He squinted into the viewfinder. After a few seconds of maneuvering the camera, he was able to frame a truncated picture.

He could see part of the operating table. Four green-capped, green-gowned people. A nurse on a high stand was handing instruments to the surgeons. He could hear the commands: hemostat, Metzenbaum scissors, forceps. . . . The green heads formed a ring around Tench. From the reporter's high angle, the camera eye did not reveal the open area on Tench's chest. No matter, O'Boyle thought. He had most of it. No one else had come close. He turned the camera to the right. A smashed glass wall. Why? Then he understood. He had been in operating rooms before. Some contained a viewer's gallery. O'Boyle inched the Filmo upward. Despite the metal bars of the grille, the newsman could see a short heavyset man in a green gown. He wore a surgical mask, and he cradled an automatic rifle with a long magazine. Two round objects rested on the bench beside him: grenades.

He panned left with the camera—not shooting yet, but analyzing what could be filmed. There were supposed to be two armed men in the room according to the FBI—a tall man calling himself John and a small dark man. But the camera's field of vision ended short of the opposite wall where presumably John was standing guard. But the viewfinder did reveal a foot and part of a leg and the edge of a metal table or desk. Tubing emanated from the metal object, up to the operating table. Heart-lung machine, O'Boyle thought.

O'Boyle inhaled and felt the sweat ooze under his arms. He wondered if the buzz of the camera would be heard. Winding it would be a greater hazard. It was a hand-run apparatus, the simplest camera they used, operated without batteries. And it tended to be noisy.

O'Boyle sighted through the viewfinder. There would be no

time to flip lenses. No time to worry about focus, lighting, angles. He would get what he could and hope they would not hear him. Then he might try to fulfill his promise to Reinhold and appeal for their surrender. He might.

Bracing his arms and elbows on the floor of the passage, the reporter framed the scene around the table—gloved hands moving, heads nodding, a nurse moving about—and depressed the button. Inside the cramped space, the Filmo buzzed with alarming loudness. There was a hundred-foot roll of high-speed film in the camera. He would have no time to reload. It was a hundred feet—about three minutes—then nothing. He knew that after running twenty-two feet the camera had to be rewound. He stayed on the master shot—the table, the overhead lights, the movements of the five people in green. Once he thought he saw a glimpse of a bloody patch on the table. Maybe Tench's heart.

Rewinding was not as hard as he thought. He was able to move the camera to his side, muffle the noise of the key twisting the spring. He was ready to film again. He would get the stocky man in the gallery this time. He shivered in anticipation. He turned to the right, resting his back against the metal side of the duct. He framed Rashid in the viewfinder. A husky guy, brown-skinned, standing up now. Rashid scratched his crotch, rested the gun by placing the wire stock on the bench.

The Filmo buzzed as O'Boyle exposed another few feet. He had an absolute bead on Rashid—the dark head, the thick body. Maybe Reinhold had been right: a fast-shooting cop could have dropped the invader with one shot. But across the room, out of range, was John.

"Not bad, not bad," O'Boyle said to himself, controlling his excitement. He was looking into Rashid's black eyes, the black eyebrows, the ridged forehead. Take off your mask, the correspondent wanted to say. Smile, you're on "Candid Camera," you little bastard.

8

"John, I hear something," Rashid was saying. He was craning his neck.

"What?" Trask called.

"Like an electric current. Something has been switched on."

"It could be the isolation transformer," Motzkin said. He, too, had heard the camera buzzing. "Over there. It grounds the electrical gear." Motzkin had little knowledge of how it worked. It had been Jimmy's province.

"There she is," Lake said. His scalpel, deep in the heart, had revealed a section of pinkish artery. He had seemed to be cutting blindly.

Licata whistled. "You gotta see it to believe it."

Mihrab was clucking in admiration. "Eric, you never miss. Not once. Flor, a sponge, please."

Rashid was listening, ears cocked. His head swiveled, trying to find the sound. Again he head the humming noise. It stopped. He looked confused. "John, I want to look in the next room. Let me listen at the walls."

Trask nodded. "Lake, you others. Move aside when Rashid walks by. I'm covering you. You especially, Licata. You saw what happened to Baggs."

Rashid paused at the doorway leading from the gallery. Now he heard still another noise. It sounded like a ratchet being turned. It was not continuous, but with intervals between each scratchy sound.

Eight feet above the Arab, O'Boyle was winding the camera again. He cursed his cameraman. Now the damned thing was squeaking just as he'd feared.

Below him he could see the man with the carbine standing very still, listening. O'Boyle held his breath, then released the key. He could expose another twenty-two feet without rewinding. But Rashid would not move. He was staring into the grille. He could not possibly see anything. The correspondent drew his head back and froze.

"Stay back where you are," Rashid said to Trask. "Do not come closer. Watch the doors."

"What is it?" Trask called.

Rashid had seen light glinting on something inside the grille. Shiny metal. He had not seen it before.

"Watch the doors, John," Rashid said hoarsely. "They may . . ."

Firing the carbine from chest level, the Arab leaped backward, out of range of any weapon that might be hidden in the vent. The shots shattered the enclosed space, reverberated against the tile walls, the ceiling.

"Down!" Licata shouted. He grabbed Sally, pulling her from the pedestal. Mihrab ducked below the table. Flor, screaming, fell against the wall. Motzkin tried to rise from the low bench, stumbled, pressed himself against the metal flank of the heart-lung machine.

Trask, gun in hand, was staring at the grille.

Rashid had fired three times. O'Boyle, drawing back, protecting his head with the camera, had not been hit. Two shots had ricocheted inside the passage harmlessly. Another had bounded off the exterior frame. Rashid, firing at a forty-five-degree angle, upward and at a small area, was frustrated.

"In there," Rashid said. "John, it is a trap."

"Hold it!" O'Boyle screamed. "For Chrissake stop it! I'm not a cop!" He retreated another yard or so.

Rashid raised the carbine again. Motzkin tumbled from the bench, buried his head in his arms.

Lake remained standing at the operating table. His scalpel was over Tench's heart. *Control*, he told himself. *Keep control.* He turned to Flor. "Take my glasses off." Shivering, she got up and reached for the glasses.

Rashid was standing under the grille. "John? A grenade?"

"No," Trask said. "Tell him to stay where he is. Not to move."

"John!" O'Boyle bellowed. "It's me. Brian O'Boyle. The TV reporter. I talked to you on the phone. I'm not a cop. There isn't any cop anywhere. I want to make a deal with you."

"Go!" Rashid shouted. "Go back! I will kill you."

"Hold it," Trask said. He glanced at the door. No sign of a rush. But he could not leave his post. He flattened himself against the wall near the telephone. He could watch the door and shout across the room to O'Boyle. "Get out, O'Boyle. I told you, no deals. Tell Cardone to get the money here. I'll phone my final instructions. You stay there or we'll kill these people one at a time."

"John, I'm here to help you. Tell your friend to put that gun down. I have to talk to you."

"Cover him," Trask said. "From the gallery. O'Boyle, you have two minutes. Talk."

The reporter inched forward. The cassette kept rolling. Everything was on tape. "Trask, you'll never make it out of here. You might get out of the hospital grounds, but they'll get you. I can make a deal for you. Tell your message to the world. I've got a tape recorder. It can be on the air in fifteen minutes. Then you walk out the door, you won't be hurt. I've got an agreement from the chief of police. You can plea-bargain later."

"Hah!" Rashid laughed. "Let me shoot him, John."

"Listen to me," O'Boyle shouted. "Listen to me. You can be defended. You can plead manslaughter, no intention to kill that guy. An accident. He was a brother. All you have to do is tell me you'll walk out unarmed and I'll arrange the rest."

"No chance," Trask yelled. "We're taking this all the way. The police sent you. Rashid, hit him again."

The Arab fired two more rounds into the grille. One smashed through the metal and buried itself in the camera. The other bounced away. O'Boyle cursed. "You crazy bastards, I'm offering you the best deal you can get. Don't shoot again. I'm not armed. I want to help you, get you out in one piece, make sure no one else is killed. There'll be five hundred feds around this dump when you move out."

"They won't shoot if we have company," Trask shouted. "Now get out!"

O'Boyle hesitated. He had it now. The year's biggest story. On tape, every word. The shots, the threats. And the film. The camera housing was smashed, but the film magazine was intact. "Trask, don't blow this. I can help you. For Chrissake, don't you want to get your message out? The FBI keeps running this stuff about you and it's got to be full of lies."

Motzkin struggled to his feet. He felt a numbing pain in his left foot. He looked down. The green paper slipper had been torn. Underneath it, his tennis sneaker had been snipped at the toe. He began to whimper. "Oh, my God, Eric. I've been hit. My toe. My toe. Look, it's bleeding."

Lake barked at Cho. "Go over and take a look at Dr. Motzkin." He turned to Trask. "We're finishing up. That reporter seems to be alone. You don't have to fire again. He can't hurt you. He wants your story. Talk to him."

Lake spoke to the air duct. "You . . . O'Boyle. I always thought you were a sensible man. You damned near got us killed. Talk to John but let us finish our work." Lake shook his head in bafflement. "They'll be selling souvenirs in the hallway next. Alan, how is your foot?"

Motzkin was hypnotized by the bloody stub. What had he lost? A quarter-inch of his little toe? Cho was swabbing it with Betadine. The antiseptic burned. Motzkin grimaced. But in the very pain, he felt strength and confidence. *Under fire Motzkin did not flinch.* Was it the young Churchill who wrote about the glorious thrill of riding into battle, hearing bullets whine overhead, and surviving? The charge at Omdurman. Kitchener of Khartoum avenging the death of Chinese Gordon.

"Does it hurt, doctor?" Cho asked.

"Yes . . . no. Not too bad. Let me sit down. I have to look at the gauges."

Flor was on one knee. She was holding a misshapen leaden slug. Mine, Motzkin thought. For my children and grandchildren.

"Trask, listen to me," O'Boyle said. "I'm sticking my face out."
He had moved to the open duct. They could see the golden hair,
the tough white face. "Trask, and you with the carbine. I've got
a recorder. I'm here to help you people. I can make sure no one
else is hurt, your message broadcast to the world. The cops will
let you out. . . ." He was babbling for his life, but still under
control.

Trask hesitated. He heard voices in the corridor. He motioned
to Rashid to change places with him. If they were rushed, better
to have the rapid-firing weapon at the door.

9

In the corridor, lingering at the water fountain, Reinhold had
heard the shots. The blasts surprised him. He did not think the
gunmen would shoot at the reporter. He had expected O'Boyle
to make his presence known, convince them to hold fire. Reinhold
ran toward the door. He had intended to take cover across the
hallway in a men's room, leaving the door open, ready when the
gunmen walked out.

But the decision had been forced on him. He drew his Colt and
ran to the barricade. A half dozen men, some in green surgical
dress, some in white coats, were racing to the doors with him.

"Stade's army," Reinhold mocked.

"Hold it, chief," Lief shouted.

They were armed with handguns. But they did not appear
ready to rush the room.

"Hold it, my ass," Reinhold said. His foxlike face, all points and
angles, was raging. "I'm ready to go in. Whose going with me?"

"No way, chief," Lief said. "We go in shooting, there'll be a
lot of corpses."

The agents pressed against the wall on either side of the door.
Two stood opposite it. Reinhold choked back his fury.

Lief put his ear against the door. "John?" he called. "You hear
me? Why are you firing?"

Around the bend in the hallway, fifty feet away, Olmedo came out of the closet, checked the magazine on his carbine, walked to the right angle formed by the green tile walls. He stopped, glued himself to the wall, and listened.

Olmedo wondered if Trask had miscalculated. Maybe the police were attacking, risking everyone's life, the way the Israelis did. A half dozen men were outside the barricade. All except one, a tall man in a blue uniform, were dressed in hospital whites or greens. One man was pressing his ear to the door, trying to talk to the people inside.

Olmedo retreated. A single policeman, perhaps two, he could handle. But there were six, all armed, all professionals. These were not elderly physicians, unfortunates who might get in his way. He could hear one of the men shouting.

"John? John Trask? What's going on? Give us a signal, something. Who fired the shots?"

Another agent was on a handy-talky, relaying instructions: "Mr. Stade says don't move in. It could have been an accident."

Trask's voice came through the door. "Stay away. Nobody's hurt. But we'll kill someone if you try to come in."

"Tell us what happened, John."

"Is Mr. Tench all right?"

"I said nobody's hurt," Trask yelled. "Gun went off by accident. Next time it won't be an accident."

The man on the handy-talky nudged the agent at the door. "Stade says to stand by. They may have lost their nerve."

"You sure, John? You want to talk to us?"

Inside the room, Trask shouted to Rashid. "Show them. Take the paper off one of the windows. Take the Korean."

"Hey," Cho protested. "What for?"

Flor covered her face. Sally drew her close. Lake cautioned his assistants. "Stand still, everyone. Don't get involved."

Rashid, balancing the carbine, ripped the cardboard from one of the windows in the double door. They could see the faces of the agents outside. The Arab yanked Cho across the room and jammed the carbine in his side. He dragged him to within six feet of the door and exhibited the cringing man to the agents.

"He goes first," Trask shouted. "Then one at a time. Show them how, Rashid."

Rashid raised the muzzle of the carbine and poked it against the carotid artery in Cho's neck.

"We'll do it. Now, get away." Trask's voice rose. It assumed a womanish quality. *"Out! Get out!* Lake, tell them no one's hurt!"

The surgeon looked toward the faces in the window. "It's all right," he called. "Nobody was hurt. Let us finish."

"Nobody except me," Motzkin muttered. He studied the bloody stub of his toe. Cho had been bandaging it when he was dragged away. It hardly hurt.

Outside, Lief looked at Reinhold. "Why were they shooting?" He recalled the chief's strolling in a few minutes before.

"I dunno."

"You were near. Hear anything?"

"No. Three, maybe four shots. I can't figure it either." Reinhold cursed O'Boyle. Where was he? How far had he gotten? He could be dead. Someone would have to crawl in and haul him out. Or had he made a deal with Trask and the Arab? You couldn't trust these media freaks. An old police reporter was one thing; they were usually decent men. But these kids, these long-haired pukes! Reinhold would have a little explaining to do when the story got out.

"Take the gun off him," the agent called in. "We're leaving."

Rashid, shoving Cho aside with the barrel, taped the cardboard to the window.

Cho was stumbling back to the anesthesia cart when there was another noise overhead.

O'Boyle had slammed his fist against the grille. It was old. The flanges were rusted. It loosened, sending puffs of rust into the operating room.

"Hey!" Lake shouted angrily. "This place is sterile! Flor, clean up that mess."

The metal disintegrated and fell to the floor. O'Boyle held the recorder as low as he could, pointing it at Trask.

"You're on, John. This is prime time. Have your say."

Trask's eyes were gleaming. "How soon can you get it on the air?"

Licata sneered, "You can get a better deal from NBC, Trask."

"It'll be at the network ten minutes after you finish. We'll break in with it."

10

"We can't figure it out,' Stade said to the people in Rockewicz's office. "Three or four shots. Nobody hurt. My men had a chance to look in. They were threatening the assistant, pointing a carbine at him. But nobody had been shot."

"Nerves," Rockewicz said.

"Steve, I want Eric out of there," Martha Lake said.

"Sure, sure, Martha."

Stade took Rockewicz aside. "There's something goddamn fishy going on. I don't know what. Reinhold shows up in the corridor, disobeying orders—"

"Arnold, he's the local boss."

"That's why Lief let him walk in. A few minutes later there are shots inside the OR. As far as Lief could see, Reinhold didn't talk to anyone and didn't draw his gun until after the shooting. But then they had to restrain him from blasting in."

"This is insanity," Martha Lake said. She walked toward Stade. He was at the window, frowning at the TV trucks, the crowds across the street. A uniformed policeman was engaged in a shoving match with a black man in olive drab clothing.

"Mr. Stade, you tell them to let my husband out as soon as he's finished. He won't be needed there. Give them their money and let's get it over with."

"I wish it were that simple, Mrs. Lake. I really do."

Cardone was talking to the treasurer again. He was pacing the floor, cradling the receiver against his neck. "Seven million?" he was asking.

"To make the deadline, yes," Gallatin said. "I'm here at the Federal Reserve. They can probably make the balance in smaller denominations, but that may take time. We may be late even then."

Cardone looked at his watch. It was 11:28. "What if you use the smaller bills?"

"Very, very close. The director says perhaps another forty minutes. Surely you can ask those people to wait. I seem to recall they negotiated with those Japanese in Holland for several days. Why we agreed so quickly—"

"The helicopter is ready?"

"Yes. It can be airborne in minutes."

Cardone turned. Martha Lake was glaring at him. He could understand. But why focus on him?

"So if we wait for the full sum it may not get here until twelve-thirty?"

"Or later."

"I hate to test them. They're irrational. They might—" He stopped as the surgeon's wife came toward him.

"They won't stop to count it in the hospital," Gallatin said. "Why don't we send over what we have? Back-timing it, so we're sure we meet their deadline. They'll want to get away as quickly as they can. All we need is an assurance they'll leave Mr. Tench in the hospital unharmed."

"Make that Plan A," Cardone instructed. "If the helicopter is on the roof at noon, that should give us time to get it below. Send whatever you have by then. We'll worry about the rest once Mr. Tench is safe."

"Are you having trouble with the ransom?" Martha asked him. Her voice was cold.

"Some. I ordered them to get what money they had here. Nothing matters except that Mr. Tench survives this nightmare."

"Nothing?"

Cardone looked abashed. Ruddy splotches of hypertension colored his face. "I shouldn't have said that. Of course I am concerned about your husband and the other people. God knows I wish I could bring back that poor man they've murdered."

"Yes, I'm sure." Martha stood facing him. "I heard you just now. You're concerned only with Walker Tench. They'll leave him and they'll take my husband hostage. Then they'll count the money and find it's short. What will you do to save him?"

"Anything I can, Mrs. Lake." Cardone stepped back. In the board room no one dared address him in such a manner.

"I've overheard some of Mr. Rockewicz's conversations with the FBI agent. They think it's quite possible that those insane people will try to move Mr. Tench out on a stretcher in an ambulance."

"We—we really can't predict—"

"No, we can't. But I tell you this, Mr. Cardone. I hope they do take Walker Tench out. For most of his life he's been a parasite. My husband is worth fifty Walker Tenches, and if he's made to suffer because you or the FBI or anyone else is intent on saving only the Tench corporation, I'll make you regret it."

Cardone thought of several responses, but said nothing. Judgments on the worth of individual men were tricky things. He owed his career to Walker Tench—and he had never met Eric Lake. But he would have a difficult job trying to convince her that he was acting in everyone's best interests. Or convincing himself, for that matter.

11

Lake placed the second section of vein next to the incision in the diagonal branch of the artery. It had been touch and go for a time. The heart could sustain only so much handling. Most surgeons would have quit on the buried diagonal. Someday his luck would run out, he thought.

Licata began to suture the vein to the healthy part of the artery. His big hands moved dextrously over the heart.

"You found it, Eric," Licata said.

"A procedure. I've done it before."

As they worked, heads bent, Trask had moved beneath the air

duct and was dictating his credo to O'Boyle's recorder.

"The pigs lie!" Trask sounded manic, his voice rising. "We are the Wretched of the Earth, who will take over and destroy the oppressors. We have bombed and robbed banks and now we will begin to hold the imperialists for ransom. Tench is the first. We are unafraid of their hired killers. We are the gook, the wog, the nigger, the spic, the slope—but soon we will be running the means of production, the factories and farms, for the good of poor people everywhere. No child in India will starve in your world, because when the Walker Tenches are eliminated—"

"Does he have to shout that shit here?" Licata asked.

"Tight on the sutures," Lake said.

"We will harm only those who stand in our way. We will accept anyone who supports our revolutionary battle for the good of humankind."

"You're beautiful, baby," O'Boyle said. "Anything else?"

"Yeah," Licata growled. "It was a great fight, Mom, and I'll be home in twenty minutes in a pine box."

"Jack, Jack," Mihrab cautioned.

The phone rang. Rashid took it. It was Cardone. He wanted to speak to Trask. The Arab held the phone toward him. Trask finished his speech. He again asked for an assurance from O'Boyle that the words would be broadcast on the network.

"Everywhere, John, all over. You'll be heard in a few minutes. Radio, nightly news, the *Today* show, and reprinted in all the newspapers." O'Boyle looked at the surgeons and nurses. "Listen. You guys will be all right. You're terrific. I'll put a little pressure on the fuzz. Why should anyone have to die so Tench can have so much money? Give 'em the dough, I say. It's deductible." He looked at Lake. "Dr. Lake, it's been a pleasure. When this blows over, I'd like to come back and do a take-out on you. Ten minutes, maybe, on some new gimmick you have. Okay?"

Lake nodded his head. "See what they can do about winding this up. Tell my wife I'm all right."

"Right on!" The TV man disappeared, crawling backward,

inching toward the hatch in the supply room.

In OR number three, Trask took the phone from Rashid.

"The money is being packaged and counted," Cardone told him.

"All of it?"

"That's why I called. I've got to ask you to extend that twelve-twelve deadline. It is unreasonable."

"By how much?"

"An hour perhaps?"

"No. Our timetable is rigid. Our demands are nonnegotiable."

"You have to give us some leeway. We can't get the money precisely as you demanded, in hundred-dollar bills. Not by noon. We'll surely have seven million. The rest—"

"You want to delay so you can set a trap."

"You're wrong, John, I swear it!"

"This hall was filled with police before. I had to convince them we were serious. Cardone, you have no options."

"We'll send over every last dollar we have by twelve-twelve. I'll see to it that you get the rest. You name the place, the time, the security. I assure you there will be no pursuit, no interference, no attempt to trick you. This assumes, of course, that Mr. Tench is released . . ."

Martha Lake was watching him. Cardone knew what was expected.

". . . as well as everyone else in the operating room. Trask, you can't keep adding to your crimes."

"These are not crimes, Cardone. It shows how far apart we are. I've made a statement for the media. You'll be hearing it soon. You don't seem to realize that you're doomed. You and all the rest of your crowd."

"Listen to me, John!" Cardone sensed a quivering hysteria in Trask. "We'll get you all the money we can by twelve-twelve. It's a fortune. It's been an effort to raise it. You let Tench go. And the others . . ."

"You're saying there will be a delay. You're working on some kind of stunt with the FBI. Cardone, stay on the line. I'm putting the phone down." He laughed. "I want to show you that I mean what I say. Wait."

Lake had finished sewing the vein to the artery. Now he stretched it and let its open end touch the aorta. He would sew the vein into the aorta an inch below the first graft. A simple engineering principle. The blood would flow directly into the grafted vein, into the healthy section of the artery, bypassing the diseased part, then into the left ventricle.

Trask walked from the phone and pointed the gun at Motzkin. Rashid, back in the gallery, covered the room.

"No, please," Flor cried. "Dr. Lake . . . make them . . . tell them . . ."

"What do you want?" Motzkin asked. "I haven't done anything to you."

"Leave him alone," Lake called. "Trask, I'll do what you want. I'll talk to Cardone. Put the gun down."

"Let me around the table," Licata whispered. "Eric, this fucking thing has to end. Everyone else dive. Screw Tench. Let him get hit."

"Jack, no," Mihrab said.

"Stay at your jobs," Lake ordered. "Trask, will you talk to me?"

Mihrab's eyes found Rashid. *"Rafik,* friend? This is wrong. This is bad."

"Don't move," Trask said to Motzkin. "Stay in your seat."

Trask walked to the wall and yanked at the plug connected to the heart-lung machine's cable. It was a three-pronged plug that locked itself with a counterclockwise turn. Trask tugged at it. It held firm.

"You're going to kill him," Motzkin gasped.

"Eric, he's going to knock out the pump," Licata said.

"Pull the vein tight. We're ready to take it to the aorta."

Trask yanked at the outlet again. Motzkin wondered, Tell him? A full turn left? The decision was made for him. Trask put the barrel of the gun in the anesthesiologist's ear. There were rolling noises in his eardrum. "All right. But you forced me."

Motzkin got to one knee. The ache in his wounded toe did not bother him. The world's only nine-toed gas-passer. Fear blotted out pain. He tried to turn the plug to the left. It resisted. Had Trask jammed it with his frenzied yankings? His hands shivered. "Cho," he called. "Help me."

The assistant walked over from the ventilator, got to one knee, and put his hand on the plug. He moved it firmly to the left, pushing in slightly. It came out.

"He's off," Licata said. "No pump, Eric."

The arterial pump shuddered and halted. The plastic tube, full of Tench's blood, stopped throbbing. No more blood could enter his body.

"Please, please," Sally begged. "Put it back."

Trask leveled the gun at Lake. "You. Get on the phone and tell Cardone what I've done."

"Tell him yourself."

"He has four minutes to live," Trask said. "You said so yourself. Or he might survive and be a vegetable. I won't be to blame. Those pigs out there, that bastard Cardone. And you, too. You and your three hundred and fifty thousand a year. You'll be to blame, you're one of them. Go on, tell him."

"Eric, do it," Licata said.

Lake hesitated. Then he glared at Trask. "You. Hold the phone for me. I'm sterile. You want to move this along, don't you?"

Trask obeyed him. He took the phone off and held it to the surgeon's ear. "This is Dr. Lake. They've stopped the pump. We have about four minutes left before Tench starts to die. Agree to anything they ask if you want to save Tench's life."

"I've agreed already!" Cardone cried. "Doctor, for God's sake, do something, talk to him."

Trask took the telephone. "Cardone?"

"Anything. Anything you say."

Motzkin's hand reached for the plug. He heard Rashid's clotted voice warning him. "No. Do not touch it."

"I was just getting ready, that's all."

"My terms?" Trask was asking. "All of them met?"

Cardone was agreeing. They would have to take their chances on the rest. He prayed that Rockewicz was right, that wheeling Tench into an ambulance and maintaining him en route was impossible and that the gunmen would choose members of the medical team as hostages.

Trask finished with a final warning to Cardone. "This should be a lesson to you, Cardone. We are not fringe dissidents, or helpless amateurs, or a small group of insane radicals, as your FBI claims. We have power. We will use it. How much time left, Dr. Lake?"

"A minute, maybe a minute and a half."

"Cardone, listen. The revolutionary committee is permitting the prisoner Tench to have his life. We note your surrender and your agreement to full payment of reparations. All of this is to be published and broadcast, so that our brothers will know about our triumph."

"I've agreed, I tell you. Give Tench a chance, will you?"

"Did he give the peasants of Vietnam a chance? The Arab villagers in Palestine? Did he give Che a chance?"

Lake reached for the phone. "That's enough of that soapbox nonsense. The man's agreed. I won't permit you to murder one of my patients." He pulled the phone from Trask's hand. "You can make all the speeches you want after he's back on bypass."

Trask's head jerked backward. "Be careful, doctor."

"I'm not afraid of you. I'm not afraid of that guy with the gun up there. I have a job to do. You want to shoot us, get it over with. It'll be the end of your revolution."

"You'll challenge me once too often," Trask said.

Lake ignored him. "Cardone? Eric Lake."

"Is there still a chance? They won't dare—"

"He's going back on the pump. He'll be all right."

Licata touched Tench's flesh along the thigh. Cold. It was a good sign. He needed less blood, less oxygen. The four minutes were up. Cooled he could survive as much as eight minutes, maybe more, without blood.

The room was silent. Occasionally a suction tube hissed. The ventilator sighed.

"All right. No one move." Trask shoved the gun against Lake's side. "Get back to the table. Motzkin, plug him back in."

Motzkin picked up the three-pronged plug. He tried to make contact with the outlet. His hands shook. No, that wasn't the trouble. It was refusing to go in. "Something's wrong," he said. "Something happened to it."

"What happened?" Lake called. He was stitching the vein to an incision in the aorta.

"Prong," Motzkin said. "He bent it." He was squinting at the three metal rods.

"Unbend it."

"I can't, Eric. When he pulled at it. It's bent out of shape."

Motzkin was on his knees. Once more he tried to marry the prongs to the triple holes in the outlet. Ticks sounded in his terrified mind. With each passing second Walker Tench was dying. Anoxic, bloodless, he would approach the vegetable state —no brain, no kidneys, no lungs. Motzkin wondered if he had failed, if he had not acted quickly enough. Should he have unscrewed the plug at once? Forestalled the man from forcing it? But he had been defying him, flaunting his new bravery.

"How about it, Alan?" Lake asked.

"Impossible. I can't . . . it's ruined."

Cho walked over. He took the plug and studied it. He began to tug at one of the prongs. "Maybe I straighten it," he said. He began to worry the bent prong.

"Hurry it up," Trask said.

"You fucked it up, you fix it," Licata said.

Lake held up a cautioning hand. More than four minutes had passed. They would have to gamble on Tench's cold body.

Flor moved to Mihrab's side. She was weeping. "They will kill him, Gamel. They don't care about anything."

"No, no, Flor. We will be all right."

The soft gasping of the ventilator sounded like Tench's last breath.

Cho took a small pliers and began working at the prong. Suddenly he was holding the plug in one hand and the pliers in another. In the teeth of the pliers was a metallic scrap. A prong had come loose.

"Do something, damn it," Trask raged. "You're responsible for this."

Licata looked up from the bloody cavity on Tench's chest. He and Lake kept suturing the vein to the aorta. "Eric? It's our move."

Lake did not answer. The hemostats, the strands of sutures, danced as he tied small knots.

"He's dying," Trask shouted. "You're doing this deliberately. If he dies, you all die."

12

O'Boyle, coated with dust, struggled through the duct. His feet found open space—the hatch through which he had entered. The reporter lowered himself to the table. Clouds of dust kicked around him. A flashlight blinded him. It was Reinhold.

"You fucking liar."

Two of the chief's men stood in the shadows. They looked doglike and sullen. Each carried a rifle.

Reinhold grabbed the young man and shook him. "You were some help. You got your story and you screwed me."

"No, I didn't," O'Boyle said. "What the hell are you talking about?" He pulled away from Reinhold's hands. "I tried to make a deal with them. I told them they didn't stand a chance and to come out without their pieces. That guy Trask is crazy. He wanted to make a speech."

Reinhold wanted to smash a fist into the arrogant face. The long hair had infuriated him again. And this was the kind of trash the network paid a fat salary to stir up radicals.

"Now I'll make a speech, you bastard." He grabbed O'Boyle's arm. "Give me what you made in there. The tape. The films. Olenik, grab his camera."

"Get your hands off me, Reinhold," O'Boyle said. He spun at Olenik. "You, too. Reinhold, I said get your fucking hands off. You're in more trouble than you realize."

The chief released him. "You threatening me, you little queer?"

"You stop me from getting this on the air or from covering this story, you'll be working as a guard in a defense plant the rest of your life. You helped shove me into that hole. You're a conspirator. Obstructing justice. I'm a journalist. I've got a right to cover a story. You're a cop. You're supposed to obey orders, and you double-crossed the FBI. They'll have your badge in five minutes. Now let me out."

Reinhold's fists twitched. Ah, the sheer joy of cracking him across the nose, doubling him up with a few kicks! But O'Boyle was tough. He knew the angles. Reinhold had himself to blame for letting the reporter con him.

"Okay, O'Boyle." Reinhold motioned to his aides to move away from the door. "Anyone hurt?"

"One of the doctors got hit in the foot. It didn't look bad. He was moving around. There's two guys in there with guns. At least that's all I could see. Trask and some Arab, I think. He fired about four times. Bastard hit my camera." He held up the ruined Filmo. "But the film is safe."

"Listen," Reinhold said. "You better tell what happened to Stade, the Bureau guy. He's in Rockewicz's office."

"Sure. You think I'm not a good citizen? But first I got to find my courier."

In the foyer, O'Boyle located his crew. The cassette and the film were given to a motorcycle messenger. The sound recording could go on radio at once. O'Boyle would phone in a report to go directly on the air.

"Come on," Reinhold said. "We better see Stade." He was furious with himself. The scheme had not worked, except to the reporter's advantage. Now, he was obliged to report to the FBI. At least they would know how many men were in the room, how they were armed and positioned. They might even decide to move in. And without any help from him.

"You screwed everything up," Reinhold said to O'Boyle. They trotted down a stairway. "Goddamn queer."

"The hell I did. I found out more than any cop around here." He brushed back his blond fall of hair. "And one other thing, Reinhold."

"Yeah?"

"Just stop calling me queer, huh? I get more ass in one night than you do in a month."

13

Hooks walked out of the toilet in the luncheonette and found a rear door into a yard piled with debris. An alley was the only exit, unless he wanted to climb fences, but this was no time to look conspicuous. Trask may have been a genius, but his planning wasn't so great. Hooks felt he could have done a better job. The Irish bitch was on the grounds, making excuses at the drug clinic, probably twitching her ass at the guy who ran it. Olmedo had cased him, said he had a hard-on for young chicks. But where did that leave Bateman?

Hooks walked down the alley, slung the sack over his shoulder, and emerged into the street opposite the hospital. He would keep circling until he made his move.

"There's the big spade give me lip," the policeman said.

The sergeant looked down the street. The rain had turned to snow. The crowd was lumped in excited groups behind the barricades, pressed against store windows. They were getting soaked, but they did not seem to mind.

"You," the sergeant called. "Hold it."

"Me, boss?" Hooks stopped and grinned. A foolish black man.

"Yeah. That's better. My friend says you got snotty with him." The sergeant studied Hooks: broad-shouldered, no waist, thick thighs. The OD clothing suggested a veteran.

"Not me, boss." Hooks scratched his shaved head and pushed the watch cap forward.

"Got any identification?" the sergeant asked. His handy-talky crackled. Someone was trying to reach him. Reinhold had set up his own communications in the cubicle in the lobby.

"Sure, boss." Hooks went for his wallet. "Hon'rable discharge. Fo'ty-ninth division. Three years in 'Nam. I lookin' for a buddy. Me an' him was supposed to git jobs today."

"Should we bust him?" the policeman asked.

Hooks feigned fear. Arrested, he would be useless. And they would find the weapons in the sack. He should be feeling real fear, but he was beyond it.

The sergeant smiled. "Nah. He sounds like he learned his lesson. Beat it. Don't show your face here again."

"Thanks, boss." Hooks envisioned the two of them, face down in a ditch, stitched with red stains from his Armalite.

"Shooting again," the sergeant said. He had the handy-talky pressed to his ear. "Someone's shooting the hell out of the place. Reinhold wants everyone to stand by."

Hooks listened with one ear as the policeman talked. *Shooting.* He could guess. Rashid. The Arab killed and enjoyed it. They had almost come to blows—Hooks and Rashid—when the Arab began boasting about his deeds. He had tried to forge a bond between himself and Bateman Hooks—men who had killed without hesitation, asked no questions, made no excuses.

Walking down the wet street, feeling the slush oozing into his boots, Hooks nursed his anger at Rashid, at Trask, at the Ashanti League officers who had loaned him to these fucking honkys.

"You know what you are, Ratshit," Hooks had taunted. "You are a fuckin' coward in your heart. You shoot up tourists and kids and some Jew farmer, and you a hero in your country. You fuckin'

Ay-rabs kill people, run off to other Ay-rabs, and all them cats at the United Nations vote you a medal, all them people in blankets say you a hero. You ain't no hero, Ratshit. You a yellow ass. . . ."

Hooks let the snow hit his face. Like when he was a kid, shining shoes, running errands. All finished. He was angry at the thought, no matter how things came out, of Rashid being hailed as a hero by millions of suckers who didn't know any better.

He wondered why he hung on. He knew. He owed it to the people in the ditch.

14

O'Boyle told his story to Stade. They all listened—Cardone, Rockewicz, and Martha Lake. The reporter said that as far as he could see, the medical team was unharmed. Motzkin had sustained a small wound in his foot.

The FBI agent got up and confronted the long-haired man. "You can be arrested. Disobeying police orders. Endangering lives. You have one hell of a nerve."

"You wouldn't, Mr. Stade." His voice was full of polite appeal. "I can help. You know there are only two of them. I can talk to Trask for you. He trusts me. Wait till he hears himself on radio. He'll want me to come back so he can do an encore. Maybe we'll have a chance to get him to surrender."

"How is Dr. Lake?" Martha asked.

"He's fine. Didn't even move when that guy started popping. And believe me, I was the only one he was shooting at." O'Boyle paused. Careful. He did not want to tell them too much. Certainly nothing that would involve Reinhold.

"How'd you get to that duct?" Stade asked. "Who showed you?"

"Ah, come on, Mr. Stade. You know we don't give away sources."

Stade told Harris to post agents at all points of access to the ventilating system. It was unlikely they would use it as an escape route. But all exits had to be covered.

"I'll be around if you need me," the reporter said. "Remember, I can mediate. I'm not armed. People like that don't kill reporters."

"No," Rockewicz said. "They use them."

O'Boyle smiled. "Nothing wrong with that. It's an electronic age. Everybody wants to be a TV star. Even crazies with guns."

When he had left, Martha turned to Stade.

"That young man bluffed his way in," she said tautly. "Why doesn't the FBI?"

"He was lucky, Mrs. Lake. He's lucky his head wasn't blown off."

"Alan got nicked, Martha," Steve said. "Bullets were flying around. Mr. Stade's right."

15

"He's dying, isn't he?" Trask shouted.

"How about it, Eric?" Licata asked. "Now?"

"Another few seconds. Tench's good and cold. He hasn't lost anything off the pump." He spoke softly.

"What are you saying?" Trask cried. "He's dead already, is that it? Think twice, Lake. You'll be worth as much money as Tench. You don't mean a damn to us."

"You have unnerved him," Mihrab whispered. "Eric, maybe now—"

"Didn't someone mention an emergency procedure?" Trask called. He moved closer to the table. Tench's heart looked dead —flat and immobile. The vein grafts were two pink sandworms, looping from the heart to the aorta. But they were nonfunctional now that no blood was entering the heart.

"Go into your act, Jack," Lake said.

Licata walked from the table to the heart-lung pump. "How's the foot, Alan?"

"I'll manage. Funny. Hardly any pain. The tension, I guess. Bodily changes in fear, pain, hunger, and rage. You ever read that in neurology?" He was babbling, but unaware of it.

"Sure." Licata winked at Motzkin. "By Walter B. Cannon."

"What are you two doing?" Trask shouted. He waved the gun at Licata. "Get back. It's a trick."

Rashid was pointing the carbine at Licata.

"Fuck you," Licata said. "Fuck you and everyone on your block."

"Stay away from John," Rashid called.

Flor, terrified of the Arab, shrank to the wall, staring up at his squat figure. There was a dark circle at his crotch. The killer had wet his pants.

"You, too, you Ay-rab creep. Get stuffed."

Licata bent under the heart-lung machine and took out a heavy handle. It had a grip for turning and a semicircular housing at the other end. Licata held it as if it were a weapon in a gang war.

"Stay back," Trask said.

"Gonna ram it up you slowly, rotate it to the right and break it off."

"Start the pump again," Lake said.

"James, we'll be short. By maybe three million dollars."

"There's no choice. Send it."

Cardone had made the decision. They would have to meet Trask's 12:12 deadline. The man was irrational, incapable of accepting compromises. The data in the FBI files had contained a warning: the imposing of "nonnegotiable demands"; threats; impetuous, irrational acts. It had gotten him far in revolutionary councils.

After giving additional orders, including a statement for release that ransom would be family-funded and would not affect Tench stock, Cardone hung up. He turned to Rockewicz. "The heart-lung machine," he said, "I guess we can assume it's been reactivated."

"I would think so. Just a matter of plugging it back in."

"Any standby pump?"

"There isn't time to connect one."

"But . . ?"

Steve's patience was shriveling. "Look, they can kill him a whole lot of ways. Anyway, Lake's almost finished. Once the last bypass is sutured, they give him back his blood."

In the anteroom Steve could hear Martha Lake comforting Mrs. Baggs. The black woman sobbed in dry spasms. He had tried talking to her: useless. The director thought ahead now: Who would escape? Who would live? Would they dare wheel Tench out, tubed, wired, stitched, barely alive?

Randolph Hutchins, Tench's vice president for public relations, had joined Gallatin, the treasurer, at the Federal Reserve Bank. They watched the last of the money being stacked into the cheap valises. The scene had a dreamlike air about it.

"The joke may be on them," Hutchins said. He was a former newsman for UPI who took liberties with the tribal gods.

"On whom?" Gallatin asked. The treasurer had taken a dreadful beating on the phone from Cardone. The corporation had a life of its own, a destiny of its own. Might not Tench Industries fulfill itself more gloriously without both Tench and the unspeakable Cardone, with his notions of "community action" and "inner-city thrust"?

"On those revolutionaries."

"Oh, yes. They'll be dead by nightfall. There'll be no mercy shown. If they leave Mr. Tench behind, I have it on good authority they'll all be shot dead. If the hostages have to be killed, so be it."

Hutchins surveyed Gallatin's saurian face. A lizard. A swamp turtle. How vast were the rewards of mediocrity! Great companies were filled with untalented, bland men, attending meetings, writing memos, nodding their heads.

"I didn't mean it that way," Hutchins said. "All this money . . ."

"Why is the joke on them?"

"The money may be worth nothing in a few months. Inflation, exchange rates, our collapsing economy. Maybe they should have followed their own philosophy—no money, just power."

"You are joking, Randolph."

Hutchins was, of course. And it was a feeble joke.

16

"Are you getting anything on the EEG?" Lake asked.

"Cho!" Motzkin cried.

"Oh, sure, sure." He flicked on the machine. A jagged light danced on the screen.

Licata glanced at it. "He's alive, Eric. But its not normal."

"But he's still alive!" Trask cried. "See that you keep him alive."

Licata got on one knee next to the heart-lung machine's silvery chassis. He fitted the housing to a gear that connected with the motor. He agitated it to make sure it was secure. "What are you going to need, Eric?" he asked.

"I'm not sure. Fifteen minutes. Maybe less."

"I see," Trask said. "A hand pump. Why didn't you move faster? You're killing him. You'll blame me. None of you will live if that happens."

"Will you shut your mouth?" Licata said. "What a *bacalà*."

Licata began to crank the handle. The pump was resistant and stiff. He turned rhythmically, knowing that he was in for a great deal of pain. Jimmy had been the best at running the machine by hand.

"You're terrific, Jack," Motzkin said. "Thank God for you. I couldn't hack it, never."

"Nor I," Mihrab said. He was ambivalent about Licata's strength: the power to run machines and to subdue women. Flor was also watching the chief resident. Licata worked himself into a steady rhythm. His forearm bulged with the effort. Motzkin watched the arterial monitor.

"What are we at, Alan?" Licata asked.

"Fifty rpm's."

"You want seventy, huh?"

"Close to it."

Licata got down on his knees. The tile floor sent jolts of pain into them. Too many football injuries. Sweat poured from his forehead and flooded his eyes. "Flor, a fast wipe," he said. She came to his side. Straining, breathing heavily, he caught a whiff of perfumed soap on her hands. No. Evil thoughts. Not again.

"You're at sixty," Motzkin said.

With an athlete's controlled movements, Licata turned the handle. He used his back, his shoulder, his arm.

"Beautiful," the anesthesiologist said. "The blood flow is steady."

"When this is over," Licata said, "I'll never call you gas-passer again."

"You'll think of something worse, Jack."

The arterial tube wobbled, then stretched into a bright red line. The blood streamed into Tench's femoral artery once more.

Motzkin prodded, "Would you like to try for seventy?"

"Big-hearted Alan." Licata grunted as he increased the tempo. "Eric, you sure you need fifteen minutes of this?"

Lake ignored him. He and Mihrab raised the aorta. The chief surgeon indicated the point on the aorta where he wanted the second vein-graft attached.

Licata's body appeared to have married itself to the machine. He spaced each breath with the revolutions of the handle, bracing his legs against the base of the pump. He wondered how long he could keep turning. The motion was unnatural, a strain on the musculature. Some years ago, he had seen Jimmy Baggs run the pump by hand. For how long? Ten minutes? Twelve? His assistants had helped out—Musgrave, Rios. Three of them. How long had they run it?

"Come from a long line of organ grinders, hey Alan?" he puffed. "It's in the blood."

"Save your breath, Jack," Lake said. "And start rewarming him, slow and steady."

They were making tiny stitches around the upper end of the vein, sewing it to the aorta. Hemostats ringed the graft. The green, steel-tipped sutures flew in and out of the living tissues. Minute knots anchored the vein to the great vessel.

"How much longer?" Trask asked. He was back at the high stool, more composed, still suspicious.

"Maybe fifteen minutes," Lake said. "But the patient has to remain in here another hour and a half. He has to be closed."

"When will you be able to tell if he's suffered damage?"

"He hasn't." Lake glanced at Mihrab's solemn eyes as if cautioning him to say nothing. Both knew that there was no certainty that Tench was out of danger.

"You were lucky. If he had. . . ."

Lake ignored him. *No, not lucky, you idiot.* But there was no point in baiting the gunman.

"How do you feel, Jack?" Motzkin asked. "Want some help?"

"Nah, I'm great."

"You sure?"

"It isn't as good as screwing. But it grows on you."

Flor overheard him. She turned her back and counted sponges on a table.

Licata, feeling the pain radiate into his shoulder, his back, his neck, discovered that his mind was on other pumpings and turnings. How many women had he made love to in City General? In how many rooms? Regret over his tomcatting was marginal. It was good fun. He regarded his triumphs as ritualistic diversions. Who had suffered? Surely not the Finnish inhalation therapist with thighs like bowls of whipped cream who even smelled like dairy. Or the slithery Puerto Rican paraprofessional, Miss Sanchez, redolent of plantains and *cuchifritos*, wiggling like a speared porgy, her behind moving on ball bearings. Or the lady intern from Singapore, a spicy stew of English, Chinese, and Malayan, delicately moustached, wailing like a banshee when she came.

And his hideaways: old locker rooms, linen closets.

In the grip of exhaustion and tension, he sedated himself with memories. The color of a pair of panties. A mole on a belly. An undone bra. The souvenirs were pleasant. Except for the time he had taken Flor, made her cry, ruined something for Gamel, his friend and colleague. Flor never passed him without a shy movement of her head. A little girl from the provinces. She'd lived the part until he, stud, chief resident, had demanded his tribute. Thoughts of Flor gave him no strength. *Switch channels.* A new memory surfaced: an assistant dietitian, an angular midwestern lady, at night on a table in the bakery. Puffs of flour as they thrashed away . . .

"Nicely done, Eric," Mihrab said.

"Less compliments and more work," Licata groaned. "My arm is about to fall off."

"I'll take over," Motzkin said. "Really, let me."

"Nah, it's fun."

He knows, Motzkin thought, I'd last two minutes.

Lake examined the grafts. "We've just set a new indoor record. Considering how far we had to go for the diagonal branch, I think we should all be proud."

There was a bumping noise in the hallway. Rashid was on his feet, aiming the M2 at the door. Trask flattened himself against the inner wall, out of range of the door. He extended his right arm with the .38 special. There was a second noise.

Rashid picked up a grenade. He balanced the carbine with his right hand, pressing the wire stock against his hip. Trask edged into the scrub room. He called to the operating room, "No one move. If they come in, Rashid will release the grenade. You're all finished."

"Mistake," someone called from outside. "Don't panic. We're moving patients out. We hit the door by mistake. Don't shoot."

"Stay away," Trask yelled. His head seemed to operate on an eccentric gear deep in his neck. It jerked from the door, to the table, to Rashid who stood ready with the grenade and the carbine.

"Sounds upset," Licata grunted to Motzkin. "Maybe he's got a little yellow in him."

Lake was lifting the second bypass gently. "There's a kink in this one. I'm not satisfied with the way the vein is resting. No big deal, but if we can't do it perfectly, why do it?"

"What do you suggest?" Mihrab asked.

"Stitch it to the wall. Lift the heart, please."

"Eric, what a time for details," Licata said. His mind was spinning: Baker Field, wind sprints and one-on-ones, cursing the coaches, hating football, bruised, puking behind the bench.

"You're finishing?" Trask asked. He was pacing now, from the outer door to the gallery and back.

"That's it," Lake said. "One more stitch should do it. What's his blood pressure?"

"Ah, seventy-two," Cho said.

"EEG?"

"He's got brain waves."

"Somebody—Flor—look at his urinary output."

The circulating nurse bent beneath the table. "He is passing urine, doctor."

"All right," Lake said. "As soon as he's warm enough we'll take him off the pump. See how the new plumbing works."

"How about right now?" Licata gasped. His arm was a cement block. Like a car engine deprived of oil, with the pistons freezing in place. For what it's worth, he thought, I'm Walker Tench's heart. Heart for a corporation, a thousand employees, a half dozen millionaires. Small consolation. It didn't lessen the tearing in his arm and back. Pain was pain. You had to accept it the way you breathed air. He had learned it years ago, starting against Yale with a shoulder separation.

"Flor," Licata said. "Towel on my forehead again."

Rashid was speaking Arabic to Mihrab: soft guttural sounds. The senior resident was completing the sutures that would take the bend out of the vein, but he listened carefully.

"What is he asking?" Lake asked.

"He wishes to know if the operation is a success."

"I'll send him a written report."

Trask seemed in control again. He walked to the phone and dialed Rockewicz's extension. "I want Cardone. The Revolutionary Army of the Wretched of the Earth is sending further instructions. It is now eleven-forty-two and we are preparing our withdrawal."

17

The director of the FBI reached Arnold Stade in Rockewicz's office. He wanted a briefing. There were reports on the radio of a TV man who had gotten into the operating room and phoned in a conversation with the terrorists. Moreover, the reporter said he had a taped statement by John Trask which would soon be on the air.

The director was merely upset. But the Attorney General was enraged. He was a political appointee, a man of some intelligence, but he had meager background in law enforcement and an over-developed fear of public attitudes. Discreetly the director told Stade that the Attorney General was frustrated. How could a reporter get into an enclosed room, talk to these maniacs, get a tape from one of them, but the FBI could not?

"He went against orders," Stade said. "He didn't give a damn about innocent people getting killed. We do."

Reinhold walked into Rockewicz's office in the middle of the conversation. His quick eyes, his pointed ears, absorbed it all. Someone in Washington was tear-assed. Stade was doing a lot of explaining. The chief would keep his mouth shut. No one except Parolo and two of his own men knew that he had sanctioned O'Boyle's attempt to breach the OR. Rockewicz had looked at him peculiarly. Stade had asked a few questions. He played dumb. Good with a gun but not much brains. They'd find out.

"All right, sir, we'll examine our options," Stade was saying. "I understand how the Attorney General feels. I agree that these terrorists have no right to dictate terms and make us dance. Trask is a bad one. A long record. But the people in—"

He was being reamed out, Reinhold could see. Someone wanted blood. Someone wanted a wagonload of dead freaks. He wasn't through, Reinhold thought. There'd be other chances. When those animals started their escape.

"Flak?" Rockewicz asked the FBI man.

"Some."

Reinhold drew a chair up and sat arrogantly in front of Stade. "I heard some of that. You got a problem."

Stade tried to ignore him. He half-turned his back and was discussing with Harris the need for warning the kidnappers about the arrival of the helicopter. Trask was not to assume that it was a police operation. He was not to panic.

"Or try to use it to get away," Harris said.

"I said you got a problem," Reinhold persisted.

"Beg pardon, chief?" Stade asked.

"Your boss in Washington. He's right. If that reporter could worm his way in, why can't we? There's a million stunts we could pull. I'll be glad to go in first." He yanked the .357 Magnum from his holster. "Just this is all I need. Blow those bastards apart before they know I'm there. I go for the guy with the carbine first. Then the guy near the door."

"How do you know they'll oblige you?" Stade asked.

Martha Lake was shaking her head in firm, negative movements. Steve cautioned her with his hand: It's okay, we're indulging him.

"Hey, chief," Rockewicz said, "didn't the state legislature rule those Magnum revolvers illegal, even for cops?"

"Did they?" The fox was on guard. He stroked the six-inch barrel.

"Citizen groups objected, didn't they? Hollow-point bullets, the kind that expand. Aren't they against the law?"

"Are they? Been using one for over a year. It stops them faster than a thirty-eight. A helluva lot faster."

Cardone came to Stade's desk and turned his back on Reinhold. "This man has to be stopped. He cannot be permitted to roam the hospital putting everyone's life in danger."

Stade's phone rang again. It was the FBI director once more. The Attorney General had just heard Trask's voice on the radio, boasting, threatening, mocking the country. It was an intolerable situation. He wanted results. If any of the kidnap party escaped, he warned ominously, there would be a grim accounting.

"And nobody listens to me," Reinhold said. He shoved the blue-black gun into the holster. "But I'm just a city cop."

18

"Listen carefully," Trask said on the phone. "These are the instructions for delivering the money."

Cardone asked, "Is it all right if Mr. Rockewicz listens? He knows the hospital layout better than anyone."

"All right. Put anyone on you want. Is the FBI man on, too?"

"Of course. If that's all right, John."

Reinhold stood in the doorway, furious with them. *John, is that all right?* Talking to the germ as if he were the governor!

"The money's been collected?" Trask asked.

"It has," said Cardone.

"All of it?"

"Yes. We're flying it in by helicopter."

Rockewicz broke in. "If you hear the chopper, don't get excited, don't make any moves. It's only the money. No cops in it. Just the loot."

"Reparations." Trask sounded louder. He was on the verge of triumph.

"Sure, whatever you want to call it," Steve said. "But don't start shooting when you hear it. Is everyone okay? When that reporter sneaked in, I heard someone got hit."

"That was the reporter's responsibility. Your anesthesiologist has nine toes." His voice became warm and confiding. "We could have worked this out. The CIA tried to intervene. That's how Baggs died. He was sent in to kill me."

"Tell that to his widow," Rockewicz said. "She's next door. Want to talk to her?"

"No. That would be counterproductive. Cardone?"

"Yes?"

"The four suitcases are to be placed on the rear loading platform. Just to the right of the kitchen area. It leads from the postmortem rooms and the morgue."

Rockewicz calculated: He'd have an elevator held at the top floor. They could get the valises out in minutes.

"At eight minutes past noon one of our assault team will enter the parking area. He will approach via the entrance driveway. He will be wearing Army clothing and a black watch cap. He is a black man. He will be carrying a bag. He is armed and ready to die. He must not be stopped or interfered with or shot at. We will kill Dr. Lake if this man is harmed."

"Understood," Cardone said. "The gentleman from the FBI is nodding his agreement."

"He had better. You will make available to this man a hospital ambulance. It must have a full tank of gas and two-way radio contact with Rockewicz's office. Park it in the middle of the area."

"No problem," Steve said. "We can patch you in right here."

Trask paused. He appeared to be stroking his power, dressing himself in robes. "There will be a second member of our team in the parking lot. A young woman. She is white, wearing a tan coat. She, too, must be left alone. No sniper fire, no arrest, no attempt to stop her. If she is harmed, we will kill Dr. Motzkin."

Harris was leaning over Stade's desk. They were pointing to a diagram of the inner court, the entrances, the exits, the ambulance garage.

"Understood," Stade said.

"We're all in accord," Rockewicz added.

"I'm not finished. You may have guessed that the only way we can make our withdrawal secure is by taking members of the enemy as hostages."

"We anticipated that," Stade said. "We'd like to change your mind. We'll give you our word that you can leave unhindered."

"You think I'm a fool?" Trask asked. "To shoot our heads off? Blow us to pieces as you did the Symbionese brothers? The Panthers in Chicago? Our brothers in Palestine?"

Reinhold was nodding his head. He turned to Martha Lake. "That's my idea. I could get those people out alive, including your husband."

She had turned deathly pale. But her features were calm. Her hands were locked on her breast.

"We will leave the operating room at noon with our hostages," Trask said.

Cardone cleared his throat. "Does that include Mr. Tench? Even if the surgery is complete, it takes an hour to sew him up. You can't mean that you'll wheel him into an ambulance—"

"Anything is possible, Cardone."

"Okay, John," Steve interrupted. "Who are you taking?"

"Our options are open. All that should concern you is that any shooting will mean the death of hostages. We may die, but so will they."

Rockewicz raised a hand to stop Cardone from talking. "John, this is nuts. I'm no capitalist pig. You know I pushed a minority training program here? You know I have the best record in the east for raising hospital workers' salaries and benefits? You and I got a lot to talk about. Maybe we aren't so far apart."

"It's too late."

Cardone broke in. "Don't hurt anyone else. We've promised you there will be no shooting, no ambush. The ambulance will be there. The money will be there. Now, you are obliged to fulfill your part of the bargain. As far as Tench Industries are concerned, if you leave Mr. Tench alone, we will forget this happened."

"You don't expect me to believe that."

"Hey, fella," Rockewicz said, as if talking to an orderly caught stealing Ace bandages. "What did Dr. Lake ever do to you? What did Motzkin or Licata ever do to you? You don't want to hurt people like that."

"Lake is a millionaire. The world wouldn't miss his kind."

Rockewicz stared at the ceiling. He was grateful that Martha could not hear it all. She was sitting on the edge of a chair, massaging Mrs. Baggs's hand.

"John, I'm gonna make you a hell of an offer," Steve said.

"I'm not interested."

"This is a good one. Forget about Cardone and Tench and the FBI. You and me, one on one. Ever play school-yard basketball?"

"No deals."

"This is a good one. I'm no cop. I'm a guy trying to run a hospital. Here's a way we can work this out. I'll be your hostage. . . ."

Trask hung up.

Martha got up. "Steve, I want Eric. I want him out of there. Let them take Mr. Tench, with or without his chest open. He's the only one with ten million dollars."

Stade and Harris were making lines with a blue pencil on the hospital diagram. "They'll come through here," Stade said. "This elevator, if they use the stretcher with Tench, these stairs if they don't. The two outside will have the bags in the ambulance and the motor running by the time they get there."

"There are ten places we can hit them from once they're in the courtyard," Harris said. He was marking Xs on the plan.

"No you won't," Rockewicz said. "It's my hospital, god-damn it!"

"We won't shoot unless there's certainty the hostages won't be harmed," Stade said.

"I won't tolerate it," Martha cried. "Steve, make them give their word. I'll go down there myself and get Eric out."

Rockewicz agreed with her. With Reinhold. With the Attorney General. They couldn't just walk out. Some feint? Some fake? He shouted to Estelle, "Call the garage and tell them to move the Chevy out. Full tank of gas. Keys in." He stopped in the middle of the floor. He looked at Martha. "I just elected myself."

"What do you mean?" she asked.

"I'm going down to surgery. I'll have a talk with them. With luck they'll let me in. I once talked a platoon of Japanese into surrendering on Tarawa through an interpreter, would you believe it? This shouldn't be as hard."

"I'd advise against it," Stade said. "You don't talk John's language either."

"You can't stop me."

"I can."

"But you won't."

Stade got up. "I have agents down there. Harris, tell Lief and his men to cover Mr. Rockewicz."

"Tell them to stay away. Far back."

Stade was shaking his head. "Rockewicz, think about it. You may do a lot of harm."

"Stade, this is my turf. Those are my people in that room. I owe them everything in the world. So does this community. No maniac is going to walk Eric Lake or anyone else out of this hospital with a grenade tied to his back and a gun in his ribs. I am going to make damn sure of that."

The big man hugged Martha Lake. "He'll be okay, Martha. You'll see. Eric and I will go to the Schlosser kid's bar mitzvah tomorrow."

Outside, Reinhold had been listening. The chief watched Rockewicz's bulky, white-shirted figure leave the office. Reinhold pretended to be conferring with his riflemen for a moment, then followed the director.

PART FIVE

1

". . . We have bombed and robbed banks and now we will hold the imperialists for ransom. . . . We will be running the means of production, the factories and farms, for the good of the people. . . ."

Trask held the transistor radio up. The volume was high. The abrasive sound of his ranting voice flooded the operating room. He rotated the radio so that all could hear.

"Listen," he said. "The world is hearing it. You can be useful to us. You can side with us. Join us."

"I've heard of ego trips," Licata gasped. "But this tops them. I wish this was like Cooley's OR. We could pipe in rock music and drown him out."

"Ignore him, Jack," Mihrab said. "We are almost finished."

"That's what worries me. The second act."

". . . Anyone who supports our revolutionary battle for the good of mankind will be accepted in our ranks. But there will be more bloodshed, more violence if we are resisted. . . ."

Trask nodded, approving his own words. They were hearing him everywhere—in Washington, New York, London, Paris, the power centers. Yes, and in Moscow and Peking. The old left had sold out, the labor movement was lost. They bought appliances from Walker Tench. They were all soft, stupid, blinded to the truth. He, Trask, and his followers saw the way the world was going. They might die, but their deaths presaged a new, beautiful, and just world.

"My pantomime act," Lake said, closing his ears to the radio. "Looks like I'm stitching but there's nothing there. Green sutures over green drapes. For years I've been crusading for yellow sutures but to no avail."

"You can still joke?" Mihrab said.

"Force of habit."

Rewarmed, Tench could soon be taken off the pump. If Lake would restore the beat with electrical paddles. And Licata could end his labors.

"Fast two-minute quiz," Lake said. Trask had turned the radio down. They had finished broadcasting his speech. "Flor, why do we warm the patient before giving him back his heart?"

"Ah . . ." She made an effort to concentrate. "We had that in class. So arrhythmias can be corrected. If he's cold, it's harder to stop tachycardia or bradycardia."

"A-plus, Flor," Licata grunted. "Eric, wind him up!"

"Cho, more hot water. Turn the faucet." Motzkin pointed to the wall: Jimmy Baggs's system. The Korean walked to the wall and turned the hot water on.

The drain was removed from the vent in Tench's heart. Mihrab placed a suture in it. He took out a blood-soaked sponge and swabbed the space below the heart.

"How warm is he?" Lake asked.

"Mmmm. Thirty-five on the nose." Motzkin patted Licata's back. "Our hero. Lou Little would be proud of you."

"Less compliments, just get me off the rack." The chief resident's eyes were blind with sweat. His body had become a giant motor, a power plant activating one moving part, his right arm. "My arm is going to drop off. Wingy Licata."

They had been on emergency power for eleven minutes. How, Licata wondered, had Jimmy Baggs kept it up for *fifteen* and never complained? It was love, Licata decided. Baggs had loved Lake, the OR, the heart-lung machine. The room was his temple, his church. No wonder he had gone for Trask's throat.

"Turn, turn, you stiff bastard," Licata muttered. "Eric, this is what they call regression. Organ grinder to organ grinder in three generations."

"Easy, Jack," Lake said. "We're going on partial. We'll give him back half of his blood."

"Good. That means I work half as hard."

"Put a charge on the machine," Lake said. "I'm going to defibrillate him."

Cho was sitting with his head in his hands.

"Alan, wake that assistant of yours up!" the surgeon shouted. "I'll have a few words for anesthesiology when this is over."

"Cho!" Motzkin cried. "Pay attention! A charge on the machine!"

The Korean threw a switch.

"Defibrillating paddles," Lake said.

Trask studied his watch. It was 11:51. In nine minutes they would begin their move out of surgery.

Cho gave the surgeon the paddles—two black-handled rods, each terminating in a metal disk.

"Mean pressure?" asked Lake.

"Just got to fifty-eight," the anesthesiologist said.

"Get him back on his own power," Licata said. He looked gratefully at the electrified paddles. "That's it. Use the ultimate weapon."

Lake held up the rods for a moment, poised.

"Hang in, Jack. I'm going to start it beating."

He placed one disk in the cavity below the heart, the other on the surface of the heart. "You . . . Cho?" he asked. "Ready?"

"Yes, sir. Ready."

"Hit it."

The assistant pressed the button. There was a humming noise. Tench's heart did not react. It remained still.

"Again."

This time the heart began to flutter. Then it beat feebly.

"He's back," Lake said. "Not as strong as I'd like." He raised the heart and scowled at the scar.

"He's dead," Trask cried. His head was jerking. "You killed him."

"You shut up," Motzkin shouted. "Let Dr. Lake run this." He stared at Trask. He wanted to taunt him. Mock him. Ego for ego, he wanted to say. Eric Lake saves lives, and you, you world-saving nut, you kill.

"He's beating," Lake said. "Jack, Alan. Put him on partial."

Motzkin reached forward and fastened a clamp on the venous line. Licata slowly reduced the frequency with which he turned the handle. Both men watched the blood reservoir at the side of the heart-lung machine.

"Arterial inflow reduced?" Lake asked.

"Sure, sure," Motzkin said. "I can see the level going down. How far, Eric?"

Lake studied Tench's heart. How fast the body responded! Already blood was moving back into the right atrium, from which the venous lines had been draining, into the right ventricle, the pulmonary artery, the aorta.

"Give him twenty-five hundred cc's," Lake said.

"He's got it," Licata said. "I'm turning this thing at thirty-five rpm's. It's still not as much fun as tennis."

Lake felt the pressure in the aorta, the pulmonary artery. "Looks good."

Rashid descended to the bottom row of the gallery. He was watching Tench's heart fill with blood.

"All right, Jack," Lake said. "Your moment of deliverance is at hand. I'm about to take him off by-pass altogether."

"About time." The chief resident rested his head against the machine's metal flank. "You'll have a cardiac arrest on your hands if you keep me turning this monster."

Lake approved of the heart's appearance. The vein grafts were strong. Blood was coursing into the left coronary artery and the left ventricle.

"We're going off the machine, Alan," Lake said. "Ready with clamps?"

"Ready."

"Set."

"Set."

"Off."

"Off, and I thank San Giacomo and the feast of Mount Carmel," Licata moaned.

Motzkin fastened another clamp on the venous line, cutting off the drainage from the heart completely. No more blood would drip into the machine.

Licata slowed his pumping, keeping an eye on the reservoir of Tench's blood. The level descended slowly, the bright red line sinking.

"Give him five hundred cc's," Lake said. "He's doing well."

"You have it," Licata said. He stopped rotating the handle.

"Beautiful," Lake said. "I hope all of you observed the working of Starling's Law. The output of the heart increases as the load of blood and the filling of the chambers increase."

"Christ, my arm's paralyzed and Eric's giving us a first-year med school lecture," Licata complained to Motzkin.

"What you get paid for, Jack," Motzkin said.

"Like hell. My wrist is dead. There goes my fast ball." Licata flexed his arm, kneaded the wrist and forearm. He had functioned as Walker Tench's heart for thirteen minutes. There was still some blood in the cardiotomy tank. But the bulk of Tench's blood had been returned to his circulatory system.

"How long was he on?" Lake asked. "Including Dr. Licata's labors as the world's fastest human pump."

"Eighty-seven minutes," Motzkin said.

"Not bad. Not great."

Stretching, Licata walked back to the table. He was working on his shoulder with his left hand.

"Don't get too close," Trask warned. His head bobbed away. He backed toward the phone as Licata passed by.

"As we used to say in the Bronx, John, 'Screw you and your whole family.'"

"Don't antagonize him, Jack," Mihrab said. "We have a lot of work ahead of us closing the patient."

"Today we install a zipper," Licata said.

Sally Moorhead patted Licata's arm. "Doctor, you were wonderful."

"We're all wonderful, Sally. Look at poor Dr. Motzkin. The nine-toed wonder."

"Funny," Motzkin said. "It hardly hurts. Is it stress, adrenalin, or the absence of nerves in the toe?"

Hysteria, Alan, Jack Licata thought. But he didn't say it. He began trimming loose bits of tissue. What lay ahead was largely mechanics. Lake had done the crucial work. The assistants would finish.

Lake spoke to Licata. "When these people let us go, Jack, you beat it and get some rest. We'll arrange for another resident to help Gamel. Or I may stay and do it myself."

Trask stepped toward the operating table. Cho shrank from him. "We'll decide who stays and who doesn't. Dr. Lake, you still don't seem to understand."

"What's his aortic pressure?" Lake asked Motzkin.

"Seventy systolic."

"His cardiac output isn't bad. But I would like to see it just a little stronger."

"If it's any help," Motzkin said, "his systolic just went to eighty."

Lake nodded. "Run some Isuprel into him."

Motzkin looked at Cho. The Korean was oblivious. Truly, the slowest assistant he'd ever been burdened with. The department was a disgrace. "Isuprel," Motzkin said to Cho.

"Hunh?"

"Oh, dear." He got up and released the clamp on the overhead bottle. The drug flowed into Tench's veins.

"Magic," Lake said. "Look at that heart go. Hell, let's douse him with it," Lake laughed. "Look at that left ventricle take off. Did we fix that heart!" He had a vision of Walker as an undergraduate: fat and angry, a loner, befriending a starved premed in a torn sweater.

"Alan, you're shortchanging us," Licata said. "That clamp on the Isuprel line is stuck."

"I've only got two hands. And one foot."

They had the feeling it was over, that they would be free. The regeneration of Tench's heart, the satisfaction of the gunmen's demands, meant they would be allowed to walk out. Who cared if the corporation was short ten million dollars? Not Tench, at least not at the moment.

Trask called across the room to Rashid. "In seven minutes we leave."

"I guess we're through," Licata said. He was helping Mihrab ligate vessesls, snipping and cauterizing.

"Think of it, Jack," Lake said. "In a year you'll be a chief attending and you can get residents to turn the pump handle for you."

"Damn right, Eric. And I'll hire nothing but weightlifters and linebackers."

Trask gestured to Rashid to join him.

No one around the operating table spoke. Sally put her arm around Flor.

"What will they do?" the Filipino girl asked.

"They won't hurt us."

2

Rockewicz walked the near-empty corridors of his hospital. Once he chased a nurse back to the island. Once he admonished a patient peering from a room.

"Are they out yet, Mr. Rockewicz?" a floor nurse asked.

"No. But they will be, Mildred."

"It's so terrible. About Jimmy Baggs."

"I know, Mildred. But they won't get away with it."

Against his orders, a medical conference was taking place in one of the meeting rooms. He thought about stopping to read the riot act. But what did it matter? They'd have the good sense to stay inside. Besides, it was on the second floor, out of harm's way. He could hear the agitated voices. O'Hara, a brilliant young kidney man, was arguing angrily with Radosek, an elderly resident, a Czech who had been a big wheel in Prague and had had to start all over in America. "Drain her and you might kill the patient," O'Hara was yelling. "Nonsense, nonsense, doctor . . ."

God, how he loved them. From the chiefs of surgery to the bed-pan jockeys. The miracle to Rockewicz was that the inefficient, sprawling place got through every day as well as it did. So many jobs had to be done well by so many people working closely together.

Dave Buttram stopped him at the stairs. "Steve, is this a good idea?"

"If that reporter sneaked in, so can I."

"Sorry about O'Boyle. He got to someone."

"Find out for me. I'll burn Parolo's ass if he was involved. And I have my doubts about George Reinhold, our friendly fuzz."

"Is it true, Steve?" Buttram asked. "Those lunatics are threatening to wheel Tench out before he's sewed up?"

"Nobody knows. That's why I'm going down there."

"I wish you wouldn't."

"Somebody's got to. I was always the most valuable officer in the first wave. I carried the platoon's cigarettes."

Buttram was bothered by something else. "Steve . . . Dr. Fess has sort of vanished."

Rockewicz's eyes retreated. "Huh? Old Harvey?"

"Well, his assistants figured he went home. Estelle called his house, but there's no answer. You know Dr. Fess. He wants to be in the middle of everything. Maybe some of the FBI people down there could, ah, look around."

Steve hesitated. "Harvey may be taking a snooze somewhere. He's no kid any more. Let me make some deal with those dedicated heroes, then we'll find Harvey. I'm sure he's okay."

Buttram watched Rockewicz's bulky figure go through the door. In minutes, the executive director, armed only with his cunning, would be in surgery.

George Reinhold also saw Rockewicz go through the door. Then he heard a familiar voice—Brian O'Boyle talking into a tape recorder. He was refusing to remain in the press room.

"Hey, O'Boyle," Reinhold said. "Go where you belong."

"Sure, chief. What's Rockewicz up to?"

"He had to take a leak."

Parolo came running up to them. "Chief, you gotta get me off the hook. Mr. Buttram knows I let that guy in. You gotta tell him you okayed it."

Reinhold grabbed the maintenance man's collar. "Is there another way into surgery? An entrance at the other end?"

"The OR?"

"The whole surgery. The whole area."

"Yeah. Through the recovery room."

"Take me there."

"George, I'm in trouble enough. You ain't—"

Reinhold shoved him roughly. "Move, Parolo. I'll worry about the FBI. You worry about me."

"Rockewicz'll break my chops."

"I'll do worse than that."

3

"Look at those contractions," Lake said. "That's damned near a healthy heartbeat. Alan, more Isuprel."

This time Cho responded and unloosened the clamp. Motzkin smiled at him. When the crisis was over, he would see about some in-service training for the Korean.

There was a sharp rapping at the exterior door. Rashid aimed the carbine. Trask leaped from the stool. "No one move," he shouted. "Rashid, keep them covered."

They could hear Rockewicz's voice. "John? John? This is Stephen Rockewicz. Got to talk to you. I'm here by myself. No guns. No cops. Nothing. Let me in."

"Get away, Rockewicz. We'll start shooting people."

"John, be reasonable. I want you to get out of here safe. The money's being flown in. I want to make a deal for Dr. Lake and the others. It doesn't hurt to talk."

"We'll kill one of the nurses."

"What good will that do? John, uncover a window, you'll see. No guns, nothing. I warned the cops to lay off."

"Get away, Rockewicz." The voice was going higher.

Steve leaned against the stretchers. The barricade was not secure. It could be ripped apart in seconds. But it would make a racket. He pressed his body against the wall to the right of the double doors. At the distant end of the corridor, in Miss McCarran's office, he could see Lief and two of his agents watching him.

Steve motioned them back into the office. He did not speak but his red face registered his fury. They had agreed to stay out of sight.

"John, we got time. You say you didn't mean to kill Baggs. I buy that. You have a mission, right? You don't want to screw it up with pointless deaths, right? I'm no cop. I'm a dumb Polack trying to run a hospital. Give me a break."

"I said no deal."

"This is between us, John. What do you think I am, a fascist animal? I want to play ball with you. I want to keep people from getting their heads blown off."

Inside, Lake shook his head in wonderment. Licata rolled his eyes. The oil, the unction, the soothing quality in Steve's voice, were beyond belief. The man was a scam artist, a flimflam expert. Given the chance, the surgeons knew, he would have happily wrung Trask's neck, squashed the Arab under his heel.

"Get away. Last warning."

"No such thing as a last warning, John. You don't want to kill anyone and you know it. You're a man with an education. You're goal-oriented. A high achiever."

"Don't joke, you'll regret it."

"Who's joking?" Ah, how stupid they were. The world was a fouled-up mess, but you gained nothing by terrorizing people. You worked the big con on them, gave them all the wrong reasons for doing the right things.

Trask's voice rose to a scream. "Lake, tell him to get away!"

Rockewicz could hear Eric Lake's strained voice. "He's right, Steve. I'm winding up. Tench is going to be all right. Let them make the moves."

"Sure, sure," the director said. "That's what I'm saying. I want John to make the decisions. John, you with me? Better alive in a courtroom than dead in that ambulance. Christ, when those oxygen tanks blow—"

There was a ripping noise. Trask had pulled the cardboard from the window. Rockewicz could see his burning eyes and sweat-beaded forehead.

Rockewicz held up his hands. "No guns. Nothing. Nobody in the hallway. Just me."

"You've got ten seconds to get out of here, Rockewicz."

"Come on, kid. You need help. I haven't run out of deals yet."

4

Parolo led Reinhold up a stairway, then to the doors to the recovery room. An FBI man was on duty outside. He was using a handy-talky.

"Sorry, chief," he said. "No one goes in."

"I do."

"Orders from Mr. Stade."

Reinhold's pointed face tightened. "I got a call. One of the recovery room nurses is getting hysterical."

"I was just in there. They seem okay."

"Couple of minutes and I'll be out. Beat it, Parolo." The maintenance man shuffled away, his keys jangling as he vanished down the stairs. Reinhold pushed past the agent and through the swinging doors.

Two nurses came toward him. A radio was on full blast. A half dozen patients, wired, tubed, monitored, taped, all in various stages of postoperative misery, lay on the beds.

"Which way to surgery?" Reinhold asked. The nurse pointed to a closed door. Reinhold walked through. He took the .357 from its holster and held it in his right hand. The corridor was empty. Only two ORs were still in use—the one with the gunmen and the orthopedic case. The orthopedic case was nearer to him, four doors away. Then the corridor took an L turn. At the distant end, the terrorists were holding Tench and the hospital people. By now, he calculated, Rockewicz was on the scene.

Reinhold hugged the tile wall, walking silently on crepe-soled shoes. He could hear Rockewicz's voice, but not what the director was saying. He had to hand it to the guy, walking into that nest unarmed, depending only on his mouth.

Reinhold needed to stay on the scene unnoticed. He opened the door of the OR in which the surgeons were finishing the orthopedic case.

"Who . . . what? What do you want?" the resident asked. He moved back. The people at the operating table stared at him.

Reinhold held his finger to his lips. "It's okay. I'm Chief Reinhold. City Police."

"What's happening out there?" the resident asked.

"It's all right. They'll be leaving soon."

A huge black man in greens came forward. "What happened to Baggs, chief?"

"They killed him."

The man wiped his forehead. "Dirty mothers. Jimmy was my Main Man. He trained us."

Reinhold's eyes darted around the room. It was twice the size of most of the other ORs. One end of it was used for storage. On the wall was an array of gleaming surgical instruments used to crack and saw and manipulate bones.

Beneath it was an unused stretcher. Reinhold looked at it. A plan jelled in his mind. He started to take his shirt off.

"Listen," the orthopedic surgeon pleaded. "Don't start anything in here. We just want to get out."

"It won't concern you. All of you stay in here, finish your job." He threw his blue shirt and shield on a table. Then he took off his undershirt. The black giant was watching him.

"What's your name?" Reinhold asked.

"Musgrave. Baggs's team." He had a West Indian accent.

"You want to make it up to him?"

"I do, mon."

"Grab that stretcher and some green sheets." Reinhold took off his shoes and socks. Then he rolled his trousers up.

The surgeons and nurses looked at him as if he had gone mad. One of the nurses had read about him. A cop who walked into gunfights.

Musgrave rolled the stretcher across the operating room.

"Okay," Reinhold said. "I'm getting on it. You're going to push me through the hall, get it? You see me start to sit up or make any move, run like hell or hit the floor."

"I can't let you do this," the orthopedic surgeon protested. "You can't endanger this man—"

"It's okay, doctor," Musgrave said. He was tucking the green sheet around Reinhold's body. The chief had taken the long revolver from the holster. He held it in his right hand under the sheet.

"You got a piece for me, mon?" Musgrave asked.

"You won't need one. Just beat it when you see me draw."

Reinhold's head and shoulders were all that were visible. The sheets were bound tightly around his lean body. He tried maneuvering his right hand to see how quickly he could get it out from under the green covers. "Loosen the sides," he said to Musgrave. "Now, push me into the corridor. Anyone gives you any lip, think of a reason we're there."

"You coming from recovery room."

"Atta boy."

The West Indian got behind the stretcher. He moved it like a child pushing a toy cart. They went through the swinging doors.

5

Olmedo opened the supply room door an inch. He pressed an ear against the crack. Had Rockewicz come down alone? A tricky man, he was surely capable of setting an ambush. He would maneuver Trask and Rashid with his tongue, get them off guard, shoot them down. Olmedo was puzzled. What had really happened in the OR? There had been a second volley of shots—and no one understood what they meant. John or Rashid might be injured, encouraging Rockewicz to try something.

He opened the door another inch. He heard Rockewicz's voice, wheedling, bargaining. Why was he hanging on? Trask would reject any proposals. Olmedo unwrapped his carbine. It was a duplicate of Rashid's, with a wire stock and a pistol grip. It carried a thirty-round magazine. He hid it under his tunic and stepped out the door, pressing himself against the wall.

The gambler played his last card. "Best offer you'll get all day," Rockewicz said. "Take me as hostage."

"You?"

"Right. Come out of that room now, you and your friend, shove a gun in my ribs and a grenade in my mouth, and take me. You got yourself the best hospital director in the city, S. Rockewicz."

Trask hesitated. Rashid was shaking his head. He was furious with Trask for delaying. Olmedo had warned them about Rockewicz. Trask's head snapped backward from his neck in short, spastic movements. The director was unnerving him.

"Tell him no," Rashid said.

"I can see you're considering it," Steve said. "John, I'm your best insurance. Dress me in greens, tie me up, anything. I'll go instead of anyone in there."

Rockewicz found himself soaked in sweat. His hands were icy, the hairs on his neck itched. It was like being in the landing craft approaching Tarawa. Wanting to crap, pee, vomit. The hole widening in his gut, water flooding his eyes, all the while trying to look cool in front of his teen-age Marines. Never again, he had told himself, never play hero again. And here he was, risking his size seventeen neck. If he got out of it, carried off the bluff, Wanda would never forgive him. Probably manage to blame it on

Martha Lake or Bev Motzkin. Wanda was no friend of physicians' wives; she considered them a snooty bunch.

"I don't have a gun, nothing," Rockewicz said. "You can blast me any time you want. I'm the perfect hostage. They can't run the hospital without me. I got all the keys, John. And I'll go anywhere with you guys."

To his right, out of the corner of his eye, he saw Lief and another agent inch out of the chief nurse's room. He waved an arm at them to get back. They had their police specials out, and, in spite of their boss's warnings to avoid firing, they seemed ready to pull triggers. He waved again. Lief moved back. But part of his white coat could still be seen.

"Rockewicz," Trask said finally, "no deal."

"Why? Nobody'll shoot if you have me. You can come out this second. Or I'll come in. Tie me up, gag me, walk me out to the ambulance. I'll show you all the shortcuts."

"Start cleaning up," Lake said to his assistants.

Olmedo, the carbine under his green shirt, walked into the corridor. Tense, wary, he did not tie the yellow mask over his mouth. When he opened the OR in a few minutes to help Trask and Rashid with the hostages, he would hide his face.

Glued to the green tiles, he padded along the hall and stopped at the right angle. He poked his head out a fraction. He saw Rockewicz standing at the flimsy barricade. The director's head was close to the blocked door. He had shoved aside a filing cabinet. He was shouting at Trask, offering himself as a hostage.

Olmedo weighed his options. For a fragmented moment, he found his revolutionary ideals in conflict with certain observations and judgments he had made at the hospital. Rockewicz was no oppressor, no police torturer. He was a clever technician, sympathetic to the poor. *Must he die?* What profit in killing such a man? Not for the first time Olmedo reflected that they seemed to be killing the wrong people.

He squinted at Rockewicz. Not an easy shot. But the carbine, on automatic, could spray bullets all over the corridor. Just one would bring him down.

There was no further response to his pleas. Rockewicz felt his knees wobble. He heard steps, movements, inside the OR. Trask moving out of the line of fire?

"John? You still there?"

There was no answer. Rockewicz could hear Licata's voice, then the sound of a woman weeping. The Filipino girl.

"John, don't turn me down."

Inside the OR, high in the gallery, Rashid raised his carbine and fired a round at the door. It cracked across the table, over Tench's body, lodging in the metal below the blind windows. The door shivered.

"Son of a bitch," Rockewicz said. He jumped aside and flattened himself against the wall.

Lief and his aide were running toward him. Both were ready to fire.

"Beat it," Rockewicz shouted.

A second shot pinged against the door.

Rashid was aiming the carbine straight ahead. He held the wire stock in the crook of his shoulder, sighted down the barrel as if on a firing range. He was ready to empty the magazine, but Trask held up his hand: enough.

"No one is hurt," Trask shouted. "Those were warnings. We're coming out in a few minutes and we'll shoot anyone out there."

When Olmedo heard the shots, he drew his carbine from under his tunic and turned the corner, exposing just enough of his body so that he could fire.

He saw Rockewicz hugging the wall. An easy target, the vast white shirt an invitation. Two men in white coats were running toward him. Each carried a revolver. Police. So it was an ambush. All of Rockewicz's gentle words, his offers, his pleadings, his bargaining, added up to a man of infinite cunning and deceit.

But now that he had all three of them in his sights—what should he do? Olmedo was supposed to cover the outside area, intercept any attempt to storm the room, die if necessary, to convince the police that they were in earnest about their mission.

But the shooting had stopped. There had been two shots, apparently from inside the room. Now the three men—the hospital director and the agents—seemed hesitant, pressing against the wall out of range of Rashid's weapon. Olmedo was puzzled.

An overhead light glinted on the barrel of Olmedo's weapon. The tip protruded around the blind corner.

"Someone's down there," Lief said. "That's a gun."

"He claimed they had people outside," Rockewicz said.

Lief hesitated. It would be best to warn the man first. They did not want any more shooting. "You!" he called. "Stay where you are! We don't want to hit anyone. We're letting them out in a few minutes."

Olmedo inched forward.

Lief fired twice. The bullets skidded and ricocheted in the corridor. Chunks of green tile flew from the walls, leaving white gouges.

Olmedo dropped to one knee and raised the carbine. He quickly fired two rounds toward the OR, but he was barely able to aim. The shots were nowhere near target.

"Hold it," Lief cried again. "Can you hear me?"

Olmedo pulled back.

Musgrave pushed Reinhold down the hallway. They had hidden in an alcove for a few moments. At the sound of Rashid's first shot, Reinhold told the orderly to move him out. Then he heard the second shot, shouts, and sounds of men running.

"Move it," Reinhold said. "Fast!"

Musgrave maneuvered the stretcher down the hallway.

Musgrave was the first to see Olmedo. He knew Olmedo well. A friendly little guy. They used to kid about life in the islands. Sounded educated, smarter than most of the other PR's.

"Something wrong here, mon," he whispered to Reinhold.

Reinhold raised his head a few inches. To his astonishment, he saw a slender man in a green suit at the corner of the two corridors. He was holding an M2 carbine. Reinhold knew the weapon well. A batch had been stolen from an Army reserve unit a few months ago. The things were showing up everywhere—bank heists, stickups.

His immediate reaction was that the man was one of Stade's FBI men in hospital clothing, securing the hallway. Then he saw the man level the carbine and pump off shots.

"Who the fuck is that?" he asked Musgrave. They were thirty feet away.

"Olmedo. Orderly."

Reinhold's mind spun. "Orderly? You sure?"

"He's in surgery. Works here."

He worked there. He was armed. John had boasted that he had people all over the hospital. Here was one of them.

Olmedo was on one knee, aiming.

"Freeze!" Reinhold shouted. "You're covered!" He yelled at Musgrave. "Push me hard and dive!"

The orderly shoved the stretcher. It rolled noiselessly on greased wheels.

Olmedo spun around. His starved yellow face seemed calm, as if he had come to some kind of ultimate decision.

He saw the stretcher rolling toward him. A slender naked man, wrapped in a sheet, was rising to a sitting position. It seemed wonderfully absurd. And why was Musgrave, the black man from Baggs's team, scrambling away?

The illogic stunned him for a moment. The thin man on the stretcher was leveling a weapon at him. Olmedo raised the carbine.

Rolling silently, bracing himself on his left elbow, firing with his right hand, Reinhold squeezed off three shots into Olmedo's astonished face.

The force of the hollow-nosed bullets slammed Olmedo into

the wall. The carbine remained clenched in his hands, unfired. He appeared for a moment to be nailed to the green tiles by the mutilating power of the .357 rounds. Expanding as they struck his forehead, his nose, his cheek, they shattered skin and bone, brain, eye, skull.

Shoeless, half naked, Reinhold vaulted from the moving stretcher and ran to the dead man. There was nothing left of Olmedo's face.

The chief peered around the corner. Lief and another agent, crouching against the tiles, were hurrying toward him.

"It's me, Reinhold. I got one of the germs."

Inside the operating room, Trask and Rashid heard the shots. They assumed they were about to be attacked.

"Mistake, John," Rockewicz shouted. "Shooting's over. I got your message. Don't shoot again. You win. Do what you want, but don't hurt anyone. I'm getting out of here. The cops got nervous when you tried to wing me. Truce. John?"

"I will fire again," Rashid cried.

"Hold it," Trask said. "Let him answer. Rockewicz, are you leaving now?"

"Sure, sure, John. The offer stands. Me instead of anyone in the room. I promise you, nobody gets hurt if you play fair."

Trask walked to the door. He lifted the edge of the cardboard blind and peered into the corridor. The director was gone. He could not see down the hallway. There were voices outside, movements, but they were retreating down the hall.

"Is it all right?" Rashid asked.

"They've gone. They know they have to let us out."

Rashid grinned. The weapons. The power of death. That was all that mattered.

6

Lake looked at the wall clock: 11:55. He stepped back from the table and asked Flor to wipe his forehead. He wondered how long he could hold his people together. The shooting had almost destroyed them: Flor weeping, Sally shuddering, ducking every few minutes, Motzkin limping around dazedly.

"All right, everyone stay with it," Lake said. He put all the strength he could muster into his voice.

Licata began to cauterize vessels in the chest wall. Mihrab put sutures in the femoral artery. They would soon be able to close the incision. The heart pumped strongly. Bradycardia had cleared up without the need for medication.

"Are you finished?" Trask asked. He was at the doors, calmer now.

"I am," Lake said. "But there's still work for the others. Pacemaker. Drains. His breastbone has to be wired together."

"He's in good shape?"

Lake breathed deeply. "If you're thinking of taking him out of here. . . ."

"We might."

"Impossible. He'd be dead in half an hour."

"Not if we took the great Eric Lake along to look after him. And some of the famous Lake team."

Lake watched Licata working on the chest wall. He realized, now that the crisis of surgery had ended, that he was dreadfully frightened. When Trask had walked into his office a few hours ago and pointed the gun at him, he had been confused, angry, resentful. Complete immersion in his work had forestalled fear. But now he understood clearly what was to come. These visionaries, these world changers, would surely take him. Nobody was innocent, Trask insisted. Least of all surgeons with six-figure earnings.

"Dr. Lake," Trask said, "stand next to the sink. Right here." Trask pointed to the scrub room basin with his gun.

"You bastards," Licata shouted. "Leave him alone. I'll go."

"I said *Dr. Lake*. Now."

Lake stepped back from the table. "Jack, take over. Everything seems to be in order. The usual procedure."

Loud popping noises had broken through the anesthetic fog that smothered Walker Tench, the thick cloud of Demerol, nitrous oxide, pain-killers, and sleep inducers. The noises exploded inside his numbed brain, sounds from nowhere. Then they were softer, more distant.

Tench would remember nothing when he awakened. But now, in the last hours of his surgical ordeal, sensations slipped through the thinning wall of anesthesia. Images long forgotten and to be forgotten again colored his brain—a drunken weekend in Atlantic City. A shooting gallery on the boardwalk. Metal ducks riding by, pinging as the 22s struck them. And later, he and some of his "white-shoe" classmates shacking up with whores in a hotel suite. A blond prostitute in lavender brassiere and garter belt. He was twenty-one. The pictures shivered, vanished, and an idea cracked the mosaic of images. My suffering heart, my offending prick. He had experienced his first pain during intercourse a half year ago. How would it be the next time out?

Rockewicz, Lief, and a half dozen agents raced down the corridor where Olmedo had fallen.

"Get him out," Steve said. "I don't want anyone to see him."

Musgrave and Reinhold loaded the corpse on the stretcher and covered it. They wheeled it out by way of the recovery room. The nurses cringed and whispered.

"It's okay," Rockewicz said. "A little accident."

In the outer hall he grabbed Reinhold's bare shoulders. "What the hell did you do? Who was it?"

"Olmedo, Mr. Rockewicz," Musgrave said. "The mon had that big gun in his hand." He indicated the M2. Reinhold was holding it by the pistol grip.

"Some orderly," Reinhold mocked. "The bastard was with them. He was their lookout." He glared at Lief. "Now tell me he's with the Bureau."

Lief was on the handy-talky with Stade, reporting the killing.

"Those hollow-nose bullets do a job," one of the agents said.

"He hasn't any face left." He was not shocked, just professionally interested.

"Tough," Reinhold said. He was putting his shoes on. "We got one of them. I got one, anyway. Who's going in with me?" He pointed to Lief. "Ask your boss. Tell him I'll be the point man."

Lief was holding his hand up. "No way. The helicopter's arriving with the money. We're going along with them. This time, chief, you stay with us."

"Candy-ass cops," Reinhold sneered.

"Easy, George," Rockewicz said. "You earned your medal." He could not look at Olmedo's ravaged face.

Reinhold buttoned his shirt. He was inserting rounds into the .357. "I'm gonna use them on those germs," he said. "So fast they won't know they're being blown apart."

"No, you're not," Lief said. "That's an order. You violate it, I'll place you under arrest."

"Calm down, George," Steve said. He turned to Lief. "We can put the body in the morgue. Jesus, Olmedo! I can't believe it."

"You better believe it," Reinhold said. He pointed at Aaron Musgrave. "There's my witness. The scumbag was on one knee, aiming the piece at you people."

"I'll take the carbine," Lief said. He held his hand out. "It's a federal case chief, and it's evidence. So's your Magnum."

Reinhold surrendered the M2, but defiantly jammed the handgun into his holster. "Not till we're finished."

"Okay." Lief smiled. "Mr. Rockewicz, Mr. Stade would like you downstairs."

Stade needed no convincing that the orderly was part of the gang. He decided not to inform Trask. "Let him sweat it out," he told Steve.

"He may be waiting for him," Rockewicz said. "Is that a good idea?"

"When he doesn't show, he'll move out anyway, less one gun. He'll have to figure that either we've caught the man, killed him, or he's turned yellow."

"Maybe he'll decide to shoot someone," Reinhold said. Uninvited, he had run down the two flights with Steve. "Figures if we got one of his, he'll knock off one of ours."

"All the more reason for letting him operate blind," Stade said. He looked at his watch. "Chopper's landed. My men will be bringing down the valises any minute."

Martha Lake joined them. "I don't understand. . . . You're just letting them go?"

"We have to run that risk," Stade said.

"But aren't you going to bargain for those people in there? I heard what Mr. Reinhold said about their shooting someone in revenge for their man who was killed. My husband is in that room."

Rockewicz took her hand. "Martha, I told them I'd go. I asked them to free everyone else. They wouldn't buy it."

Cardone got up and walked toward them. "Mrs. Lake, even when they do take hostages, these activists go out of their way to see they aren't harmed. So long as they're not threatened."

"You can afford to be confident, Mr. Cardone. Mr. Tench has been operated on, and now it looks as if he's out of danger, thanks to my husband. It's always like that with the Walker Tenches of the world, isn't it? They manage to escape. And others pay the price."

"I am sorry you see it that way."

"How else am I to see it? Those insane people came to threaten him and take his money, and bystanders like my husband die for it." She turned to Stade. "I am not satisfied that you're doing enough to save Eric. The concern here all along has been for getting Walker Tench out. What kind of offers can we make for Eric's life?"

Rockewicz tried to touch her again. She took her hand away.

"Would Tench Industries offer another ten million dollars for Eric Lake?" Martha asked Cardone.

"Of course."

"But Martha," Rockewicz said, "they're going to take hostages, we know that. It's too late. They wouldn't take ten million dollars for each one of our people. Because they know that without them they'd be dead ducks the moment they appeared."

"I understand, Steve. And so does Mr. Cardone. That's why he said yes to the second ten million for Eric so easily. He knew it wouldn't happen; he wouldn't have to go to his board for it. Isn't that so, Mr. Cardone? Isn't it?"

Cardone had no ready answer. "If you see it that way, Mrs. Lake, I couldn't persuade you otherwise."

"It might not be Eric," Steve said. "They take too many people, they'll be in each other's way. They might take Alan, or one of the nurses. Christ, it's no picnic, whoever goes. But they don't gain a thing by killing anyone. Besides, Stade says there will be no shooting. They'll be allowed to go wherever it is they're planning. Right?"

"My word of honor," Stade said. He did not tell her that in his last conversation with Washington, the Attorney General, raging at the FBI director, had ordered no more concessions to the gunmen. "The government doesn't pay blood money." This was not a government case. Tench was a private individual. Tench Industries made its own rules on the payment of ransoms. "Think again," the Attorney General warned. "We don't want any precedents set."

Martha Lake walked to the window and wept silently, not bothering with a handkerchief. Cardone started toward her, stopped, said nothing. Stade nodded at Rockewicz and Harris. They left the office. From a higher floor they would be able to observe the courtyard and oversee the positioning of the sniper teams.

7

Trask listened for Olmedo. It was thirty seconds past the agreed upon time when Olmedo was to thrust aside the barricade.

Rashid caught his eye. "What is it, John?"

"Come here."

Lake had been ordered to stand with his face to the wall in the scrub room.

"Tape his hands," Trask said to Rashid. He took the carbine from him.

Motzkin was staring at the EKG monitor. A jagged yellow tracing danced across the scope. "Eric . . . he's showing something."

Lake turned to Trask. "I have to look at the EKG."

Rashid was yanking adhesive tape around the surgeon's wrists, locking them securely behind his back.

"I said I have to look at the monitor."

Trask pulled his mask down. He seemed to be short of breath. He walked to the door, listened. No sign of Olmedo.

"Let him look at it," Trask said. His voice was clotted. He was rigid, mechanical in his movements.

Rashid shoved Lake toward Motzkin. The surgeon studied the EKG. "He's got an SA nodal block."

"We didn't jab him," Licata said. "No nerve damage, I'm sure."

"Start pacing him," Lake said. "We handled his heart a lot, Jack. You can give them a block just from that."

Motzkin nodded. The impulses on the oscilloscope were slow. The intervals were too long.

"He'll come out of it," Lake said. "Did he get his protamine? We don't want to lose the patient because his blood wouldn't clot."

"Yes, Eric." Motzkin stumbled to his feet. The maimed toe was angry with pain whenever it touched the floor.

"Get back here, Lake," Trask said. "We're leaving."

"I'll finish my job first. Pace him again, Alan."

The tracings on the scope assumed a more rapid and regular character.

"That's better," Lake said. "I knew his heart was sound."

Trask nodded at Rashid and pointed to the ceiling. The Arab fired a round.

"The next shot will be at one of you," Trask said.

"What the hell?" Licata protested. "We have to finish—"

"Get against the wall, all of you."

Sally helped Flor. Mihrab came over and put his arm around the Filipino nurse.

"Face away from us," Trask said. "Lake, come here."

"Don't do it, Trask," Licata called. "You won't gain a thing. Take your money and go."

Trask was whispering with Rashid. Their green-capped heads were close.

There was a hitch of some kind, Licata sensed. He muttered out of the side of his mouth to Motzkin, "Something got screwed up for them outside."

"I hope it doesn't make them reckless."

"Motzkin, come over here," Trask said.

"Me?"

"Yes, you. Fast."

"Why? What do you want from me?"

Licata turned around. "He's wounded. He's got a bum foot. Take me instead."

"Get back," Rashid warned.

Licata stared at Rashid's trousers. The dark wet circle around his crotch had widened, a spreading stain on the pale green. "You turd," Licata said. "You lousy cowardly turd. You peed in your pants. Mihrab, tell it to him in Arabic if he doesn't understand."

Mihrab shook his head; he was overcome with shame and fear.

Motzkin limped away from the wall. "It's all right, Jack," he said. "I can manage."

Rashid shoved him around rudely. The Arab taped his hands, yanking at the adhesive, twisting it around the anesthesiologist's wrists and fingers.

"Flor, will you stop crying?" Lake called. He and Motzkin were standing shoulder to shoulder in the scrub room.

"I am sorry, doctor."

"Jack, after we go, get Burns or one of the other residents down here. Get some of Jimmy's people in to help out."

"Don't worry about us, Eric."

Trask walked to the doors and opened them. He peered out. There was no sign of Carlos Olmedo. It was silent and deserted in the corridor.

When he spoke to Rashid again, his voice shook. He did not try to disguise his words. "He won't be here," Trask said.

"Ah, waiting for a buddy," Licata said.

"A third?" Trask asked the Arab. "Now?"

Rashid nodded at the people against the wall. "It does not matter. Any one."

Lake was ignoring them. "Jack? You hear me?"

"Yes, Eric."

"Get blood-gas tests immediately. Keep an eye on his urinary output and get a serum potasseum. If Tench wakes up and wants to know what happened to me, tell him I'm on an emergency case. I'll see him as soon as I can."

Trask and Rashid were whispering, nodding at the people against the wall.

Lake went on, "Leave the pericardium open. Evans will come by when he's in the recovery room."

Mihrab shivered. They were selecting their third hostage the way a housewife would pick a carp from a tank in the market in Cairo. Unbelievable. Why one and not the others? He could guess why they had not taken Jack Licata. They saw he was strong and hot-blooded and could be dangerous. And perhaps some shred of civility would prevent his kinsman from taking a woman. And Gamel Mihrab, M.D.? He should have volunteered. Rashid and he—the same people. But he had stood silent. Had anyone thought less of him for it?

"I shall go," Mihrab said. "It is not fair. Dr. Motzkin is wounded. Please." He looked at Rashid. *"Rafik,* I'm of your blood."

Rashid ignored him.

"All right," Trask said. "You. At the end." He pointed to Cho.

"Me?" the Korean asked.

"Yes. Come here."

"But I'm new. I just come work today."

Rashid yanked him by the arm and dragged him to the scrub room.

"Turn," Rashid said.

Then he taped the third hostage's hands.

8

Rockewicz had taken Stade and his men on a tour of the possible escape routes. There was a flight of stairs to the left of the main entrance to surgery. It led to the basement, past the morgue, the postmortem laboratory, and the old classroom, to the loading platform.

"If there's only two of them," Stade said, "they'll have trouble handling four valises and keeping the hostages covered." He was looking at the loading platform.

"They'll have help," Lief said. "They've been bragging about all the hidden men they have."

Stade studied doorways, elevators, stairways. He had a hundred men around the courtyard, some high, some low, snipers using Lyman sights on Winchester rifles. From the maternity wing, a man could cover the loading platform. Another stationed in the kidney research unit had a clear shot at the ambulance. But to all of them it was made clear that only Stade should give the order to fire. Each sniper was accompanied by a second agent, awaiting orders on a handy-talky.

Back in the office, forced to tolerate a gloating Reinhold, Stade repeated his instruction. "The safety of hostages is our first priority," he told the men. "We will be in a position to observe the withdrawal. Pursuit will be conducted in the same way. Covertly, with no danger to the hostages."

"Pursuit?" Rockewicz asked.

"Don't ask me any more about it."

Reinhold walked over to the desk. "What about me? What about my men? You closing us out?"

"Just for the time being."

"But I got one of them. You got nothing."

"You did a good job, chief. But you were lucky. Inside that operating room you might have gotten everyone killed."

An agent had been studying Olmedo's personnel file. "Says he's a Cuban," the agent said. "Age twenty-seven, came here six months ago, no family, lives in New York."

"Does it say what weapons he qualified with?" Reinhold asked.

". . . Unconfirmed reports that a second man has been killed in the kidnap-siege of an operating room at City General Hospital, where armed gunmen are holding millionaire Walker Tench for ransom. . . ."

The director of the methadone clinic turned the radio up.

Who was it? Fiona wondered. Damn them, why did they not give the name? Had Rashid been killed? Trask? She was operating blindly. In minutes she would walk down the steps across the courtyard.

Someone had driven the ambulance into the middle of the yard. It was blockish, vanlike, painted orange and white. It had three flashers on the roof and sirens front and rear. There were red crosses on the rear windows. Hooks claimed he had driven similar vans. "I drive anything," he bragged. "Yeah, and shoot from the window, pickin' off slopes the same time."

Two men were standing to one side of the ambulance. They seemed to be talking about it, pointing to the chassis. They looked concerned. Then they returned to the garage.

"Jesus, what a mess," the director, Fat, said. "Another guy killed. I hope it's one of those bastards."

Fiona was the only person left in the clinic. She had moved the duffel bag and the oblong package near the front door. The director had asked her to leave, but she pleaded dizziness. He gave her a dose of methadone in a paper cup. When he turned away, she'd emptied it into a wastebasket.

Her eyes searched the courtyard for Hooks. His broad-shouldered olive-drab figure would be unmistakable. There were still a few minutes left.

"Why in hell are they leaving the ambulance out there?" Fat asked. "I get it. I bet those people are gonna use it for something. Or maybe they're laying a trap for them."

Fiona wondered if he might be right. "Trap?"

"I dunno. If it was me, I'd blow the whole thing up. Booby-trap it, send them up in smoke. Or you could hide cops in it and blast them when they come in."

She gauged the distance from the clinic to the loading dock to be about forty yards. The platform was empty except for some battered trash cans. A short walk. She could drop the packages in the ambulance, help Hooks with the valises, coordinate their moves with the arrival of Rashid, Trask and Olmedo.

She stood at the door and waited. Her eye caught a silhouette on a roof opposite the clinic. It was a man holding a pole. No. A rifle. He had come into view momentarily, then disappeared. Now she saw him again. A brimmed hat, a short coat. She thought it was an odd getup for a sniper—so neat, so middle class.

She wrestled with her packages, slung the bag on her shoulder, her left hand holding the oblong box.

"Hey, you better stay here. Something's going on out there. There's orders to stay out of the courtyard."

"I'll be all right."

Across the inner court, the doors of the loading platform opened. Four men in business suits walked out. Each carried a green plaid bag. They walked to the edge of the dock and set them down, neatly aligned, identical, forming a single green block.

Trask shoved Motzkin with his gun. "Move. The three of you face the door. In single file. Motzkin first, then Cho, then Lake."

Lake asked, "Can the others return to the patient?"

"As soon as we leave."

"We'll be okay, Eric," Licata said.

"Look . . . can't we do this another way?" Motzkin asked. "You think I'm not sympathetic—"

"Alan, don't start debating with him," Lake cut him off.

Rashid opened the double doors. He kicked at a stretcher, shoved a file cabinet. Then he looked into the hallway. When he turned, his eyes were filmy. "I don't see him."

"Damn," Trask said. "Damn those bastards." He was trembling. "We . . . we . . ."

Lake and Motzkin stood quietly, waiting.

"It's too late to worry," Rashid said. "He is dead, or he betrayed us."

"Anyone but Carlos," Trask said. "Anyone but him."

Lake said suddenly, "Let's go—if we're going."

"Goddamn it, wait," Trask said. He was choking, trying to suppress a disabling anger. He left Rashid guarding the men in the scrub room, took the phone and dialed Rockewicz's number.

Lief answered.

"Where's Stade? Where's Rockewicz?" he shouted. "You bastards. What did you do with Carlos? Where is he?"

"I don't know what you're talking about. John, there's still time to come out unarmed. No one will be hurt."

"You know what I mean. Where is he? Don't believe anything he tells you. He's a liar. He's pathological. What did you do? Bribe him? Put a police spy on him?"

"John, who is Carlos?" Lief asked. "What's it all about?"

"You murderers. Don't try anything when we leave. You'll have dead doctors on your hands. We'll go, but so will they."

Rashid called to him. "We will be off schedule. The others will be waiting. Maybe Carlos had to change his plan. He will be at the ambulance."

Trask put the phone down.

Licata watched, fascinated. He said to Mihrab, "They had a guy outside—"

Trask pointed the gun at Licata. "Maybe I'll even things up."

Licata said, "I told Dr. Mihrab that Tench's heart needs pacing. You object to that?"

"Carlos," Motzkin said. "Isn't that Olmedo's name? The Puerto Rican?" He looked at Lake.

"I don't know, Alan." He wished Motzkin would shut up.

Rashid opened the doors again. He braced each with a table.

Trask touched Lake with the gun. "Lake, you will walk abreast of me. The gun will be in your side. Cho, you walk behind Lake. Motzkin, you walk next to Rashid. His gun will be in your side. We will stay close together. Keep masks and caps on. One move by any of you and we start firing."

"Stay loose, Eric, Alan," Licata called. "You guys will be all right."

Trask shouted at Licata, "As soon as we leave, call them. Just tell them we have left the operating room."

From a tenth-floor window, Stade, Rockewicz, and Cardone had a view of the inner parking area. They could see the overpass connecting the wings, under which the road led to Kennedy Boulevard. Across from them, at ground level, was the methadone clinic and the garage. Opposite it was the old loading dock.

The orange-and-white ambulance had been moved into the center of the court. Several dozen cars had been removed, towed away when the owners could not be located.

There were snipers on the tenth floor, at either side of the windows where Stade had posted himself. There were other men on the fifth floor setbacks and at ground level.

"Snowing," Steve said. "Is that good or bad?"

"Good for us. They won't be able to hit high speeds, at least not without risking a crash."

"Did I hear you talk about pursuit?" Cardone asked.

"Of course, but they won't know it. You don't think we're going to let them have it all their way?"

"But Mr. Tench . . . Would they dare wheel him out, in this cold weather, the operation unfinished? Maybe his chest is still open?"

"Human body is tough," Rockewicz said. He understood Martha Lake now. Yes, let them have Tench. But not Lake, or Motzkin, or any of his people. She was right. The Tenches of the world had it their way. Money created luck, breaks, winners. Everyone else paid their dues. Not a bad man, Tench. But hardly a great man like Eric Lake. Rockewicz felt no shred of sympathy for the armed lunatics willing to bomb and kill to bring about a new society, but he resented the way the Tenches always managed to get off the hook.

Below they could see Stade's agents placing the valises on the platform.

"What was the last count?" Stade asked.

"About seven million dollars," Cardone said. "They're getting the rest together. I'll have to keep in touch with these people somehow."

"That would buy a lot of Demerol," Steve said moodily. He'd get his people back. Jimmy Baggs was dead, but the others would make it. Out of the horror, he'd sneak some winnings. He wasn't Stephen Aloysius Rockewicz for nothing, organizer of the Polish Falcons Eyrie, veteran of the Second Marine Division, an honors graduate of Penn State—the human baling wire, glue and Scotch tape that held this goddamn wonderful dump of a hospital together.

A notion dazzled him as they waited in silence. He would put the bite on Cardone for a memorial in Jimmy Baggs's name. A room. A lab. A wing. No, the top. A building. *The James Baggs Memorial Heart Research Center.*

"Why is that girl coming out of the clinic?" Cardone asked.

Fiona, looking tiny, lost, with her two burdens, walked down the steps and started toward the dock.

"That jerk of a director," Steve said. "I know he's dumb, but he should have kept her—"

"She's theirs," Stade said. "Trask said two people. A black man and a girl. That's the girl."

"You gotta be kidding," Rockewicz said. "She looks like a kid."

"White, small, and armed," Stade said. "That's her."

"I wonder what she has in the packages." Cardone stroked his nose. "A frail little thing like that. And she's got us all tied in knots."

"No one is to fire," Stade said into his handy-talky. "I repeat; no one is to fire."

9

Bateman Hooks had circulated in the neighborhood, three times around the block, stopping again for coffee, buying cigarettes, checking his watch. The place was full of pigs. Uniformed men, flat-faced guys in unmarked cars. He felt no fear of them.

A young black man walked by with a transistor pressed to his ear.

"What happen?" Hooks asked him. He was on a side street on his way back to the hospital.

"They kill someone else. They say two people dead."

Hooks nodded. "Who? A brother?"

"Only one. They ain't sayin' who is the other."

He could guess. That asshole Ratshit probably shot someone. Lost his cool and pumped lead into some nurse or doctor. Ratshit enjoyed it. He got his jollies watching people die.

Hooks checked his watch again. Time to move in. The wet snow would be a problem—braking, cornering, picking up speed. He walked toward the facade of the hospital, keeping his distance from the wet shivering crowd at the barricades.

He wondered about the black man who was shot dead. Baggs. A nurse said he was a good man, one of the best. If Rashid had killed him, he'd want to know more about it. Have a talk with that Ay-rab dude. Always the way. Do whitey's work, get the shit end of the stick. Like in 'Nam. Kissing white ass by shooting yellow people.

But the Ashanti boss warned him: "We stayin' with them on this one, so you stay, too, Hooks. We do our own thing soon enough, but you stay with this. You be our Main Man, then we tell Mr. Charlie go screw himself. We help them change the world, but then we do our own changing."

Hooks approached the barricade. He would not walk out on them. He had nowhere to walk. Maybe he had contempt for Trask and the Irish chick, sometimes he detested Rashid. But he could work with Carlos Olmedo. Olmedo had something. Olmedo had suffered. There was some kind of good light in Olmedo's eyes. He did not enjoy seeing people dead, even his enemies. They had talked. Hooks thought he understood Olmedo.

"Where you think you're going?" It was the young cop who had tangled with Hooks earlier.

"Into the parkin'."

"Like hell. Come on, move."

Hooks had one leg over the wooden barrier. The bag was slung on his shoulder.

"I'll knock you on your ass," the cop said. "Hey, sergeant. This guy is back."

"Don't call no sergeant," Hooks said amicably. "Call them FBI cats yonder." He pointed to the front entrance of City General. "Them pigs there with the radio. They knows me."

The officer looked at the agents.

Hooks arrogantly waved his arm. "Hey, pig. It's me. The Main Man."

One of the agents was talking on the radio. He was studying Hooks—the watch cap, the Army clothing, boots. He signaled the city policeman and called across the street. "It's all right. Let him through."

"You damn said it, man."

Hooks climbed over the barrier and walked across the street. A few members of the crowd looked at him curiously.

"What the fuck is going on?" the young cop asked.

The sergeant sucked his teeth. "Beats me. Maybe the spade is with the Bureau. They use a lot of them now."

"Everything's screwed up."

Hooks half heard them. He swaggered into the driveway, walking at a slow pace. You wants to shoot my black ass, baby, do it now. Trask swore they would not touch him. Not with some of their rich doctors with grenades shoved up their asses. No way. He looked at the rising towers of the hospital and thought of the strange way everything came around if you waited long enough. He had been born here, screaming, shitting, unwanted. Ahead of him he saw the courtyard and the big ambulance. You come in shit and you go out shit.

"I can't believe she's one of them," Cardone said. "She looks about sixteen."

"Wouldn't it be something if she was a free-lance crook from the clinic?" Rockewicz said. "Walks off with their loot. Seven million bucks."

"I doubt it," the FBI man said. "They described her—the tan coat."

At the side door of the ambulance, Fiona stopped. She opened it and deposited the long box and the sack. Then she continued toward the platform.

A half dozen snipers had her small head in the cross hairs of their telescopic sights.

Stade repeated, "No one is to fire."

At the dock, Fiona picked up two of the valises, saw Hooks approaching, and started back to the ambulance.

"What's the range of that radio in the ambulance?" Stade asked.

"Oh, seven, eight miles." Rockewicz frowned. "When you can hear it. It isn't the world's best system."

Stade clucked. "We'll get them long before they're seven miles away."

The instant Trask and Rashid marched their hostages out of the operating room, Licata dialed Rockewicz's office. He got the assistant director, Buttram.

"They're on their way, Dave."

An agent picked up an extension phone and listened.

"Who'd they take?" Buttram asked.

"Eric."

"Jesus. Anyone else?"

"Alan. And Alan's assistant, some Korean kid."

"Three?" The agent broke in. "And how many of them?"

"Two. The same two who were here all the time. The skinny guy Trask, and the Arab."

"No one else hurt?" Buttram asked.

"No, we're okay. Operation went fine. Tench is in good shape. I need some help. Get me one of the senior residents—Burns if he's free. And a gas-passer. And an assistant for him. Some people from Jimmy's team. Musgrave is around. I saw him this morning."

The agent interrupted again. "How are they armed?"

Licata paused. "The Arab's got what looks like a carbine. It's an automatic. He did all the shooting in here. Shot Baggs in the back. The tall guy has a handgun, maybe a thirty-eight. They've got grenades."

"Anything else you remember?" the agent asked.

"They started acting funny at the end. As if they were waiting for someone to join them."

"They have a long wait." The agent hung up.

Licata kept Buttram on. He wanted Baggs's body removed, the labs alerted, recovery room ready to receive Tench in an hour.

"The big bastard slept through it all," the chief resident said. "The world comes apart at the seams and Mr. Walker Tench the Third is under the whole time."

"How was Eric?"

"The old master. Operating with two guns on him. . . . Move on those people, will you, Dave? See if Abe Gilad is in. Next to Alan, he's the best anesthesiologist we have."

Buttram relayed Licata's requests to Estelle LeBlanc. Then he saw Martha Lake standing in the doorway. "I heard," she said.

"I'm sorry, Mrs. Lake. They have Dr. Lake. They won't dare hurt him."

"Stop saying things to make me feel better!"

Stade looked up. "They have their money, Mrs. Lake. Once they feel they can get away, they'll turn the hostages loose. It isn't as if they're holed up in an embassy or an office building. They have to stay in motion. Three extra people become a burden."

"I don't know why I should believe you," Martha said. "I've heard nothing but optimistic predictions—and now the worst has happened."

"Not the worst, Mrs Lake," Stade said.

"No—" her voice broke. "Not yet."

The hand radio crackled. "They've picked up the money," the agent said. "A girl and a black man. They're in the ambulance."

"Where is my husband?" Martha asked.

"The gunmen and the hostages are on their way down. They should be leaving in a few minutes."

Buttram saw her put her hands to her forehead. She wavered for a moment. He got up from the desk. "Are you all right, Mrs. Lake? I'm sorry."

He went to her. She backed away. "I'm all right. *Just don't touch me.*"

10

The five men, three with their hands taped behind their backs, walked out of the doors of surgery. They walked past the sign that read AUTHORIZED PERSONNEL ONLY and through the shabby waiting room.

Trask, his .38 jammed into Lake's ribs, walked first. He looked into a storage room. A man in a blue windbreaker was standing just inside the door. He stared at them but made no move.

"Keep walking," Trask said. "Nobody talk."

The man in the windbreaker called after him. "None of us is armed. You can surrender at any point from here to the ambulance. You won't be shot at. You will have all your rights."

Trask ignored him. He was breathing noisily. Carlos Olmedo had been a crucial part of the plan. Olmedo knew the hospital.

"Which is the fastest way down?" Trask asked.

Lake said, "Take a right and then the first flight of stairs on your right."

A nurse pushing a wheelchair saw the procession. She darted into a room. At the windows of the ICU, a half dozen people stared.

Trask opened the door to the stairs. He held it open until all five were inside. Then he returned to the head of the procession.

"Could you walk a little slower?" Motzkin asked. "I have this sore foot."

Rashid barely heard him. He was sweating. His eyes were wide, alert.

Motzkin stumbled as he started down, bumping the banister.

"I said slow down," the anesthesiologist cried. "You people are your own worst enemies."

On the stairs, Cho turned his dazed eyes around to face Rashid. "Why are you taking me? I'm no good to you."

Rashid jabbed him with the carbine. "Move. No one will be hurt if the police stay away."

Trask stopped at the first floor. The stairwell was dark and dirty.

"The platform is one more flight down," Rashid said.

"Is it?" Trask asked. He had been depending on Olmedo to take them out.

"Yes," Lake said. "But you can get out here and walk through the cafeteria and the kitchen, then down a flight. It doesn't matter. There are police all over the place."

Trask opened the door. Outside they could see a wide doorway leading to the cafeteria. A man in a dark suit ducked away as he saw Trask. "Alongside me, Lake," Trask said. "Same order. Cho between us, Motzkin and Rashid at the rear. Remember, the carbine is an automatic. He can kill everyone in seconds."

"Walk closer," Rashid said. "John, do not get too far ahead. They would like to separate us."

Trask led them into the cafeteria. A woman screamed. A tray clattered to the floor.

"Behind the counter," Lake directed. He was too weary to be frightened. "Through the doors and all the way through the kitchen, and then down the rear steps."

Hooks, entering the courtyard, could see Fiona lifting two of the valises from the platform. Beyond her he could see the ambulance. It was a Chevyvan 20. He would drive the wheels off it.

"Take it, baby," he said. Fiona was a gutsy chick. No good in bed, didn't like to ball, hard to turn on. But she wasn't afraid. Her trouble was she didn't understand that her people in Ireland were niggers, that her people in the United States hated niggers more than anything in the world, and would never send a dime or a gun or a body to help them in Belfast. At least *we* got us an organization, Hooks thought.

"I am here, mother-fuckers," Hooks said. His eyes scanned the tops of the hospital buildings, the setbacks, the doorways. He sensed that a thousand eyes were on him. Gunsights. Barrels pointing. Ready to blow Bateman's head to a black mash. But they wouldn't fire. Not with Trask and Rashid and Olmedo holding guns on their doctors. He would be glad to see Olmedo.

"Hooks," Fiona said. "Help me."

"Yeah, I help you." He pulled the M2 out of the bag and raised it high. "Here come Bateman Hooks, the Mighty Avenger."

In the dispatcher's office, drivers and mechanics watched Hooks's performance. Fury boiled in them. They were more enraged with the police, the FBI, and the hospital authorities than they were with the Negro. "Goddamn Rockewicz," one of them said. "That's what he gets for sucking around spades."

"Someone oughta shoot that black bastard right in his fucking head."

"Maybe they will. When the lead starts flying, hit the deck. Eight to five they blow his brains out."

Hooks took a valise from the dock. Fiona, having placed two

in the ambulance, returned, picked up the last, and walked with him to the van.

"Where they at?" he asked.

"They will be here. Go in and start the engine. Can you work the radio?"

"I do it all, baby. And you stop giving Hooks orders. This ain't dumb-ass Belfast. You keep your mouth shut from now on. The only one I wants to hear is Carlos. I tell Trask and ole Ratshit to fuck off same way."

Fiona climbed in the rear of the ambulance, leaving the door open several inches. Two stretchers were covered with gray blankets. The driver's compartment had two seats and was separated from the rear area by a sliding glass panel. Immediately behind the glass was a padded bench. There was ample room. There were phones in both the rear and front sections of the van. Metal glistened, plastic covers were spotless.

Hooks stretched. "Man, that snow feel good. Got the whole world lookin' to shoot me down, but they ain't gonna." He saw a gun barrel on one of the setbacks and sneered. Then he got into the cab and sat at the wheel.

One of the mechanics, less than thirty feet away, shouted at him. "Say your prayers, spook. They're gonna blow your head off."

"The FBI is gonna shove TNT up yer ass."

"Jungle bunny."

"Nigger bastard."

Hooks spit at them. He turned the ignition key. The engine exploded with life. He jammed his GI boot against the accelerator. It roared, full of mechanical power. The gas tank was full. The battery was on charge. Hooks shoved the watch cap forward until it almost covered his eyes. "Big mama, you sound beautiful."

Looking down on the courtyard, Stade said: "That's the second one. Just as Trask described him."

"Does he look familiar?" Cardone asked.

"No. But he's getting his picture taken. We may know who he is in an hour or two."

"They're all nuts," Rockewicz said. "Damned fools."

"Despair does strange things to people," Cardone said. He was feeling autumnal, philosophical, now that Tench was safe. Ten million dollars had bought his life. And Cardone's future. Of course it wasn't fair that two doctors and some obscure Korean were under the threat of death. But life was never fair. He would have paid twice ten million to end the dreadful business for everyone. He had said so.

The parking area was empty of people again. Snow settled on the asphalt. The girl and the black man were in the ambulance.

"You'll follow them, of course," Cardone said.

"Forever," Stade replied.

Hooks looked at the radio, the phones, the two-way communications lash-up. It was no big deal. Push this, push that. An AM/FM radio. A tape deck. Man, they went first class. He began to push buttons. Rock music blared from the radio.

"Hooks," Fiona called from the back section. "Turn that bloody thing off."

"Nah, I needs me some music."

"I said turn that off."

He ignored her. She feared and hated him more than ever. Ah, the endless complexities. He was supposed to be on her side: oppressed, hungry, victim of prejudice. Need threw them together, but it wasn't enough. Opening the first valise, hypnotized for a moment by the vision of the green bundles of American currency, she wondered if Trask's grand view of history had gaps in it. Like Hooks. Like the men in mustard-colored helmets who had mocked her that morning. If she and Trask and Rashid were the leaders, who were the followers? Che had died with a half dozen supporters around him, the peasants deaf to his call to rebellion.

Up front Hooks jerked his head back and forth to the music, his big palms beating on the steering wheel.

11

Aromas of Salisbury steak, tuna fish salad, macaroni and cheese, the inevitable institutional odors, filled the steamy air of the cafeteria. Men and women in white uniforms stopped working and stared.

"Oh, my God, it's them."

"They got Dr. Lake. Isn't that Dr. Lake?"

"And Dr. Motzkin. He's limping."

Trask waved the gun. "Stand aside. Don't get in our way. Stand aside."

Ed McFeeley, nursing his sixth free cup of coffee, sat with the bakers in a corner. He got up, slicked back his gray hair, and followed the five men. "Yellah bastards," he called after them. "Somebody stop them guys. They got Doc Lake."

"Why don't the cops do something?" a woman wailed.

The kitchen was cavernous, lofty. Huge aluminum wagons impeded Trask's progress. He looked for the exit to the stairs Lake had mentioned. McFeeley skipped a few yards behind the party.

"Somebody stop them guys," he said. "They're the radicals who shot up surgery. Somebody grab 'em. Shoot their heads off."

"Straight ahead," Lake said to Trask.

"Tell that lunatic to get away," Trask said.

The surgeon called over his shoulder. "McFeeley! Keep your distance. You're not helping us."

In her glassed-in office Miss Diener, director of food services, saw the green-gowned men pass by. She was preparing her dinner menu. Miss Diener was a slat-thin woman in a starched pink uniform. She wore her rimless glasses on a black string and had learned all she needed to know at Manhattanville College. She feared no one in the world—neither Rockewicz, nor the board of managers, nor a dishwasher who had gone berserk a month ago and threatened to slit a pastry cook's throat. Miss Diener had disarmed him.

An FBI agent in whites was in the office with her. He saw the men approaching and talked to the command post. "They're coming through," he said.

McFeeley began to yell. "Hey, Miss Diener. Them guys got no permit to cross the kitchen. They got Doc Lake."

Miss Diener got up. Her uniform crackled. She adjusted her eyeglasses. Cooks and bakers were scrambling for cover. An orderly released a cart of lunch trays and it rolled against a stove. Cups of cherry Jell-o flew against the wall like red birds.

"You men," Miss Diener said. "You men, stop at once."

"That's tellin' 'em," McFeeley crowed.

The director of food services, ignoring the pleas of the agent, strode out of the office and walked toward the intruders. The kitchen was her domain. She had thrown a city councilman out a few days ago for daring to interrogate the salad men.

"Turn around and get out," she said to Trask.

Trask waved the gun. "Stay away."

"I said get *out*. No one enters this kitchen without written authorization from the executive director."

Jigging, McFeeley clapped a hand to his gapped teeth. "Tell 'em, Miss Diener," he cackled. "Tell 'em. We ain't scared of them."

"I am telling you to get out," Miss Diener insisted. She planted herself across Trask's path. It was a narrow area, hemmed in by two of the multishelved metal carts.

The FBI man walked to the door. "Miss, let them go!"

Rashid pointed the carbine at him. "Stay there. Don't come out."

"I'm trying to get her back," the agent said. "We've got orders to let you through."

"Miss Diener, this is Dr. Lake. You'd better get out of the way."

"Absolutely not. Rules were made to be obeyed." She glared at Trask. "You made enough trouble here for one day. I run City General's food services. No one breaks my rules. You will turn around—"

Trask smashed the gun against her jaw. Astonished, she sank in slow motion. Blood trickled from her mouth. The eyeglasses tottered, fell from her nose, dangled from the black string. She was on her knees, still protesting.

"John, move on," Rashid said. "We have lost three minutes."

McFeeley danced behind them. "Lousy cowards! Afraid of a woman! The old Eighty-second Airborne woulda handled you rats! Where's the cops?"

The agent in the office talked into his radio. "They're going out."

"They comin'," Hooks said. "Trask and Ratshit and three others."

"Olmedo?"

"Can't see for sure. That him in the middle?" Hooks squinted through the wet windshield and saw that the man walking in the middle rank was not Olmedo but a stranger with his hands tied behind his back.

"So there were five of them altogether," Rockewicz said. "The two guys who were in the room, the girl, the black, and Olmedo."

"And only four now," Stade said.

They could hear the engine of the Chevyvan racing. They could see the hulking black man in the driver's seat.

"You could get two more of them right now," Cardone said. He was liberated, quick to give advice.

"And then what?" the agent asked. "We shoot them, and in a few seconds the others come out, and who knows which doctor they'll shoot first?"

The doors on the loading area opened. Five men in green came out.

"That's Eric in front," Steve said. "Alan's in the back. Christ, the guy can hardly walk. I guess that's his assistant in the middle."

"I have a line of sight on the front man," one of the snipers said.

"Orders stand," Stade said. "No one fires."

Rockewicz found his hands trembling. He had memories of a break from a California jail: desperate men on trial, walking out a white-haired judge with a shotgun taped to his neck. Someone had opened fire. He had killed three convicts. And the judge's head had been blown off.

Cardone could see the men in the dispatcher's office waving fists at the party, shouting at them. And Walker Tench—Cardone's meal ticket—lay dozing upstairs. He felt his guilt, but mildly. On the steps of the methadone clinic, a man in a sweatshirt was yelling something through cupped hands.

The girl was holding open the rear door of the ambulance.

"That's Lake going in the back. And Motzkin. And that's his assistant." Rockewicz felt as if he were strangling.

Fiona got in. Rashid was last, looking around, as if daring the snipers to shoot him now that he was detached from the hostages. Then he hopped up the step and slammed the door.

Trask climbed into the cab next to Hooks.

"As casually as a bunch of tourists going on a bus tour," Steve said.

"What now?" Cardone asked the agent in charge.

"We'll be after them."

"Will they know it?" Rockewicz asked.

"I doubt it. But they'll suspect us. We have to run some risks."

With a defiant blast, the orange-and-white ambulance skidded off the wet asphalt and lurched under the walkway. In seconds it had vanished from view.

PART SIX

1

Musgrave and another of Baggs's men, Rios, were sent to the operating room to help Licata and Mihrab finish the work on Tench.

"I cannot believe it, mon," Musgrave said. "Why Jimmy?"

The Israeli anesthesiologist, Abe Gilad, arrived to take Motzkin's place. He was a dour, brooding man who had vanished during the Yom Kippur war, then returned, more somber than ever. Gilad had been listening to the radio. Scattered Arab groups were claiming Rashid as their own, though most left-wing organizations had disowned the Wretched of the Earth. "The United Nations will give him a medal," Gilad said to a nurse as he dressed for surgery. "The General Assembly will give him a standing ovation for shooting Baggs in the back." She didn't understand what he was talking about.

Another resident in cardiac surgery, a Dubliner named Maurice Burns, arrived to help sew up Tench's chest. Minutes later Dr. Burt Evans, the chief attending physician in cardiology, joined them.

"Femoral artery is closed, Jack," Mihrab said. "Shall I remove the clamp?"

"Sure. Look at that heart go."

The surgeons stitched the incisions in Tench's left leg. Dr. Burns took the metal retractor from Tench's split sternum. The resilient bone came together. Soon they were threading metal loops through the split bone.

"How is he going?" Licata asked Gilad.

"Slow getting back, but okay. We should keep him on pacing. Is Motzkin badly hurt?"

"Lost part of his toe," Licata said.

Gilad nodded. He respected Motzkin as a medical man and had learned a great deal from him. But he'd always felt he was soft, indulged, a man who treasured his luxuries too much. Not a Jew he could really admire.

Mihrab yanked the heavy wire through Tench's sternum, looped it, drew the bone together.

The halves were united. Humpty Dumpty back together again, Licata thought. But something much bigger, more complex, than Walker Tench's heart and chest was in trouble—unstuck, unglued, not responding to treatment.

The armed crazies who had invaded the OR and killed Baggs were surely not objects of pity or sympathy. But in some imperfect way Licata, a nonpolitical man, realized that they were symptoms of an invasive disease, a pathology in the world that needed medical maintenance, perhaps a surgical solution.

"I'd like to get him off pacing," the chief resident said. "Abe, more Isuprel."

From Rockewicz's windows, the people in the director's office could see the sky darkening, heavy with a stew of rain and wet snow. It splattered against the high glass. Outside, the crowds and the police assumed an underwater appearance. Sodium lights had been turned on early. The hospital was functioning at full strength again.

"They're heading west," Harris said to Stade, as the latter entered the room.

"Are we on them?"

"As close as we can get without giving it away. Half a block back, and on parallel streets."

The speaker on Rockewicz's desk had been patched into the dispatcher's radio system, which had two-way communication with the ambulance.

Martha Lake was standing next to Rockewicz. "How did Eric look?" she asked.

"Cool. Old procedure. They'll never hurt him, Martha. He's too overwhelming."

Harris was listening to a handy-talky. "They're doing it in style. All three flashers are going. And the klaxon. These people have a sense of drama."

"No, just a plan," Stade said. "It clears the streets ahead of them. The cops know they've got hostages. Everyone else clears out of the way."

Rockewicz was stroking his golden fuzz. "How're they going to get rid of the money without attracting attention? They're crazier than I thought."

Outside, Estelle LeBlanc was sobbing. Buttram was talking heatedly to chief nurse McCarran. Orderlies had discovered Dr. Harvey Fess's body in the supply room.

"Fess is dead?" Rockewicz whispered. "Harvey? Jesus. It can't be. . . ."

Buttram sat down, shaking. "Steve, this is unbelievable. The cops think Olmedo killed him. When Harvey came around to clear everyone out, he must have stumbled on Olmedo. . . ." Buttram's eyes were wet.

Rockewicz put a hand to his forehead. "Oh, my God. I sent him down there. How did I know what would happen? I should have gone myself. Was he . . . shot?"

"Strangled, as near as they can figure."

Chief Reinhold came in. He had been out in the corridor where O'Boyle had interviewed him for the TV cameras. He was in uniform again. The Colt Magnum that had blown apart Olmedo's head was in the holster. "I should have gone in, Mr. Rockewicz. You lost a doctor because you didn't listen to me."

"Shut your goddamn mouth, chief," Steve said hoarsely.

Reinhold persisted. He looked at Martha Lake. "I could have gotten your husband out, Mrs. Lake."

"That's enough, Reinhold," Stade said. "That's all I want to hear from you."

Something in Stade's voice finally reached the chief. He backed off.

The speaker crackled. There was a sustained scratchy hum. Then they heard Trask's brittle voice. "Let me speak to the FBI man."

"This is Arnold Stade speaking."

"Listen carefully, Stade. You will not pursue us. If you do, we will kill a hostage every ten minutes, and keep one man until the end, until we feel we are safe."

"We understand. No one is pursuing."

"As soon as the money is counted, we will proceed to our escape vehicles, and we are not to be followed. When we know we're safe, we will release the last hostage."

"Understood."

There were confused sounds on the other end of the system. Trask appeared to be speaking to someone else. Once they thought they heard him say: "Wait, wait, not now."

A new voice came over the speaker. It was loud, angry. "What you do with Carlos, mother-fuckers?"

"Who is this?" Stade asked.

"You find out, pig. This is Bateman Hooks, the Main Man. What you do to Carlos?"

Stade looked at Rockewicz. "Who are you talking about? Carlos who?"

They could hear Trask arguing. "Hooks, shut up. Don't . . ."

"I tear your fuckin' head off, Trask, you touch me oncet more. Hey, pig. His name Carlos Olmedo. What you do, shoot him dead?"

Rockewicz looked at Stade for approval to respond. "Mr. Hooks? This is Mr. Rockewicz, the hospital director. We do have a Mr. Olmedo here. He's an orderly. But he hasn't been around for hours. When the OR was secured, we told all nonessential personnel to leave. He must have left. No one's seen him for a few hours."

"What you do? You catch him? You gonna run wires up his

ass make him talk? It ain't gonna help. Olmedo twicet the man you is."

"Shut up, Hooks. Give it to me." Trask sounded strident.

"May I talk to them?" Cardone asked the FBI men. "I want to tell them the money is short."

Stade nodded.

Cardone talked into the two-way. "John, this is Cardone. I want to be honest with you. The money is short several million. We did our best. We collected all we could. The Federal Reserve just didn't have it all in hundreds, and it would have meant another hour's delay. I promise you that I will deliver the balance if you do not hurt those people in the ambulance."

There was another pause, static on the line, the sounds of an argument. Trask spoke again. "You violated our agreement. We can't be responsible for what we do now. We freed Walker Tench. We kept our word. We did not hurt him. It was your agent Baggs who attacked me. You have been the aggressors. You always are."

"Where's Carlos, pig?" Hooks shouted. "Trask, you fuck him up. They got him now."

"We may have to make an example of someone." Trask's voice was rising.

"We don't know anything about Olmedo," Stade said.

"Not for that," Trask said. "For deceiving us about the money. Cardone, you lied to us."

Then the speaker went dead.

"They're not what you'd call a harmonious group," Rockewicz said. "Wow. That Hooks."

Harris was reading the computer print-outs. "His name doesn't show anywhere."

"We'll keep them guessing about Olmedo," Stade said.

"Why not tell them he's dead?" Reinhold asked. "Let them sweat a little."

They ignored him. Cardone was phoning his treasurer. He

wanted the additional money packaged as fast as possible. He would find a way to get it to them.

Steve sat down next to Martha. "Go on, you can be bitter. I know what you're thinking." He nodded toward the executive. "His man is home free and Eric and his people are still in the fire."

"He didn't intend it that way."

"No, but it's how things seem to break. Those guys land on their feet."

Martha brushed her hair back. "I'm not becoming theological in middle age, Steve, but maybe there's some kind of crude justice in this whole thing."

"I don't get it."

"Eric and I never thought about being rich. And the money's just been getting bigger and more unmanageable every year. It surrounds us, it suffocates us. Could people be reminding us of something?"

"Martha, you and Eric don't owe anyone apologies. And you don't need any lessons in values. Those people are psychotic."

"Yes, they are," she said. "But aren't they partially right about some things? Why should people like Cardone and Tench own so much, and run so much, and have everything their own way? And what do Eric and I need with all that money?"

"You can't change things by killing people. Or by getting the whole world angry."

"How do you change things, Steve?"

"Don't look at me, Martha. I got my troubles running a hospital."

They could hear Stade conferring with his men. One man was drawing lines on a large map of the city.

"They can't hide an ambulance forever," Stade was saying. "They'll have to ditch it somewhere."

"They don't even seem to be trying," an agent said. "They pulled out of here with the klaxon on and all the flashers. Everybody in town is going to know where they are."

Estelle poked her head in. "We've located Dr. Motzkin's wife. I think someone should talk to her."

Rockewicz looked up. "Volunteers?"

Martha stirred beside him. "I'll—"

"No, not you, Martha." He got up and went to the phone, not at all concerned about who saw the tears in his eyes.

2

Hooks drove wildly, but with absolute control of the ambulance. A carbine rested at his side, against the communications panel between his seat and Trask's. Trask held the .38 in his lap.

Lake surveyed the inside of the ambulance. It had been years since he had ridden in one. The new ones were elaborate, beautifully equipped, carefully designed. In back of the cab was a sliding glass panel. Trask opened it so that he could talk to Rashid and the girl. The Arab was seated on the left-hand stretcher, near the rear doors, his carbine leveled at the three hostages.

Lake noted the girl's Irish accent. She was seated on the blue bench under the glass panel, apparently unarmed. On the stretcher where the Arab sat they had stacked the valises. The hostages were jammed together, Motzkin near the rear door, Cho in the middle, Lake near the cab, on the right-hand stretcher.

"There's an old Marx Brothers movie," Motzkin tentatively tried. "All of them on a park bench and they shove Groucho off, and Chico says, 'Now there's room.'"

A bad joke. He had tried anyway.

Lake looked at Fiona. Pretty. Young. Pale skin. Did she have legitimate complaints? Martha would know, would be able to explain it, the religious bitterness, the ancient hatreds. He could not understand any of it. It was not measurable, like blood output or central venous pressure. "I could use a cigarette," Lake said to Fiona.

"I'm afraid not, doctor."

"Dangerous," Motzkin said. "Oxygen all over the place."

"Maybe they'll stop, Alan, and give me a cigarette break."

Second bad joke. They needed Licata.

Motzkin's eyes sought Rashid. The Arab had dropped the surgical mask. His face was furrowed and pitted. There was a black stubble on his chin. The anesthesiologist looked for a hint of humanity. The black eyebrows joined over Rashid's forehead. Yes, a trace of a smile, an acknowledgment. Motzkin feared him. There was a great deal to fear in men who were zealous, fanatic about their manhood, deprived of victories too often.

"Listen, Eric, if something happens," Motzkin said. "If the worst happens. You know what I mean."

"Nothing will happen. We'll be of no use to them after a while."

"It happened to Jimmy. Eric, if the worst happens, tell Bev and the kids that I behaved decently, right?"

Lake's exhausted eyes stared at the roof of the ambulance. "Alan, you and Bev watch too many movies on the late show."

"Maybe, maybe."

"If you fell asleep during the news, the way I do. . . ."

"You know what I mean. Why did they take me—and this poor guy? Because we won't be any trouble. You, you're the big fish. No one will try to get them while you're here. Jack Licata they wouldn't touch. Jack's brave. Eric, shut me up if I talk too much. But you know what I'm saying."

"You don't have to apologize. For God's sake, Alan, you're the best gas-passer City General ever had." He paused. "Now be quiet."

Trask turned around from the cab. "Fiona, blindfold them."

The girl got up. She took a roll of bandages off the shelf above the stretcher and, beginning with the anesthesiologist, wound the gauze around their eyes.

"Young lady," Motzkin said. "You look intelligent and educated. What are you doing with these . . . these . . . people?"

She did not respond. There was something warm and innocent in the man's voice. She forced herself to ignore it. A woman who had worked with her in Belfast had taught her to blot out personal sentiments. The ones they bombed and killed and maimed were not people. They were objects in the way.

The ambulance was speeding through a crumbling part of the city—small factories, boarded-up stores, sagging tenements. Above them was a superhighway. Olmedo had marked out a route —Plan A—that would keep them on obscure streets, enabling them to turn, double back, and finally disappear.

"You hear somethin'?" Hooks asked Trask.

"Like what?"

"Chopper. They followin' us. Goddamn, we need Carlos. He know the city."

Trask opened the window and looked into the soggy gray sky. The air was full of thickening wet snow, lazy flakes. "I don't hear anything."

"You don't hear. You don't see. What the fuck good are you? You got Carlos killed."

"We don't know he's dead."

"Yeah, they got him. You put him outside, save your ass. Carlos a better man than you and Ratshit together, right Ratshit? So you stick him out where the pigs waste him, and you and Ratshit split."

"That's not true. Drive the car, damn it. Stay off the sidewalk."

"Then you make deals with the pigs. Some deals. They on top of us with a chopper. I hears it. We need Carlos tell us how to get out. Plan B, huh? And now where Carlos?"

Motzkin whispered to Lake, "Seems to be a strain in the family tie. Is that good or bad?"

"I wish I knew." Lake yawned. His mouth stretched and trembled. He could feel fatigue devouring him. It hit him in the back first, tearing at his muscles, tormenting his nerves. In his mind, he was reviewing all that had to be done for Tench: no strain there. Licata and the others would take over. Walker Tench would live.

Motzkin kept trying to crush the terror in his gut with small talk. "Cho? You with us still?"

"Yes. Right here."

"Tough on you, kid. First day on the job. You heard what Dr. Lake said. They won't hurt us."

It was crowded and uncomfortable on the stretcher. Lake tried to uncross his legs, rest against the wall. It was no use. Between fatigue, discomfort, and the blindfold, he could not pull himself together. Still, he reasoned, his malaise was an asset. He could not be truly frightened, not with spasms in his legs and pinched nerves in his back.

Fiona, returning to the seat in back of the cab, opened the box she had been carrying. It contained five collapsible canvas valises, of the type sold in luxury luggage shops. They were of various pastel colors—tan, blue, gray. None was green.

Rashid moved down the stretcher toward her. He opened one of the green plaid bags. At once the two of them began counting the bundles of hundred-dollar bills and transferring them to the folding bags.

Trask turned around. "Assume the bundles are accurate. Just count each bundle, and forget about the odds and ends."

Rashid nodded. He had set the carbine at his feet. Blindfolded, the hostages were no threat. He worked swiftly, making clucking noises as he counted the sums.

Hooks watched them handle the money through the rearview mirror. He laughed. "Man, look at ole Ratshit work over that money. Buy hisself a whole Ay-rab tribe, camels, tents, all that shit."

Cho was leaning forward on the stretcher. His head was lowered in his hands as if he were going to topple over.

"I'm carsick," the Korean said.

Lake said, "There should be a bucket or a plastic bag on the shelf. This man has to throw up."

"Get back," Rashid said. "You." He picked up the carbine and jammed it into Cho's left shoulder.

"Ow. Ow. I'm sick."

But the threat seemed to cure the assistant's upset stomach. He made crooning noises, then slumped against the wall.

"I have an operation this afternoon," Lake said. "When can you let us out?"

"That depends on the FBI and the police," Trask said. "You may never get out."

Trask had turned the car radio on. On the all-news station, he heard his own voice again, O'Boyle's recording of the statement he had made in the operating room. ". . . we are revealed now as stronger than the secret masters, the governments, the oil companies, the corrupt agencies of oppression, the lying media, the two-faced universities. We speak for all people, all the oppressed, everyone, the Asians, and Latin Americans, and Africans. . . ."

Hooks exploded with laughter. "You don't speak for no Africans, man."

Trask's face reddened. "Hooks, I warn you."

"Enjoys hearing his own voice," Motzkin whispered to Lake. "A true paranoid."

"Another bag," Rashid said. He and Fiona had filled the first. They unzipped a second plaid valise and began the hasty counting and repacking. The idea was Trask's. Pack everything in new containers, discard the old ones.

"You and your fuckin' plan," Hooks was saying. Defiantly, he had rolled the window down. Every now and then he scanned the sky, watched the side streets. There was little traffic. No one appeared to be tailing them, but he wasn't sure. He thought he heard the helicopter again. Everything had to go perfectly for Trask's plan to work. Now they needed Olmedo. He knew the dark places. Hooks couldn't shake the suspicion that Trask and Rashid, jealous of Olmedo's status, had contrived to get rid of him. They get rid of me, too, he thought, if they gets lucky.

"It's working so far," Trask said. He cocked an ear to the newscast. There was some vague information about negotiations between the police and the kidnappers, and the departure of the gunmen in an ambulance. Bad, bad. He should have forbidden that. A loose end. But the press would have been a problem in any case. Whores like that O'Boyle played both sides of the street for a story. They'd go also.

"Yeah, I bet it work. What you do with all that money, Trask? Start the big revolution? You say you gonna teach Ay-rabs like Ratshit what has the metals and gold and all that shit, you teach them to keep it from Genral Motors, so we can take over? You shittin' me, Trask? Them Ay-rab kings and that nigger president think they God. Maybe they as bad as the boss of Genral Motors, you dig? They all busy killin' other niggers, cutting their feet off. Man, if you think them Ay-rabs and them nigger kings with *us,* you crazier than I think. They starvin' their own people."

"He's got a point," Motzkin said happily.

"Alan, lay off," Eric muttered. "They'll do better without your help."

"Ole Fiona got her a special problem. Tell her go up to Boston and see what her Irish people doin' to niggers. She can paint her ass black and be a real nigger for oncet."

We will have to kill him, Trask thought.

Hooks spun around a corner. The van skidded. Its blockish chassis swung wide, righted itself, sped on. Inside, the hostages fell against each other. Packets of bills slipped to the floor.

"Damn you, slow down," Trask said.

"More family troubles," Motzkin said to Lake. "Ah, sorry."

The surgeon did not respond. He was resting his head against the side of the ambulance. If I were not so damned exhausted, I would try to get out. Although his eyes were bound, he could tell that Rashid had moved away from the rear doors. Had he been Licata, or Jimmy Baggs, he would have calculated his chances, leaped for the doors, and out. But he was not Licata or Baggs. He was Eric Lake. So he thought about his ASD that afternoon. He assured himself he would be back in time for Angela Ramazotti.

"Start giving out the clothing," Trask said.

Fiona opened the duffel bag. She pulled out thin nylon-shell jackets of varying colors and assorted caps.

"We will only need four," she said to Rashid. "I wonder about Carlos. . . ." Her voice trailed off.

Rashid continued counting the money. "Be quiet."

"Carlos, Carlos Olmedo was with you?" Motzkin said wonderingly. "And he was such a nice fellow."

Trask had the radio on again. There was biographical information on him. They had unearthed a great deal: NYU, the secret meetings in Berlin, contacts with the Red Army of Japan, the Tupamaros, the PLO. They knew nothing about Rashid.

Trask peered into the rear of the van. "Rashid, Fiona. Start changing clothes." He swiveled his head back. "Hooks, kill the klaxon and the flashers."

"Nah, I get my jollies makin' noise. *Wah-wah-wah*, this heah Mighty Hooks, the Avenger!"

"I said cut them. We needed them only to clear traffic in the hospital area."

"No way, Trask. I goin' out flashing and howlin', like a fuckin' rocket attack on a gook village. *Wah-wah-wah—!*"

Trask reached across the communications console. His eyes sought controls, found the button that silenced the bawling klaxon. It was suddenly quiet inside the ambulance.

"Keep you fuckin' hand on yoah side, whitey."

"Do as you're told. Cut the flashers."

"Cut yoah ass."

Trask got to one knee, steadied himself on the console, and looked for the buttons. There were two sets: one for the twin lights on the rear of the roof, another for the long bar in front with its multiheaded rotating lights. He pushed both buttons. The red-and-white bursts of light ceased.

"Man, you reach in oncet more, you have one less hand."

Fiona turned her head. "Hooks, obey orders." She untied the duffel bag.

"Fuck yoah face, honey," Hooks called back.

3

"They've turned south," Harris said to Stade.

"Are we on them?"

"As close as we can get without making them suspicious." He was listening to a field telephone. "The chopper is under orders to stay out of sight. Luckily, it's overcast. The cars are following."

Stade studied a map of the city. They'd have to abandon the ambulance soon. But where? Somewhere in the city they had parked vehicles, cars they would transfer to when they felt safe. And the hostages? How soon would they let them go? He had a notion that they would hang on to at least one of the three men until the end. Maybe when they were in a foreign country. He had alerted the airports. A plane hijacking was not outside the realm of possibilities.

Their plan had been a daring one. Except for the loss of Olmedo, it had worked. Masked, gowned, they had been able to melt into the hospital. Now they had protection—a great surgeon, two other men, people valuable to the community.

"It's none of my business," Steve said. "But how can you stay with them if you have to keep your distance so they won't be suspicious?"

Stade's face cracked a small smile. "Before we moved the ambulance out, our wire man put a sensor on it. It transmits a beep. The pursuit cars can follow it even though they can't see it."

"Sounds good."

"When it works," Harris said.

Steve looked apprehensive.

"With or without it, we won't lose them," Stade said.

Will I lose anyone? Rockewicz wondered. He envied Cardone, home free, his benefactor saved. What was ten million to them? Cardone appeared subdued. He was in a corner of the room, talking on the phone to an underling. They had located Tench's daughter at a commune in New City. A limousine was bringing her to the hospital.

Cardone wondered about her. Another young one, disaffected, jumping ship, opting for the rural life, Eastern religions, vegetables, faith, Jesus, retreat. They were as wrong as the muddle-headed revolutionaires who had seized the operating room, except they were peaceful. But who was right? Who had the formula?

"They're on the pipe again," Stade said. The speaker hummed.

"This is John."

"I hear you. Stade, FBI, here."

"We heard a helicopter."

"Impossible. Maybe a city chopper, but we've warned them to stay away. Chief Reinhold has called them off."

"You're lying, Stade. You're observing us."

"John, why not stop this right now? You can't get away in that vehicle. What will you gain by hurting anyone? You stop somewhere, I'll arrange for an intermediary to talk to you. That reporter, O'Boyle. He's outside. He was fair with you. He ran your speech. You can come out with him. No guns, just a talk."

"Don't make me laugh."

Steve asked if he could get on the microphone.

"John, this is Rockewicz. You know you have no backing. All the radical groups are staying away from you like you got the mumps. Why not call it off? It won't work."

"Those people have been brainwashed by the CIA and the KGB. They are no longer part of the world revolution."

"Okay, have it your way." Rockewicz was learning when to back off from Trask.

"We may decide to let some of our people off. But I'm warning you. The hostages will be under continuing threat of death. So don't try to pick anyone up."

"We won't," Stade said.

Martha Lake was in the room again. She put her hands to her face. Cardone looked at her and quickly away. He was drowning in guilt, in his good luck, but now he was powerless. He did not like being bereft of the magic to change lives, move men around, control situations.

The speaker went dead. Cardone read from more print-outs. The man called Olmedo, shot down in surgery, was actually named Vasquez. He was neither Cuban nor Puerto Rican, but a law student from Buenos Aires widely respected in left-wing intellectual circles. It seemed inconceivable to Cardone that he should come to this end—his face blasted apart in a hospital corridor. But Olmedo-Vasquez had sought it. And all that intelligence and courage had been wasted.

4

Trask had stopped talking to the hospital. Lake heard rustling, the sounds of zippers. They were changing clothing.

Fiona tucked her hair under a short black wig, donned eyeglasses. The men wore caps. The surgical greens were piled in a corner.

The money had been transferred to the smaller valises. It went quickly. Rashid and Fiona had stopped counting after they had noted the number of hundred-dollar packets. Rashid shoved the packed bags to the rear.

"Sounds like they're getting ready to leave," Motzkin whispered. "Eric, you okay?"

"My back is killing me. I need a cigarette."

Fiona moved to the rear doors. She was carrying a pale blue valise. It contained about two million dollars. Calmly she tucked stray hairs under the wig. She had replaced the tan sheepskin with a burgundy nylon coat. She had rolled up her black slacks and lowered a gray skirt over her knees.

"When he turns the next corner," Rashid said, "I will open the door for you. Step out, then hide for a few minutes."

Rashid opened the door. They were racing through a slum street, rather like the street on which the group had lived while planning. The Arab checked his watch. It was 12:45. The street, piling with slush and snow, appeared deserted. The poor stayed indoors. He held his carbine by the pistol grip, and with his left hand opened the door about a foot.

The ambulance swung wide, grazed a parked car, and spun around a corner. Hooks pumped the brake twice. Motzkin and Trask were hurled forward. Rashid braced himself against the bottom of the stretcher mount.

"Now," he shouted at Fiona.

The girl held the valise with one hand and jumped from the rear of the careening van. She fell against the curb, gasped in the icy air, and got to her feet. Her knees felt bruised, perhaps bleeding. To her left was a row of decrepit stores, doors leading to the tenements above. She ran to the first door—next to a church of some kind—and hid in the dank corridor, shivering.

"It will work," she thought. "Trask was right."

She rested against the peeling wall. Cat piss and cheap frying oil again: the aromatic inevitabilities of the urban poor. There would be time to enjoy success later. Trask spoke of an even grander scheme involving the money. When they met, several hours from now, he promised to reveal it. Still, she wished Olmedo were with them. Trask was rigid in his planning. Carlos could improvise.

Catching her breath, she lingered in the hallway. Outside, the snow was settling more heavily. Gray and brown, sagging buildings, defeated people. Like Belfast. She peered through the misty glass to the street. It could have been Bogside, except that the passersby were black. On a scabrous wall she read: FUCKEN BASTIDS WEST SIDE KILLERS SUCK COCK.

There was a bus stop two blocks away. Disguised, carrying the new bag, she was to take the bus, change to another, and meet them later. She was no longer the long-haired woman in a sheepskin coat and black slacks who had entered the methadone clinic.

Snow was general all over Ireland. The line tingled in her head. No time for that any more. Bloody little poetry left in the world. Only power mattered. But she could not suppress a shimmering memory of the first time she had read *Dubliners.*

As she started down the wet street, two boys came out of a candy store. They were black. One was beautiful, his skin the color of desert sand, his eyes full of wonder and light. The other was taller, inky black, with a drowsy face. They wore knit caps and ragged jackets, and they could not have been more than twelve. They were smiling at her. In the doorway of the candy store, a fat black man in a white apron stood cursing the weather. On a wooden newsstand were three soaked copies of a morning paper.

"Lemme help you carry that, lady," the boy with the angelic face said.

"No thanks. I can manage."

"Hit look heavy," the darker boy said. "Me and Loftus, we carry hit for you and you give us a dollar."

"It's all right. I'm only walking a few blocks."

They were standing athwart her, looking bigger and more menacing. Loftus was laughing. The drowsy boy was nudging him. An odd resonant fear, an unfathomable sensation that echoed inside her head, gripped Fiona. She had faced down B-specials and Welsh guards. Why did these street boys frighten her? Then she understood. They were the people she and Trask wanted to save. She knew how to deal with her enemies, but not her friends.

"Let me by," she said. "I'm going around the corner. I warn you, I'll scream. I'll call for police."

"Sheet, you scream," Loftus said. "Bishop, she talk funny. She a furriner."

"We rides in Cadlacs. Ain't no bus. Gimme that fuckin' bag."

He reached for the handle of the valise. Fiona pulled her arm back. But the boy was tenacious, gripping his small hands around hers, trying to bend her fingers. She struggled with him, cracking her loose hand against his neck. The bigger boy watched as if half asleep.

"Loftus, he fight like a chick," he said.

"I'll pay you. Let me go. Stop." She brought her bare knee into the boy's crotch. He bent over, hissing and spitting. Then he leaped at her again. Fiona rammed her fingers into his face, digging them into the eyes, the flat nose, feeling his teeth cut into her thumb.

They wrestled, rolling in the snow. She would not release the bag. The taller boy, hooting, enjoying the brawl, got to one knee and smashed his palm against her nose. The pain was like an electric shock. *My beloved wretched of the earth . . .* The agony inside her skull was a thousand detonations. Bishop kicked her in the leg, again in the side. He picked up the valise.

"Let's go, Loftus."

The small boy scrambled to his feet and kicked Fiona in the thigh. "Fuckin' pussy. Nex' time we kill you." They began to run.

She shook her head, spit blood, staggered to her feet and began to run after them. It was useless. "Damn you, goddamn you, come back." She wanted to explain that she was on *their* side. She pitied their poverty and unhappiness. She kept running, feeling the blood turn icy and thick on her lip, the wet snow freezing her feet.

A white delivery van was riding alongside her. It pulled ahead. The rear doors opened and a man in a brimmed hat and a raincoat stepped out, then a second. They were pointing guns at her.

"Don't move, miss," one of them said.

"Go to the wall, turn your back, and freeze."

"Dirty pigs."

"It's all right. Don't move. That's a good girl."

"You were following us, you bastards. Trask will kill the doctors when he finds out."

"He won't find out."

The truck picked up speed. The agents were putting handcuffs on Fiona, frisking her for a gun. She had left it on the ambulance. She was unarmed. That was part of the plan.

Two blocks away, the white truck caught up with the boys. An agent pursued them on foot. They saw the flash of his gun, dropped the valise, and with a chorus of "mother-fuckers" vaulted a fence, ran into a house, out another door, and vanished.

"They've got the girl and one of the bags," Harris said. "They've been transferring the money to different valises."

"Shooting?" Stade asked.

"No. She wasn't armed. Wig, different clothing. They've planned this thoroughly."

Stade nodded. "But with no alternatives. It's almost too easy." He looked up at Harris. "What are you smiling about?"

"Two teen-age hoods tried to steal the valise. They beat her up pretty badly. Our men got the valise back, but the kids got away."

The FBI chief nodded at Reinhold. "We'll make the juvenile delinquents Chief Reinhold's problem."

Reinhold did not think the remark funny. He muttered something under his breath and walked out of the office. In the hallway O'Boyle was waiting for him. "Why are you taking that crap from them?" the reporter asked. "Why aren't you out there chasing those bastards?"

"It's their case."

O'Boyle stroked his long hair. "That didn't stop you from getting Olmedo. Want to live dangerously? You know this city better than the feds. Why don't we do some free-lancing? You and me. You catch that ambulance, you'll get a medal at the next police chiefs' convention."

The foxy face listened. Stade's last insult had burned. Sending him after a couple of punks! "Let's go, O'Boyle," he said.

"I need one guy. A cameraman."

"And a driver. We'll show the scumbags."

Rockewicz listened to Martha Lake talking to Motzkin's wife. She was calm, tender, reassuring. Steve had tried to reason with Beverly—Alan was not badly hurt, he was a hero of sorts, he would be free soon—but his best efforts had been rewarded with wails. It was astonishing how Lake's wife had lowered the decibel count, stopped the tears. Abruptly it occurred to Steve that they were ignoring the third hostage.

"Hey, Estelle," he called. "Who was that third fellow they took?"

"The man from anesthesiology. His name was Cho. Cho Park."

"You know him?"

"No. You know that department. They come and go."

"Try and find out if the guy has a wife or a family," Steve said. "Poor kid comes to work and walks into this mess."

5

Rashid was wearing a black nylon jacket and a black baseball cap. He had put on eyeglasses. He dragged a valise toward the rear doors and waited as Hooks sped through the city.

"Fiona is safe," he said.

Trask called to him from the front seat. "You're next, Rashid."

"When I makes the turn," Hooks snarled. "Trask, you ain't givin' orders when I drivin'."

"Hooks, we have to cooperate. We're not out of this yet."

Motzkin leaned toward Eric. Blinded, their hands bound, they could only guess at what was happening. "Eric," Motzkin whispered. "I heard him tell the Arab to get out. We'll be alone here. You and me and Cho."

"What can we do?" Lake asked. "We've got no eyes or hands."

"Not safe," Cho said.

"What?" Motzkin asked.

"Not safe even if he goes. No escape."

"I guess he's right." The moment of heroic possibilities vanished. Motzkin rested against the side of the van.

"You ain't givin' no orders, heah?" Hooks was still furious.

The ambulance bounced and vibrated.

"All right, I'll ask your permission," Trask said sarcastically. His voice shook.

"I hope they kill each other," Motzkin said.

"To hell with them," Lake said. "I want to get back to the hospital."

Trask said, "There's a traffic island around the next street. Across from the factory. There should be a taxi there. Rashid, you hear me?"

"I am ready." The Arab shoved the M2 carbine under the blanket of the stretcher. He looked at the captives. They could not see. Cho was edging away, trying to hide in the corner near the cab.

The ambulance went into a wild swerve as Hooks turned the corner. It drew screams from several people waiting for a bus. People scattered. A lunch-hour group of factory workers shouted at Hooks to straighten out.

Seconds after the van had righted itself, Rashid opened the rear door and stepped out with the valise. He had jammed a .38 into his belt under the nylon jacket. Bespectacled, stubble-faced, dark, he ran toward the taxi stand. A yellow cab was parked at the curb. The driver was reading the *Daily Racing Form.* Rashid opened the door and threw the suitcase in, then climbed in after it. He had to urinate again. His kidneys were on fire.

"River Avenue and Tenth Street," he said to the driver.

The hackie put down his newspaper. He turned and stared at the brown furrowed face. The features were large and thick, the hair black and curling. And the accent—a foreign accent. He pushed a switch and put down his flag. "Sorry, Gonzales. I'm off duty."

"I beg your pardon?"

"I said I'm off *doody.* Whatsamatta, Lopez, cancha read? My sign on toppa the cab says off *doody.* Out."

"You just put it on," Rashid said. "This is an urgent matter. I must get across town."

The driver (a card revealed his name to be Salvatore Connetta) smiled at Rashid. "Look, pal, it ain't personal. I got my own rules. No spics or spades in my cab. I mean, go find a gypsy somewhere. You can help him steal hubcaps."

Mr. Connetta knew his Puerto Ricans. No mistaking this baby —baseball cap, black jacket, three-day beard, dark skin. And the cheap valise. Probably selling blouses with lace trimming or scarlet bikini panties door to door.

"Come on, get out, Juan."

"You have no right to do this," Rashid gasped. He was deadly tired.

"Pancho, I gotta make a living, see? I gotta wife inna hospital and three kids. I take people like you to the West Side, I get mugged. My goombah Charlie got it from a Porto last week. A shiv right inna short ribs. Now do me a favor and get the fuck outa my cab before I break your chops."

Rashid took the .38 from his belt and pointed it at Connetta's eyes. "You do as I say. Drive off."

"Fuckin' bastard," Connetta said. "I coulda guessed. Goddamn PRs."

"Drive."

Mr. Connetta turned the key and gunned the motor. As he tried to drive away, a blue sedan rammed into him from the right. He was trapped between the car and the traffic island.

"Drive over it," Rashid said.

Two men leaped from the sedan. One opened the door of the cab. The second leveled a double-barreled shotgun at Rashid. "Drop it," he commanded. "Police officers."

For a fraction of a second, Rashid thought of firing, going out in glory, dying a hero. Two things changed his mind. He had to urinate terribly. He did not want to die with his bladder tormenting him. Secondly, he was sure that, like his glorious brothers, he could never be hurt. There were friendly nations, oil countries, desert princes, great governments in the world, that feared and respected him, airports where he could be landed safe from punishment, hijackers who would demand his release so that he could return to the glorious revolution. Why die?

"Drop the gun," one of the men ordered.

"Of course, of course."

"Get out and get against the cab. Legs out, hands over your head. Move."

Rashid, stiff, pained, dragged himself out. There was a damp spot on the taxi seat. An embarrasing way for a warrior to surrender. With wet trousers.

"Thank God for you guys," Mr. Connetta said. "That spic had a .38 special on me. Can I work him over once or twice?"

"Two down," Harris said. He had just received a radio report on the capture of Rashid. "He didn't resist."

"He didn't have a chance to shoot someone in the back," Stade said. "I thought I gave orders for no shotguns?"

Harris laughed. "You know how it is, Arnold. They run for the shotguns first."

Rockewicz was pacing the floor. "It's crazy. Can't put my finger on it. Your men say that the black and John are up front. They've dropped the girl and the Arab. See what I'm getting at?"

"Yes," Stade said. "The hostages are alone in back of the van."

"Why would they leave them like that?"

The FBI agent shook his head. "They're bound. Maybe blindfolded. Trask can cover them from the front seat if they break for it."

"It's still nutty. After the way they've guarded and threatened them. They killed Baggs when he made a move. I don't get it."

The speaker crackled. Trask was on again. "Stade? We're going to release a hostage. To prove that we're honorable people. We won't tell you who."

Rockewicz came to the set. "Why not release them all? No one's tailing you."

"No?"

Hooks's raging voice blasted through the speaker. "Maybe we shoot some doctor right now, make things even, huh?"

Stade broke in. "Can you tell us where you'll release the hostage? Just give us an idea."

"No." There was a pause, as if Trask were weighting a stratagem. "Stade? Rockewicz? We're going to keep one man to the end. Once we're safe, we might discuss a prisoner exchange. Olmedo for this man."

"Olmedo?" Stade asked. "He isn't around. You seem to think he was working for you. If he was, he's double-crossed you."

"You fuckin' liar," Hooks shouted. "Carlos never rat on no one."

"Damn it, Hooks, give me the phone," Trask was saying. "You drive and let me handle this."

The speaker went dead again.

Steve said, "They should want to keep *everybody* for the trade." He pounded a fist into his hand. "I can't figure it. There's a gear slipped somewhere."

"Let's take him off pacing," Licata said to Abe Gilad.

Licata and Dr. Evans, the cardiologist, studied the tracings. Evans measured the peaks with his calipers. "Not bad. Not bad at all. Maybe this bypass was justified."

"Burt, your confidence in the Lake team is underwhelming," Licata said. The Lake team. Would it be the Lake team tomorrow?

Mihrab was suturing the incision in Tench's chest. He worked swiftly, glancing from time to time at Flor. She seemed to have recovered. Her friend Imelda, who came from the same village, talked to her in their native language, *Cebuano*. They sounded to Mihrab like singing birds. The Egyptian was intoxicated with her. What a magical combination they would make! A union of two ancient cultures—Middle East and Far East.

"Abe," Licata said. "Give Rockewicz a call and see what's doing with Alan and Eric."

Gilad dialed, staring at the bullet holes in the ceiling. He would have handled it differently. Take the losses, kill them. Encourage them and they will only do it again.

"They are still in the ambulance," Gilad said. "But they dropped off two of their own gang and the FBI got them."

"Dead, I hope," Licata said.

"Alive."

Licata grunted and took a set of hemostats from Sally. Tench's chest was almost sewn together. There were still tapes on his eyelids, where Cho Park had placed them a few hours ago.

"That poor sucker of a Jap," Licata said.

"Korean," Mihrab corrected him. He pulled the sutures tight. "Alan greeted him in Japanese and then had to apologize."

"Did he? It seems like something that happened two months ago. Spray him, Flor."

6

"Motzkin!" Trask shouted. "You're getting out. When we turn the corner jump."

"How? I'm blinded. My hands are tied. Somebody take the blindfold off, please. Untie my hands. This is crazy. I'll be helpless."

Trask yelled at Cho. "You! Get over here. Crawl to the window."

The Korean was huddled, fetuslike, in a corner of the stretcher. He struggled to the glass panel.

"Turn around," Trask said. "I'm cutting your hands free. You can take off your blindfold. Then open the door for Motzkin. But don't jump or I'll shoot."

Trask reached in with a hunting knife and cut the adhesive tape binding Cho's hands. The Korean ducked, as if afraid of a blow, then tore the bandages from his eyes. The ambulance skidded and he fell to the floor.

Trask yelled, "Get to the back. When we turn the corner, open the door for Motzkin and shove him out. Motzkin, move to the rear. You'll get only one chance."

Cho got up, fell again. He rose, flexing his fingers. He took Motzkin's right arm and shoved him gently toward the rear. The vehicle careened around a corner, went into a skid and slowed down.

Cho opened the door. A snow-drenched iron-gray sky hovered over them. He pulled Motzkin by the arm, guiding him to the rear steps. He lowered the bandages on Motzkin's face. "It's okay, doctor," he said.

Motzkin saw the buildings and the street tilting crazily. He wanted to yell at Hooks to slow down. The driver was a madman. The physician jumped to the sidewalk, fell, got to one knee, conscious of how stupid, incongruous, inexplicable he looked—a stout man of middle age, limping around in a light green suit and cap, his hands bound behind him.

Two women carrying shopping bags stared at Motzkin as he rose in the snow, exchanged horrified looks, walked away. Not for them any involvement. Motzkin felt ice and water seeping into his wounded toe. Bad business, it could get infected. He needed a phone, a change of clothing, a warm place. He had information for the FBI—two of the kidnappers had been released. Trask and the black man were engaged in a bitter argument. And he had to assure Bev he was safe.

"What in hell is he supposed to be?" a man standing at a street crossing asked.

"Beats the hell out of me, Charlie."

Stores had been closed, boarded up, in the decaying neighborhood. After dragging his foot about fifty feet, Motzkin saw a dim light in a shop. People too poor to relocate. It was a dry goods store. A cluttered, flyspecked window reminded him of the market block on Prospect Place in his youth. A sign read: D. TEITELBAUM, PROP.

The anesthesiologist, shaking as if he had parkinsonism but savoring the delicious taste of freedom, kicked the door. A bell tinkled. A bearded Orthodox Jew presided over a counter laden with bolts of cloth. He wore a wide-brimmed black hat, sported earlocks and a lush black beard.

"Please . . . please . . . I'm from the hospital . . . you heard on the radio?"

"As a matter of fact, I have. You are a physician?"

"Yes. They took me in the ambulance. There are others. May I use your phone? Will you please free my hands?"

"Certainly, doctor."

"Thank you, Mr. Teitelbaum."

"I'm Mr. Klarsfeld. Teitelbaum's son-in-law."

"You speak excellent English." Dialing, Motzkin realized he had committed another *gaffe*. The beard had set him off. Never assume stereotypes, he should have known.

"I'm a graduate of Yeshiva University."

"A terrific school. My wife took courses in learning disabilities there." The anesthesiologist waited for Rockewicz's gruff voice. He prayed for Lake, for Cho.

A man in a gray topcoat entered. One of Stade's people. "Are you all right, Dr. Motzkin?" he asked. "How's that foot?"

"Fine, fine. I'm calling the hospital." He felt heroic, larger than life. There were more important things than tax shelters and professional corporations.

7

"Can't we figure out where those germs would go?" Reinhold asked. He nudged the driver. "Ram the accelerator to the floor. Hit the siren. They've dropped two of their own and one hostage. That leaves four. I like the odds."

The blue-and-white prowl car, siren shrieking, raced through lights, crisscrossing the wet, slippery streets. O'Boyle was in the back with his cameraman.

"I'll owe you a few for this, George," the reporter said.

Reinhold said nothing. He let the revolver with its long barrel rest in his lap. It looked to O'Boyle like a hunting rifle.

"Jesus, keep that thing on safety," the TV newsman said.

"Don't worry. I know guns."

"The gun that got Olmedo. Great title for a special." He jotted something in his copybook. "What do you call it?"

"Colt Trooper Mark III with a .357 Magnum and six-inch barrel. It's got a short hammer throw and a big cylinder latch."

"Standard issue? Isn't there a big stink about those hollow-nosed bullets?"

"It's standard issue for *me*," Reinhold said. "My mother-in-law gave it to me for Christmas. Guess what it cost."

"I'm not a gun lover, George."

"Goes for a hundred and forty-two bucks without tax." His face looked sharper than ever. "You could do a TV feature on gun control, O'Boyle. Show up the commies and liberals, right?"

He was insane, O'Boyle thought, but useful.

The prowl car blasted across an intersection. In the distance there was a flash of white.

"That's them," Reinhold said. "Step on it."

Harris was jiggling a phone. He was trying to reach an FBI man in the dispatcher's shack. There had been a foul-up; they were losing contact. He spoke to the man, then turned to Stade. "We've lost them."

"How?"

"You know those sensors. Some interference knocked it out. They never work as well as they do in the movies."

"Lost them?" Martha Lake asked.

"Will it start transmitting again?" Rockewicz asked.

"It might," Harris said. "The things aren't bugproof. They can glitch out on you. Something else isn't helping."

"What's that?" Steve asked.

"Some idiot in a police car is flying around town. We asked them to lay off, but our people have sighted it. Possibly his radio jammed the sensor."

"Oh, brother," Stade said. He looked at Rockewicz. "Anyone seen our friend the chief of police?"

Rockewicz shook his head. "George's got a wild hair up his keister. It could be him."

Martha's eyes were wide with anger. "Is this how you get things done? My husband's life is in danger, and the FBI and the local police are fighting over who can get him killed? I can't believe it! Get on the radio and tell them it's a mistake. Tell them the police car isn't after them at all. Lie. Make something up."

Steve thought, She's looking at me. She knows I can lie, deceive, hustle, see around corners. He took it as a compliment. But now the game was being played in Stade's ball park.

Cardone took Rockewicz by the elbow. His principal was free, out of danger. Some of the old boardroom authority was back in his voice and manner. Rockewicz did not like the firm grasp on his arm, but he did not resist.

"I'll make this up to you," the president of Tench Industries said. "I heard about those membrane oxygenators before. You'll get them. As soon as this mess is over, I promise you."

Rockewicz held his tongue. He wanted to say, Thank you for your membrane oxygenators, sir, but I'll take the James Baggs Memorial Wing . . . or possibly it would be the Eric Lake Memorial Wing, God save us.

"Dr. Motzkin's on the outside line," Estelle cried. "They let him go. He's safe."

Rockewicz jumped up and applauded. "Martha? See? It's going to work out. Alan's out. Eric'll be next."

"It's working," Cardone said. "Try to raise them, Mr. Stade. Tell them that this act of good faith is what we've been waiting for. Tell them that I personally will see to it that they get the balance of the money. . . ."

Blowhard, Rockewicz thought.

Stade and Harris tried to contact the ambulance again. There was no response from Trask or the driver. The FBI men spoke in subdued voices. They were disturbed by the failure of the sensor, angered at Reinhold's mad chase. With his siren and flasher, waving his damned Colt Trooper, he could blow everything sky high.

"I mean it," Cardone was gushing at Rockewicz. "You can write your ticket."

"Glad to. We need everything here. Other day the chief attending in gastroenterology demanded ten thousand dollars for a colonoscope. It goes up the rear end. An hour later the chief of medicine waltzes in. He wants seven grand for a duodenoscope, a gimmick you shove down the mouth. They were almost ready to fight. I calmed them down."

Cardone looked blank. Was he being mocked? "How?"

"I told 'em," Rockewicz said, bringing his face close to Cardone's, "I told 'em, 'Flip for it. I'll buy you only one, and you can wipe it off between uses.'"

Cardone did not smile. No one dared talk to him that way at the corporation.

Hooks and Trask heard Reinhold's siren. They switched on the two-way radio and Trask talked to Stade. "Someone's out here with a police car."

"It's a local cop, John. He's on some other case. We're trying to get him off the road."

"I don't believe you. We set a hostage free. Now you've got a police car on our tail."

"Believe me, we appreciate your releasing Dr. Motzkin. He called in. There is absolutely no pursuit." It was partially true, Stade felt. Their electronic beeper was still failing to transmit.

"Get that police car off the road or we'll shoot Lake."

"We'll do our best, John. You must believe me. He's after a speeder or something. The city police have been told to stay away from any ambulance."

"I don't believe you."

Hooks, his hands spinning the wheel, his feet light on the clutch and brake, raged at Trask. "You dumb-ass honky. You let them trick you. We git to the place and it be full of pigs. Tell them you shoot somebody *now*."

Trask looked into the rear of the cab. He shouted under the blast of the klaxon: "Cho. Move to the back. Don't try to jump or I'll kill you."

"Don't do anything stupid, Trask," Lake cried. "We're helpless. You can't do anything but hurt yourself."

The surgeon, blindfolded, his hands taped, racked by fatigue, fought the fear in his chest. A stupid way to go. A pointless way to die. He tried to be calm, procedural, orderly. He had seen patients behave with dignity in the face of death. Many of them knew it was coming. They were not deceived by the optimistic chatter of surgeons and internists. And so they put things in order, arranged matters, made it easier for their families. He would try to be as calm.

"Trask," Lake called. "At least take my blindfold off. Untie my hands. If you want, I'll get on the radio and beg them to call that car off."

"Cho," Trask shouted. "Go on."

The Korean hesitated. What did Trask want? Trask was on the radio, threatening Stade again. Cho went to Lake's side and cut the tapes on his hand, watching as the doctor removed his blindfold. Trask took no notice.

The surgeon rubbed his eyes and flexed his fingers. Something was cockeyed, out of joint. It was too easy. All he had to do was dive for the doors, hurl himself out, and be rid of them. The Korean could do the same. Hooks was speeding down a highway bordering the river. Trask was haranguing someone on the radio.

Lake edged forward. His back creaked. His knees seemed to make grinding noises. He caught the Korean's eye and pointed to the door. Then he pointed to himself. He edged along the stretcher another foot, wondering how best to fall, how to avoid a fracture.

Then he pointed to Cho and again the door, as if to say, *You first.*

Motzkin's assistant skidded to the end of the other stretcher. He lifted the gray blankets and took out the carbine Rashid had left. Lake signaled with his hands as if to warn him that it wasn't needed.

But Cho was pointing the weapon at him. "Stay where you are, Dr. Lake."

8

Beverly Motzkin arrived. She was torn between hysterical laughter and racking sobs. Guilt nibbled at her. Eric Lake was in the ambulance.

"And they have one of Alan's people, don't they?" she asked Rockewicz.

"New kid. Estelle, where the hell's the file on that guy?"

Miss LeBlanc hurried in. She had just forced her way into the anesthesiology department, ransacking files. "Here's some data," she said. "It was on top of a cabinet."

Rockewicz squinted at the yellow card. "Cho Park, Korean national, educated at Berkeley, twenty-six. One year training at the San Francisco Medical Center. No phone number. Nearest relative Mrs. Cho Sung, Pusan, Korea. An aunt. That tells us nothing."

"The secretary in anesthesiology said he was new," Estelle said. "He was just hired."

Rockewicz frowned. He turned to Motzkin's wife. "One of these days, Bev, Alan will do me a favor and take that department over."

Harris was signaling to Stade. "I've got city police headquarters. They're going to get that car off the street."

"What about the sensor?"

"It's out. We've got five cars tracking them, but nobody's seen them for the last five minutes."

"Who's left in the ambulance?"

"Trask, the driver, Dr. Lake, and the Korean fellow."

Stade turned to Rockewicz. "What were you saying about the Korean?" Steve slapped the yellow card. "Look at this. This guy barely qualifies. I got nothing against brown or yellow people or people with turn-up shoes, but they have to be competent. Licata says Cho was more trouble than he was worth."

Stade was listening attentively. He got up from the desk, leaving Harris shouting at a city dispatcher to silence the prowl car and get it off the streets. "How long has this man been with you? This Cho?"

"Two weeks or so."

"And he was hired by a committee?"

"Three or four people pass on him. Tests, interviews."

Stade looked puzzled. "How do they get them?"

"Oh, applications, advertisements. Recommendations."

"How are they scheduled for their work?"

"Another committee."

Stade held his hand out. "Mind if I take this for a minute?" He gave it to one of his aides. "Call the Bureau in Washington and see if they have anything on this man."

Rockewicz squinted. His eyes were lost in his pink ham of a face. "Wait a minute. I'm getting a message. What good . . . ?"

"That's what I'm trying to figure out," Stade said.

Estelle held up a phone. "Mr. Rockewicz, for you. I've located someone on the anesthesiology committee. Irene DeFord."

"Hunh?"

Estelle covered the mouthpiece. "The Amazon who leads the pickets."

"Oh, yea. Refers to me as the resident fascist pig." He took the phone. "Hi there, Miss DeFord. This fellow Cho in your department? Cho Park?"

The city dispatcher reached Reinhold's flying car. He conveyed the FBI's message: He was not to roam the streets looking for the ambulance with his siren shrieking.

"Tell him I'll meet him halfway," Reinhold laughed. "We'll turn the siren off."

"They're on the river road," the chief's driver said. "Where the hell are they going?"

Reinhold shut his eyes as if trying to envision a map of the city, main roads in and out, the airport, the terminals, isolated areas. "Maybe the park."

"Park?" O'Boyle asked.

"Sure. In winter who goes to a park? It's empty even in summer. It's a place you go to get laid, pick up a fag, or get mugged. Let's try it."

The car bounced up on a sidewalk, slid across a patch of wet snow, and turned around.

"What the hell is this?" Lake asked. "What are you doing?"

Cho looked shamefaced. With the mask lowered, the surgeon could see that he was young and soft-skinned. "Sorry, doctor. Just sit down. You can't get out."

Lake slumped on the stretcher. He rested on one elbow. "You're with them. I'm not sure I understand. Weren't you . . . aren't you . . . on staff?"

Cho held a finger to his mouth. "Don't ask me. It's important. We need you for a while."

"Don't tell him anything," Trask called over his shoulder. "We'll keep him as long as we have to. We'll kill him if we have to." His head bobbed, moved in that strange pecking way. "I don't hear the siren any more. They've called that police car off."

"Yeah, they 'fraid of Ole Hooks." Bateman began to laugh. "Sheeet, I show them who got a sireen. We goin' out first class." He flicked the button for the klaxon. "Yeah, an' all them big lights on top, too. Let 'em know we ain't pussy."

"You crazy bastard," Trask shouted. "Turn them off!"

"Fuck you, Trask."

"Hooks, you'll get us killed. Listen to me. We're almost there. They're going to let us get away. Turn them off."

"Nah. This my fun for today. Sheeet."

Trask got up and reached into the driver's section, his shivering hand turning off the button that controlled the klaxon, then the one that activated the flashing lights. Hooks cracked down on Trask's wrist. "You mother-fucker, stay where you b'long. This my side. This my turf." But he did not touch the buttons again.

"Hooks, you have to stick with me. We need each other."

"You needs me more 'n' I needs you. Ole Ratshit the only other gunner you has, he gone. Ole Ratshit take his million bucks and buy hisself a oil field and a Cadillac and a whole lot of dumb-ass camels. He tell you go shove yo rev'lution up yo ass."

Lake listened to the black man's wild chatter. There was a kind of gleeful fatalism in him, something vigorous and strong turned crazy, running amok. Trask was having his problems. But where did that leave Eric Lake, M.D.?

In the rear window behind Cho's head, Lake could see the boulevard bordering the murky river. The waters were a ratty gray, spotted with chunks of late winter ice. Gulls wheeled and dipped, squabbling and squawking over garbage.

"We near the park now," Hooks said. "Them mothers never find us."

Trask took the phone and signaled. "Stade, this is Trask. We have a gun on Dr. Lake. He'll be the first to go if you try to ambush us."

"You will not be interfered with."

"What about that prowl car?"

"We've stopped him." Stade looked at Harris. The latter shrugged, as if saying I hope to hell we have.

An agent came running in. "One of our cars picked up the signal. The sensor's working again."

Stade got up. "Tell him to follow. I think they're getting ready to ditch the ambulance."

9

In the recovery room, Dr. Licata bent low and shouted into Walker Tench's ear. "Mr. Tench, this is Dr. Licata. If you can hear me, wiggle your toes."

Tench, naked, dyed yellow, sprouting tubes, wires, monitors, and drains, emerged from deep sleep and obliged. His toes wiggled.

"Dr. Lake will be here any minute to look at you. Okay? Wiggle them again."

Tench's toes responded.

Licata looked at Mihrab and spoke softly. "I hope to Christ he gets here. I'd rather see Eric's face than this monster's toes."

Mihrab touched Licata's arm and angled his eyes toward the entrance to the recovery room. Rockewicz, escorting Cardone, was entering. The president of Tench Industries sagged at the knees when he saw the chairman of the board, his patron, naked, intubated, wired, patched. Three nurses hovered around the bed. They seemed pitifully small and weak to Cardone, decorative more than functional. Rockewicz introduced the executive to the surgeons.

"I'm indebted to you," Cardone said. "Not only the operation, but that ordeal."

"We made it," Licata said laconically. He did not like the look of Cardone: flared suit, dandy's shoes, artfully cut hair. *Cardone?* A *paisan* who had made it.

"We hear Dr. Motzkin is safe," Mihrab said.

"Yes," Rockewicz said. "We hope they let Eric go in a few minutes. And the assistant."

Dr. Evans walked in and checked the charts and the EKG. "Patient's fine," the cardiologist said. "He may have a soft systolic murmur, but I don't think it's a matter for concern."

Cardone stared again—in mingled horror and relief—at the bloated figure of his benefactor. A narrow escape. For both of them.

Dimly, fuzzily, Tench heard voices, but apart from the loud command to wiggle his toes, he had not been able to distinguish words. He began to think he was dying. He was back in a duck blind near Stuttgart in Arkansas, forced to hunt green-headed mallards with his father and his uncle. He hated shooting ducks. Hated killing anything. Big, rich, strong, he was supposed to like to hunt. Who had been pop-popping a shotgun? Once. Twice. Again. A misfire. Something in his chest. Had he been hit?

The surgeons were at the door with Rockewicz and Cardone when they heard one of the nurses say, as casually as if she were announcing the time, "Oh dear, he's fibrillating again."

And another girlish voice: "Dr. Licata?"

The chief resident, bleary-eyed, arm weary, turned. "Yeah?"

"The patient is fibrillating."

Licata and Mihrab appeared more annoyed than frightened. It would be painful to lose a patient with Eric Lake gone. He would demand explanations.

"Christ," Licata said.

"Is this . . . serious?" Cardone's voice was a croak.

"Routine," Steve answered. He said a few silent prayers.

Licata and Mihrab walked back to the bed. Licata took the fibrillating paddles—bright metal disks on plastic handles. He placed one on Tench's taped chest, the other under the left armpit.

"Hit it," Licata said.

The nurse sent a charge through Tench's chest. The tracing fluttered erratically.

"Hit it again."

"Not much change," Evans said.

Cardone cried, "Is that all you can do? Why are they so casual about it? Why are they so indifferent?"

Rockewicz took his elbow. "Hysteria won't help."

Licata gave the paddles back to the nurse. "There are other ways to cook a minestrone," he said.

The chief resident leaned over Tench's chest. "Mr. Tench, this may leave you with a bruise, but it's for your own good."

Cardone looked horrified.

"It's okay," Rockewicz said. "I doubt Mr. Tench understands anything as complex as that."

Licata placed his left palm over Tench's chest. Then he slammed his right palm on top of it. Cardone almost rose vertically out of his shoes. All he could think of was Tench's abused chest and heart—cut, sliced, stitched, repaired, full of tubes, so fragile. And now this muscular man was administering karate chops to it!

"Is . . . is that necessary?" Cardone gasped.

"It's a tough muscle," Licata said. Once again he slammed his right hand on top of his left.

"Got him that time, Jack," Dr. Evans said. He clapped his hands.

"Good move," Mihrab said. They were both studying the tracings with evident pleasure.

Licata did not need the EKG to tell him that Tench's heart was back on a coordinated beat. He felt it under his hand, felt the power, the life, all the things Eric Lake had given back to the man.

"Put him back on pacing," Licata said.

Tench's cottony brain wondered, Who is jumping on me? Why are people jumping on my chest?

Back in his office, Rockewicz was getting information on the phone from Irene DeFord, the chairwoman of the anesthesiology committee. Miss DeFord explained that Cho had come with excellent references from California. She conceded that none of the physicians had seen his records. The committee alone had the right to hire and fire.

"Who?" Steve yelled. "Who was on this committee?"

"Community representatives, technicians, nurses. We can outvote the doctors any time we want, you know."

"You're damn right I know. But was this man qualified?"

Miss DeFord had cleared her throat. "Professionally and politically. Mr. Cho gave evidence of genuine concern for a restructured society."

"I'd like the names of some of the people on that committee. No punitive action, I promise you. I'm just curious how such inept assistants get hired. That man—I'm sorry he's in trouble—screwed up all morning. Who picked him?"

"Myself. Mr. Davis. Miss Lugan. Mr. Olmedo."

"Who?"

"Mr. Olmedo. Carlos. The orderly from surgery."

"He's on your committee?"

"Yes. We wanted someone from surgery and we certainly didn't want one of your surgeons."

Rockewicz slammed down the phone.

Stade said, "It's crazy."

"You thinking what I'm thinking?" Steve asked.

"It's a new one for me. The hostage that isn't a hostage. Why?"

Rockewicz tapped the desk. "What does it do for them?"

"When they make the final run and change vehicles, or pick up a plane, they've got an extra gun rather than a hindrance, someone to worry about."

"Even better," Rockewicz said. "We keep trying to free some guy who doesn't want to be freed."

"And we can chase them forever or until they disappear, to no purpose. He's one of theirs and they don't let him go no matter what."

Harris nodded. "And we keep holding fire."

"It has one fallacy," Stade said. "If we find out, they have no insurance once they free Lake."

Rockewicz smiled. "Maybe their policy just lapsed."

Stade asked Harris, "What about the two we picked up? Are they talking?"

"No. We read Miranda to them, told them they had all their rights and didn't have to say anything. The girl, I'm ashamed to report, has an Irish accent, right out of the old sod. She won't give her name and doesn't have any identification on her."

"And the Arab?"

"He's a barrel of laughs. He admitted he's Rashid Ali, Palestinian."

"Did he say anything about the others? About Cho?"

"No. But he's made a nonnegotiable demand. He insists he has the right to take his case before the United Nations General Assembly. He says that's the only place he can get a fair hearing."

10

"Whut you do now, wonder man?" Hooks asked.

"Just as we planned. Take the next turn into the park." He turned around. His starved face contorted with rage when he saw that Cho had removed the surgeon's blindfold and freed his hands. He was covering him with Rashid's carbine. "Who told you to take his blindfold off?" Trask shouted. "Are you crazy?"

"You told me to."

"I did not. You idiot."

Hooks roared. *"Haw-haw!* You got you one more fuck-up, Trask. That slope ain't good for nothin'!"

Trask's mind tried to untangle his problem. He moved bits and pieces, like a child's puzzle where little numbers have to be jiggled to get them in sequence. He could not free Lake if the surgeon knew the Korean was one of them and that the police had no reason to hold fire. He reached for the telephone.

"Stade? This is Trask."

"I'm on."

"We've released Dr. Lake. He's free."

Hooks squinted at him as he blasted the van through two stone pillars and into a swirl of damp snow. They were in Weaver Park. The wheels sent up rooster tails of slush as they sped down the main road. The park was empty.

"Where is he?" Stade asked.

"You'll find him. He'll call in. We keep our word."

"Now why not let Cho free? Then we can talk. There's no need for anyone to get hurt."

"He stays with us until we're convinced we're clear. We may keep him a day or two. He'll be decently treated." Trask was trying different combinations. It kept narrowing down to one. Lake might have to be killed to keep him from telling the police.

"I'm sure you'll treat him properly," Stade said. "He's one of your own."

Trask felt fear rising from deep in his bowels, up his tract, clotting his throat. It was a white cold sensation; the way men must feel before they die.

"What are you talking about?"

"Cho Park was sneaked into the hospital by your friend Olmedo. Cho Park is a member of the Japanese Red Army. We have a file on him and we'll get his real name. You can keep him forever. Why not spare everyone the trouble, stop the ambulance, and come out peacefully?"

"You dumb sumbitch Trask!" Hooks yelled. "You fuck up again! They know who the slope is. They kill Carlos, they find out who the slant is, they git us now!"

The van skidded as Hooks raged. He bounced it on to a narrow road and hurtled through the snow toward the car he'd parked earlier.

At the park entrance Reinhold sighted the ambulance as it vanished into the trees, and he went after it. The chief rolled down his window. He readied his Magnum.

In the ambulance, Trask waited a few seconds. "Stay on, Stade. You just told me all I have to know. Lake, get over here."

The surgeon bent low, walked through the van, and stuck his head through the open window into the cab.

Trask gave him the phone. "Tell them."

"This is Dr. Lake. That was a fake. I'm still here. Keep your cops away. They won't hurt me, so long as they need me. I'll talk to them."

Trask grabbed the phone. "One up on you, Stade. If you try to stop us, you'll have a dead surgeon on your hands."

"John, listen. You don't stand a chance. Let me tell you how it is. Olmedo is dead. He got his head blown off when he tried to shoot it out. We've picked up the girl and Rashid. They're under federal custody and they're talking. All you can make is more trouble for everyone, including yourself."

Martha Lake ran to his desk. "You fool. You'll get my husband killed."

Steve held her. "He knows what he's doing, Martha."

"Don't you see, Steve?" she cried. "That lunatic tricked him. He told him Eric was free. They've got him. He's all they have for insurance. He's all they have left!"

There was a roaring noise at the end of the phone. Trask was struggling with someone. "Mother-fuckers" and "sumbitches" soiled the air. Then the speaker was silent.

"I'm sorry, Mrs. Lake," Stade said. "It was time to let them know. If they know we've picked up two of them, they should be ready to bargain."

"Or kill." She leaned into Rockewicz's arms.

"Goddamn wonder-man Trask," Hooks howled. "Git us all kilt. Yeah, you got a big plan. Change the whole world. Knock off all them guvments, all them big people. You can't change your fuckin' underwear."

"We'll get out of this. We still have him."

"Fuck him. I ain't got nothing against him. You wanna kill him, you kill him, or ask that slant to kill him."

"No one's seen us," Trask said. "Hooks, listen to me. We can make it. We've still got half the money. We're out of trouble as soon as we get in the Buick."

Hooks drove the ambulance past the dirt clearing where he had left the getaway car. He braked, skidding through a grove of poplars, then went into reverse.

Lake pitched and rolled inside the ambulance. Cho was having the same trouble. He had braced his body against the stretcher trying to keep the gun trained on the surgeon.

Across a snow-soaked meadow, Hooks and Trask saw Reinhold's blue-and-white car speeding toward them. The siren was screaming again, the beacon whirling. Reinhold itched to finish them off in one long burst.

"Fuzz," Hooks said. He spit out the window. "City fuzz. It look like you fuck up oncet too often, Trask." He stopped the ambulance in back of the Buick.

"Cho!" Trask shouted. "Take the bags and run for the car!"

"What about him?"

"I'll cover him. He won't move. Watch it, Lake. You're all we have. Just be still when he runs out."

Cho slung the carbine over one shoulder. He scrambled across the ambulance floor, picking up the two valises. Ducking low, he opened the rear doors and struggled down the steps with the heavy bags. Shivering, he landed in the snowy mud, fell to one knee.

Cho had only a few yards to run to the Buick with the valises. But the sudden cold, the soft underfooting, slowed him. He pitched forward again in his eagerness to get to the car. His thin green surgical garments turned dark brown. He struggled to retrieve the suitcases.

"On your feet, germ," Reinhold shouted.

O'Boyle and his cameraman leaned out of the patrol car windows.

The camera hummed.

Cursing, Reinhold ordered his driver to turn off the maintenance road and swing wide around the van and the Buick. He had to assume the people in the cab would be firing.

"Come in the sights, pig," Hooks crowed. "You gon' be a dead pig." He aimed the carbine.

Lake fell to the floor of the ambulance. He tried to isolate his problems and act on them. First, get out of range. With a swift sliding motion, he darted under the right-hand stretcher. He knew that the mattress was fairly thick. Bullets might lose their force if fired into it.

Shots were being fired—modest, popping noises, firecrackers. Lake wondered if his life would pass in review—the old wives' tale about the moment before death. But he did not feel at all like dying. There was work to be done. Angela Ramazotti's ASD was scheduled for that afternoon. Someday he would teach full time, do his own research on prosthetics. Now he was less afraid than disgusted, frustrated by his immobilization. Killers repelled him. It would be good to punish them.

Something flitted through his mind. Something Jack Licata had said an hour ago in the OR. A weapon? An ultimate weapon Jack had joked about. . . .

Reinhold ordered the driver to slam on the brakes. The prowl car skidded across the soaked field, stopped. The chief flew out of the door and took cover behind the hood. He raised the .357 Magnum and drew a bead on a green-gowned figure. A small man staggering toward a snow-mantled car.

"George, for Chrissake, how do you know who it is?" O'Boyle screamed. "It could be—"

"He's got a gun. That's good enough for me."

Cho had dropped a valise and was tugging at the Buick door. The icy rain seemed to have frozen the catch.

Reinhold steadied the revolver with two hands. Thirty-caliber slugs from Hooks's carbine danced off the hood, pinged into the motor. O'Boyle, the cameraman, and the driver were on the floor.

"At least hold the camera up," O'Boyle gasped.

"Brian, those bastards are trying to kill us," the cameraman whined.

"They'll kill Reinhold first. Get the pictures."

The man raised the camera high but kept his head below the door.

Reinhold squeezed off two shots. The long barrel flashed orange twice. A giant palm seemed to slam Cho against the side of the Buick. He appeared pasted to the metal flank when a third shot smashed into him. He disintegrated, melting into the snow, as the hollow-nosed bullets devoured him.

"Oh, Jesus," O'Boyle wept. "Oh, Jesus, we'll all get it. Let's get the hell out of here."

Reinhold, still behind the hood, directed his fire at the ambulance. "Take a walk if you're chicken, O'Boyle. You wanted to come along."

"We'll kill Lake!" Trask screamed from the ambulance. "We'll shoot him!"

"Lay off him, asshole," Reinhold shouted. "You're all dead, scumbags! Throw out the guns and walk out."

"Are you getting all of this?" O'Boyle asked.

The cameraman peeked over the edge of the door. "More than I want."

"They're in the park," Harris said. "Reinhold found them first. They've stopped the ambulance."

"What about our cars?" Stade asked.

"One unit picked up the signal pretty clear. They must be getting there. There's been shooting."

Martha Lake covered her eyes. Rockewicz had his arms around her. He opened his mouth to console her, but for once there were no words.

"Yeah, you screw up everything, Trask," Hooks raged. He had trouble sighting the carbine. The honky policeman was a smart one. Staying out of range, keeping covered. Hooks longed for the M16 Armalite. That would have shown the pigs. The carbine was a piece of junk, okay for people like Ratshit or the bitch, people who wasted civilians. You went against professionals, you needed a professional piece.

"He outa range." Hooks scanned the sky, heard the helicopter again. *You come in shit and you go out shit.* He could step out of the ambulance and get a good angle. He could start the van again, circle, look for a better shot. Trask was holding his .38 special, his hands trembling, his face paler than a bleached dog turd. Hooks grinned at him. "You no fuckin' good. You got big ideas but you yellah."

"Come on. We'll get out and take a chance. The money's in the car."

"Not yet it ain't. Cho got his back blowed off. Bags is outside. Who gonna pick 'em up, and who gonna cover?"

"We'll make Lake go out with us. I'll use him as a shield."

"You show your ass, that cop blast you."

Trask got up and pointed his .38 at the back of the ambulance. "Lake! Get up! We're getting out!"

Lake had a childish desire to bash their heads together.

"Get out, you bastard," Trask shrieked.

"It's too late," Hooks said. "They all here. You kill him, they kill us anyway. Besides, he ain't movin'."

"Drag him out."

"Sheeet. How I get to him?"

Lake evaluated his options. None appealed to him. He disliked being at the whim of others. He ran his own shop like a dictator. He knew that other chief attending physicians thought him stiff-necked, intransigent, too demanding, too insistent on loyalty. Old Procedure.

Perhaps he would not die.

A black sedan sped across the field toward the van. Another was ten yards behind it.

This revolution that goes nowhere, Lake thought, has got to stop. At least the part that involved him.

A man was shouting from a bullhorn.

"John, we're federal agents. You can't get away. Drop your arms and come out."

Hooks boomed his response, "Fuck you, pig. We die like men."

There were more shots, a splintering of glass. Lake wasn't cooperating with his captors. The script called for him to be sacrificed, but he was unreachable. The glass partition with the sliding panel was too small for Trask to crawl through. The stretcher shielded him. They couldn't see him, much less get a decent angle to destroy him. He considered the chances of his rolling out, breaking for the doors. Evidently the Korean was dead. Someone had shot him as he raced for the car.

Suddenly it was quiet. The shooting had stopped.

"Trask, we both goin'," Lake heard Hooks say.

"Not yet. If one of us drags that bastard Lake out, we can make it. He's all we have left, Hooks."

"You the one fuck it all up. You get him out."

"I can't see him. Is he still back there?"

The voice boomed again out of the gloom. "John, we've stopped the police car from firing." Lief's voice on the bullhorn was patient, cajoling. "You can come out now."

Reinhold, cursing, mocking the agents, reluctantly put the Colt Trooper .357 into his holster. He had his kills for the day. Two of them. He would enjoy the next protest from civil libertarians about the brutality of his hollow-nosed bullets. He would have some choice answers for them. Perhaps he could have some plaster molds made of the wounds caused by the slugs, the kind of thing ammo manufacturers bragged about in his favorite gun magazines. "Cast of the wound cavity made by standard .38. Compare with the cast of cavity by our special .357. . . ."

O'Boyle and the cameraman were out of the car. They knelt behind it. There were four unmarked sedans surrounding the ambulance. "Christ," the TV reporter said. "The whole FBI." He counted fifteen agents. More cars were speeding down the maintenance road.

"Who was the guy you just killed?" O'Boyle asked. Cho's body seemed to be sinking into the mud, flattening into a green-brown blob.

"I dunno."

"He had a surgical rig on. He could have been a hostage."

"With a carbine on his shoulder?"

The firing halted for a moment.

Trask was making a final attempt. "We're coming out with Lake," he screamed. "He'll die if you try to fire. You must let us get into our car and get away."

Hooks stuck his head out. The snow felt cold, fresh, a reminder of his wild boyhood. He hated hot weather, had hated it since the day in 'Nam when he offed the slants.

"That won't work," the bullhorn responded. "Why hurt Dr. Lake?"

Lake edged closer to the aisle. His eyes scanned the shelf above the opposite stretcher. The ambulances were far better equipped now than when he was a young intern. They carried everything, including a radio setup that permitted personnel at the hospital to monitor an EKG from the ambulance. And all sorts of life-supporting gear. His eyes discovered a large white box at the foot of the stretcher opposite him. A battery-operated portable defibrillator. Licata's joke darted through his mind again: *the ultimate weapon.*

Lake was not a daring man. But he had isolated the problem and could now act on it. It would require timing and deft moves. If he fumbled it, he would be dead. But his legs were resilient and his coordination good enough. He slid further into the aisle, pulling part of the blanket with him.

"You'll fuck it up, Trask," Hooks said. "You use that slope for a trick, but they know he one of us."

"Fire a round at Lake," Trask said. "If we can't take him, we'll kill him."

"Shit, no. I ain't gonna kill the doctor." It did not matter what side they were on, red-neck or radical, they gave you the shit and took the glory.

The bullhorn blared at them. "We'll give you two minutes. Turn Dr. Lake free. Come out without guns."

In the lead car, Lief turned to another agent. "We'll give them two more and two after that. We'll stay here all afternoon if there's a chance to save Lake."

"You see, Trask? They don' give a fuck. They gon' come out shootin'."

"Hooks, there's still a chance." His head bobbed. "Empty a magazine into the back. Something will get him."

"Nah. I done shootin' for whitey. See how brave you is."

Trask's long head jerked around. His eyes seemed filmed, unfocused. As he turned, looking for Lake in the rear, Hooks slammed the panel of the glass partition over Trask's half of the cab, leaving his own section open.

"Goddamn you, Hooks. You dumb nigger."

"Yeah, that's always my trouble."

Lake listened to their rising voices. Then he heard two muffled explosions. Trask slumped slowly down and out of Lake's view.

"We all goin' anyway," Lake heard Hooks say. "Me, Trask, ole doctor. We all be shit."

The surgeon rolled from beneath the stretcher. In one swift move he leaped to the white box. It took him a second to lift the lid, throw the switch, put the dial at maximum—*400 watt-seconds*. Then he grabbed the two black-handled **paddles**.

Hooks heard the noise. With a puzzled frown on his face, he turned. Lake saw the barrel of the gun rising above the partition, but it was not pointing at him. What was deterring him? Some buried sense of right or wrong?

"What the fuck you doin'?" Hooks looked insulted.

Lake leaped upward, one knee braced on the blue bench. As Hooks stared at him, he slammed the silvery disks of the defibrillator into the man's face. One struck Hooks's right ear. The other cracked against his left cheek.

The electrical charge blasted through Hooks like a lightning bolt. He shrieked. His body flew upward in convulsion. His skin sizzled. The carbine fell from his hand. For a few seconds his upper torso seemed to dangle in space, his head wobbling and shuddering as if made to dance by invisible strings. Insensate, burned, his limbs rigid, he collapsed slowly. His huge eyes were frozen by shock. His tongue protruded stupidly. The powerful body fell forward against the dashboard and twitched.

Lake retreated to the stretcher and rested his head in his hands.

"What's going on?" he heard the bullhorn. "We told you not to fire."

The surgeon opened the back door of the ambulance and shouted to the cars. "It's okay. This is Lake. I'm safe. For God's sake, don't shoot. One's dead and one's out."

Then he walked back to the cab, reached into Hooks's pockets —the man was rigid in a wide-eyed scorched sleep—and found a pack of cigarettes and a book of matches.

He slumped onto the stretcher and lit up, letting the smoke fill his aching lungs. All around the interior of the ambulance were large NO SMOKING signs.

"To hell with it," the surgeon said. This was one time he wasn't going to follow procedure.

Lief's face was peering into the opened doors. He was covered with a dusting of snow. There was a shotgun in his hands.

"Dr. Lake?"

"Yeah, yeah. I'm all right. Somebody look at the driver. The black man. I shocked him out of his shoes. He won't be happy about it, but he's alive. Trask's probably dead. The black man shot him. They began to get on each other's nerves."

"You're not hurt?"

"No. Just get me back to the hospital."

PART
SEVEN

Lake went directly to the recovery room. Buttram kept the reporters and photographers away. Licata and Mihrab, hearing that he
was en route, left the cafeteria, where they had been having lunch
with Flor and Sally, and ran to surgery. Motzkin, sporting a cane
from the orthopedic department, came hobbling along.

"Tench began to fibrillate," Licata said. "I had to smack him
a few times."

Lake studied the oscilloscope. "His P-waves look good," he
said. "Girls, keep a close watch. We handled his heart a little."
He bent under the table and examined the urine receptacle.
"Looks okay. He is a Lake patient and he should get my usual
procedures."

They giggled.

"Watch out for any postoperative hypertension. And he looks
cold. If he begins to shiver he might develop circulatory stress. A
little curare or chlorpromazine would be indicated. And plenty of
morphine if he complains of pain. Understood?"

"Yes, doctor."

"And I need a hot shower and some clean clothes. And about
four cigarettes."

Martha was standing at the entrance to the recovery room.
Behind her was a tall dark woman in her twenties. She had long,
disheveled black hair and a solemn, shadowed face. She wore an
Indian blanket over denim coveralls.

Lake saw his wife. He walked to her, and they embraced. "Eric
. . . Eric. You're all right? No—no wounds?"

"I'm okay, Martha." Her arms locked around his neck. "Let's
go, honey."

"Why?"

"Well, I mean, in the recovery room, in front of the nurses and . . ."

Her face drew close. "In front of the nurses. Exactly." Martha put her hands on his gaunt cheeks. She kissed him on the lips—a long, soft kiss. She held his head close to hers with one strong hand. "God has been kissed in public." She was resisting his efforts to shake free. "He will never be the same to his worshipers."

"Cut it out, Martha. This is undignified."

"But I love you."

"I'm aware of that." The nurses were staring. Motzkin was laughing.

"Kiss him again, Martha," Motzkin said.

She did. She put an arm around his starved waist and refused to let go.

"Look, Martha, there's a whole day ahead of us."

"Come home now."

"I've got another operation this afternoon. A little girl. She's been waiting for months."

She would not let go of his hand. "Steve has a bottle of bourbon on his desk," Martha said.

"Stop raping me in City General's recovery room, and I'll do anything."

"Kiss me."

Lake pecked nervously at her cheek. "Enough."

Martha noticed the dazed-looking young woman in the blanket and coveralls. "Oh, dear. I forgot about Miss Tench."

Martha led her by the hand toward the surgeons. "Eric, this is Dee-Dee. Walker's daughter."

Lake shook her hand. The girl was dark, slender, with a vacant look in her brown eyes that might pass for peaceful. "You were a little girl when I saw you last. At Newport? Your grandfather's place?"

"I don't recall. That part of my life is gone." She fingered an *ankh* on her chest. There were a dazzle of rings designed with signs of the zodiac on her brown hand.

"Ah," Lake said, "you live nearby?"

"I am from an *ashram.*"

Eric looked blank. An ash can?

"Oh," Martha said. "A commune. I read about them. Where?"

"Well, ah, like, geographically in New City. But we exist on different levels of consciousness."

Licata whispered to Motzkin. "Miss Dee-Dee Tench is stoned out of her kugel. I think she's been smoking dried grasshoppers."

"Don't kid around, Jack. That's millions on top of millions. She'll get it all someday."

"Not worth it. Those people don't have sex, they have awareness." Licata turned toward Mihrab. "How about you, Gamel? You helped save the old man's life. You get to know Miss Dee-Dee better, you could buy your own heart clinic in Cairo."

"She is not my type, Jack."

And I know who is, Licata thought.

Lake led Miss Tench toward the stretcher. Her father was naked as Noah before his sons. He was a frightening sight.

"Don't be afraid," Lake said. "He's fine. He can even hear a few things. Go on, you can yell in his ear."

"That . . . that's . . . father?"

"I guarantee it."

"But . . . it's been so many years. And seeing him this way. I'm not sure who it is."

Licata clapped a hand to his mouth and shoved Motzkin to a corner.

"Alan, if that isn't her Daddy, we're in real trouble. We've thrown a Tench in the works."

Motzkin winced. "Yeah, Jack. That's your worst joke *ever.* Absolutely the worst."

"It figures. This has been my worst morning. Absolutely my worst."

"I guess it *is* Daddy," Dee-Dee Tench said dreamily. "What stage of awareness is he in? Is his consciousness higher than his awareness? Is he on a transitory or a creative level?"

"I'm afraid that's not my specialty," Lake said.

"Daddy looks so *strange*," she said. Her voice was inflated, full of warm air. She was staring at Tench's long limp penis, with the catheter winding from the aperture.

"Daddy's got himself a whacked-out little girl," Licata muttered. "Ah, to be so rich you can talk sheer crap all the time."

"It's no different from what goes on at an executive meeting," Motzkin said.

Lake put his mouth next to Tench's ear and shouted. "Walker. This is Dr. Lake. Wiggle your toes if you hear me."

Tench's toes wiggled.

"Walker. Your daughter is here. Dee-Dee. She came down to see you. If you understand what I said, wiggle your toes again."

Dee-Dee Tench's hazed eyes studied her father's toes. They wiggled more vigorously.

"He's doing wonderfully," Lake said.

"The big toe smiled," Licata said. Miss Tench looked at him blankly. "Well . . . it looked more *aware*, if you get my general meaning."

Motzkin dug him in the ribs. One did not joke with believers, especially if they were heirs to fortunes.

Flor Aquino was waiting for Licata and Mihrab outside of surgery. She had switched to a starched white pantsuit. It did not obscure her willowy figure.

"He is all right?" she asked.

"Oh yes," Mihrab said.

Licata moved past them, waving.

Mihrab took her elbow. There was time left to finish their soggy lunch—or at least a cup of coffee—before the next call.

Mihrab could not find the words, and he would not for a while, but he knew that ultimately she would love him—as sure as Allah was in his heaven and Eric Lake in his operating room. Jack would be his best man.

"How's that guy Hooks?" Rockewicz asked.

"Medium well done," Lief said.

They were in Rockewicz's office, reviewing the events of the last hour.

"Leave it to Eric. Blasting the guy with the defibrillators. And he had it on high—400 watt-seconds."

"Hooks must be made of hardwood," Lief said. "It knocked him out, scorched him, and he's still alive."

Rockewicz walked around his desk. "Know what I think? I think Lake saved his life. You people would have ended up shooting him dead. You or Reinhold."

"What about Mr. Trask?" Stade asked, changing the subject.

"He's in the emergency room," Lief said.

Estelle came in. "They thought he was dead when they brought him in, Mr. Rockewicz. There are life signs now."

"Who's with him?"

"Dr. Burns."

Something wicked gleamed in Rockewicz's eyes. They worked their disappearing act. He went to the speaker on his desk and flicked the switch for the PA.

"I can't say this often enough," Cardone said. "You people have been marvelous. All you've done for Mr. Tench. And I'm sure Miss Tench joins me."

They were seated at a long table in the cafeteria. The room had resumed its noisy, dirty ambience. Gusts of steam rose from the kitchen, where earlier Miss Diener had tried to stop the gunmen. She had allowed a Band-Aid on the corner of her mouth where three stitches had been necessary.

The OR number three people had come down together for coffee—Licata, Mihrab, the nurses, Lake and Martha, Motzkin and Beverly (weeping, laughing, and squeezing her "hero"). Cardone and Dee-Dee Tench had asked to sit with them.

"Miss Dee-Dee Tench looks like she's somewhere else," Motzkin muttered to his wife. "I heard her say she barely knows her father. Probably remembers his hundred million, though."

"Alan! Be generous to people." Beverly Motzkin nibbled his ear. Was his foot all right? Would he limp forever? Motzkin assured her he would not. The toe would heal. Nothing at all. As a boy in Brooklyn Motzkin had read all of Sherlock Holmes. He recalled how Dr. Watson spoke of the "Jezail bullet" he carried in his hip, a souvenir of a colonial war. So instead of the nine-toed gas-passer, he would play Watson to Lake's Holmes.

Cardone kept trying to engage Miss Tench in conversation. He had never met her. She would drink no coffee, no tea, sipped only skimmed milk, fingered her *ankh*. Cardone felt a vague terror. What was in Tench's will? Who was this intruder, this creature in a blanket who mumbled about states of awareness?

"This, ah, community . . . is it Indian?"

"It is all things. There are no more nations, no more separate peoples. We are one in the cosmos."

At the summit, Cardone understood, one's problems never ended. He would have to visit the *ashram*, perhaps donate a prayer wheel or a set of cymbals. Who knew when Miss Dee-Dee Tench's goodwill might be needed?

Brian O'Boyle approached Lake and Martha. "Camera is set up outside, doctor. Can I interview you?"

"Go on, Eric," Licata said. "Only make it *your* story. You can't be background music to a lousy shoot-out."

"Anything you want to talk about," the TV newsman said. "I've been asking around. You're not just a hero. You're one of the best heart surgeons in the world. People tell me you're every bit as good as DeCooley and Bakeley."

"It's DeBakey and Cooley," Lake laughed. "And you better get their names right if you don't want to be sued."

"Go on, Eric," Martha said. She stroked his neck. "You weren't the world's best-known heart surgeon this morning, but you may be tonight."

Lake got one leg over the hard bench. He would increase his

annual donation to CGH. Some of the money could be diverted from the heart research unit to buy decent chairs for the cafeteria.

The loudspeaker on the wall was blaring at them. Lake cupped one ear. It was Rockewicz's voice, full of honey.

"Will Dr. Eric Lake please go immediately to the emergency room? Male patient suffering what appears to be a penetrating heart wound and hemorrhaging. . . ."

"Since when am I a trauma man?" Lake asked.

"Steve's sense of humor," Licata said. He got up. "Let's do it for old Rockewicz U." He halted, straddling the bench. "Jesus. I can guess who that male patient is!"

Lake was stunned. "It can't be."

Mihrab ran after them. Motzkin hobbled behind, using his cane. O'Boyle trotted alongside Lake. "It's one of them, isn't it? Maybe your friend Trask?"

"I have no friends," the surgeon said. "Only patients."

Outside the cafeteria, Rockewicz was ready to pounce. When Cardone emerged, shepherding Miss Tench, he grabbed the executive's elbow and waltzed him to the elevator.

"I apologize for our rotten coffee," Steve said. "But I hope everything else was all right. I know how you felt when you found Mr. Tench in this old dump."

"I am more than satisfied. You have magnificent people here."

"That's what I keep telling the board of managers."

Rockewicz looked over his shoulder. Martha Lake was walking with Dee-Dee Tench and Bev Motzkin. Good, good. Out of earshot. This was between himself and Cardone, a little one-on-one.

"I understood you to say you'd like to make some contribution to City General," Steve said. When in doubt, the frontal assault was often the best. "In Mr. Tench's name, of course. Or in the corporation's."

"Yes. I heard about your need for new oxygenators."

"Mr. Cardone, a membrane oxygenator costs about six hundred, maybe seven hundred bucks. I had something a little more ambitious in mind."

"Really?"

"A heart-research wing. We have the people. Lake has the program. Eric's got ideas on heart surgery nobody knows about. But he needs space and equipment."

"You aren't shy, Mr. Rockewicz."

"Everyone calls me Steve."

Cardone smiled. It would be fun bringing this hustler to a board meeting. "I'll think about it. How does the Tench Heart Institute strike you?"

"It's nice, but I had another idea."

"Did you?"

"The James Baggs Memorial Institute. No need to make a fast decision. I'll call you tomorrow. Maybe we can meet with our architect. I've got him standing by."

James P. Cardone, president of Tench Industries, stopped dead in the hall and allowed himself his first belly laugh of the day.

"Steve," he said. "If you ever need a job, come to me first."

Chalky white, naked, Trask was placed on the operating table in the emergency room. There was a red hole the size of a walnut in his chest. Only one of Hooks's shots appeared to have struck him.

Maurice Burns had made a deep incision between the fourth and fifth ribs. When Lake entered with his assistants, Burns was shaking his head. "I don't get it, Eric. Why isn't he bleeding more?"

"He probably developed a clot in the pericardium. Jack, grab that spreader. Flor! Gamel! Get him at forty-five degrees and lift his left arm."

"But it's crazy. He doesn't seem to be losing much blood."

"He's lucky," Lake explained. "The clot is probably keeping blood out of the pleural cavity. We'll find out." He squinted at Trask's insenate face. "Stick the spreader in, Jack."

Licata shoved the metal instrument between the ribs and turned the ratchet. The incision widened. "Depend on Licata for semiskilled labor," he said. "Does this animal have any idea who's trying to save his miserable life?"

"He will," Lake said. "Alan, start dosing him with sodium bicarbonate. As soon as the IV is in, perfuse him with whole blood."

"Right, Eric."

"Everybody stand back," Lake said. "I'm cutting the pericardium. I have a hunch it's full."

He reached in and made a long incision. A sheet of crimson gushed out, flooding the table, the floor, their gowns. The nurses flew about, mopping and throwing towels.

Lake plunged his right hand into the widened space between Trask's ribs. His fingers grabbed Trask's dying heart. He touched it, palpated it, explored it for the damage.

"I've got it. A clean wound through the left atrium."

"Shove a firecracker in it," Licata said.

Lake put his thumb on the bullet hole and pressed. He could feel the oozing of blood stop. His right arm was solid red with the blood of the man who had tried to kill him.

"Gamel, get ready with sutures. I'll rotate the heart until you can see it. There it is. Start sewing."

"He doesn't have much of a beat, Eric," Licata said.

"Start massaging. Seventy squeezes to the minute. If you go for more than three minutes, it's a new indoor record. Try to keep out of each other's way."

"Steady, Jack," Mihrab said. "I can barely see. Clamps, please."

Licata grasped Trask's heart and began to massage it. "I may be getting something," he said. "No. My imagination."

"We've got to improve cardiac performance," Lake said—as if discussing a malfunctioning carburetor. "Good, transfusions are going in. Perfuse him, don't stop. Keep massaging, Jack."

Licata's weary hand opened and closed over Trask's heart.

Didn't he see a movie years ago with Robert Taylor as a prize-fighter, flexing his right hand over a tennis ball to develop strength?

"Let me," Mihrab said.

"Nah, there's only one source of coolie labor around here."

Lake nudged Motzkin. "Don't cheat on the sodium bicarbonate. He's acidotic. Every little bit helps."

"Right."

"As soon as it's beating, Jack," Lake said, "rush him to the OR. I don't like emergency rooms."

"It's coming on," Licata said. He felt the heart come to life in his hand, reacting to massage, new blood, medications. "Jesus, it's beating."

Lake moved Licata away and put his arm into the incision. He held Trask's heart and began squeezing it. "Yes, it's coming around. Cardiac performance is improving. Now listen everyone. When he comes to, he'll be in pain. I mean *pain*. Alan, load him with morphine."

"Do I have to?"

The heart pumped faster. Trask's eyes opened. They were glazed with fear. Flor moved his right arm away from the table and swabbed it. Motzkin rammed a syringe full of morphine into the vein. "It won't hurt long," he said.

Before he succumbed to the narcotic, Trask had a blazing vision of lights, faces, machines, tubes. He heard metal instruments snapping and clicking.

"Get him up to surgery," Lake said. "Drains, a nasogastric tube, an indwelling Foley catheter. Give him blood gas tests and saline irrigation. We'll look for the bullet later. It's probably in the chest wall. His lungs seem functional."

Blood poured into Trask's body from the suspended bottles. The orderlies began to move him from the soaked table to a stretcher.

Chief nurse McCarran was standing in the door, looking at Trask as if she would happily cut off his plasma supply. "What about the Ramazotti girl, Dr. Lake? Do you want to go ahead with her? Shall I keep her scheduled for two-thirty?"

"If my assistants aren't quitting."

Licata yanked his mask down and looked at Mihrab, Motzkin, the nurses. "What else do we have to do this afternoon?"

"Dr. Lake has an interview with the world this afternoon," Brian O'Boyle said.

Eric Lake stared at him. The nervy kid had walked right into emergency with them. Lake nodded and smiled, ever so faintly.

ABOUT THE AUTHOR

The Hostage Heart is Gerald Green's fifteenth book and tenth novel. His previous works include such bestsellers as *To Brooklyn with Love, The Lotus Eaters, Tourist* and *The Last Angry Man.* Among his nonfiction books is the recently published *My Son the Jock,* and also *The Stones of Zion* and *The Artists of Terezin.*

In addition to his career as a writer, Gerald Green was a pioneer in television news and documentary programing. Among his credits are *The Today Show, Wide Wide World* and scores of documentaries including such award-winning programs as the Toscanini centennial and the Joseph Wood Krutch nature series.

A native of Brooklyn, Mr. Green lives in Connecticut with his wife and three children.